I0729096

Division One: Tourist Trap

by Stephanie Osborn

Chromosphere Press

Huntsville, AL

Table of Contents

Chapter 1

It was rare enough for two Division One agents of Earth to honeymoon; rarer still when they honeymooned on another planet. But when they did, they tended to pull out all the stops and have as much fun as they could legally find to get into. When those two agents were the heads of the Alpha Line, the most badass department in Division One, and arguably in the entire Pan-Galactic Coalition, they proved amazingly childlike—in the best possible way.

"What's on tap for tomorrow, Ace?" Omega asked her partner, a tall, dark, and handsome Agent whose Apache mother's ancestry blended well with his Texan Celtic father's genetics. The pair were preparing for bed together in the suite's luxurious bathroom, a couple of days into their sojourn. Division One Director Fox had ensured they had one of, if not the, best honeymoon suites in the Gwesti Tŷ Preni, the poshest resort hotel and spa in the capital city of 'Eden'—also known as Zeta Aurigae Four to Earth scientists, or Tiniken to the locals. The fact that it happened to be right on the beautiful silver beach, and that their balcony overlooked that scenic vista, only enhanced the experience.

"Well, Meg," Echo noted to his lovely, svelte, platinum-blonde partner and bride as she washed her face in one sink; he had just finished brushing his teeth in the other. "I thought we'd start off the way we have been for the last couple days, with room-service breakfast on the balcony—I already put in an order for that omelet you loved this morning, for both of us, plus coffee, arng juice, and the local version of waffles—then we'd spend a few hours on the beach. You can finish teaching me the finer points of bodyboarding!"

"That sounds like fun!" Omega agreed. "All morning?"

"Yeah, at least until we need to come inside so you don't get sunburned," Echo noted. "I can't believe the special 100+ SPF sunblock we got from Medical still isn't enough for your pale Celtic skin, baby. And Zebra said they didn't have anything stronger."

"I know. But it's the fact it's a different spectral type star, and we're out in it a lot longer, with a lot more skin exposed."

"Yeah, I reckon so. But I'm glad I realized you were turning pink that first day, and scuttled you inside before you DID burn."

"Me too. That woulda ruined the last few days, especially given we forgot the bottle of Rejuvic."

"Yeah, I know," Echo noted, then smirked. "Never mind ruining the nights, when I couldn't even touch you for the sunburn."

"Hey now! My bikini isn't THAT revealing!"

"I know; I was just teasing. I wouldn't have let you loose on the beach if it was—that's MY scenic view of you now, baby, and mine alone. NOBODY else sees you like THAT but ME. Right?"

"Damn straight." Omega thrust out her jaw, then considered for a moment. "Well, I guess Zebra, during my physical."

"All right, then. And that doesn't count! I was just givin' you grief about the almost-sunburn, I swear."

"Okay, okay. What about lunch and the afternoon, then?"

"Lunch is down the street at that little 'Tinikenii Café' we've been wanting to try," Echo noted. "I made reservations when we came in this afternoon, before dinner. Not that they normally TAKE reservations, I think. But I figured it was better to do it and be sure we'll get in, than not do it and wait in line all afternoon. An' they understood, and said they'd make sure to save us a table."

"Ooo! Nummy! And good idea on getting in."

"Then I thought we'd go for a little hike. Remember the cab flying over that flowering forest reserve, on our way to the hotel from the spaceport?"

"Yeah? The one with all the huge blue and purple flowers all over the trees instead of leaves? We're gonna hike through that!?"

"That's the plan, baby."

"Oh, that sounds gorgeous, Echo!"

"Yup. They have several walking and hiking trails of various lengths and degrees of difficulty, it turns out. So I thought we'd take one of the hiking trails that goes back into the foothills a little ways, through the densest of the floral regions. Along with a picnic basket with an afternoon snack. Or maybe a backpack; I haven't decided yet. I was hoping for a recommendation on how rugged that trail is from the park reserve management, but they haven't contacted me yet."

"Snack from the Tỷ Preni restaurant here at the hotel?"

"Yeah—or the café, if you'd rather."

"Either one ought to know which carrier is appropriate to the trail, I'd think."

"Good point. I'll ping the concierge in the morning and ask. Then, after our hike, we'll come back here for a soak in the hot tub on the balcony before we dress up and go to a late dinner at Prenihohni, upstairs. Then I have a surprise for you. I've had this one in work for a while, I just had to adjust the timing, once we got here." They headed out of the bathroom and into the bedroom proper.

"What? What? Tell me!" Omega begged, and a tolerant, cheerful Echo capitulated.

"I bought us tickets to see a production of *Ey Rhai Diflas*; it's kind of the Tinikeni version of '*Romeo and Juliet*.' Which seemed appropriate on our honeymoon, because *Ey Rhai Diflas* has a happier ending," he told her.

"Ohhh, Ace, that all sounds wonderful," Omega said with a dreamy smile, slipping off her black silk robe and hanging it on the hook beside the bed, placed there for the purpose.

Echo eyed the skimpy blue négligée she wore underneath with some appreciation—said appreciation was more for the way it strategically covered, yet enhanced, what was underneath it, than for the garment itself—then doffed his own robe, hanging it on the corresponding hook, and slid his nude body between the sheets.

"C'mere, baby," he murmured, holding out one arm. "We have hours to go before we have to get up and do any of that stuff. And I got other plans in the meantime."

"I could go for that," Omega decided, joining him in the big bed.

* * *

In a tenement dwelling in a different, older and more

run-down part of Zeta Aurigae Four's capital city of Preni, a Ke!endarian doffed the uniform of the Gwesti Tŷ Preni Hotel, removing his ill-fitting uniform boots and flexing his bare claws, before cladding himself in a kind of long, belted, draping vest, a style that was rarely found on either Ke!enda!ar or Tiniken. He ensured the door of his dilapidated apartment was locked, engaging no less than three locks—only one of which came with the flat—then he moved back to the tiny bedroom and opened the closet door, pulling a small black chest from the floor in the corner. He sat it on the dresser and opened it, revealing a compact interstellar communications device. Activating it, he programmed in a specific frequency and direction, then picked up the microphone and murmured into it.

The fact that the language he spoke was NOT Ke!endarian... was telling.

* * *

(Outcast to Leader. Come in,) he said, sotto voce, then waited. After several moments a response came back to him.

(Outcast, this is Leader. Report.)

(I believe I have found Public Enemy Number One, Leader.)

(Ah! Really?! Very, VERY good. We shall be heroes on the homeworld! Have you matched the sensor data for a proper verification?)

(No sir. I do not have access to a portable sensor bank, nor would it fit into the uniform I must wear while undercover. Can you please provide a scan of his image, so I may verify?)

(Ah yes. Stand by, Outcast. We should have his imagery filed somewhere in the data banks.)

After several more moments—which wait was largely occupied in signal travel time, even with the sophisticated 'warp bubble' blip transmissions commonly used in the Great Spiral and the galactic neighborhood—a small printer on the side of the comm device began to spit out a little printed image, about the size of a typical Earth snapshot photo. When it was complete, the 'Ke!endarian' picked it up and studied it.

It was a photograph of Agent Echo.

(Leader, this is Outcast. I confirm—I have located Public Enemy Number One.)

(Where?)

(At the hotel where I am working undercover. He is apparently staying there in the special elite nuptial suite. The housing computer in the hotel indicates he will be there for at least another quarter of a standard lunation, as it is reckoned in the Great Spiral. More, the cost of the stay is being covered by none other than the Director of Division One, which argues that it is a mission, not a pleasure trip.)

(Understood. He is said to regularly associate with Public Enemy Number Two. Have you seen her? Stand by for image.)

Moments later, another agent's image had landed atop Echo's. The strange being picked it up and studied it. It was that of...

...Agent India.

(Negative, Leader, I have not seen Number Two. I will watch for her, however. Given he is in the nuptial suite, it is just possible that they are no longer working together, and that he has taken a mate. Or they are still together, but looking to entrap another, perhaps with the aid of a colleague...which would be my surmise, given the fact that the Director is paying for the trip. Or perhaps Public Enemies One and Two have become mates and left the Division One, and he is merely keeping her within the nuptial suite, as befits a female.)

(Mm. Any of those are possible, I suppose. And I take your point regarding the source of payment, and tend to agree. Notify me as soon as possible, should you see her.)

(I will do so. Do you wish to take action?)

(Definitely. We are some two or three systems away, and will have to use stealth in arriving; I will divert the *Orktes* from our intended mission—it will wait—and be there in three days. Then we will take Public Enemy Number One into custody. If you see Number Two in the meanwhile, note her location. We will thereby take them both at once, if possible.)

(I understand, Leader. I will keep watch.)

(See that you do. Leader signing off.)

(Outcast signing off.)

* * *

The purported Ke!endarian took the small images and tucked them into what passed for his wallet, then he powered off and packed up the comm unit, and returned it to the dark corner of his closet.

Then he prepared for roosting. His shift at the hotel came early the next morning, and rest was required, so he might be as alert as possible...now that he had an actual mission.

* * *

Several hours later, Alpha One cuddled together, content, in the big bed. Omega's silver-blonde head rested on Echo's bare shoulder, and his arms wrapped around her nude form, cradling her close to his own naked body, as the fingers of his left hand idly played in her hair. He pondered for a few moments, then addressed her through the nd't'lq.

Hey, baby?

Yeah?

I was wondering something.

Shoot.

Bang.

They snickered.

Seriously, Ace, she said. *Go ahead and ask. I think I know what it's gonna be about, anyway, just on account of the nd't'lq.*

Probably. Hell, as well as you've always read me, you'd probably know, even WITHOUT the nd't'lq. Well, so anyway, I know that you were kinda scared of, of intimacy, after what Slug did to you when you were a kid, an' all. I just... Echo broke off, then tried, *I wanted to make it as enjoyable for you as it is for me. I was wondering...*

If you'd succeeded?

Well...yeah. I mean, you don't LOOK like it's bothering you now, but...

You wanna make sure.

Right. If I need to do something different, I need to know.

You're doing fine, Ace, she told him, then looked up at him and grinned mischievously. *In fact, I think we can now officially put paid to THAT particular reaction.*

Meaning it doesn't bother you any more?

Meaning it doesn't bother me any more. At least with you. I can't say it wouldn't with somebody else, I guess. But since I can't imagine having anyone else for a lover, let alone husband, I think that's a moot issue anyhow.

Mmm. Okay, that works, I guess.

Quite nicely, I think. She planted a kiss on the skin of his shoulder. *Now, since I know you're gonna wake me up in a few hours to do this again, never mind at oh dark thirty in the morning, could I suggest a bit of sleep right now? Especially with the busy schedule we've got lined up for tomorrow?* she asked him in a pert tone. He laughed.

Oh, I suppose, he decided. *G'night, Mrs. Bryant.*

Good night, Mr. Bryant, she responded with a smile.

Moments later, they were both asleep.

* * *

Sleep was, as Omega had noted, somewhat intermittent; being newlyweds, they tended to do what newlyweds most often did. However, the days on Zeta Aurigae Four were longer than Earth days by nearly twice as much, and since they were used to 48-hour days anyway, it worked reasonably well, and they were able to obtain enough rest for all the activities—both 'extracurricular,' as Echo put it, and not—that the couple had planned.

The next morning, an alarm on Echo's cell phone woke them in time to be up and robe-wrapped well before room service arrived with their breakfast. A knock on the door heralded breakfast. A local Tinikeni trundled the food cart into the room as Echo opened the door; far down the hall, a Ke!endarian porter in the hotel livery paused briefly, looking down the corridor at the human, as it attempted to maneuver a fully-loaded— Earth bellhops would have said OVERloaded—luggage cart through the door of another room, which happened to be the secondary bridal suite; it was not as large and luxurious as the one in which Alpha One currently stayed, but it was very nice, all the same. Echo chuckled and gave the porter a thumbs-up before closing the door behind the server, who already had the food cart halfway onto the spacious balcony, ready to provide their breakfast in the scenic dining nook in the corner opposite the hot tub.

Moments later, the waiter had been tipped and departed, leaving Echo and Omega to enjoy a delicious breakfast for two on the balcony overlooking the ocean, with a delightful salt tang in the breeze that gently ruffled their hair.

* * *

An hour and a half later, the pair was on the beach, swimming and bodysurfing, as Omega taught her groom the finer points of that sport. Enthusiastic whooping and yelling sounded over the beach, and several other grinning vacationers decided they wanted to take lessons from the platinum blonde human, rather to Echo's apparent amusement.

On the hotel's pool deck, which overlooked the beach, a Ke!endarian in the hotel livery paused in serving drinks, to glance across the beach at the cavorting couple...just as Echo, who was trying to sandboard along the edge of the surf, lost his balance and fell backward into a big wave, creating a tremendous splash that soaked his laughing bride...and several amused Tinikeni taking lessons from her, into the bargain. The Ke!endarian extracted a battered old wallet, pulled something out and checked it, then clucked, shook its head, and tucked the wallet back into a pocket of its uniform.

Then it resumed serving drinks from the poolside bar.

* * *

Omega and Echo headed back to their room from the beach, where they cleaned up and dressed in shorts and t-shirts, then headed down to the lobby and out the front door of the Gwesti Ty Preni Hotel, en route to the little café where they had luncheon reservations.

A certain Ke!endarian hotel employee, whose work schedule had placed it back at the porter/luggage office, stood in the door of that office and watched them go.

* * *

After a delicious and filling lunch of the local cuisine at the Tinikenii Café, the café packed a substantial afternoon snack in the Tiniken equivalent of a picnic basket—a lovely, intricately-woven container of naturally-shed bark from the local flowering trees, which was almost as fragrant as the flowers—and Echo and Omega caught a cab to the information center at the Eleiea Flowering Forest Reserve. After studying the maps and conversing briefly with one of the reserve's 'rangers,' Echo chose a little-frequented walking path, and the pair set out.

After about an hour of walking, they were deep in the forest, and the sweet scent of the flowering trees enveloped them, as did the bright colors of the blossoms. There were only a few red, yellow, or orange blossoms; most were in shades of teal, blue, and purple. Even the foliage had a slightly blue tint to the green leaves—principally, Omega explained, because the star was larger and hotter than the Sun, so tended to emit peak energies in the blue end of the spectrum.

"This is just beautiful, Echo," Omega murmured, looking all about, even as she drew in a deep breath of the delightful sweet, slightly resinous, almost spicy fragrance. Echo, lightly swinging the picnic basket in one hand, reached over with his other hand and took Omega's near hand in his, holding it gently. She glanced at him and smiled.

"Good, baby," he replied in a soft voice, returning her smile. "I'm glad you're enjoying it. I, uh, I guess I have something I should confess."

"Oh? What would that be?" she wondered.

"Well, this walk...as soon as I realized we were coming to Prini on Tiniken for our honeymoon, I knew I had to try this," he admitted. "Remember last spring, when we were crashed on that protoplanet, and we first started talking about visiting Eden?"

"Yeah? And then Fox turned around and sent us here on a mission, as soon as we were both healed up and fit for duty again," Omega recalled. "But, fun as that was, I still don't think we saw nearly as much then as we already have, on this trip."

"Yep, and nope," Echo agreed. "But the thing is, I dreamed about us visiting Tiniken, several times, while we were crashed...and at least once after we got home, while we were recovering, I think. And in one 'a those dreams—which unlike several fever dreams I had was a GOOD dream, a happy dream—it was just you and me, hand in hand like this, and I knew that, in the dream, we were lovers. And we had a picnic, under a flowering tree..."

"Aha. So I guess that, since it was your dream, an' it was a really 'GOOD dream,'" Omega said with a grin, "I suppose that dessert was probably me. Assuming you'd fallen for me by then."

"Uh, you might say that," Echo said with a sheepish grin of his own. "And yeah, I had."

"So now I know why you picked one of the less-frequented paths!"

"Aw! Well, come on, baby. I didn't mean it like THAT." Echo shrugged. "After all, this is a public park an' reserve. I just wanted to feel like we had the place to ourselves, is all."

Omega raised her eyebrows and bit her lip, scrunching it to one side; Echo wondered if he only imagined her expression looked vaguely disappointed. His question was answered the next moment, though not audibly.

If we can find a nice hidden spot, I wouldn't object, she told him through the nd't'lq. *I think it would be twenty-five kinds of romantic. But we HAVE to be outta sight! I don't wanna be found, like that.*

Me too neither. I don't think it would do our Agent reputations any good, either, newlyweds or no. I guess we'll play it by ear. I didn't intend to re-enact THAT part of the dream, though, honest. It was just so nice, with the two of us walking hand in hand through the pretty trees, and it was quiet and peaceful, and then we sat down together and had a picnic in the shade... He shrugged. *I thought it would be great for our honeymoon, to do something like that.*

I do too. And I'm good with it, either way, Omega said. *I really like the idea of making a literal dream come true for you, Ace. And if that's all we do, have a picnic together like in the dream, it'll still be wonderful, so don't feel like you have to search and search to find just the right secluded spot for, um, shenanigans. We can always go back to the hotel room for that.*

Okay, he said with a chuckle. *We'll see what we run across, and how far we make it before we get hungry.*

Before I get hungry, she noted. *'Cause with my 'enhanced' metabolism, I'll probably get hungry before you do, even though that was a big lunch we had.*

Which is fine, he decided. *I just have to make sure I keep enough fuel in you, especially now I'm your husband; I feel like it's that much MORE important to look after you. But I've already kinda gotten used to that, at least since we found out about it, anyway. I want you to be healthy, honey. And stay that way, as nearly as I can manage helping you do it.*

I know, and I appreciate it. And the feeling is mutual, I

guess you know. And I LIKE looking after you. It feels...special.

Yeah, I know, and I understand it an' agree. We're good, you an' me. Like usual.

Yup.

* * *

Several hours later, Alpha One returned to the Gwesti Ty Preni Hotel thoroughly sated in many senses of the word, Echo having managed to find the perfect, deeply secluded spot for their picnic. The hotel lobby was busy as they crossed it en route to the elevator bank, and the concierge nodded a friendly greeting just before turning to help another hotel guest, but no other familiar faces met their trained eyes.

"Oh, that's nice an' cool," Omega murmured as they entered their bridal suite and the cool breeze from the highly-efficient air conditioner system washed over their perspiring bodies; the afternoon had turned hot, and their walking path had had some steep parts...never mind certain 'extracurricular activities' that added to the exertion. "Oh, but wow, I'm gonna get chilled fast, Ace!"

"Why?"

"I'm all sweaty, an' the AC is cranked!"

"Cooling down too fast?"

"A little, yeah." She shivered.

"Well, then it's a good thing I'd planned on a hot tub soak," he decided. "Lemme nudge the thermostat up a little, too."

"Okay."

They sat the lovely picnic basket aside; it had been part of the purchase at the café, and would go home with them in their luggage as a souvenir of the trip, to be used on other occasions. Echo turned on the 'one-way' viewing field around the balcony, and the pair disrobed, then slid into the hot tub on the balcony, opposite the breakfast nook. Omega sank into the hot water, stretching her legs—a bit tired from hiking over uneven terrain—across several jets, as Echo slipped an arm around her shoulders and pulled her lightly against his side.

"Mm," he hummed, relaxing. "I knew bein' married to you would be great, baby. But I still didn't manage to imagine just how much I'd enjoy it, or how RIGHT it would feel."

"I know," she agreed. "I feel the same way."

"Good. I'm glad. Happy?"

"Very."

"Great. Just relax for now, maybe even take a short nap on my shoulder if you want to. Then we can go inside, dry off, and start getting all gussied up for a fancy evening out."

"I can't wait!"

* * *

Their dinner reservations were at the posh Prenihohni restaurant, on the roof of the hotel. Echo wore his Suit with tuxedo accoutrements, to include a bow tie, pleated shirt, and cummerbund, and Omega wore the 'Marilyn dress' she had been given for her birthday, and which she had not had occasion to wear, as yet. He gave her an approving once-over, then smiled and offered his arm; she took it, and they were off.

Their table offered an incredible view of the city, the beach, and the surrounding mountains. Echo selected a delicious five-course meal for them, and they ate and chatted their way through it, sometimes audibly, and sometimes telepathically.

Which I'm really gettin' into, Echo told Omega in private, via the mental bond.

Who knew the reserved Agent who valued his privacy so much—who originally didn't even wanna tell me what STATE he was from—would ever enjoy telepathically conversing with his wife? Omega teased in the same fashion.

When his wife understands him about as well as he understands himself? And he already learned a long time ago to trust her with his life? Why not? Echo wondered.

It works both ways, you know, she responded, sobering.

Yeah, it does, at that, baby, he agreed, as they polished off dessert.

Echo charged the meal to their room, and they slipped out, headed for the historic theatre that would be presenting the latest production of *Ey Rhai Diflas* that night.

There were, for a wonder, no Ke!endarians in evidence.

* * *

Ey Rhai Diflas was, as Echo had said, similar in plot and theme to Shakespeare's *Romeo and Juliet*. However, whereas the Earth play was a tragedy, *Ey Rhai Diflas* was more of a suspense drama. The male lead was indeed badly injured in the fight with the rival clan, but his love for the female lead kept him going, and he managed to overcome his injuries with her help, leading to a happily-ever-after in the end.

The acting was excellent, as was the fight choreography and the set design, and Alpha One found they could immerse themselves in the show and briefly lose track of the real world. So it was something of a shock when the curtain closed and the lights came up for intermission; they both started somewhat, then shook themselves out of the story.

"Wanna go to the bar for some drinks and a snack, baby?" Echo wondered, glancing at his wrist chronometer. "It's been a couple-three hours since dinner. I bet your metabolism could stand a little something, by now."

"That might be nice, Ace," Omega replied with a smile, and they stood. "I'm not REALLY hungry, at least not yet, but yeah, by the time the show is over, I probably will be."

"Let's go, then," he said, offering his arm as they made their way along the aisle. "And we can stop off for an after-show something before bed, too."

"Then let's make this snack light, and do something a little heavier for an after-show," Omega suggested.

"That works," Echo said. "We won't have long to wolf down food before the last act, anyway. Do you want a glass of that ploom wine that we had for our picnic, if they have it?"

"Sounds delish," Omega immediately decided. "And maybe just their version of a croissant-thing...those seem to be common snacky-foods here, and they're light..."

* * *

Several hours later, the pair returned to their suite at the hotel, tired but happy, and well-fed.

"Did you like the show, Meg?" Echo wondered, as they prepared for bed.

"I loved it, Ace," a smiling Omega said in a soft tone. "I could easily imagine that was us, 'cause it sounded like several chunks of our last missions all strung together, or something."

"Me too. Whatcha wanna do tomorrow?"

"Well," Omega said, seeming a bit uncertain, "I did something I hope you'll like."

"What's that?"

"I scheduled us for an all-day couples spa session. Massages, saunas, facials, all that stuff."

"Whoa. I've never had a facial before. What the hell do they do for one 'a those?"

"Oh, for you, since you shave, they probably won't do an exfoliation, but they will on me. And they'll probably do a deep cleanse, an' a facial massage and moisturizing, then maybe a mask on top of the moisturizing cream, to help it push into the skin. OR," she considered, "they could do a purifying mask, then the moisturizing on top of it."

"Uh," a nonplussed Echo said, hesitant to admit that he didn't know what half of that meant. "If you say so, baby."

"It's okay. It all feels good. An' your skin'll feel GREAT afterward, I swear it will. I told 'em to make it the pampering kind, not the 'my face is a wreck an' I really need this' kind." Omega laughed. "Since you like having full-body massages, I think you'll like this. Oh! Hey," she added, as a memory surfaced, "remember when you had the makeup put on you at the movie set last Christmas, an' your skin got all irritated?"

"Yeah? Oh, you mean when you put the windburn shit on my face after finally gettin' all the makeup offa me? The ointment stuff?"

"Yeah. It'll probably feel a lot like that."

"Oh. Well, that's all right, then. That felt good. Never had anybody do that before." He paused, opening his mouth to say more, then he decided to let it go.

"What?"

"Nothing."

"Nuh-uh. That was another thought you aborted there, Ace," Omega protested. " I saw it in your eyes. I—wait."

"Huh?"

"I think I just picked it up through the mind thing," Omega told him. "You want it to be me massaging your face, don't you?"

Echo felt his cheeks heat.

"Um," he tried, then realized he wasn't likely to be able to force it out of his mouth. So he resorted to 'the mind thing' himself, given he had promised himself—in her presence—not to hold back his thoughts and feelings from his wife. *Yeah,* he admitted. *I love the feel of your hands on my skin. And you give great massages. So I just wish you could do it all, instead of somebody I've never met before. But then YOU wouldn't have it done to YOU, which isn't fair. An' I get that.*

Well, you could return the favor after, I guess, Omega pointed out. *I can cancel the appointment, and we can just stay here. Uh, I guess we'd need to run down and actually buy some of the products to use on each other...but I can do that, and you can get things ready here.*

No. Because by the time you were done with all that on me, I'd probably be asleep. And then we're back to YOU wouldn't be pampered the same way, never mind that I dunno how to do those facial things an' shit. Leave it. I'll learn what it feels like to have all that done to me, then we can maybe work out how to do 'spa days' for each other, when we arrive back home, if I like all of it. He shrugged. *Even if I don't like all of it, I can learn how to do it for you, if you want me to.*

I like that idea. A whole lot. She gave him a brilliant smile.

Echo lost himself in shining, sapphire-blue eyes.

* * *

The next day was a rip-roaring success, much to Omega's delight. Despite being what Omega sometimes teasingly referred to as 'Agent Badass Tough Guy,' it turned out that Echo loved the pampering.

"Because it relaxes parts of me that I didn't even realize needed relaxing," he explained to her, when the aestheticians had stepped out to allow the pair to unwind quietly together over their delicious, healthful, and very filling lunch, which was included in the package Omega had booked, and which had been created by the Prehnihohni restaurant on the roof.

"Ee-zackly," Omega agreed. "And now ya know why us females like having it done, now and again."

"Well, I do. It makes sense."

"Game for learning how to do it, then buying the right things to do it for each other, once we get back home?"

"Sure."

So for the rest of the day, he and Omega both questioned the aestheticians and therapists about the techniques. Those same spa workers, understanding that the pair were not from

15

Tiniken and therefore would not have ready access to the spa's facilities once they returned home, cheerfully explained, then taught, the various techniques. The massage therapists were especially pleased to discover that both were certified massage therapists on Earth—Omega having completed her certification at the end of the summer—and shared a few trade secrets.

Then Alpha One purchased several large product bundles to take home, and headed back to their suite arm in arm, wrapped in spa robes, talking quietly.

An avian porter watched as they exited the spa, headed across the lobby, and climbed into an elevator.

* * *

"Hey Meg?" Echo said, as they entered their suite.

"Yeah, Ace?" Omega looked up. "Wanna opaque the balcony and climb in the hot tub for a bit, before we see about dinner? Which meal I did NOT plan, by the way; I thought we could just wing it, tonight, depending on how relaxed we were after the spa. An' I dunno about you, but I'm pretty relaxed."

"Yeah, we can do that, alla that," he decided, moving to the wall control and doing as she'd requested. "I was just wondering something..."

"What?"

"I keep seeing this guy, all through the hotel, an' I'm not sure if I'm imagining things or not," he considered. "Have you noticed that Ke!endarian hotel staffer that keeps showing up? It was downstairs in the lobby just now, over by the bellhop station."

"Well, I have," Omega admitted, "but only because it kinda stands out, what with the bright plumage an' whatnot. The Tinikeni are more standard humanoid, after all. Umm, Opdip, according to that new morphology classification the sociologist on Aleancë came up with a couple months back."

"Yeah. That's true, I guess..." He chewed on his lower lip, considering. "Maybe that's all it is, then."

"What's wrong?"

"I dunno. I think it's probably a case of what Zz'r'p warned me about—my situational awareness is a little wonked, yet."

"Mm. It's possible," Omega decided. "After all that went down in the last couple weeks, at least. Galactic presidential assassins, an' space planes nearly blowin' up, and bein' mostly dead, then the brain core dump an' the fight between the nd't'lq download/re-upload and what was left of your mind after the dump, an' ALL that shit. It'd be enough to throw anybody off at least a little. Is the guy following you around? Is that what's bugging you?"

"It's hard to say," Echo noted, as they doffed their robes and slipped into the hot tub, gazing out at the lowering sun as it neared sunset. "I mean, if it is, it's not bein' obvious about it. I just keep SEEING it everywhere."

"Yeah, I hear ya," Omega said. "It could just be a solicitous hotel staff member...or it could be one of the last of the H!nar kre Naese!en!Re, who's recognized us, and either wonders if WE'RE after IT, or..."

"Right," Echo confirmed. "And it's the 'or' that concerns me. I don't want us to be blindsided by some bad shit on our honeymoon."

"Fair 'nuff. And no shit. Okay," Omega suggested, "what say we keep our eyes peeled for the guy, you an' me both, and see if, between us, we can figure out what's goin on? An' a quick query of the hotel manager might not be amiss, either. I mean, we don't wanna get the guy in trouble if we're just bein' too suspicious, but like you said, we don't wanna be blindsided, either. So I think a few discreet inquiries are warranted, here."

"That works," Echo concluded, settling into the hot water, finding a jet for his back, and pulling Omega into his side.

* * *

Late that evening, in the same run-down flat in a poorer neighborhood of Prini, the same Ke!endarian doffed the uniform of the Gwesti Tŷ Preni Hotel and clad himself in the same long, draping, rather threadbare vest he had worn before...and which he wore every evening after returning from work, rather like a robe or dressing gown. He ensured the door of his dilapidated apartment was locked—engaging all three locks—then he moved to the bedroom and opened the closet door, pulling a certain small black chest from the floor in the shadowed corner. He sat it on the dresser and opened it, revealing the same compact interstellar communications device he had used

17

before. Activating it, he programmed in a specific frequency and direction, then picked up the microphone and murmured into it.

In Cortian.

(Leader, this is Outcast.)

Moments later, the response arrived.

(Outcast, this is Leader. Continue.)

(I have been able to track Public Enemy Number One over most of his activities since we last spoke. However, the female with him is NOT Public Enemy Number Two; it is another human-like female that I do not recognize. I do believe that this is his mate, however; they are always together, and as nearly as I can determine, spending a good bit of their time together unclothed and frequently procreating.)

(How did you determine this? Have you managed to enter their hotel room?)

(No, not as yet, though I am working on that. The hotel has damnably strict rules regarding guest contact, however, so it may be necessary to find...alternative means.)

(Then how do you know this?)

(They went for a walk in the flowering forest near the hotel yesterday as I was going off shift at the hotel. I followed them and watched from a carefully-hidden location.)

(You saw them copulate?)

(I did.)

(Then yes, you are correct—this is not his former partner. They did not have such a relationship, but were very business-like with each other.)

(No, not according to the dossier I studied about them. Are you still interested in the mate?)

(Negative. If it is not Public Enemy Number Two, then it is merely an ordinary female, and beneath our interest. I care nothing for those. For now, we only want the male.)

(Very good, Leader. I think this should be doable without too much difficulty; he seems to be...preoccupied, I assume with mating rituals.)

(Excellent. How do you recommend we apprehend, Out-cast?)

(I am formulating a plan. However, I recommend we do so

the day before their scheduled departure. It will time out best that way, and given their intended departure, possibly no one will notice for some time that he has even gone missing, leaving us with more than sufficient opportunity to get well away.)

(Do you desire to utilize the standard methods and procedures for taking a new acquisition?)

(Just so.)

(Very well. I will ensure you have a team available for that day. You have adequately proven yourself, so you will be in command of that team. Keep up the good work, and I shall assign them to you permanently.)

(Thank you, sir.)

(Do you have any other information?)

(Negative, Leader; not at this time.)

(Then we shall see you on the designated day. Leader signing off.)

(Outcast signing off.)

* * *

Over the ensuing days, the newlywed pair explored Prini and the surrounding area. This included visiting a local theme park; climbing the possibly-dormant, probably-extinct volcano on the outskirts of the city, and bathing in the hydrothermal springs associated with the volcano; taking a guided tour of the entire region; splashing their way through a nearby water park; going on a vineyard tour and sampling the local wines—though the fruit being used was not a grape, but something called a ploom; bar and restaurant hopping to thoroughly sample the local cuisine; and snorkeling and scuba diving with the local underwater wildlife. This was interspersed with swimming and bodysurfing at the hotel beach, splashing in the pool, another visit to the excellent hotel spa, two more plays on the Prini equivalent of Broadway, and plenty of soaks in the hot tub on their balcony, both with and without swimsuits.

Subsequent discreet discussion about the Ke!endarian hotel employee with the various members of the hotel hierarchy—to include the concierge, the head of security, the luggage services manager, the night manager, and the hotel manager—had left the pair somewhat perplexed about the situation.

"On the one hand," Omega observed, "it's just a hotel

worker. And we've never seen it anywhere other than where it's supposed to be. And you know we asked, that time."

"Yeah," Echo agreed. "But there's just that off chance it's more than it seems. And...it's entirely possible that it's BOTH—a member of the cult who escaped the whole mess after we took out Slug and it was revealed, who came here, got a legit job, and has been working hard at it...but who recognized us when we showed up, and resents us for what it had to give up on its homeworld."

"That's a definite consideration," Omega asserted. "I guess we sorta need to keep an eye on this guy, just in case."

"Yeah. But it sucks having to be on our guard on our damn honeymoon," Echo grumbled.

"No doubt. But better that, and completing our honeymoon and getting home okay, than the alternative," Omega pointed out.

"Yeah, yeah. I know. I don't have to like it, though."

"Nope. But that's the nature of our job, honey. And you know we both love the job."

"True. Don't sweat it; I'll deal. Hey, let's go jump in the hot tub."

"Okay."

* * *

Their honeymoon sojourn wound down all too soon. The morning before they were due to leave, Echo set a soft alarm on his cell phone, and sat up when it went off, somewhat earlier than they had been rising during the trip...which was considerably later than their work schedule, in any event.

"Mmph," Omega muttered, as Echo crawled out of bed. "Where ya goin', Ace?"

"Shush," he murmured. "Roll over and go back to sleep, baby."

"Nuh-uh. Where ya goin'?"

"I'm just gonna run down to the front desk and make sure everything's ready for us to check out tomorrow," Echo noted, pulling on a pair of shorts and a t-shirt.

"Hang on an' I'll go wif," she said, slurring her words a bit, but starting to sit up anyway. Echo put a hand on her shoulder and pushed her back into the bed.

20

"No," he told her, kissing her nose with a grin. "You need a little more sleep, baby. You're groggy as hell, an' it shows. I kept you up pretty late last night...and woke you up several times overnight into the bargain...and I fell asleep after the hot tub soak yesterday and took a nice nap, but you didn't, 'cause Ms. Got-A-Crapton-Of-Degrees was lookin' at the travelogue book from the volcano park. So right now, I want you to just stay here and snooze. I'll take care of matters."

"You sure?"

"I'm sure. I just wanna check that everything is in order, the bill gets paid, an' whatnot."

"I thought Fox an' the guys 're payin'...that 'uz their gift..."

"They are...for the hotel. But we have a buncha incidentals, too. Room service, restaurant visits, spa stuff, an' all kindsa shit like that. An' that's gonna have added up pretty damn fast; I don't wanna stick them with all that. So I need to make sure the hotel has a means to bill US for that—an' we'll have to sit down, once we arrive home, and finalize our joint finances an' accounts an' stuff, so we CAN pay it off properly, and not piss off the hotel at us. Plus, I need to find out the best way to send our luggage over to the spaceport and see it's loaded onto our ship in the morning." He shoved his feet into flip-flops. "Hopefully they can arrange that for us, without our having to do it, so we can make a few last-minute stops for souvenirs an' shit."

"Oh. Okay. Jus' log-logis..." Omega broke off, and Echo suddenly realized with some amusement that her eyes weren't open...and hadn't been, throughout their entire exchange. "Logis-tics," she finally managed to force the word out of her sleepy brain and through her mouth.

"Yup. Shouldn't take long. So roll over there and go back to sleep, sweetheart. When I get back, I might just slip back into bed with you."

"An' wake me up again?"

"Depends on if you wanna be woken up or not."

"Hmm..."

"Meantime, I'm off," he said, heading for the door.

"Hokay. 'F I'm not in bed, I'll be inna bafroom."

"Right."

And he was gone.

Seconds later, Omega was sound asleep.

* * *

As he had expected, it did not take Echo long to settle matters with the hotel's front desk, explain about the different charges, and provide a way for the hotel to place the incidentals on his *carte noir* account. This would, in turn, send a receipt back to his Division One files, and Accounting would separate it out from the standard expense account charges. He would then receive an invoice from Accounting, and he would pay it like a bill, from his personal banking account; as yet, he and Omega had not had an opportunity to set up a joint account, largely due to considerable travel offworld, combined with assisting in rescue after the space plane accident and subsequent events.

"And your luggage will be taken care of, as well," the concierge told him. "We have the records of your personal-use spacecraft in our files, so all you need do is contact...I think you call it 'the bellhop' on Earth, though I have never understood why...when you are ready to check out. Luggage services will come to your room and collect your bags, take them to the appropriate area of the spaceport, and leave them with Division Seven personnel, who will see that it is all loaded onto your spacecraft in plenty of time prior to your scheduled departure. There will be all due paperwork to see that the handover occurs smoothly, so fear not on that account. While this is occurring, you can shop, eat, walk on the beach, or whatever last things you wish to do."

"Great! How long will it take for our luggage to be loaded on board?" Echo asked. "We have quite a few hours' flight in front of us, but there ARE a few last things we wanted to do..."

"I would allow about four of your hours," the concierge decided. "That will permit for the transfer of possession between our service and the Division Seven spaceport personnel, as well as time for them to load it aboard your craft."

"That sounds good."

"Is there anything else I can do to help you?"

"No, that should be fine," Echo decided. "Is there anything else you need from us?"

"No sir. We have everything on record now, and will take

care of matters pertaining to separating the charges appropriately."

"Good deal."

"We hope you have enjoyed your stay and that it has provided you with pleasant memories of your nuptial trip," the concierge said with a smile.

"It's been great, the hotel is terrific, and we've both really enjoyed it, thanks," Echo said, returning the smile. "So on that note, I'm going to run back up to the suite and join my bride before room service arrives with our breakfast."

"Very good, sir."

And Echo headed for the elevator banks.

* * *

The bridal suite where the couple was staying was in a more remote wing of the hotel, intended to ensure privacy thereby— and though there were some six or eight such suites, all in the same wing but grouped on different floors by pairs, Fox had ensured that Alpha One was given the most luxurious, up on the top floor of the bridal wing. So Echo got off the elevator on the correct floor of the hotel's main tower, then walked down the corridor, headed for the dog-leg connector at the end that would take him into the honeymoon-suite wing.

But as he stepped around the corner of the dog-leg, a sudden blow landed on the back of his head, and he dropped to the carpeted floor, unconscious.

One presumed Ke!endarian, wearing the hotel's uniform, stood over him...

...Flanked by nearly half a dozen avian beings with bright-yellow plumage, in a military uniform that, had Echo been conscious, he would have recognized instantly.

And with extreme prejudice.

* * *

The Cortians moved swiftly. Three of them searched his body for weapons or other telltale devices, and removed his wrist chronometer, his special Agency cell phone, and his hidden Winchester & Tesla. These were tossed aside, under a nearby decorative cabinet, where they would be difficult to find. Their undercover operative confiscated Echo's wallet, complete with *carte noir*, tucking it into a hidden pocket of his uniform...a pocket which was NOT standard-issue.

Then they hoisted the human between them, and the under-cover operative led them to a service door nearby.

Within moments, the Cortians had vanished with their pris-oner.

Chapter 2

Back in the honeymoon suite, Omega woke with a start. *Oh shit,* she thought, concerned. *What just happened? Something is wrong, something is BAD wrong.* Then she reached through the nd't'lq. *Echo? Honey, are you there?* Then she waited for a response.

Nothing.

Well, not QUITE nothing, she decided. *I'm picking up a sense of his presence, just...no thoughts. Which may mean he's unconscious. Which means something IS wrong.*

Omega leaped from the bed and frantically began throwing on clothes.

* * *

She ran down the corridor toward the elevators, then stopped dead in the dog-leg.

Here, she thought. *He was here.*

Omega turned her experienced Agent's eagle eye on the area, noting several things...

The grip of a Winchester & Tesla 'death-ray' pistol protruding from the shadow under the nearby cabinet.

The faint glint from something else metallic under that same cabinet.

A certain scuffing of the carpet, notably two narrow drag marks that went for some three or four feet before disappearing.

Three small feathers—two yellow, and one that was teal green at the base, transitioning to bright blue at the tip.

"Oh, shit," Omega whispered, horrified, as she pulled out her cell phone.

* * *

"Madam, I am very sorry," the local police officer, having been summoned by hotel security, told Omega in a disparaging tone nearly an hour later, "but there is no real evidence that anything untoward has happened to your spouse. I am sure he is elsewhere in the hotel, perhaps getting a bite to eat, or maybe on the beach."

"And I'm telling you that you're wrong," Omega declared. "AGENT Echo wouldn't simply go off like that without telling me. And he specifically told me he was coming back to the room, after he discussed some business with the concierge."

The police officer sniffed and offered her a condescending smile.

"And do you always claim your spouse is a secret agent?" she wondered.

"No," she said, gritting her teeth, "he happens to be a PGLEIA Agent of Division One, as am I." She whipped out her *carte noir* and showed it to the officer, who only glanced at it perfunctorily before turning away.

"Madam, placing an emergency call when there is no emergency IS an offense on Tiniken," she noted. "Be glad I am not choosing to take you into custody; I do understand how newlyweds can become...agitated."

And she walked away.

An annoyed and deeply worried Omega whipped out her cell phone and hit the speed dial to Director Fox of Division One.

"Fox?" she said, as soon as the other end answered. "Something bad has happened, and I need some help, as fast as you can, 'cause I'm sure not getting it here..."

* * *

"Oh HELL no," Fox declared, when Omega had ended the phone call. "That won't do AT ALL." He hit the intercom on his desk. "Lima? Bravo? Who've I got?"

"It's Lima, boss," came the response.

"Lima, put me straight through to the chief of police in Presti, on Tiniken, and make it FAST. Emergency channels, please."

"On it!"

* * *

Five minutes later, and having hung up on the police office in Presti, Fox hit his intercom again.

"Lima, get me Yaacrun Elyryqoli this time, on an emergency max secure link."

"Director of Division Seven?"

"The same. And this IS an emergency."

"What the hell has happened?"

"Get Elyryqoli on the line and I'll tell you after."

"Roger that, Fox."

* * *

"Wait, wait, wait," Elyryqoli said, a few minutes later, after Fox had explained the situation. "Your newly-espoused assistant director has disappeared, and his Agent spouse cannot even locate him? And then the local police force representative refused to even recognize her, let alone assist her?"

"Worse—my agent, who happens to be the assistant chief of our Alpha Line special forces, was threatened with arrest for filing a supposedly false emergency report," Fox elaborated.

"Arniquat and argdun!" Elyryqoli cursed. "Argit self-important idiots! And to the Alpha Line assistant chief, no less! All right, let me think. Presti, on Tiniken, you said? Excellent! MY assistant director is currently there on Division business; I'll contact him right now and tell him to head over there with a team and help your Agent, as fast as he can get there."

"That would be MUCH appreciated, Yaac," Fox averred. "Aside from professional considerations, Echo is one of my oldest friends. I'm hoping nothing bad has happened to him."

"ECHO?! The missing agent is ECHO?? Argit, gronk, ale arniquat!" Elyryqoli cursed even harder. "All right, Fox, I'll send Vaea post-haste. If that does not do it, contact me again on this mode, and I will go to Tiniken PERSONALLY. If you decide you need to take a small force there to help search, by all means, do so. I will welcome the assistance; the regional crime lords have been...difficult, of late."

"Understood, meyn khaver, and thank you. Fox out."

"Elyryqoli out."

* * *

Fifteen minutes later, Division Seven personnel were swarming the hotel corridor, reconstructing the crime scene, and the snarky police officer was receiving a VERY thorough reaming-out by the PGLEIA team lead...who also happened to be the Division's assistant director. Omega watched from farther down the corridor as the Tinikeni officer flushed a deep purple, hung her head, then nodded to the Division Seven agent. The agent delivered a curt order, then spun on his heel and headed straight for Omega.

"Idiot," he grumbled. "Self-important, overconfident imbecile! She did not even look at your *carte noir* to register it as proper identification, let alone PGLEIA special-issue! And so is this equipment, according to what my people are telling me," he added, waving at the chronometer, pistol, and cell phone, now lying bagged and tagged on top of the cabinet, as the team swept the corridor for additional clues. "Oh, forgive me, Agent Omega. I am Vaea Kilinisi of Tiniken, and I am the assistant chief, ah, the assistant director, the proper terminology makes it, for Division Seven—which means I am your spouse's equivalent, in your Division. Our chief thought it only proper to ensure top personnel responded, but he is himself based on Ryynqitsk and Director Fox indicated this was an emergency—I hope you understand how it is."

"I certainly do. You were close, and he wasn't. Pleased to meet you, Agent Kilinisi," Omega murmured, taking his proffered hand and shaking.

"Call me Vaea, if you would," the tall, humanoid agent with the lightly teal-toned skin noted, giving her a slight, friendly smile. "You have begun on a bad note with our local law enforcement," he cast an irritated glance over his shoulder at the chastened police officer, who flinched, "and have uncharacteristically lost track of your mate and partner. The least I can do is to offer my friendship and help."

"Thank you, and that's GREATLY appreciated, all of it," Omega sighed. "I take it, you've identified the equipment as Echo's?"

"Without doubt or difficulty," Kilinisi averred. "The registries on the chronometer, the weapon, and the communications device are all very plain. But I note that his wallet and *carte noir* are not to be found. Evidently his kidnappers did not realize that these devices are as easily identifiable as his personal identification."

"Yeah," Omega agreed. "Listen, Vaea, I'm worried. I mean REALLY worried."

"Why? Your husband is quite capable."

"Let's step into the foyer of my hotel room for a moment, so I can fill you in on a few things, in private," Omega suggested.

* * *

"Oh great Maker," an alarmed Kilinisi exclaimed, when Omega was done. "So you FELT the event, and it woke you?"

"Exactly," Omega noted. "But I can't communicate with him now, which means he's unconscious."

"Forgive this question, but are you certain he is not dead?"

"Positive," Omega declared. "I'd feel that, for sure. Think... think carrier signal, but no comm. That's what I have right now."

"Ah. Well, there is something, at any rate."

"Yeah. And those feathers? Make sure Forensics gets on those five minutes ago. I'd lay odds that the yellow ones belong to the Cortian species, and the blue one is either off a Ke!endarian from the Naese!en!Re cult, or else it's been dyed and is really from a Cortian in disguise."

"Oio! Akri tiri!" he exclaimed in his native language, cursing, then stuck his head out the door and yelled down the hall. "Ikirinu! Awai! Send those feathers to Forensics IMMEDIATELY! Tell them to check for dyes on the blue one, and to identify the genetics by species, as fast as they can! The iniwiki Cortian slavers may have Agent Echo!"

Everyone in the corridor froze in horrified shock, then erupted into a coordinated frenzy of activity.

Omega sighed, deeply worried.

* * *

"No, it doesn't sound good," Fox acknowledged a query in the Alpha Line Room.

He had called an emergency all-hands meeting of that department to brief the situation, and invited Crutch, head of the standard field agent department, new recruit Chi and his recently-assigned partner Genova, and as many of the Medical department physicians as could get away, to join them. This included Zarnix, chief of staff; Fox's mate Zebra, assistant chief of staff; as well as a few medtechs, to include Yorker.

Dihl, Echo's mother and a fine medtech in her own right, was NOT there, since she had already returned to the Ranch—

their family rancho down in western Texas, which currently served as a safehouse and guest ranch for visiting agents and offworld diplomats, as well as the occasional unaware human family—where she was the resident medico, splitting her time between the Ranch and Headquarters. Given she had a doctorate in nursing and had worked in several different medical fields, including emergency room work, this was considered an excellent use of her skills.

Uncle, head of the Security department, also stood by, listening to the briefing. Several of the Deltiri embassage, including Ambassador Zz'r'p ob Tii'rkin, his assistant, envoy Mm'l'n ag Mii'laa, and a handful of others, were also there at Omega's specific request. Lima and Bravo sat in the corner, taking notes; Fox had told them to attend so they could hear what was happening without the need for him to explain multiple times.

"Wait," Monkey said then, biting his lip and seeming torn between seriousness and whimsy. "You mean we just got him all back to normal an' married off to Meg, an' Meg's done lost him?"

"In a manner of speaking, yes, though it was certainly not her fault, Monkey. According to the information she fed me, they both had instinctive negative reactions toward a particular hotel staffer," Fox explained, "a Ke!endarian who always seemed to show up when they were around. They suspected the being might be a former member of the H!nar kre Naese!en!Re cult. They never were able to determine that anything was wrong with the being, and the hotel vouched for it as a legitimate staff member. But when Omega picked up on an event involving Echo earlier today through the nd't'lq—"

"The wha?" Uniform wondered, puzzled.

"Uhm, the telepathic bond that Ambassador Zz'r'p created at the end of their wedding ceremony," Fox tried, "well, she ran to the site that she picked up in the telepathic link, only she found no Echo, nor anyone else...but what she DID find was his concealed-carry weapon, his chronometer, and his cell phone. Tossed under a decorative cabinet in the hallway. No wallet, though. And she found three feathers...one in the teal-blue crest color of a Ke!endarian...and the other two in the canary-yellow of a Cortian."

A wave of murmured cursing in several languages swept the room.

"Director Fox," Mm'l'n piped up, "you said Agent Omega 'picked up an event.' What kind of event? What was Agent Echo communicating to her when this event occurred?"

"That's the problem," Fox noted. "She doesn't know. According to what she told me, Echo rose up early this morning to run down to the front desk and arrange for the luggage to be transferred to their spacecraft tomorrow, for the return home... and didn't come back. Meanwhile, and at his insistence, she was still asleep in bed."

"Ah," Zz'r'p observed. "So she was herself soundly asleep, and it was this...'event'...that awakened her. Only...because she was asleep when it happened, she does not know WHAT happened. Only that something was, and is, wrong."

"Exactly."

"I hate to ask it, especially after...recent events, but...is she certain Echo is still alive?" Zz'r'p pressed.

"That, she was positive about," Fox noted. "Apparently not conscious, but alive. She said it was like a carrier signal, but without an actual communication overlaid."

"Ah," Zz'r'p murmured. "So background brain activity, but no thoughts."

"As best I understood it, yes."

There was a long silence as everyone pondered the implications of that information.

"Whadda y'all need?" Romeo asked then.

"Well, it seems that the local gendarmes were rather less than helpful," a wry Fox informed them, "let alone respectful, when Omega reported her husband and partner missing. In fact, they refused to act at all, declaring Omega to be, basically, a flighty young bride...and actually threatened her with arrest for falsely reporting an emergency. Nor did I receive any better response, when I called the local police directly, in an effort to speak with the Prini Chief of Police—the receptionist or dispatcher, I never was able to determine which, had evidently had news of Omega's report through channels...or possibly gossip...and tried to claim that I must be the husband, and that she and I were attempting to perpetrate an illegal hoax of some sort." He shook his head in disgust. "Eventually I had to go through channels to report the matter to the Division Seven chief as an emergency situation and send some PGLEIA agents over there before the crime scene was spoiled by housekeeping or some such. Omega has specifically asked for any of the Deltiri embassy personnel that can be spared to come to Tiniken and help her try to track Echo...who is apparently still unconscious, and it's now been close to three hours, possibly four..." he glanced at his wrist chronometer, "no, make that definitely four...since the 'event' that woke her...which I take to be likely when he was knocked out and captured. I pinged her right before this meeting commenced, and verified that she still has no communication with him."

"Wait—still unconscious, four hours later? He's still alive, though, right?" Yankee wondered, concerned.

"She swears he is," Fox told the once-recalcitrant Agent. "She specifically said to tell Zz'r'p that business about how it was like a carrier signal with no comm."

"If he is still unconscious after four hours, then he is likely being KEPT unconscious," Zz'r'p averred. "His captors are likely attempting to prevent a telepath tracking him, while they escape with him. Which means," he added, "that we need to start on this right away, or we shall lose him, possibly forever."

"Zz'r'p, I will be glad to help," Qq'k'l ob Sii'stek, an interrogator with PGLEIA, formerly assigned to Division Five but recently transferred to Division One, volunteered. "All of us in the embassy know Agent Omega at this point, and most of us know Agent Echo. And the embassy is, finally, fully staffed. I think we can ensure that Fox has not one, but a team of telepaths to assist, while still keeping the embassy running properly."

"Agreed," Mm'l'n averred. "I will gladly go to help Omega find Echo."

"And I am free as well, and my pupil and patient—Omega—needs me," Zz'r'p observed. "Mm'l'n, do you and Qq'k'l gather a team of at least three more of our people, and prepare to depart as soon as Director Fox determines."

"Which will be as soon as we get an overall team of volunteers together, and the *Genesis* ready to depart," Fox noted. "Her crew is gathering and transferring aboard even as we speak. It won't be a full crew, but we'll have all positions staffed and ready. I already have a forensics team lined up and ready to go, as well. But I need at least a couple of physicians, to ensure nothing harmful has been done to Echo—and treat him if there has been, and some field agents, whether from Alpha Line or Crutch's standard Field department. Preferably some of both. Plus any security teams that Uncle can spare."

"I cannot go," Zarnix sighed. "I have several important patients in the various embassies that will need seeing to in the next few days. It could be a diplomatic incident, several times over, were I to leave now."

"I can go," Zebra volunteered. "If I can have Yorker and a couple more medtechs, and if Alpha Two comes along so I can have India as a backup, I think we're good for medical."

Romeo and India, the Alpha Two team, exchanged glances.

"Done," India declared.

"Yah-bo," Romeo agreed.

"Chi, do you and Genova want to come along?" Fox wondered. "Omega is your old friend..."

"I'd really like to, Fox, more than I can say...but I think I have some major training scheduled, in order to ensure some stuff is properly certified," Chi said. "Crutch? Any chance I can waive that?"

"Not and follow PGLEIA regs," Crutch pointed out. "Which you need to do, if you're aiming for membership in Alpha Line."

"All right," Fox said. "Crutch, can you send us a few teams? Uncle, what about you? We might have a bit of a fight on our hands if the Cortians really do have Echo, and I'd like enough field agents on the *Genesis* to ensure a crap-ton of boarding parties, if it comes to that. I don't WANT us to have to fight our way through to Echo, but I will if I must. And for what it's worth, I WILL be there, fighting beside your agents. Echo is the chief of Alpha Line, my Assistant Director, the future Division Director...and my oldest human friend still living. And I want to keep it that way."

"Consider it done, Fox," Crutch said. "As many as you

need."

"Ditto," Uncle averred. "As many as we can cram aboard your flagship. Do you plan to bring out the fleet?"

"Not this time, not unless I have to," Fox said. "But you lot need to be ready, in case I DO have to. I WILL have a few small escort craft, fighter types—corvettes and whatnot. Whatever can readily fit into the spacecraft hangar bay, or can keep up. Because the *Genesis* will be hauling ass. Again." He let out a sigh. "I swear, of late I've been thinking about putting emergency running lights and markers on it; ever since Pul nearly got himself gelatinized on the transfer station at Emdali, I never seem to use her as a flagship, just an emergency response vessel."

"Roger that," Crutch agreed with a bleak chuckle. "And don't worry, old friend—we'll be ready. Whatever we need to do. I'll put the entire department on alert, world-wide, all facilities."

"Us, too," Uncle added.

"Good. And thank you both. Alpha Line, volunteers?" Fox asked.

The entire department present in the room stood, and all of the video links to the other Office branches bleeped, depicting rooms full of standing Agents.

"Right," Fox said with a wry, but pleased, chuckle. "Romeo, draw straws or something, please. I want at least a half-dozen Alpha Line teams going with me. Alpha Four, I know you want to come along, but if Alpha Two is coming—and they are, because we need India's medical expertise—I need you two here to run the department."

"Yes sir," Golf accepted the order.

"What he said," Easy agreed. "We'll help wherever we're needed, Fox. You know that."

"So they're exempt," Romeo noted. "Got it."

"Good. Everybody else, go get ready to head out," Fox ordered. "We leave dry dock in not longer than two hours. Agents dismissed."

* * *

"Forward view on screen. Hail dry dock," Fox ordered exactly two hours later, and Cast brought up the large viewing screen. Sail nodded, tapping a few controls before murmuring into his mic. Seconds later, the response came, and he put it on audio.

"This is Lunar Farside Drydocks Control for the *Genesis*. Admiral Director?"

"Affirmative, Control, this is Fox. Take her out of dry dock, if you please."

"Tractor beams locking on, sir."

"Docking clamps disengaged," Fox made the call even as he signaled Cast to release the clamps, "now."

"Copy that. Locking beams...now," Drydocks Control replied. As usual, there was a slight shifting of the deck beneath them, but otherwise there was no evidence of the tractor beam lock until the dry dock's structure began to slide past the viewing screen. The huge saucer moved farther and farther away from the docking superstructure with each second that passed.

"Drydocks Control to *Genesis*."

"*Genesis* here," Fox replied.

"You are clear, sir, and ready for interplanetary drive. As per *Genesis* Protocol, all other traffic has been halted until you depart."

"*Genesis* copies. *Genesis* Protocol engaged. We are go for interplanetary drive; all other traffic halted."

"I show good copy. You may engage interplanetary engines at your discretion, sir. We all hope you find Agent Echo swiftly."

"Amein," Fox murmured in response. "Aaand...engaging interplanetary drive...now." He nodded at Übermut, whose hands already hovered over the appropriate controls.

And the *Genesis* shot away from the Earth-Moon system, en route to Tiniken.

* * *

Fox took the *Genesis* out, well past the asteroid belt, with full cloaking and sensor scrambling to avoid detection from Earth, angling above the ecliptic plane into the galactic plane. As soon as Cast reported clear space and all significant masses far enough away, Fox ordered an Alcubierre warp bubble raised, and the *Genesis* headed straight for the Zeta Aurigae system, and its fourth planet, Tiniken, more commonly nicknamed 'Eden,' as fast as it could travel.

* * *

Just over four hours after the *Genesis* left the Lunar Farside Drydocks and dropped into emergency Alcubierre warp, Fox, Romeo, India, Zebra, and Zz'r'p were on 'Eden,' meeting with Omega and Division Seven Assistant Director Vaea Kilinisi, in the hotel security staff's conference room.

"So you are all right, tekhter?" Fox verified, as Zebra and India both checked Omega with their medscanners.

"Other than fifty-eight kinds of upset, Fox, yeah, I'm okay," Omega murmured.

"I confirm," Zebra said.

"Me, too," India added. "Omega, have you taken your meds today?"

"Not yet," the distressed Agent confessed. "I usually do it after breakfast, and this all went down before...Echo was supposed to be back in time for breakfast, see..."

"Ah," Zebra said, and she and India both nodded. "Is it in your room?"

"Yeah. Which is up on the top floor, I think, in a different wing."

"So not close," India confirmed.

"Nope."

"No worries," Zebra said. "I thought about this, and brought extra." She fished out a small case from her medikit, extracted a tiny tablet, and gave it to Omega, who swallowed it dry. "There we go."

"Medications?" Kilinisi wondered.

"Ah. Omega has been stalked, nearly raped, mind-raped, sexually assaulted, physically assaulted, and several other such assaults, all in the last, mm, say three-ish months," Fox explained. "She is suffering from PTSD, and a certain amount of free-floating anxiet—"

"Great Maker!" a shocked Kilinisi exclaimed. "In no more than three lunations?! Female, why are you even HERE?! You should be at home, resting and recovering!"

"This was supposed to be a bridal vacation," Omega murmured ruefully.

"Ah, yes, yes," Kilinisi recalled. "You and Agent Echo are

mated. So that was NOT a cover story."

"No," Fox confirmed. "She and Echo were here on their honeymoon, having left right after the wedding recep-uh, the nuptial reception. We had hopes that this would prove beneficial for both of them, as Echo also suffered near-death in an accident recently, as well. We...hadn't counted on yet another of their old enemies getting to them."

"So...this has all been a concerted effort by their various enemies, to exact revenge?" Kilinisi queried. "All these events in recent lunations?"

"Yes," Omega replied. "For the most part, at least. Not necessarily all the SAME enemies, nor even working together. But at least one of 'em played off another."

"True," Fox agreed. "And even though this is our top team, there is only so much a being can take, after all."

"That, I shall grant you," Kilinisi acknowledged. "And now this latest blow. So we need to ascertain who, where, and what to do about it."

"Yes," Fox concurred. "I think—"

Just then, there was a knock on the door. Kilinisi held up a finger.

"Come in," he called.

The door opened, and a Tinikeni wearing a Division Seven-styled Suit—which was cut slightly differently from the Division One Suits, to better accommodate slightly different anatomy—entered, followed by several members of Fox's hand-picked forensics team.

"Please forgive the interruption," the Tinikeni agent apologized, "but we thought you would want this information at once."

"Go," Kilinisi ordered.

"We have completed the analysis of the feathers Agent Omega found on the floor of the corridor, at the point where Agent Echo was apparently abducted," the agent continued. "And we have confirmed that they are ALL Cortian, from three different individuals, and the blue feather was in fact dyed; it is yellow beneath. The dye was not particularly sophisticated, for it showed readily in our chemical analyses, but apparently it was sufficient to the purpose. No one suspected he was NOT a Ke!endarian...except Alpha One, apparently."

"So...that means the Ke!endarian hotel employee was a plant," Omega observed, "like Echo an' I figured. 'Cause he's the only Ke!endarian we've seen."

"It sounds that way, tekhter," Fox agreed. "Which is not good news."

"No, it is not," Kilinisi averred. "Thank you, Awai. Please continue to work with our Division One colleagues whenever necessary, as necessary."

"Yes sir."

The group departed. The room was silent for long moments.

"Well," a pale Omega said then, wry, "I guess that answers 'who.'"

"Indeed," Kilinisi agreed.

"Now we need to figure out 'where,'" Fox declared.

"An' figure out what to do about it, when we get there," Omega added.

* * *

After half an hour of quizzing Omega regarding her perception of the event, with little more information determined— "I just don't KNOW," she insisted, "I was asleep!"—Ambassador Zz'r'p raised a thin blue hand.

"I think there is little more to be gained by interrogating Omega any more, except in that it will only upset her further," he said. "With her permission, I have already perused her memory of the incident, and there is very little that even I can obtain from it, except to note that Echo was likely struck on the back of the head to render him unconscious."

"Huh," Omega grunted. "That was my impression, yeah, but I'm not used to all this, so I wasn't sure."

"Well observed, then," Zz'r'p commended. "What else have you ascertained?"

"Not a lot," Omega sighed. "I still can't reach Echo, though I AM picking up faint sensations. Beyond that, I can't really tell."

"If you wish, I can enter the bond with him and see if I cannot locate him, or at least determine his condition."

"I think that'd be really good," Omega agreed immediately.

* * *

Assistant Director Kilinisi watched in curiosity as Omega and Zz'r'p settled down in their chairs, closing their eyes and relaxing as much as possible. Gradually the human and Deltiri faces both blanked, all expression fading, and they slumped a bit in their seats as their respiration slowed. The room became completely silent.

"Wha—" Kilinisi began.

"Shh!" the others shushed him, verbally and with vehement hand gestures. A slight smile crossed Zz'r'p's face; Omega slumped deeper in her chair. Fox motioned the other male out of the room.

* * *

In the corridor outside, with the door to the conference room closed, Fox explained.

"Omega isn't a full-on telepath, Vaea," he noted, recognizing the Tinikeni from the times the other male had filled in for his superior on the Directors' Conferences. "That's why she needed Zz'r'p's help. She has definite abilities, and she can be quite strong with some of 'em, but humans aren't natural telepaths, and she needs Zz'r'p's help to do this. And we've all found that it's better to just be as quiet as possible when either of 'em tries to do something like this. Oh, I'm sure it doesn't bother Zz'r'p, unless it's a really delicate task...which he had, recently...but Omega needs the quiet to be able to concentrate and ensure she does things properly."

"Mm. I see," Kilinisi pondered. "If I am understanding correctly, this is the agent who was...tampered with...by an interstellar criminal?"

"The very one," Fox confirmed. "And this ability is one that was induced in her by those tamperings. 'Enhancements,' she calls 'em...though she doesn't mean it as a positive thing. So, while the things that were done to her—which were performed in such fashion as to be essentially tolly torture, let me add—have placed her easily in the top percentile of the human species, there are still limits to what she can do. That said, if she is determined enough, I have seen her at least temporarily exceed those limits, exceed the norms for our species," he admitted. "Sometimes, by a goodly amount. And, given how much she cares about Echo, it wouldn't surprise me to find out that this will be one of those situations."

"So she needs the silence in order to concentrate, and accomplish what would normally be impossible," Kilinisi couched the query as a statement.

"I dunno if 'impossible' is quite the right term, but 'improbable' certainly works," Fox said with a shrug. "'Difficult' is probably the best descriptor; really, really damn difficult, even for her, with her altered abilities. She has a massive intellect—which is natural, by the way; the alterations didn't give it to her—a great heart, deep love, and a strong, powerful will. If she can't determine a way to find Echo, especially with the Deltiri helping her, then he can't be found."

* * *

When the pair re-entered the conference room, it was to find Omega and Zz'r'p already 'coming to,' and becoming aware of the people around them once more.

"What's th' word, guys?" Romeo wondered.

"Indeed," Fox joined his voice to the Alpha Line Agent's. "What information were you able to ascertain, Zz'r'p?"

"I reached into Omega's mind, to the location of Echo's mental 'clone,'" the Deltiri explained. "It was largely unresponsive, which I expected, but I was able to reach out along the connection and ascertain a few things."

"Keep going," India said.

"I must agree with Omega, and with my original surmise, back in Headquarters," Zz'r'p decided. "Echo is being kept unconscious until he is well away from the scene of his kidnapping. However, based on what I could pick up and interpret, which is a bit more than Omega, as I have many decades more experience doing so, I am afraid I have some bad news."

"Tell us, alter khaver," Fox urged.

"Very well," Zz'r'p said with a sigh. "I sense that Echo is already off-planet. I do not think he is far; with some help from my colleagues, we may even be able to track him. But he is moving farther away even as we speak, and we must move swiftly if we want to catch up to them. But that will also mean that he is aboard a Cortian vessel, and I do not know how to rescue him from the depths of one of those."

"I got me some ideas about THAT," Omega declared with a scowl.

"So do I," Fox averred, just as firm, and just as angry.

"Great," Omega said. "Based on past events, you an' I work pretty synergistically together, Fox, so we oughta come up with some damn good stuff this time. Don't worry about getting him out, Zz'r'p. Just find him. You find him, and I'LL get him out."

* * *

When Echo finally awoke, headachy and sluggish, he had been stripped naked and shackled, spread-eagled, to a wall by wrists, ankles, and waist. His feet were barely on the floor, thus making for an uncomfortable semi-suspension from the shackles, which therefore tended to cut into his skin.

He was in a dank, dirty, tiny cell somewhere in the depths of what seemed to be a ship; from time to time he could feel the sensation of motion. This impression was heightened by the sound of invisible machinery all around him, and a light thrumming in the floor beneath his bare feet. Taken together, this indicated to the experienced, knowledgeable Agent that he was not likely still on Tiniken.

Oh man, he thought in dismay. *Where am I, and who the hell got me?*

Ace? Ace, honey, is that you? he suddenly heard in his mind. *Are you finally awake?*

The nd't'lq! he realized. *It's Meg!*

Yes! came the eager response. *You've been kidnapped, honey, we think by Cortians. Are you okay?*

So far, he decided, feeling a chill wash through his guts at the information.

Abruptly a flashback to a memory from earlier that autumn hit.

* * *

"...Let's say the Cortians had actually gotten you," Omega had told him. "From what India has told me of the short an' ugly communiqués the Agency had with the Cortians while you and I were crashed on that protoplanet last spring, one of the things they wanted you for was your genetics. They intended to 'harvest' 'em."

"They what?" a shocked Echo had said, voice flat in disbelief.

"Yeah, you got it," Omega averred then. *"They were gonna breed you. Probably whether you wanted to or not. Which means they had ways of getting around the 'respective equipment' issues."*

"Shit," Echo had whispered, his eyes widening. His face must have paled at least slightly, for he remembered feeling the blood drain from it.

"So let's use that as our scenario. Assume you got taken by 'em, and it took us a while to rescue you. They'd likely have stripped you down to skin, shackled you, and..." Omega considered, *"based on my experience with Slug, shot you up with a buncha junk to ensure things proceeded the way they wanted, whether YOU wanted it or not."* She met Echo's gaze, her own steady. *"You can decide whether or not we rescued you before anything more happened or not—before it progressed further, I mean. And you can decide whether it makes that much difference to your sense of personal autonomy, whether they'd actually succeeded in raping you or not."*

A horrified Echo had merely stared at her, aghast.

* * *

And here I am, he thought, coming back to the present, *stripped down to skin and shackled. All that's left is to shoot me up with shit to get the family jewels going, and...*

He fought back a shiver of dread.

Ace? Hon? You there? Is everything okay? Omega's voice broke into his morbid musings.

Uh, yeah. Sorry. I, uh, I was just remembering...something you told me, once...

Yeah. The discussion you and I had about the Cortians raping us, back when everybody was tryin' to convince me to do counseling. I see that now. Sorry. I didn't mean to scare you, honey.

It's okay. No, I, I'm fine, at least for now. Got a little headache, I guess where they klonked me to knock me out, but other than that, I'm okay, baby. But without some help, I'm pretty much stuck here. No equipment, no clothes, and shackled pretty thoroughly—just like you said, during that rape discussion—so

I have no way to get loose. Where are you?

Aboard the Genesis, *flyin' low,* she told him. *Fox showed up with Alpha Two leading an Alpha Line contingent, a buncha field an' security agents, some medics in case we gotta fight our way to you, an' even a Deltiri delegation led by Zz'r'p! India an' Romeo helped me throw all our stuff into our suitcases, then Fox had 'em loaded up, and we even moved the* Republic *into the hangar bay of the* Genesis! *The Deltiri are trying to use the nd't'lq link to track you through me!*

That...sounds promising, Meg. Just how long have I been out, then?

Oh, you've been out some hours, Ace. Pretty nearly an Earth day, I'd estimate at this point, though I haven't really been looking at a clock or anything. We think they mighta done something to drug you after they klonked you, though, to ensure you stayed out until they could escape off-planet with you, 'cause that's a long time to be out from only a knock on the head, with no serious concussion symptoms presenting now. Which means they were worried about telepaths, I guess. But apparently they have no way of actually detecting 'em. Let alone knowing that you an' I have a telepathic link.

Yeah, kinda figured as much. The next question becomes, what do they have in mind to do with me?

How much do you wanna think about it, hon? Omega wondered. *If they have you shackled...an' it already unnerved you a little, there, finding out it was the Cortians that got you...*

I need to know, Meg, so I can at least try to come up with some options, Echo told her. *Try to plan something. I need to survive and try to avoid too awful many...complications...until you and the others can reach me and get me outta here. And I haven't forgotten you telling me that they planned to, uh, 'harvest my genetics,' either.*

Yeah. Her sigh was audible in Omega's thoughts. *I've been discussing it a little bit with Fox. JUST Fox. And the way we figure it, you're most important to the Cortians as breeding stock. Only after successful breeding—whether old-fashioned or high-tech breeding, they probably wouldn't care—would they take step two, and that's selling you to the highest bidder.*

Which would probably end up being an old enemy, one way

or another. Which means I wouldn't survive long.

Yeah. Unless we manage to scare 'em all bad enough that they decide to stay away. After all, remember the curse-promise thing that the Rrgllbrrgll made to Uncle Pul.

True. So if they don't have any, like, bounty hunters or something out to buy me, what then?

Well, Fox is looking at the possibility of trying to buy you back himself, using funds from the Division One budget—regardless of who else may or may not be bidding. Kind of a ransom scenario, I guess. Given they seem to have it in for us—Division One, I mean—we're not holding our breath on that one, though. The last thing they'd do, if all else failed, would be to sell you as a basic slave—to a mining world, or whatnot. But if we don't have you back by then, we can do it pretty easily at that point. Because then we simply nail the mine owners for slave trading.

Okay, Echo sighed. *Do you know how far off y'all are?*

I don't, no, Omega admitted. *Mostly 'cause I haven't thought to ask yet. As far as I know, Zz'r'p and his team are workin' that directly with Fox an' the bridge crew.*

All right, that makes sense. So I need to TRY to avoid bein' raped, here, until y'all can arrive an' get me outta this damn ship. I guess that's my first hurdle.

Well, but if they do it high-tech, it might not be SO bad, Omega tried to offer solace. *I can try to stay here, in your head, and, and help, some kinda way. I mean, Zebra and India are fussin' at me to take some sleep, but if you need me, to hell with sleep.*

I understand what you're saying, baby, Echo told her, *and I know that you're trying to help. And definitely stay close, as much as you can without wearing yourself out. But rape is rape. I guess it would be maybe a little worse to know that I was forced into violating my marriage vows with another being, though, so I see your point.*

Well, I know, she said, sounding a little ashamed. *I was just trying to...figure out a way to...*

I know. It's okay. Don't be down on yourself. You're trying to find a way to keep my spirits up.

Yeah.

* * *

While they conversed mentally, Echo had been observing his prison cell. It was, by his estimate, a bit more than six feet by six feet and very nearly cubical, with the overhead barely high enough for his tall form—Echo was six feet, three and a half inches tall—to fit inside. One wall contained the shackles in which he was enclosed; there was a certain amount of adjustability built in, so that their positions could be shifted to account for species of varying height, size, and overall morphology. The opposite wall contained what looked like a door, of a fairly standard spacecraft-hatch-type, though rather ramshackle, it appeared; it was the only entrance. The two side walls seemed to have stowage cabinets.

Probably for the 'genetics-harvesting equipment' and shit, he thought.

Yeah, Omega agreed. *I'm looking at it through your eyes, Ace, and if the* Genesis *can take me to the ship you're on and I can sneak aboard, I can get in there and bust you loose, I think. Can you give me an angle on any of your shackles so I can 'see' 'em better?*

Yeah, baby, he said, looking at his wrists, then his waist. *I can't quite lean forward enough to see my feet, but there's that much.*

Then yes, if I can reach you, I'm ninety-nine percent certain I can get you out.

C'mon an' do it, as soon as you can, then.

Workin' on it, Ace. I love you.

I love you too, baby.

I'm gonna go talk to Fox and Zz'r'p and see what's goin' on with that, she told him. *So I'll be in the background of your head, but all you have to do is yell and I'll put you front and center immediately.*

Got it, he said. *Meanwhile, I guess I'm just hangin' around, here.*

Ooo, bad pun, Echo.

Hey, I got nothin' else to do right now.

He heard her mental laugh.

Okay, sweetheart. I'll be back soon.

Roger that.

And Echo was alone in his small cell, unable to even pace.

* * *

"So he is awake?" Fox confirmed. "Finally?"

"Yeah, Fox, awake and alert," Omega affirmed. "And analyzing the hell outta the situation. But there isn't a lot he has to work with. He's stripped down to skin and shackled to the wall."

"Damnation," Fox cursed. "By what body parts?"

"All four limbs and waist, near as I could tell," Omega noted. "Neck and head are free, but that's about it. It's exactly the sort of setup you'd expect for 'harvesting genetics,' as he put it. At least for a humanoid biped. They do NOT want him going ANYwhere."

"Farkakte, verdammt, shit, merde, cachu, khro, abdab, glagaram, og'dm'n, and gronk!" an angry Fox cursed in half a dozen offworld tongues and several Earth-based ones. "This is NOT good, tekhter."

"I know," Omega said in a low tone. "Look, Fox, I gotta admit to something. And I need you, of all people, to understand, because I need you to HELP me. See, I need somebody I can lean on through all this. Echo's leaning on ME, so I'm dealing with all the stress for both of us right now, and I..." Her voice cracked, and she broke off for a moment, regaining control of it, before continuing. "And I need someone to help me deal with all that. I know I'm Alpha Line; I'm its assistant chief. We're tough, in Alpha Line. I'M tough. But Echo's my HUSBAND now, never mind my partner and my best friend, and I'm scared, Fox. Really, really so...scared. For him. I'm trying HARD not to be, especially for his sake, 'cause I figure he can probably feel it through the bond even though I have a light block up, but..."

"Sshh, hush, meyn kind; you do not need to apologize to me," the older man soothed, putting an arm around her shoulders and pulling her into a gentle, fatherly hug. "I DO understand, and I will help to the best of my ability. Am I not your 'Abba Fox,' after all? You and I, Omega, we have been through things that no one else in the Agency has, things that no one else in the Agency CAN understand, because they have NOT been through it...or anything remotely like it, really. But neither of us would wish those experiences on another. So when you need help of this kind, I AM the person you should come to. And I think that is one reason why I tend to view you as a daughter of sorts; I understand you, yes, but...you also understand me."

"Y-yeah. And that's why I asked, I mean, why you needed to know..." Omega broke off, then blurted, "I need HELP, Abba Fox! I don't know what to..."

"Shh, shh, hush; I understand, tekhter," Fox told her, easing back, but still keeping an arm around her, hoping it would soothe. "You have all the help I can possibly offer, child. Oh! Maybe this will help ease your fear. Because I have a bit of news for you."

"I'm listening. I hope it's good."

"I think it is, very good. I've contacted Teela, Pul, and Wux and let them know what's happened. And aside from preparing to support us—it will take a while, but they are gathering a small fleet of some hundred warships, NOT merely fighters and escorts, but battleships, in case the Cortians have managed a fortified hideout somewhere in an out-of-the-way system— anyway, they've come back to me with some intel. It seems that the Cortian homeworld blockade has left what few ships are still out there, haunting our shipping and whatnot, rather hurting for supplies and equipment. And we've made things difficult enough on their raiding that the rogue Cortian ships are in a world of hurt, when you get down to it."

"Ohhh, I see where you're going," Omega murmured. "So we might actually manage to reach him before they CAN do much to him. Because they just don't have the resources to do it."

"Exactly."

"Have you heard from the Deltiri team? Or Zz'r'p directly?"

"Not in the last hour or so," Fox averred. "But they're working directly with my helm team on the bridge, and—"

We are making progress, my friends, Zz'r'p's mental voice interjected then. *Forgive my interruption; I had planned on tagging up with you both soon anyway. And when I 'heard' my name in Omega's conversation, through what she calls 'piggy-*

backing' on the nd't'lq, I thought it might be a good time for that tag. I swear to you both that there was no eavesdropping.

"Umph! Some day I might get used to that," a startled Fox grumbled good-naturedly. "Go ahead, old friend."

The fact that Echo is now awake and alert is helping us considerably with tracking him. We—my Deltiri colleagues and I—believe we now have a very good directional feed on him, even a distance estimate, through his bond with Omega, and your helmsman and your navigator both believe we should be within sensor detection of the Cortian vessel holding him in about an hour or so.

That's really good news, Omega said.

Well, it is, and it is not. Because once we find him, we must determine how to reach him and free him.

I told you...that's my job, Omega declared. *Y'all don't worry about it. I have it covered.*

You have an idea how to do it, tekhter? Fox wondered.

I do, Omega averred, confident. *The only thing I don't have figured yet is how to make it aboard their ship without being detected. Once I'm aboard, I think I can head straight for him, with them none the wiser. I'll need those electronics and such we talked about, Fox...*

I've already made arrangements, Omega. And remember how I said I had some ideas for how to do it, too? Well, I think I may just have an idea or two about how to sneak you aboard.

Good. I've really been wishing for one of those 'beam me over' gizmos like in the classic science fiction TV series.

Yes, I know what you mean, Fox agreed. *But I think that, between the two of us, we can see this through, especially with all the help we've gathered around us.*

Well, this really sounds most promising, Zz'r'p decided, heartened and encouraged. *Let us all play our parts, and perhaps Echo will be back with us very soon, safe and unharmed.*

Amen to that, Omega asserted.

* * *

Echo managed enough contact against the floor with his feet to enable him to shift positions ever so slightly and ease a few muscles that were threatening to cramp. Moments later, however, two avians with bright canary-yellow feathers entered the small cell.

As soon as he heard the rattle at the door, Echo let his body go limp, his head nodding forward until his chin almost rested on his chest. Then he watched through slitted eyelids as the pair paused just inside the door and studied him.

If I'm lucky, he thought, *they'll think I'm still unconscious and talk in front of me. Then I can maybe find out a few things about what they have planned. AND pass it on to Meg, to boot. Good thing I still remember Cortian from the first 'diplomatic' encounter.*

* * *

The slave supervisor and the captain of the *Orktes* stood just inside the door of the cell, surveying the prisoner.

(He appears to still be unconscious,) the captain observed.

(It seems so. It can be difficult to know how much of the pharmaceutical to use, for a new species,) the slave supervisor explained. (Sometimes just a little too much, and they are out longer than we expect. It all depends upon how sensitive they are, as individuals and as a species, to the particular drug being used.)

(As long as he is not dead.)

(Oh, no, he is not dead. He has a pulse. He should wake soon.)

(Good. It is a waste of the pharmaceutical, using too much; when we are out of the supply, we may have trouble obtaining more.)

(I know. I apologize, sir. I have never worked with an Earth human before.)

(Eh. Neither has anyone else, I suppose. It cannot have been VERY much over, else he would be in sick bay, being resuscitated, I expect. You did fine. He looks to be in rather good shape. Strong and powerful. Are the restraints sufficient?)

(They should be quite sufficient. But yes; this is a prime acquisition, sir.)

(Yes. He is possibly the top specimen from his homeworld, at least of the male sex.)

(You have done well, my captain.)

(Indeed. It is a pity we have not the access to the technology to harvest his genetics properly. The damnable 'Pan-

Galactic Coalition' has severed us from the homeworld, or it should be a relatively easy thing, typical limited resources at home notwithstanding. Are you certain we cannot do it thus?)

(I am sorry, sir. There is simply no more of the proper pharmaceuticals to do the thing. Perhaps we can do it in a more... natural...fashion.)

(If we can find a suitable female, perhaps. Check the genetics of the female slaves on board—not that there are many—as well as the mates which the more...permissive...of the crew brought along, and see if any of them are compatible with this...human. If so, then we will simply harvest his genetics by forcing them together, and be done.)

(Will not the crew protest the forcing of their mates?)

(What is that to me? They should not have brought women along in the first place. If they mutiny, I shall have them executed, and the females added to the slave docket; there are not enough of them to come close to overcoming the more loyal crew. Do it.)

(Yes, sir. And after that?)

(We will see what he knows that may be useful to us, one way or another. Meanwhile, we will put forth word through appropriate channels that we have him in our possession, and see what offers we may obtain for him.) The captain gestured. (Cut a clump of the strange feathers that grow from his head. That should provide us with a genetic sample to determine compatibilities, without damaging the specimen...for now.)

(Based on the inquiries we have received,) the slave supervisor said, searching the pockets of his uniform, (damage later is fully intended.)

(Exactly,) the captain noted with a smirk. (I only hope I may watch, given the difficulties this slave and his partner have caused to our people.)

Within moments, the slave supervisor had produced a small knife, cut a lock of Echo's hair, and tucked it into an envelope.

(There,) the slave supervisor said. (I will have this examined as soon as may be, sir.)

(Very good, then.)

(Do you wish to examine the slave personally? Perhaps check him for fitness?)

(What, and soil my talons on his unclean flesh? Hardly. Let us go; I have more important work to do.)

(As you wish, sir.)

They left.

* * *

Well, that's something, Echo thought, raising his head and checking the room for surveillance equipment. There was none; apparently it was considered a waste of precious resources on prisoners. He relaxed...just a little. *At least they don't get to shoot me up with shit that doesn't give me a choice. And if I have any say, I'll make it as difficult for 'em to do it the natural way as possible. And it sounds like they don't know that much about humans, anyway. I don't guess they've ever had an actual human in their possession. Lucky me.*

He sighed.

* * *

The prisoner supervisor came back a little bit later; Echo once more feigned unconsciousness. The Cortian came over to him and carefully palpated various points on Echo's body, eventually finding a pulse in his neck and feeling it with a surprisingly light, almost gentle touch.

"Mm," the avian hummed, thoughtful. Then he eased his hand up Echo's neck to the back of his head, careful not to scratch the Agent with his talons, and felt around until he located a lump on the back of Echo's head. Echo grunted in pain despite himself, but otherwise remained limp. "Ah," the Cortian vocalized then, in what sounded like understanding.

Good, Echo thought. *He thinks that, when the 'acquisitions team' whacked me on the head, they concussed me. That might help matters. Or at least get somebody in trouble.*

Just then, a high-pitched whistle sounded. The Cortian went to a small box on the wall beside the door, and hit a button. It turned out to be an intercom, and Echo listened closely to the ensuing conversation.

* * *

(Slave Keeping, this is Sick Bay,) the speaker annunciated.

(Go, Sick Bay,) the Cortian ordered.

(I have completed the analyses that you and Captain Incke specified. There is no genetic or anatomical match aboard the

51

ship. Evidently humans have genetic structures that are very different from the other species with which we are familiar. Based on the imagery taken earlier of the slave, I do not think we even have the means of taking reproductive samples. And even if we could do so, there is no female aboard with which those samples would be compatible, no likelihood of obtaining one in the foreseeable future, and no way left to preserve the samples until we could obtain such a slave.)

(Mm,) the Cortian grumbled. (That is not good news, any of it.)

(No. But at least we HAVE the slave. He should fetch a high sales fee.)

(True.)

(It is my understanding that this slave was taken during a nuptial trip? Where he brought his new mate?)

(Yes, that was what I was told.)

(Perhaps we should have taken the mate, as well. Then we would at least have a compatible female.)

(Possibly. But I would not tell the captain that, when you report.)

(Why?)

(It was his decision not to take the female.)

(Oh! I see. Yes. Also, it is entirely likely, given the way similar humanoid species procreate, this male may well have nothing in the way of gametes left. It might be necessary to wait until the gametes in his body have built back up to sufficient levels to harvest them.)

(Mm. That makes sense, yes. Contact the captain and let him know your findings. I will go to his cabin shortly and discuss with him what to do next.)

(Uh...can you not tell the captain when you see him?)

(The findings are yours, as is the expertise. Admittedly, your findings are not what he will wish to hear, but that is your responsibility, not mine.)

(Very...very well. Sick Bay signing off.)

(Slave Keeping signing off.)

The Cortian headed out the door.

* * *

Well, that's something, I suppose, Echo decided. *I guess I*

52

need to 'wake up' at some point, but it looks like rape is off the table. Thank You, God, as Meg would say. An' I mean it every bit as much as she does!

Now, he decided, *if she and I can figure out how to get me outta here before they have a chance to sell me off to the highest bidder...or else Fox can BE the highest bidder...this might end up okay.*

* * *

"Meg," India said as soon as the Alpha Line assistant chief entered the *Genesis* sick bay, "I'm gonna ask it again—when's the last time you got any sleep, honey?"

"Huh?" Omega replied, confused. "I thought this was about Echo. You called me down here..."

"It is, sorta," Zebra tag-teamed India. "You have to be in good shape, and clear-headed, if we're to have any sort of real hope of getting him back. Which means you need to rest now."

"But Zebra—"

"No buts, girl," Zebra said, stern. "When?"

"Um, I was asleep when Echo was jumped," Omega explained. "It woke me up, 'cause I felt something through the nd't'lq. And no, I haven't had a chance to sleep since then, but it's not even been quite a full Division day yet. An' it isn't like I've been running over half of Antarctica or something, so I'm doing fine."

"And how much sleep was the honeymooner getting BE-FORE that?" India pressed.

"Enough," Omega said, flushing. "It was a little piecemeal, sure, but I was sleeping almost a full night's worth every night, one way and another. And we were napping some during the daytime, too."

"And hiking all over the countryside, never mind up and down mountains, and going to the Tiniken equivalent of Broadway shows, which means staying up late, and all kinds of shit like that, according to Fox," Zebra noted.

"Well, yeah, but—hey, waitaminit," Omega protested. "How did Fox know about all that?!"

"Until Echo had the incidentals and such separated out and put on his account, Fox was being notified of the charges," Zebra explained with a smile. "No, I swear he wasn't checking up on you. But that's standard practice in the Accounting department when one agent's accounts are being borrowed by another agent—which happens more often than you might think, one way and another. That way, they make sure no one has stolen identities, or set up fraudulent charges, or whatever. Not that anybody would suspect you guys. But stuff can be stolen, after all."

"Oh," Omega noted, settling down a little. "Well, that makes sense..."

"You look tired, Meg," India observed. "There's even dark circles under your eyes."

"Um, I'm kinda stressed, guys," Omega murmured. "How would either of you feel if it was Fox, or Romeo, in Echo's shoes?"

"She has a point," Zebra noted. "But India does, too. Will you do something for us, honey? Will you just go back to your cabin and take a short nap?"

"Do you really think I could sleep?" Omega pointed out. "You know me better than that."

"Not without some assistance, no," India said. "But we can help with that. You've already taken your anxiety med for the day, right?"

"Uh, yeah."

"Then go straight back to your cabin and take this," Zebra said with a smile, handing Omega a small prescription bottle. "It's a lower dose of your regular anxiety med. Combined with the regular dose, if you take it now, you'll sleep for a couple of hours and wake up ready to tackle the universe."

"Guys, Echo an' the Deltiri are counting on me to maintain a link with Echo," Omega explained. "I really can't afford to do this."

"I already talked to Zz'r'p," Zebra said, sobering. "He says they have a pretty good fix on Echo's position, and they're working with the bridge to hone it, and come in on that position as fast as we can without being detected. And if you're going to need sleep, he said now is the best time for it. And I verified it with Fox just a couple minutes ago, and he agreed. He also said it would be good, because you were REALLY stressed."

"Well, but..."

"I CAN make this a medical order, you know. But I'm trying NOT to do that," Zebra said, growing stern once more. "Work with us here, honey."

"All right, all right," Omega grumbled, accepting the pill bottle. "I got a really bad feeling about this, though."

She turned and headed out of sick bay.

* * *

Just then, Romeo, who had been sitting in a corner, unnoticed by Omega, while his partner helped Zebra, spoke up.

"Guys?"

"Yeah, hon?" India said, turning. "Damn, I'm sorry, Romeo; I almost forgot you were there, you were so quiet."

"No big. I'm mostly along f'r the ride, nohow, just in case we need muscle, an' I know it. Look, um, I kinda think that 'uz a bad idea, babe," Romeo tried. "What you guys just did with Meg, I mean."

"Huh? Why?"

"Yeah, Romeo, why would it be a bad idea?" Zebra wondered. "Fox AND Zz'r'p indicated this was the best timing for her to get some rest. And they both said she was pretty badly keyed up, even with the anxiety medication."

"Didn' either of ya catch what she said, just b'fore she left?" Romeo asked.

"Um...well, no," Zebra admitted, as she and India exchanged glances. "She was just fussing, was all. That's...typical, when she's in the medlab. She doesn't like to be on the sick list, and she grumbles a little bit. Never mind the fact that the procedures keep reminding her of all of Slug's crap, from when she was a kid."

"What did she say, honey?" India queried.

"She said, 'I got a really bad feeling about this,'" Romeo repeated. "An' we're dealin' with th' Cortians again."

Both physicians stopped dead, jaws slack, wide eyes staring in horror.

"Oh damn," Zebra breathed. "You don't suppose..."

"That she might be doing that 'seeing future options' thing again?" India wondered. "Damn. I wouldn't wanna bet against it right now."

"Maybe we can stop her before she takes it..."

"Call Fox, and let's go—NOW," India declared.

* * *

(Come in,) the captain responded to the light rap on the cabin door, as he sat at his desk, filling out paperwork essential to the operations of the ship. The door opened, and the slave keeper—Echo's jailer—slipped inside, shutting it behind himself. (Ah, very good. You anticipate me.)

(You have heard from the genetic studies?) the slave supervisor wondered.

(I have. I take it, you have, as well?)

The slave supervisor merely nodded.

(Yes, well. It is not what I had hoped or wanted to hear, but there is no help for it.) Captain Incke sighed in disappointment. (We have customers who desire this one, and we cannot wait forever until we can find a match for the male. I do wish, now, that I had had the acquisition team bring his mate, however.)

(It was more risk.)

(I know. But we would thus have a means of breeding them. And perhaps made it go easier in the doing, while we were about it. This male was, by the testing and evaluation of his own people, at the top of the species, or VERY near it. It is a damnable shame to waste such marvelous and promising genetics. His offspring would make very strong, useful slaves. Optimally, I should have hoped to capture his former partner, as well, and forcibly breed those two; surely that would produce amazing specimens for enslavement. There is absolutely no chance of saving a tissue sample?) Incke gazed, stern, at the slave supervisor, who did not flinch.

(I do not think so, sir; at least, that is not what I understood. You would have to ask the medical team. They would know more of that than I.)

(Mm. They were underwhelming when I discussed matters with them. We may soon need a new team. What about the gametes?)

(We are not entirely certain from whence the gametes are produced, sir; we are still working on determining details of the human anatomy,) the slave supervisor admitted. (We believe that the appendages between the legs serve this purpose, though some of them also seem to be used in elimination, according to the medical examination he was given while unconscious, before being remanded to my custody. Generally it has never been a problem, as once we apply the appropriate drug, the being responds in arousal whether it would or no, and we are able to determine by its behavior what needs doing.)

(Ah. Well, you and the medical staff would be the experts in THAT procedure,) Incke said with distaste.

(Yes sir.) The slave supervisor paused. (Do you wish to postpone the auction?)

(That is possible, yes. I think we shall delay somewhat in announcing our acquisition, this time. Perhaps we will experience some good fortune and run across an acquisition that matches his anatomy and genetics. Or is at least compatible with them.)

(And in the meantime, sir?) the slave supervisor wondered, as the captain sat at his desk and pondered the situation. The captain was silent for long moments, while the slave supervisor waited patiently.

(Mm. Let us see what information we may obtain from him,) Captain Incke decided. (I will provide you with a list of questions to be asked. Use the standard interrogation techniques.) He pulled over a sheet of paper and a pen, and began to jot down the list of questions for the interrogation.

(Sir? How much damage may we risk?)

(I have already inquired of that from the most eager of the bidders,) the captain noted. (As long as he is alive and recognizable, they care not, it would appear. He will not fare well at their hands, nor live long. Which is why,) he said in frustration, (I so greatly desired to harvest his genetics. There will be no more where that came from, once they are done with him.)

(So damage is not an issue?)

(No, it is not. Well, save the appendages between the legs and do not injure them, just in case we have some good fortune, though I do not expect it.) Captain Incke handed the sheet of paper to the slave supervisor. (Here. Go prepare your interrogation tools; take your time, and do it with finesse. The longer we delay, the more chance we may have of coming across a compatible mate for him, though I hold no real hopes of it.

Obtain the information, however; that, and the auction price, are apt to be all we end up extracting out of this one, no matter the promise of his abilities and genes. DAMN this illegitimate 'Pan-Galactic Coalition'! Were it not for their blockade, we should be able to harvest his genetics indefinitely! I would cheerfully delay the auction for as long as it took, in order to obtain as many offspring from him as possible! Ah well. It is a pity, but there it is.)

(Very good, sir, and I agree. Anything else?)

(No, that is all. Dismissed.)

(Yes, sir.)

The slave supervisor exited the captain's cabin, en route to the prisoner cells.

* * *

A glum—and VERY anxious—Omega headed straight to her cabin aboard the *Genesis*. As soon as she was there, she went through to the tiny head, ran a glass of water from the tap, then knocked back the lone pill within the bottle Zebra had given her. She moved to the edge of the bed, shucked off shoes, Suit jacket, weapons holsters, tie, and belt, placing the jacket neatly on a corner of the bed and the rest beside her hygiene kit on the top of the stowage shelf that passed for a dresser, then rolled over and curled up on the bed, deeply missing her partner, lover, and spouse, and intensely worried for him.

She closed her eyes, felt the medication kick in and her whole body relax...and was sound asleep within moments.

Five minutes later, there was a knock at the door. The voice that came through was muffled.

"Meg? Meg, this is Zebra. Romeo brought something up, something important, and I wanted to ask you about it before you took your medications. Meg...?"

Omega never moved.

* * *

"She must already be out," Zebra said, turning to the three who accompanied her—her own spouse, Fox; and Alpha Two, standing in the corridor. "She followed orders, pretty much immediately."

"Which is what we told her to do," India said with a sigh.

"Well, tekhter, she is a good girl, and does as she's told by her 'parents'...and sibling," Fox noted. "And she IS tired. It may well be that true relaxation, freedom from worry, is what she needs right now."

"Yeah, th' girl looked het up," Romeo agreed. "Can't say as I blame her, neither. I jus' wish we knew what she meant by 'a bad feeling about this,' that's all."

"Given past history, I...would not argue that, in the least," Fox agreed. "I suppose we shall have to wait and trust Adonai to handle things as He wishes...for good, or for ill."

* * *

It had been several hours since Omega's last communication through the nd't'lq. Echo was still shackled, naked, to the wall of the small, dank cell. He had been provided with neither food nor drink for the entire time he had been there, and when nature had called insistently about an hour earlier, he had had no other option but to urinate on the floor of the cell, and with no hands free to control matters, it had been a bit...random. So now, in addition to everything else, he endured the ammoniac stench of stale urine. *And by the feel of my gut, Number Two may not be far behind,* he thought. *Damn, is that gonna stink.*

But at least it looks like rape is off the table, he decided with some considerable relief. *And Meg knows what's up, an' she has Fox and a big Division One contingent with her. Division Seven an' Chief Wux, it sounds like, are prepared to back 'em up, and they're trying to track me. I might actually get outta this before they have a chance to do that whole 'selling to the highest bidder' thing, because those are most likely gonna be old enemies on the purchasing end of the transaction. So my life expectancy after the sale would be...short.*

Just then, the door rattled and opened, and the 'jailer,' as Echo thought of the being, entered the cell. He saw Echo was awake, and grunted in approval.

"Englishes talk you, yes?" the Cortian male said in a thick, slightly clacking accent.

"Yes, I speak English," Echo replied.

"Good. Is talk we. Is you things me tell."

"I'll see what I can do," Echo decided. The Cortian gave him the equivalent of a smirk.

"Is you things me tell," he averred.

"I'll see what I can do," Echo repeated, thinking fast and fully prepared to make up something in order to divert the being and buy himself some time. "I don't know everything, after all. What is it you wanna know?"

"Is device gots you to sensors blind making," the slave supervisor said. "Is this wants we. Is tell you, build us."

Uh-oh, Echo thought in dismay. *I don't even have a clue where to start on THAT. I don't know anything about the engineering of the thing, so I can't come up with something that sounds feasible, even, just to stall. Well, maybe he'll buy the truth. Maybe. Otherwise, maybe Meg can send me some knowledge in an info dump through the nd't'lq, if she can do it fast.*

"Uh, I dunno," he admitted. "I'm a pilot, not an engineer or an inventor. I have no idea how the sensor scrambler is made."

"Use you it to *Trindak* destroy. Lie you."

"No, I'm not lying," Echo protested. "I'm a pilot. I know how to use the devices on my spacecraft, but that's just a matter of pushing buttons. I dunno how they actually WORK, unless I take the time to look into it. And that was an experimental device when I used it; the mechanism was classified. I never saw the design or plans for it." *Granted, I have the clearance to access it, if I'd wanted to,* he thought. *But I didn't have TIME, and haven't thought about it since. And they sure don't need to know WHY I have the clearance to access it. Meg? Honey, are you there? I need some help, and FAST.* He got no response, save a few flashes of what seemed to be dreams. *Well, shit. I bet India or somebody made her go lie down and rest. Maybe even knocked her out with some meds. I'm sure she needed it, but DAMN, is it bad timing. At least for me, it is. This might go south in a big way.*

"Lie you," the Cortian repeated. "Tell you, or regret you."

"I swear to you by the Maker," Echo used the galactic standard reference to a deity, and meant every word, "I'm not lying. I honestly don't know how the thing works, or how it's made."

"Tell you," the Cortian said, calm...

...As he went to a locker near the door, opened it, and extracted a large, kukri-style bladed weapon with a specialized grip, and crude designs etched lightly on the blade. The honed edge gleamed even in the low light.

Oh shit, Echo thought in dismay, as his head spun in sudden realization of what 'regret you' meant. *Meg, too late, waaaay the hell too late; stay outta my head, baby. I know I swore to share everything with you, but not THIS. Just...no. Oh, dear God, help me. This is gonna be BAD.*

The Cortian turned with a cruel leer.

"Tell, or regret," he reiterated.

Chapter 3

Omega had been asleep for several hours when something far worse than a blow to Echo's head surged through the nd't'lq into her sleeping brain. Omega suddenly sat bolt upright in the bunk in her cabin, eyes wide with horror.

"Oh, no," she whispered in deep dread. "No, no, no. They didn't. Dear God, help us—they DID!"

She leaped from the bunk and reached for her cell phone, lying on the nearby dresser, slapping at it to activate the emergency mode, and trying not to scream in fear for her mate.

* * *

"We got your emergency summons, tekhter! What's the latest?" Fox asked some five minutes later, fairly bursting into the cabin, Ambassador Zz'r'p hard on his heels. "I take it, you managed a bit of rest?"

"Some. But oh, dear Lord, I wish I hadn't!" a deeply distressed Omega cried, already dressed, though only in jeans and a t-shirt, sans shoes or socks. "I just knew something would happen, I knew it, I knew it!"

"What?! Why?"

"Because evidently Echo sent me a desperate request for information while I was asleep, and because we don't have this whole nd't'lq thing quite worked out yet, my sleeping brain didn't respond...again," Omega explained. "And I think that... was bad."

"Have you been able to obtain any additional information from your link with Echo, now that you're both conscious, then?"

"No," Omega murmured, nearly in tears and wringing her hands. "Something is BAD wrong, Fox! I'm way better than ninety-nine percent sure that they're torturing him..."

"WHAT?! Why do you think that?" Fox wondered, alarmed.

"Because now he's put up a really amazingly strong mental block, and I can't get through it," Omega explained, then she swallowed hard. "I didn't even know he could DO that! Not hard like this! And he's promised me he'd always share everything with me, and I promised I'd share everything with him, so there's gotta be something wrong! Something he knows will upset me, or worse!"

"Does he respond when you press, youngling?" Zz'r'p wondered.

"A little; not much," she replied. "I asked him why he wasn't letting me in, and he said I didn't need to know. And that's ALL he said! But Fox? What woke me up, was...Echo SCREAMED...at least three times that I know of, maybe four. ECHO...screamed."

"Oh, HaShem help him," Fox breathed, horrified. "I have only ever heard him scream ONCE."

"You have? What in heaven's name happened to him?" Omega whispered.

"You happened to him, tekhter."

"Huh?"

"The only time I have ever heard him scream, you were lying atop him, burning alive, protecting him from the Cortians' ion drive with your own body. He loved you by then, and he knew it...and there was nothing he could do to stop it." Fox met her wide blue eyes. "And you say he screamed at least three times?"

"Yes," she murmured, biting her lip as those same blue eyes grew wet. "Clear through his own block. Loud. And, and...sharp, and...dreadful..."

"FORCE your way through his block, meyn kind," Fox ordered. "Find out what's happening with him!"

"Yes," Zz'r'p added, urgent. "You are the only one, at this point, who can do so without any risk of injuring his mind."

"I've TRIED!" Omega cried, as the tears she had been holding back—probably for far too long, the Director decided—finally spilled over. "I CAN'T! I didn't think 'ordinary' humans," she quirked her fingers around the word, "could even do much in the way of mental blocks..."

* * *

"Mm. They cannot, normally," Zz'r'p confirmed, deciding that Omega needed a mental diversion, even if only brief. "But in recent months, I have begun to suspect that Echo may not be quite as 'ordinary' a human as we have believed."

"Huh? What do you mean?" a surprised Omega wondered, managing to stop the tears by dint of focusing on Zz'r'p's train of thought, as he gently touched certain places within her mind to help her settle.

"I mean I believe his genetics may not be standard human," he elaborated.

"How?! Bu-but," a shocked Omega tried, but the words would not come out.

"Wait," Fox demanded. "Are you telling us someone mucked with his genetic structure too, Zz'r'p?"

"No, no, not at all," the Deltiri responded. "I am saying that, rather like Omega—at least, outside of her 'modifications'—I believe he is an outlier for the human race, possibly a mutation. Quite possibly, he—the two of them together, even; Echo and Omega—may represent the first stages in the next developmental step of the species."

"How do you know?" Omega whispered, astounded. "Have you looked at his genetic scan?"

"Actually, as it happens, I have," Zz'r'p affirmed. "In attempting to help you and counsel you on your fears in the aftermath of everything that has been done to you, I asked him for permission to do so—I was thinking in terms of trying to help with your fear of having children, which is reasonable, given the 'damned gastropoid' intended them as genetically programmed Echo-assassins, as well as trying to determine workarounds to that—and in the circumstances, he gave it without question...and with his blessing."

"He...he did?" Omega whispered, stunned. "As private as he is..."

"He did," Zz'r'p attested. "He loves you deeply, my dear, and he wants a full and complete life with you. And is willing to do whatever it takes, not only to achieve that, but to make you comfortable with it. I strongly suspect that life will eventually include children...if we can figure out how to do it safely for you both."

"Um...o-okay," she murmured. "Go...go ahead."

"All right. So. With Echo's permission, Zarnix and I sat

down with Echo's genetic scan profile and studied it in some detail. And when I spotted what I suspected was the pertinent mutation—not that I am expert in such matters, but I am what you would call 'a quick study' and had done considerable research, in order to best counsel you, my dear—I pointed it out, along with my suspicions, and Zarnix dug into the matter and was therefore able to confirm it."

"Oy vey," Fox said blankly. "The man is a latent psi?"

"Not quite," Zz'r'p noted. "Echo's ability is certainly nowhere as strong as Omega's deliberately-tweaked ability, and he is only learning to use it instinctively as he and Omega interact more and more in this fashion...which likely means I need to start working with him too. But the potential is definitely there, and Echo does indeed have the capability, at least. Which is probably one reason why he has been so comfortable working with Omega, and why he survived a direct conflict with Slug as a young agent, when so many other agents did not. And it sounds as if, in his extremis, he has now learned to use some specific aspects of that capability."

"But because she's not—well, not quite—a natural telepath, Omega is unable to break through his block?" Fox wondered.

"Precisely," Zz'r'p noted. "Coupled with Echo's sheer willpower, which as we ALL know, can be quite formidable. Add to that a certain desperation, and that block is likely a mental fortress, at the moment." He cocked his head and gazed at Omega, letting his expression show understanding. "Which I suspect someone else in this room comprehends, all too well, especially after recent events."

A pale Omega simply nodded.

"But if Echo is a telepath, then why can't he just tell us where he is?" Fox continued.

"Several reasons, all surprisingly simple—he likely does not KNOW where he is," Zz'r'p explained. "After all, these are slavers and pirates, with slave holding cells somewhere within the depths of their ship. Echo was removed from Ti-niken while unconscious, and kept unconscious until he was well away from the Zeta Aurigae system. He was probably incarcerated long before regaining consciousness."

"And imprisoned in some dank, dark, tiny cell, likely constantly shackled to the wall," Omega murmured, thoughtful, "from what little I HAVE been able to get out of him...at least, before they started to work on him."

"Exactly. He has not been in a position to FIND OUT where he is."

"But he could read the pilot's mind, or the navigator's," Fox protested. "If he's a telepath like you say, and he's...'broken through,' for lack of a better term..."

"No, he cannot, because he IS not," Zz'r'p pointed out. "Aside from the fact that he has likely not been...'introduced'... to the bridge crew. Just because one has the latent genetic tendency does not mean one has the ability, Fox. Even genetically, he does not have the full ability, only...let us say, the first step toward it. He is blocking Omega with such strength for the same reason Omega was able to attack and stop Tt'l'k—Omega was protecting Echo then, and Echo is protecting Omega now. It is love and desperation that powers his telepathic block, coupled with that incredible will."

* * *

"Oh shit! Zz'r'p!" Omega exclaimed, badly upset, as a level of understanding suddenly struck. "You HAVE to help me force through his block!"

"Tekhter, that is not wise," Fox murmured, laying a gentle, restraining hand on her shoulder. "Not with what you're already dealing with. I've changed my mind on THAT."

"I must agree," the Deltiri averred. "Let me handle this, Omega."

"No," she shook her head, determined, "neither of you is getting it. You CAN'T handle this, Zz'r'p. But I can."

"Oh," Zz'r'p breathed in sudden understanding, his eyes widening as she felt him surface-read her thoughts, her reasoning...so she deliberately laid it out for him in her mind. "Oh, great Maker."

"What?" Fox wondered. "Omega, child, you're still receiving counseling—FROM Zz'r'p—for the whole farshtinkener mess you've been through..."

"Which includes what, Fox?" Omega pressed. "What was it that Slug did to me, to begin with?"

"From what I've been able to gather from our private talks, he all but took you apart and put you back togeth—" The Director broke off, sucking in a sudden deep breath, as understanding slammed into his brain, as well. "Oh, Adonai help us..."

"Bingo," Omega murmured then. "And I'm gonna need His help, so keep asking, Abba Fox. But I'm the ONLY one who can do this, out of everybody here. Because I'm the only one who's been tortured to the extent of being taken apart and put back together, while conscious and alert and feeling all of it, and come away to talk about it. So I'm the only one who can help him do the same thing." She broke off, then added, "Except somehow, I doubt they're gonna put him back together."

The room was silent for a long moment, as the males winced.

"...So we're gonna have to do it for him, instead," she appended, and firmed her jaw.

"It will not be pleasant, my adoptive niece," the Deltiri said, very quiet. "Make sure you are ready, when we do this. And," he added, "given Echo's strength of will, and the level of desperation I discern from what you are telling me, even I may not be able to break through his block without help. And doing it WITH help...could harm him."

"Well, let's try, at least."

"That, we can do. But first I want to make sure that you are in a good position, physically, mentally, and emotionally, to handle the psychic feedback from the connection. Because it will be significant, and it will be severe."

"That makes sense," Omega agreed. "I can deal with that."

"Then grab your shoes and socks, tekhter, and let's see about putting a meal in you," Fox determined, then held up a quelling hand as Omega started to speak. "No, no. I don't have to be a telepath myself to grasp that. You are deeply upset, and that does bad things to your digestive tract, meyn tekhter; I know. I know this already from my own past experience of you, and from conversations with India and Romeo, AND Echo, all of whom have been there to experience it firsthand, even though I have not, at least as yet. But we can see about putting mild, bland foods into you, a little at a time, to ensure proper nourishment, child. And we are on the *Genesis*, so we are in a position to do it, and do it well."

"And a full, maximum dosage of your anxiety medication, in addition to that, with said dosage as determined by Zebra," Zz'r'p added. "And anything I can do to aid in keeping you calm and in control."

"Won't it put me to sleep?" Omega wondered. "The meds, I mean?"

"I doubt it," Zz'r'p responded, voice low. "Not once we break through his block."

"So let's take this one step at a time, and make sure you are ready for it," Fox determined.

"But we need to HURRY!" she exclaimed. "It's horrible, I can tell even without him letting me in! He's hurting NOW!"

"No. In this instance, your condition MUST take priority, youngling," Zz'r'p pointed out. "I understand he is in great pain, and that you can help him by suppressing that pain, and by bolstering his mental and emotional strength. But it does him no good if you are not in the best possible position, mentally and physically, to help him counter what is being done to him. If you begin, then collapse under the strain, the end of that matter will be worse for him than things are now...because you will break, and he will know he is the cause. You MUST take nourishment, and you MUST take a maximum dose of your medications...or YOU will not deal with this, and may end only by making matters worse...for ECHO."

"...Okay," Omega decided, only slightly grudging. "I... guess that'll do. Alla that. And you're both right; I need to do it. For Echo's sake, if not my own."

"We ARE going to get him back, and we will patch him up, whatever the zin fun a hur have done to him, tekhter," Fox declared, determined, "and therefore YOUR sake IS Echo's sake."

"Listen to him, youngling," Zz'r'p added his weight to the argument. "Fox speaks the truth."

"Point, both of you," Omega sighed, sitting on the bunk and drawing on her socks before shoving her feet into slip-on sneakers. "All right, let's go see about making me a little stronger, and ready to help Echo handle whatever the hell the bastards are doing to him."

"That's the spirit!" Fox said, putting his arm around her shoulders and leading her toward the sick bay, en route to the ship's mess.

* * *

"Oh shit, oh shit, oh shit," Zebra fussed, as she scurried about and refilled Omega's prescription for xolafet, the galactic anxiety medication, marking the regular AND the maximum dosage instructions on the labeling. "You're saying they're doing something dreadful to him, other than just selling him as a slave?"

"Yeah," Omega murmured, taking the dose cup and glass of water the physician offered her and chugging it.

"What are they doing?"

"I don't know for sure," she admitted. "He won't let me 'in' to find out. He doesn't want me to know. Which is how I know it's bad. That...and the fact that he's screamed several times. Think about that, Zebra. ECHO screamed. Not just once. Several times. I've never..." Omega broke off, then shook her head. "I never thought I'd hear Echo make a sound like that... and I hope I never do again. We have to find him and stop this!"

"Oh, dear Lord!" Zebra exclaimed in horror, then stifled her reaction. "Mmph. All right. What do I need to do, to be ready once you bring him back? Do you know that?"

"Bubeleh," Fox said, subtly waving off Omega's response and privately signaling his mate to back off on her questioning, "I don't think she can tell you that, either, at least not yet. She simply doesn't know right now. Just be ready for anything, and we might want to consider...do you have the components to set up a regen pod here, on the *Genesis*?"

"No," Zebra said, regretful. "I thought about that, but given the emergency summons and the short turnaround time before launch, there wasn't time to pull everything and pack..."

"No worries," Fox said, holding up a hand. "Then what I want you to do is to contact Zarnix, back at Headquarters, and have him and the team ready to 'dunk' Echo as soon as we can bring him back there. Have 'em ready to deal with...whatever the Cortians have done to him."

"I'll get on that right away," Zebra determined. "Do you

want 'em to bring Dihl up from the Ranch?"

The group paused in an awkward silence, as Fox turned to Omega.

"Tekhter?" he wondered in a soft voice. "How wise do you think that...?"

"...I...don't think it's a good idea, Fox," Omega said in a low, hoarse voice. "I've gotten a few flashes from Echo—despite himself, I guess you could say. And if I'm reading between the lines correctly, I think we probably need to put him in the regen pod before she has a chance to see him."

"Oy vey," Fox breathed, even as Zebra blanched, and even Zz'r'p turned a paler shade of blue. "That bad?"

"I'm thinkin'...yeah. Every bit."

"Like..."

"Like..." Omega opened her mouth, then shut it again and turned away. "I'm afraid to say. Dear Lord God, PLEASE let me be wrong."

"Shit, shit, shit," Zebra grumbled again, badly worried. "All right, honey. You have your meds; Fox, take her off to the mess and feed her good. And Zz'r'p, you take good care of her brain while you two are trying to get through to Echo, okay?"

"Of course, my dear friend," the Deltiri agreed. "I plan on providing the support myself, personally, and making it a powerful telepathic link. She will have plenty of support...because I have already informed my team of what we will be doing, and THEY, in turn, will be supporting ME. And there are some EXTREMELY strong telepaths on that team."

"This sounds good," Fox decided. "All right. Anything else, Zebra?"

"No, hon," the physician replied to her husband. "You guys get going, and hurry and find Echo."

"All over THAT one," Omega agreed, as they rose and headed out of sick bay.

* * *

Highly attentive and very concerned, Fox and Zz'r'p both escorted Omega through the mess hall, straight to the Admiral's personal dining room, where a lone waiter promptly attended the trio.

"What may I bring you, sir?" he wondered, solicitous. "You all look worried. Perhaps some comfort food?"

"Coffee for myself," Fox noted, "black, as usual. Omega?"

"I'm...thinkin', Fox," Omega murmured. "I'm just not sure what I dare try."

"How about we start with a vanilla protein smoothie, then?" Fox suggested. "I often have that for breakfast, or after a workout, and the ship's mess does a particularly good one. Once we put something in you, and your belly settled a bit, then we'll look at something more substantial."

"That sounds like it might work," she decided.

"And you, Your Excellency?" the waiter asked Zz'r'p.

"Do you have the Deltiri drink, rn'g'td mar'l?" he wondered. "It is our equivalent of coffee, and I think I may need the stimulant in the next few hours. If you do not have it, then bring me coffee with a good deal of cream and sugar, and perhaps some coconut oil."

"I...don't think we have the Deltiri drink, sir," the waiter said, "but I can certainly provide the coffee, as well as the other items."

"Good, then," Fox said. "This is more for Agent Omega, here, than either Zz'r'p or myself, so when she's about three-quarters done with her smoothie, come back and let's see what else she can handle eating."

"Yes sir," the waiter said, then paused. "Agent...Omega? You're the partner of the agent the *Genesis* is trying to rescue, aren't you? Agent Echo? The Assistant Director and head of Alpha Line?"

"She is," Fox noted, waving off Omega's anxious start at an answer. "She is, herself, the assistant chief of Alpha Line. And they are newlyweds, into the bargain. So this is why we are here; she needs to keep her strength up, but she is understandably VERY upset, and that has thrown off her digestive tract, in a rather distressing fashion."

"Ohhh, I see," the waiter murmured. "All right. Let me go deliver these orders, then I'll consult with the chef on duty and explain matters, and see what it comes up with for her, as options for her upset belly. Rice pudding, or chicken soup...oh, maybe mac and cheese, or something like that?"

"That sounds...really good, actually," Omega sighed. "Any of that."

And the waiter was off.

* * *

Zz'r'p and Fox—with the able assistance of the mess hall team—managed to keep Omega eating until they adjudged she had sufficient calories in her to hold her for a while. Meanwhile, Zz'r'p mentally contacted Echo to let him know that he was not alone, even with the block he was maintaining, and they were still hot on his trail.

Then the three beings repaired to Zz'r'p's stateroom, where the other Deltiri on the team met them, telepathically called by Zz'r'p to the meeting. He quickly explained the situation, and grave blue faces met Omega's gaze.

"We are here for you and Echo, Omega," Kk'q'r ob Iin'i'rek, the embassy's resident bonding specialist, told her. "You should recall me..."

"I do," Omega said. "You're the nd't'lq expert."

"Indeed. And you already know Mm'l'n," Kk'q'r noted. "Zz'r'p, would you prefer to do the introductions, or shall I continue...?"

"Go ahead, Kk'q'r," the Deltiri ambassador noted.

"Very well. This is Qq'k'l ob Sii'stek," Kk'q'r continued. "He is a certified and very experienced interrogator, and understands a great many things about telepathic links as a result, including how to obtain information without damaging the mind containing that information. He was formerly assigned to Division Five, but was transferred to Earth in the aftermath of the assassination attempt against Lord Entiyti, and the concurrent accusations against Alpha One. It was felt that we might need additional interrogators to help sort things out, in case there were embedded Persan agents, given that Aggum started his takeover attempt on Earth."

"Ah," Omega murmured, understanding, as the Deltiri thus identified stepped forward and bowed slightly.

"In the end, we found there were no more as such in your Agency, though there were a few in disguise in the general population, and they have been apprehended," Qq'k'l noted, "but I stayed for the experience of working with a new Division. And now I am here to help, as much as in me lies."

"Thank you," Omega murmured, and Qq'k'l nodded.

"This is Bb'y'x ag Ogg'nii," Kk'q'r went on with the introductions. "She is an inter-species telepathy expert."

Bb'y'x stepped forward and bowed formally in deep respect, then offered Omega a simple but encouraging smile. Omega gave the female her best attempt at returning the smile, aware that her own was a little wobbly, but it was as much as she could do for the time. *And,* she thought, *these guys will understand.* At that, Bb'y'x nodded affirmation.

"And this," Kk'q'r finished, "is Jj'k'k ob Dee'kyy. He is by far the most powerful telepath among us; you may think of him as our 'power' telepath. If we need to break through a strong mental shield, he has the power to do so."

"But that will not do, here," Zz'r'p noted. "Not directly, at least, though he may perhaps 'loan' some of his power to Omega. You see, Echo is fighting desperately to protect Omega from discovering whatever horror the Cortians have done to him. This is what strengthens his unexpectedly powerful mental block. If WE try to force our way through it, we are most apt to damage his mind. And I have already had more than enough of working THAT out, of late." He offered Omega a wry, teasing grin, and she returned it. It was a weak expression, but sincere.

"But yes, I can certainly strengthen Omega in what she is about to attempt, if I am understanding your mental communiqué correctly, Zz'r'p," Jj'k'k declared.

"Good," Omega said. "And I'll take that. All of that, and all of the help alla y'all can give me...an' lotsa prayer, too. Because it's time to move on with this. I need to help Echo, get through to him, ease his pain, and help strengthen him, or the Cortians are gonna break him entirely. And he'll never recover from that, even if he survives this."

"Consider it done," Mm'l'n declared. "Let us prepare, and quickly."

* * *

Roughly half an hour after meeting with the Deltiri team, they began their attempt to reach Echo from their base of operations in Zz'r'p's stateroom, where they all congregated. The

73

Deltiri ambassador had sent Fox back to the bridge to focus on matters there, as the telepaths were still honing their fix on Echo's location, and expected to have more, when this attempt was finished.

Echo? Honey, it's me, Omega tried through the nd't'lq.

Baby, no. Just...no. Stay away. You don't need this. I'm done. Let me go.

NO. Now you just hush that, right now, Ace, Omega declared, stern. *I'm not about to let you go, EVER. Do you hear me? We're getting close, and we're formulating a plan for getting you out. I'm here now, through the bonding, to help you hang on until we can arrive there.*

Uh...huh? To...to help me? No offense, baby, but how the hell can you help me? I'm living a n-nightmare, here.

Echo, think for a second; I don't want you to actually REMEMBER it—not in your current mental state—but think about the sorta thing that Slug did to me, hon. Think about the fact that I deal with it, with the memories, every moment of every day. I can DO this, honey. Lean on me mentally, until I can make it there, literally with you, beside you, and you can lean on me physically. AND...I can do something else, if you'll let me in enough to find the right place...

There was a pause, then Omega sensed the mental block soften, just a little.

What do you mean, the 'right place'? his voice asked in her mind.

I mean that...okay, I dunno exactly what they did to you. But I know it was bad. I 'heard' you scream, sweetheart. I know you tried NOT to let me hear, and the Deltiri team say they didn't hear it, but I'm too close to you; you can't quite get away with that, not with me. I can tell you're in severe pain, right this instant, despite your block. And I can help that. I can ease that pain. I KNOW I can, because I've done it before. Remember how I helped ease the pain of your busted legs, when we crashed on the protoplanet?

Oh shit. Yeah, you did, didn't you? You think you can do that now? That...that would be...dear God, that would help, so much...

I know I can. I dunno that I can eliminate ALL the pain,

but I have Zz'r'p's team backing me up, and if I can't do it by myself, they might be able to help. At least it'll ease it a good bit. Omega paused, then said, very pointedly, *But you HAVE to let me IN. You don't have to let me 'see' everything, if you don't want to. And I promise I won't look. But you have to drop your block, at least partway, so I can find the right spot to 'make it not hurt.' Is the jailer-dude still there?*

No. He hasn't been back in a while. I think he finally figured out that I didn't have any real information to pass on—all the shit they wanted to know was stuff I didn't know anything about, or never got around to looking up, or stuff like that— and he gave up on that line of attack. Literally.

Okay. Lemme in, honey. Let me help. I CAN help. But you have to LET me.

Zz'r'p? Echo asked then. *Are you there?*

I am, Echo, but in the background, the Deltiri said; his mental voice was slightly fainter than either of the two Alpha One members. *Omega is letting me 'piggyback' on the nd't'lq link, so that I can reinforce her own abilities and help, as well as using the link to help determine your location. She has showed me what she wants to attempt, and I am convinced she is right—she can do as she says, support you mentally and relieve your pain—because this is a variation on mental techniques that have been part of the Deltiri body of knowledge for millennia. And I and my colleagues are here in order to provide the strength, endurance, and instruction she may need to accomplish those tasks most effectively. If either of you have questions about how to proceed, you need only ask, and one or other of us will answer, depending on the relative expertise we possess.*

How many o' y'all ARE there? Echo wanted to know. Omega bit her lip; Echo's mental voice was starting to slow, mumble, and drop sounds. She began to worry that the communication had exhausted his limited reserves.

There are six of us, Zz'r'p explained. *Myself and Mm'l'n you already know. Kk'q'r you have met. There are also Qq'k'l ob Sii'stek, Bb'y'x ag Ogg'nii, and Jj'k'k ob Dee'kyy. All of us have a wide variety of certain specialties, between us, that will enable us to best assist the two of you in one way or another.*

P-pleased t'...t' meetch'all, Echo slurred. *Uhnn...*

ACE, honey, lemme in, Omega demanded, *before you pass out an' you can't.*

Awright, awright. Jus' promise me you won't lookit what they did. I don' want you seein'...

I promise. I understand, and I won't go there unless and until you're ready to show me.

'Kay.

And Echo dropped his telepathic block.

* * *

Omega fairly surged her own mind through the nd't'lq link into Echo's mind, automatically and instinctively providing her strength, thankful she was rested and well-fed to maximize that strength...because the sudden, terrible pain she experienced—and knew for a fact that it was his—shocked her with its unexpected intensity. She felt Echo sigh at the sensation of her presence, just before he winced in deep pain, and immediately she went deeper into his mind.

Zz'r'p, come with me, she said, dimly aware that her physical body was trembling with the shared pain, and that it had collapsed into a chair that Jj'k'k swiftly slid beneath her, but ignoring those facts in her determination to accomplish what she had set out to do for Echo. *I need to find this spot...it's the same one I used back after our crash, I just have to find it...and then I can show it to y'all, and we can maybe tag-team minimizing his pain. I'm not holdin' my breath to think I can make it completely go away THIS time, but maybe y'all can. Or maybe we all can, together. Somehow.*

All right, Omega, Zz'r'p agreed. *I am 'with' you, and we are all watching. But I can only do so much to help you find it, because we have not tried this technique on humans before.*

Okay. Where is it, where is it... Omega hunted frantically.

Slow down, youngling. I know you want to do this instantly, and I know why...but you will be more efficient, hence faster, if you slow your frenetic explorations, relax, try to recall what you did, and search more systematically.

Yeah, I know. I need to...oh! I see it! Right over here! Ace, hang on a sec, honey...

Hangin' in t-there, baby.

And...there. Omega touched the place in Echo's mind, making the mental contact as soothing and warm as she could. She felt the reflected pain in her own body diminish almost instantly.

Ohhh...dear God, Echo groaned. *Yes.*

Better?

Much.

Still hurts though, right?

A little. But it's only about a 1 on a 10-point scale now, Echo explained. *It was about a forty-eight or somethin' before, I dunno. It was...bad.*

Omega? Mm'l'n queried. *I have worked in a hospital and have some knowledge of this technique. That you figured it out on your own is very good. Let me show you how to apply the mental 'pressure' a little differently, and we may be able to do even better for Echo.*

The others sensed Echo trying to relax both mind and body to allow them to work, even as Mm'l'n demonstrated to Omega and the rest how to do what needed doing in order to most effectively anesthetize Echo. A few moments later, Echo sighed deeply, relaxed even more, and slipped into a semi-conscious state.

Whoa, Omega murmured, worried. *Ace? Honey? Echo, are you there?*

'M here, came the very slurred response. *Jus' really, really...tired now.*

And that is understandable, and normal, Mm'l'n confirmed. *He has been in great pain for a considerable time, and is likely in shock on several levels, physical, mental, and emotional. He needs the rest.*

More, Jj'k'k noted, *if he is, or at least appears to be, in a stupor or even unconscious should the slave supervisor return, whatever means of torture they are inflicting upon him would not be effective, and so they would not bother. The usual reason torture is applied is to obtain information; an unconscious being can give no information.*

Ooo, Omega responded. *Then this is good.*

Yes, it is good, Bb'y'x averred. *Zz'r'p? Kk'q'r? Have either of you shown this pair how to...what is the word the humans use...? Ah! Have you shown them how to 'cuddle' through the bond?*

No, Zz'r'p said in some surprise. *It has been too long for me. I had not thought...yes, that would be good, especially right now. Kk'q'r, if you would be so kind as to assist?*

Of course, Zz'r'p.

All right, Omega, Zz'r'p began, *as Echo is rather too tired to be completely coherent at this point, and I think he is the one who needs it anyway, let us explain the concept of 'telepathic cuddling' to you, and then you can soothe your mate even more...*

* * *

About five minutes later, an exhausted Echo was fully relaxed, relatively free of pain, and effectively 'napping' in Omega's telepathic 'embrace.'

Very good, Kk'q'r murmured. *You learn quickly, Omega.*

She does, Zz'r'p agreed. *It is one of the reasons training her is so rewarding.*

Can he hear us? Omega wondered. *Can Echo hear us?*

No, Kk'q'r said. *We are 'tight-beaming' to your mind, and yours alone. He may hear a few distant echoes through the bond, but in his current state, he is unlikely to notice.*

Is he asleep?

Yes, he is.

Physically, too?

Yes, Zz'r'p averred. *His body will be forced to rest while his mind rests. And this is good, on several levels.*

'Cause he needs the rest, after...everything, Omega noted, *but also because, if the damn Cortian comes back, he'll look unconscious?*

Exactly.

What now? she wondered.

This has tired you, a shrewd Qq'k'l observed, *has it not? We saw you collapse in the chair...*

Yeah, to be honest, it has, Omega admitted. *Damn, I basically felt his pain, in order to locate and deaden it. And WOW, was Ace in some pain. No wonder he tried to keep me out. That HURT.*

Yes, that is how it typically works, Mm'l'n agreed. *And yes, if the patient is in severe pain, it can be very stressful and tiring to the healer. It takes either great love, or great determination, to endure it. You, my friend, have both.*

Zz'r'p, Bb'y'x declared, *I think she needs to rest, and soon.*

Aw, not again, Omega grumbled. *I had only just got done from a mandated nap when this all went down a few hours ago.*

No, no, I do not mean to sleep, Bb'y'x explained. *You will soon need a 'brain break,' I sometimes call it. Some down time, I think you humans often term it. You are not used to this as the rest of us are, and it is tiring you rapidly as a result. And you DID experience the brunt of his pain; we did not.*

You have a point, Bb'y'x, Zz'r'p acknowledged. *No, Omega, do not try to deny it. Not here, not like this. We can all sense it in you.*

All right, the Agent sighed. *What do I need to do, so that I can keep going, keep helping Echo?*

Be there for him, Kk'q'r said. *Now that you have convinced him to let you, and by extension, us, within his block, your very presence through the nd't'lq will soothe him and strengthen him. He can now lean on you without fear of harm TO you. You are his mate, his chosen spouse, and his deeply beloved. None other can calm him, provide solace for him, as you can.*

I should like to recommend that she remain 'here,' helping Echo to relax, until he awakens, Bb'y'x said. *Meanwhile the rest of us will work out a shift schedule to ensure that Echo is kept free of pain, and able to relax and look unconscious, should any of the Cortians return. In this fashion, as Jj'k'k said, whatever means of torturing him they are using will seem to them to be useless, as he will not be conscious to give them whatever it is that they want of him.*

This sounds like an excellent plan to me, Zz'r'p said. *Omega? Is this acceptable to you? You will still be in constant contact with him through the bond, and can talk to him at any time, to provide whatever connection, what communication, may be needful for you and him to make it through this. And this, only YOU can do, not merely because of who and what you are to him, but also because of how you came to be as you are. But now that we know precisely what to do, we can take over the easing of his pain for you, as we are more experienced, and it will not tire us as badly. We had simply never done it for a human before, as I told you earlier; we needed you to show us the precise location in his mind. But now we know, and can do it for you.*

...Yeah. Yeah, I think that'll work, Omega decided.

Then let me poll my team, Zz'r'p said. *Mm'l'n? Are you in favor of Bb'y'x's plan?*

I am, Mm'l'n vouched.

Kk'q'r?

Yes.

Qq'k'l?

I think it an excellent notion.

Jj'k'k?

I am for it.

Then for now, I will assist Omega, Zz'r'p announced. *The rest of you, work out a schedule for 'tag-teaming' Echo's pain relief, as he would put it. Make sure you put in time for your own rest, for we will soon need 'all hands,' as Fox would say.*

Consider it done, sir, Mm'l'n said.

Omega sighed in relief of her own.

* * *

The captain looked up from his paperwork at the knock on the door frame. The slave supervisor stood in it.

(Report,) he barked.

(The prisoner knows nothing,) the slave supervisor replied, stifling a sigh of frustration. (Full interrogation is now complete, but I could obtain none of the desired information.)

(NONE of it?!)

(None, sir. He knows nothing.)

(Impossible!) Captain Incke declared, outraged. (He is an elite agent! He MUST know!)

(I assure you, sir, he does not,) the slave supervisor answered, shrugging. (Not even under maximum interrogation techniques did he confess to knowing anything. He claims he is a fighter pilot only; he knows how to wield the devices in question, but nothing about how they are built. Which latter IS the purview of an engineer...which he is not.)

(He is lying!)

(I swear to you, sir, he is not, of this I am completely convinced. He IS tough, that one; only when I was exerting maximum pressure upon him did he break sufficient to scream. But he DID break, and he did scream. Yet he continued to insist he did not know the information, and had nothing to give us.)

(Condemnation,) Captain Incke cursed bitterly. (For all his promise, this one will end by yielding us nothing but his sell fee.) He shook his head, and clacked his beak in disgust. (You have given him all due attention? I would not have him die before our honored guests arrive. Then we should obtain NOTHING out of this damned transaction.)

(I have, sir.)

(Good. Return to your station, then. Do not bother with this ignorant Division One Agent any further. We will sell him to the highest bidder, and have done. He has proven disappointingly beneath our attentions.)

(Yes, sir.)

The slave supervisor departed. Captain Incke rose and stepped to the door of his captain's cabin.

(Communications!) he snapped.

(Sir!)

(Contact our esteemed customers, and notify them of the predetermined rendezvous point and time. I tire of wasting effort on this worthless slave.)

(Aye sir!)

(Helm.)

(Sir!)

(Set course for the rendezvous site. Initiate as soon as you have the course laid into the piloting computer.)

(Aye, sir.)

Captain Incke turned back for his cabin office.

(What a colossally damnable, disappointing waste of time and resources,) he grumbled. (That one has been nothing but trouble since our people first encountered him. Well, I suppose soon, he will trouble us no more, if the head of the Rrgllbrrgll is to be believed.)

He headed for his desk to resume the endless paperwork.

* * *

"Sir!" Sail looked up from the comm console on the bridge of the *Genesis*. Fox, who had been working out a special and

81

highly apropos design on his personal tablet as he sat in the captain's chair, glanced up at his bridge officer.

"What? You have something?"

"The rendezvous location and time!" Sail observed with a wolfish grin. "It's in code, but the code is simplistic. I don't even need to run it through a breaker."

"Show me."

Fox moved to the communications station and looked at the display over his shoulder. Sail pointed, and Fox nodded.

"Pop it to Übermut at the helm," he ordered. "Übermut, make sure the Deltiri know, then plot an intercept course, highest possible velocity. We have the sons of bitches."

* * *

"See it?" Cast asked Übermut, roughly an hour later; Fox had reached a certain point in his design work, and needed to concentrate, so he had retired to his 'captain's cabin'—really a kind of small office—just off the bridge proper. "Right there, on the edge of our sensor resolution?"

"I see it," Übermut noted. "Let us hone in on our target."

"Shall I notify Fox, in his cabin?" Sail wondered.

"Yes, please," Cast confirmed. "He asked to be notified when we were getting close."

"We are close," Übermut confirmed. "Very close."

"Wilco," Sail agreed.

* * *

"Bridge to Fox," the intercom in the captain's cabin annunciated, as Fox worked on several ideas at once. He reached over and thumbed the mic switch.

"Fox here. Go, Sail."

"Fox, the flight crew wanted you notified—we have the Cortian spacecraft on extreme sensor resolution, now. There's two of 'em, it appears, which follows what the PGLEIA has been able to determine of their protocol...but the Deltiri know which one Echo's on. We're pretty damn close. The red dwarf system their communication specified for the rendezvous is only a few tens of light years ahead."

"I copy," Fox said. "Find Omega—there are only three places she might be: Ambassador Zz'r'p's stateroom, her own cabin, or sick bay—and have her come here to my cabin, please."

"Wilco, Fox. Anything else?"

"Not for now, Sail. Tell the flight team good job for me."

"Will do. Sail out."

"Fox out."

* * *

"No, this will be tricky, meyn tekhter," Fox explained, as he and Omega met in his little captain's cabin—where he could be available to the bridge crew, yet still get other work done—just off the *Genesis* bridge. "Sail, Zero, Romeo, and I studied the, ah, the 'invitation list' the Cortians sent out in their communiqué, and there are going to be representatives from the Rrgllbrrgll, a couple of Veldorn—likely lieutenants of Xoreplirg Erushin, who was out to get you and Echo in order to tie up loose ends, and that you took down a couple weeks back with a little help from your friends—a couple of Gurgevs, some Ke!endarians, Dabanorans, Teludals, Glu'gu'ik, Delzantians, Zargothians...it's a real mixed lot. Almost all are from some half-dozen interstellar syndicates, however; just different factions of 'em."

"Wow," Omega murmured, stunned at the length of the list. "Some of those, I can figure, from the missions Echo an' I have done together, but..."

"Yes, well, he and X-ray, and later Romeo, stayed quite busy before your advent, meyn tekhter," Fox agreed. "And now that lot—the survivors, at least—are coming back to try to take revenge, or at least to see revenge done on him by, ahem, 'colleagues.' But several of those races fall into the so-called Opdip category in that new Gibheer Morphology System..."

"Meaning they're humanoid, and look a lot like us," Omega noted. "Which means I can pass as one of them, with a bit of help."

"Exactly. So what I have planned to do is going to be a bit complicated, my dear girl," Fox explained. "And not a little dangerous for you, in several ways." He paused, waiting for her reaction. Omega scowled.

"Keep going," she declared.

"All right. You'll need to wear both your solid hologram disguise unit AND the personal sensor scrambler you've ginned up—and for which, I'm preparing additional power packs, to ensure it lasts long enough—because this is a three-part plan. I then want to put you in a disposable emergency egress envelope, which is basically a structured polymer bubble with a few small life support modules and maneuvering units attached; it's the starship equivalent to an inflatable lifeboat, so it's tough and difficult to, say, puncture...but not impervious, by any means. It's next to invisible in space unless its beacon has been activated, but we're going to disable this one's beacon, because we emphatically WANT it as nearly invisible as possible." Fox paused and gave Omega a querying glance.

"I follow. Keep going." Omega's face was hard, the blue eyes bright, their gaze sharp.

"All right. The envelope will go out one of the hatches on the *Genesis*...with you inside. We'll grab you with a tractor beam, and maneuver you over to one of the hatches being used to ingress the Cortians' Opdip 'guests,' extending our own cloaking around you as you progress, just to ensure that they can't see a damn thing. Now, we'll have to wait until their spacecraft undocks from the Cortian ship...which, I gather from the communiqués, is called the *Orktes*."

"*Orktes*; got it," Omega murmured.

"At that point, you'll dock the egress envelope to the hatch, and hit the emergency airlock cycle; there'll be a panel to the right of the hatch, and it'll look like a standard numerical keypad, but with different symbols. Hit the sequence that would correspond to $8-5-2-6-5-4$. That's basically a plus sign across the keypad, starting with the vertical line, then going right to left for the horizontal."

"Okay."

"That will cycle the airlock without requiring a dock; it assumes there will be a crewman outside, in distress, and opens the hatch, providing fresh air as soon as the outer hatch begins to open, but it's automatic, so move fast. From there, you'll have assumed the disguise appropriate to whatever race we select..."

"All over it," Omega said. "I have all of those Opdips you mentioned already programmed into the solid hologram, and have ever since I first set the thing up. Just let me know which one y'all choose. An' rather than wearing a Suit, I'll go put on some different clothes to blend in—unless you think a Suit WOULD blend in—and make sure I wear my sneakers, so I can soften my footsteps."

"Good girl. No, I think in this instance, different clothing would be appropriate; you'll be undercover, after all, and our Suits could be too recognizable to this lot. That said, based on what I know of the typical henchmen for these sorts, head to toe black should fit in pretty well, so choose your clothing accordingly."

"Okay."

"And while you are ingressing the *Orktes*, I plan to have a couple of our fighter escorts do a little dance on the other side of their ship, as a diversion," Fox continued. "That way, no one on the *Orktes* bridge should see the emergency hatch entry." He waited until he saw her nod, then went on. "Zz'r'p's team is going to lead you to Echo; at this point, they have a pretty firm fix on him within the Cortian ship, using the data they're able to pull in from the quantum-entanglement aspect of their telepathy, and they'll locate you the same way, then tell you more or less where you need to go, by referencing your location, Echo's location, and general Cortian ship's schematics, based on the fact that all of the Cortian spacecraft use the exact same plans and schematics."

"Which is damn useful for us in this instance," Omega decided. "Most instances, I guess. But this one in particular."

"It is, indeed." Fox offered his adoptive daughter a slight smile, and she returned it in kind, but her eyes were still hard. "Now, once you are free of the commons areas, engage the sensor scrambler and keep going. If you're careful and quiet, no one will know you're there; our intel indicates that, while the Cortian ships used to have a certain amount of detection to catch escapees and whatnot—things like infrared cameras and the like—not only should your miniature scrambler take care of that, most of 'em no longer work."

"What, they haven't been able to return to the Corta system to have things upgraded and refurbished, 'cause of the blockade?" Omega wondered. "And nobody in the Coalition will help 'em except the criminals, and they probably don't trust each other."

"You nailed it, tekhter," Fox said with a wry grin. "So at that point, you should be able to go straight to Echo. You have all your gear, right?"

"After the Vacation That Wasn't this past summer, Echo an' I both started carrying our standard travel kits, crammed as full as we could make 'em, on every trip, even the off-duty stuff," Omega acknowledged. "Especially after y'all acquired the new space-warp kits for us field agents. You have NO IDEA what-all we have crammed in THOSE things!"

"Right. So getting in and freeing him shouldn't be a problem. Getting him OUT will be the problem, because it sounds like, based on what you've picked up through your telepathic bond, he's most likely going to be incapacitated."

"Yeah..." Omega bit her lip. Fox saw, but pretended not to, even as his heart sank.

"That's why I have this," he said, and produced a metal-mesh belt from a pocket. The buckle also held a small device. "This is an antigrav belt. It's basically like your jet belt, only without the jets. Wrap it around his waist, initiate it, and he'll float anywhere you need to take him—WITHOUT having to carry him yourself. No, no, I know you've been working out so you can," Fox said, holding up a hand as she made to protest. "I remember events last Christmas. But we also don't really know how far you're going to have to go within their ship, or how many deck changes you'll have to make, let alone how tight passages are going to be. This will ensure you don't exhaust yourself before you can get him out. AND make it easier to ease him through narrow passages, hatches, and the like."

"Okay," Omega grudgingly admitted, as he put it, and a kind of harness tether, into her hands. "It makes sense. And sounds like a pretty handy gadget, at that."

"Good. Just make sure you extend your sensor scrambler field around the both of you on the return leg, and that'll work fine for you. Then come back to the emergency egress envelope, seal it, detach from the airlock, and notify the Deltiri you're both in there; they'll relay it to me. As soon as we have the notification on the bridge, we'll return you the same way we sent you, via tractor beam behind the extended cloaking fields. Romeo and India will be waiting for you both at the *Genesis* hatch, and will take Echo straight to sick bay, where Zebra and a full team will be waiting."

"Got it," Omega said, calm.

"Oh, one more thing," Fox remembered, pulling another small device from a pocket; he had been the one to introduce Echo to warp pockets, and while he hadn't raised it to quite the art form that Echo had, Fox generally had several on his person, with who-knew-what stashed within. He placed the object in her hand. "Here. They do have cloning technology, whether they have the resources to do it at the moment or not; unfortunately, I don't KNOW if they have the resources to do it at the moment. But we do NOT want them getting hold of any tissue they can clone. Can you verify that they don't already have a clonable sample of his tissue, stored somewhere?"

"Hang on a minute," Omega murmured, and closed her eyes. Moments later, she opened them. "Okay, the telepath team has Echo kinda sedated, like, so I couldn't squeeze a lotta details out of him, but evidently they did their genetic testing on a hair sample, so it doesn't sound like it. I kinda gathered that, um, well, let's just say that no other parts of him, or body fluids, or anything like that, have left the cell they have him imprisoned in."

"That is...good news. And I assume Echo will be injured, so at the least, there will likely be blood in that cell. This is a kind of emergency flare used for signaling that a ship is in distress, if their comm is down. It's visible over VERY long distances, so it is very bright, and burns very hot. I've taken the liberty of modifying it a bit; you know me, tekhter. It now has a timer on it, good for up to half an hour. Set that timer for however long you think it will take you to carry Echo at least one hundred feet away from his cell, initiate it, and leave it inside the cell. Then, MAKE SURE you are at least one hundred feet away!"

"In other words, haul ass."

"Yes. Because when it initiates, not only will it thoroughly sterilize the inside of the cell and burn away any tissue residue, it will probably also reduce all the other contents to slag."

"It won't present a danger to the ship as a whole, will it? I'm not out to burn the thing down...at least, not until after I've managed to sneak Echo out."

"It shouldn't. It's not that big. But I can't speak to the maintenance schedule of the *Orktes*, either, so don't dawdle getting out, if you can help it."

"Right."

Just then, a *bleep!* cut through the atmosphere of the cabin, and Fox hit his intercom button.

"Fox here."

"It's Zero, sir. We're approaching the intercept point. The Xyir system is only a few light years off, and we'll be dropping the warp bubble in a few minutes. You wanted to be notified."

"Right. Thank you, Zero."

"My pleasure, Admiral-Director. Do you have any instructions?"

"Yes. The Xyir system is a binary, consisting of a red dwarf flare star and a brown dwarf. Make sure we come up on the back side of the brown dwarf; its mass will protect us from the radiation if Xyir A is in flare mode. The shadow of Xyir B should be where the rendezvous site is, anyway, if I recall correctly."

"Very good, sir, and yes, it is. Zero out."

"Fox out." He returned his attention to Omega. "That was our wake-up call, tekhter. It's almost time to rock and roll. Now, are you ready?"

"Yes." Omega squared her shoulders; the expression in her eyes was such that Fox did not wish to be a Cortian meeting up with her.

"Then let us do this," he declared.

They exited the cabin, cut through the bridge, and headed for Omega's cabin for her to change into her disguise and grab her desired equipment, en route to one of the decks containing the *Genesis'* principal egress hatches.

* * *

Omega entered her assigned cabin, Fox on her heels, and went to the little wardrobe, pulling out several pairs of pants, ranging from dress trousers to jeans, all in black, and holding them up for Fox to assess. He considered briefly, then pointed. Omega tossed the selected trousers onto the bed, replaced the others in the wardrobe, then rummaged through for several shirts—a black silk blouse, a black polo shirt, and a black t-shirt. Fox studied them, then pointed to the silk blouse. That went onto the bed next to the trousers, and Omega dove back in, fishing out a pair of slip-on sneakers in solid black.

"This too, tekhter," he said, tapping a set of body armor he had had put in the wardrobe earlier, expressly for this purpose. "Don it underneath. But use the belt for your trousers, and tuck the extra shoulder harness into a warp pocket someplace; you'll want it for Echo."

"Oh, okay," Omega agreed.

Then she went to the travel kit on the dresser and extracted more than a dozen items, including the solid hologram disguise necklet, and tucked all but the hologram disguise and her ginned-up personal sensor scrambler into various warp pockets already in her Suit. Fox watched with some interest, finding it fascinating, the eclectic selection of items that Alpha One chose to have available. Omega next extracted the warp pockets from her Suit, laying them in a line across the dresser, in a certain order.

"Abba Fox, would you mind stepping into the hall for a sec?" Omega wondered. "The head is a little too small for changing clothes, an' Zebra might not be happy if I changed clothes in front of you. 'Sides, I'd be twelve kinds of embarrassed."

"Not a problem, tekhter," an understanding Fox said, heading for the door. "You're my daughter in all but blood, and I don't think of you like that; but your privacy is paramount, after all that has been done to you."

And he was gone.

* * *

Five minutes later, Omega came out the door of her cabin, attired in the black silk blouse and black trousers, footsteps nigh unto dead-silent in the black athletic shoes, with the hologram necklet in position about her shoulders, and the sensor scrambler attached to the body-armor belt, which was threaded through the trouser belt loops. Her shoulder holster, complete with both blasters, rested atop the blouse, and Omega had added a menswear-style vest, open in the front and cut for her figure, atop it to help cover them.

89

"Oh, excellent thought, kind. What about your Winchester & Tesla?" Fox wondered.

"In my back, like usual," Omega noted. "The waistband holster tends to fit entirely inside my trousers anyhow, so it was already pretty well hidden."

"Warp pockets in place?"

"Oh yeah."

"Then let's go, meyn tekhter."

"Right beside you, Abba Fox."

Chapter 4

Fox escorted Omega to Airlock 21, on Deck 7; Alpha Two was already there, waiting. In the shadows of the corridor past the airlock, an antigrav gurney waited, as well.

"There she is," Romeo noted. "Ain't gonna be long now, Meg."

"No," she said, succinct. "Let's get going."

"You have this, Romeo?" Fox wondered.

"All over it, Boss-man," Romeo averred. "Me an' India done gone over the thang, made sure it was all workin' like you wanted after you swung by an' disabled th' beacon awhile back, an' we got it deployed outside the airlock. All Meg has ta do is go through, seal th' bag's hatch, and detach."

"Right," Fox said. "I'll head back to the bridge, then. I want to oversee this operation personally." Then, much to their surprise, he stepped forward and gave Omega a light, brief hug. "Stay safe, tekhter," he murmured. "Bring Echo back to us in one piece."

Omega opened her mouth to reply, choked, then nodded. Finally she forced out, "I'll do the best I can, Abba Fox."

"That is all I ask, meyn teyere," he told her.

And he was off.

"Okay, Meg, you're good with your meds?" India asked.

"Yeah," Omega replied, voice gruff, slightly hoarse, and somewhat deeper than usual. "I've been on the max dosage since y'all all insisted I do it to help Echo mentally. Which," she admitted, "turned out to be a Really Good Thing, all around."

"Awright, let's slip ya through here an' into th' bag," Romeo said, turning to the airlock controls.

* * *

Fox emerged onto the bridge at speed, and headed straight for the joint helm/navigation/weapons console.

"Move over a bit, Boy, if you would," he addressed the female agent at the weapons console. "I want to handle this myself, no offense."

Puzzled, Boy, Cast, and Übermut eased to the side as Zero brought the spare console chair and sat it in position for Fox.

"Is there a reason why you need to be the one to do it, Fox?" Cast wondered. "I mean, we all work hard at our jobs, and we're damn good, if I do say so..."

"Oh, that was never in question, meyn khaver," Fox noted, sitting and scanning the console. "But I am considerably older than I look, with many more decades of experience at running precisely these types of controls. And it is Omega who will be at the end of the tractor beam on the outbound trip, and hope-fully Omega AND Echo on the return trip." He drew a deep breath. "It's hard for me to explain. It isn't that I think more of them than I do of my excellent, intelligent, and highly-skilled bridge crew—because I don't. I value the lot of you just as much. But on a personal level, Omega and I relate to each other in ways that, I think, no one else on this vessel understands, or CAN understand. We have both been on the receiving end of true horror, of complete inhumanity, in ways that few humans still living have been."

"So it's true, the rumors," Zero murmured. "You DID sur-vive the Nazi exterminations..."

Fox paused and turned to look at the security chief and sometime captain of the *Genesis*. He deliberately did not re-ply...verbally. Nor, however, did he hide the knowing com-prehension on his face. Finally he chose to respond...after a fashion.

"Let us merely say that galactic medicine is a marvelous thing," he noted, wry. "And both Omega and I understand that, as no one else can...though I'm afraid Echo may be about to join that exclusive little club. But we also understand, she and I, that galactic medicine, wonderful as it is, can only do so much, and it cannot wipe away experiences, nor our responses to them. Even the brain-bleacher can only remove the memo-ries; we now know from recent studies, the traumatic responses still tend to remain. AND...he was little more than a boy when I first met him, and I tend to think that X-ray and I finished raising him, more or less...but Echo is my oldest human friend still living...and I intend to see he stays that way, if it is in my power."

"Is it because you have that 'family' thing going?" Sail wondered. "You gave Omega away at the wedding..."

"Say rather that the 'family thing' is because of that," Fox said, thoughtful. "Yes, Omega put together a kind of adoptive family, and yes, I am part of that family—the patriarch, the others call me. Because yes, I AM older than I look...by a considerable amount. But you see, Omega no longer has a family outside of the Agency, thanks to the heinous actions of a dreadful being. And I no longer have a family outside of the Agency, thanks to the heinous actions of another dreadful being...and his henchmen and followers. It's a choice, you see... allow ourselves to retreat, to become reclusive, to stop caring because we simply do not want any more pain, or create the kind of family around ourselves that cares, that understands, that refuses to let us retreat, refuses to let us become hard and callous and uncaring." He returned his attention to the weapons console and set up a specific sequence involving the tractor beam projectors, the active cloaking, and the sensor scrambler, but did not yet initiate it. "I didn't choose the family, nor did I choose to become involved in it. OMEGA chose. Though I do not think she did it consciously, really; she let her heart choose those of us to whom she could relate, who best understood. In her case in particular, you see, not everyone DOES understand, and it causes her pain, because those who don't understand most usually treat her as an unnatural creature at best, or as a monster at worst. And when she chose to include me, I debated whether to allow it...and in the end decided it would be good for her, because I had experience and wisdom to offer her, wisdom and experience that she needed in the aftermath of specific events. It was only after the fact that I discovered...it was good for me, too." He shook his head. "I want you all to know, I do my damnedest, children, not to show favoritism toward this 'family' that has developed. In fact, I consider all of you to be part of it—nieces, nephews, cousins, and what-not. And in the colloquial way of putting it, the entire Agency in its current incarnation is 'my baby'...which makes everyone in it my child, in a way. And there are non-human members of that family as well, so it's really a rather eclectic grouping of beings."

"Lord Entiyti?" Zero suggested.

"Among others," Fox admitted. "He is, after all, my oldest non-human friend. He and I were together for many, many years, traveling this big old, beautiful, amazing galaxy. Yes, ostensibly I worked for him, but he was always fairly egalitarian, 'Lord' Entiyti notwithstanding, and it didn't take long before we stopped thinking of ourselves as employer and employee and became, essentially, best friends." Fox shrugged. "But enough maudlin reminiscence. We have an operation to execute, and the situation we have now is such that it requires a very delicate touch, or the envelope tears, and we lose Omega. Or Omega AND Echo, since that would prevent her from rescuing him from the impending sale to his enemies...or if she gets him out, but the envelope tears as they are returning." He shook his head. "So many things could go wrong. And given all that background I just told you about, I will pay for it personally if I do not do this myself. Because if something goes wrong, I will never forgive myself." He glanced around. "And this protects you, because if I do it myself and something goes wrong, there is ONLY myself to blame. " He paused, then added, "I do not say that because I would in any way blame you. But I do know you all, and I know how you think...and I know that each and every one of you would try to blame yourself. I don't want that. So by doing it myself, I ensure that I'm the only one to shoulder any blame. Which I would do anyway."

The bridge fell silent.

* * *

A piercing *bleep!* suddenly annunciated into the air of the bridge, followed by Romeo's voice. They all jumped, then settled, pretending not to have noticed.

"Airlock 21 to Bridge, this is Agent Romeo f'r Director Fox."

Fox hit a toggle switch.

"Fox here. Go, Romeo."

"Okay, Boss-man, Meg's in th' egress envelope, we got it sealed, an' she's detached from th' airlock hatch. She's all yours."

"On it, Romeo. Thank you, and pass that thanks to India. Stand by there for Omega's return with Echo in a bit. Meanwhile, keep an eye on her out the nearest porthole, and make sure this is working. Yell at me IMMEDIATELY if you see anything going wrong."

"Wilco. Alpha Two standin' by an' watchin'. An' India says thanks f'r rememberin' her, an' you're welcome."

Fox hit several keys, and the tank lit with the positions of the *Genesis*, the *Orktes*, and several other large spacecraft, as well as some half-dozen of the small corvettes that served as fighter escorts for the huge *Genesis* battleship. A tiny blip, very close to the hull of the *Genesis*, showed up near the starboard side of the big spaceship; a large, fuzzy gray sphere, representing the cloaking field, surrounded the *Genesis* and the little blip. Smaller gray spheres surrounded individual corvettes. Abruptly Fox glanced at Sail.

"Sail, did we send the word to the corvettes about the diversionary tactic?"

"Aye, sir, and they report they're ready and waiting for the word. Three for the diversion itself, and three for the backup, if they're needed."

"Good." He drew a deep breath. "Let me do this, then."

He hit a few more keystrokes, and the tank showed a pale yellow line lancing out to the little blip—and the blip began to move.

* * *

Zz'r'p, are you there? Omega asked, as she clambered into the emergency evacuation envelope.

Of course, came the immediate reply. *I am unlikely to NOT be here, child, not until matters settle a bit, at least. I am aware that you are about to attempt rescuing Echo, as well. Fox notified me.*

Oh, okay. Well, good, she thought. *Is...is he...does Echo... know? That I'm coming, I mean?*

Yes, my team has notified him. I believe Jj'k'k is currently 'on duty' to keep him pain-free and to keep him company, though the hand-off to Mm'l'n will occur shortly; but he told Echo you were on the way just a little bit ago.

And? Omega sealed the envelope and detached it from the airlock.

It seems Echo was not entirely happy about it, Zz'r'p confessed. *He apparently does not want you to see him in whatever condition he is in, and urgently petitioned us to convince Fox to send someone else. We attempted to explain to him that you were far and away the best person for the job, and he finally admitted we were likely right...but he still was not happy about it.*

Yeah. And I have a pretty damn good idea why, Omega admitted, trying not to wince. *His block is good, but it wasn't quite strong enough to keep me from sensing what they were doing as it was happening. That's what woke me up, even with the meds Zebra and India had insisted I take.*

Yes, I saw that in your mind earlier. I fear you may be right. Zz'r'p paused, then continued, *I have an idea.*

Let's hear it.

I think that it might be good, perhaps, if we were to ease Echo into a deep, fully unconscious state shortly before you arrive in his cell. He is not far off it anyway, so it would not take much. And this way, you do not have to try so hard to control your reactions to the sight of him, whatever state he is in, and he does not have to endure the emotional pain of witnessing those reactions. In addition, if we maintain that state until you return him to the Genesis, it enables you to move him without inducing additional pain in him...which will be the excuse we will give him for doing it. And it would be difficult for us to adjust the pain response to a constantly-varying input, in any case, especially while still trying to direct you in progressing through the Cortian ship. It would, thereby, ensure he did not groan in pain at an inopportune time, or the like. It prevents him accidentally giving away this escape attempt.

I think...I think that's a really good idea, Zz'r'p, on a whole lotta levels, Omega decided, biting her lip. *Let's do it.*

Consider it done, then, Zz'r'p replied.

Just then, the tractor beam captured the free-floating envelope and began to move it toward the Cortian ship.

Okay, here we go, she told the Deltiri. *I'll ping you when I'm aboard the* Orktes.

I await your word, Zz'r'p responded, as Omega turned to wave at Alpha Two, whose faces she could see in the viewing port.

* * *

Alpha Two stood in front of the nearest viewing port, side by side, and watched as the emergency egress envelope began to move steadily away from the side of the *Genesis*. Omega waved at them, and they waved back, then she turned to look at the Cortian ship. Romeo thumbed the intercom switch, beside the viewing port.

"Airlock 21 to Bridge, this is Agent Romeo."

"Go, Romeo," Fox's voice responded.

"Meg's headed outbound, nice an' smooth. My compliments t' whoever's operatin' th' tractor beam."

"Thank you, zun," Fox replied, a hint of amusement in his voice. "I'll let Boy know."

* * *

"Have we made a call on which airlock we're going to use on the Cortian ship?" Fox wondered.

"Yes sir," Zero noted. "We decided to go with the Dabanorans. They're just docking—see them, over on the port side of the Cortian ship? In the big 'cracker box' Andan H34 model craft? By the time you can ease Omega's envelope over there, they'll have just debarked, and the ship will undock. And you can slip her right in."

"That works," Fox averred. "Heads up, Zz'r'p..."

I am here, and ready, Fox, came the Deltiri ambassador's mental voice.

Good. Tell Omega to select the Dabanoran disguise.

Stand by, and I shall do so, Zz'r'p said. Moments later, he came back. *She says thank you, and done.*

Excellent. Now if the damn Dabanoran ship will only hurry up, we'll have this thing taken care of.

Patience, Fox, patience.

Tell that to Echo. I'm sure he can't wait to get out. Does he know Omega is coming?

He does, but he is...not in good shape.

Will he make it?

I believe so. I gather that his wounds have been tended, though he is still refusing to let any of us in far enough to know what those wounds are. He is barely conscious.

Have you warned Omega?

I did not have to. She already knows.

Fox bit his lip.

* * *

A worried Fox alternated between adjusting his control on the tractor beam and watching its progress in the tank. When he had set up the sequence, he had ensured that the cloaking field, which was combined with the sensor scrambler—though, upon Omega's recent recommendation, he had ensured it was possible to decouple them—would extend along with the tractor beam, always remaining about ten feet in front of the emergency egress envelope.

Now, with the envelope only a hundred yards out from the hull of the *Orktes*, he paused, waiting for the Dabanoran craft to clear the airlock, and tried not to drum his fingers on the console in his impatience and concern.

A few minutes later, the running lights on the Dabanoran spaceship sped up, and the spacecraft broke away from the Cortian ship, executing a translation maneuver to its port side before moving forward.

Fox sat up and remained alert for danger of collision with the envelope or the tractor beam, either of which could be disastrous, but the *Genesis* had deliberately chosen to approach from below the Cortian craft, and most beings tended to prefer an upward motion. It was a wise choice; as the Dabanoran ship moved away, it angled upward relative to its own hull, which was aligned with the *Orktes*, and Fox deftly maneuvered the envelope, at the tip of the tractor beam, to the airlock thus vacated, after first checking to verify that no other ship intended to dock there.

Zz'r'p, he thought, *tell Omega we're coming in for a landing.*

Will do, came the response.

* * *

Be ready, my dear, Zz'r'p's voice sounded in Omega's mind. *Fox is bringing you to the airlock hatch momentarily.*

All over it, she replied.

As the egress envelope moved toward the airlock, Omega activated her solid hologram disguise and moved to the envelope's tiny control panel. There, she began to maneuver it into the proper position for its adaptive hatch to mate with the external airlock door. When she was within a couple of feet of the airlock, she felt the slight shift as the tractor beam released, and she took full control of the movement, slowing her forward momentum and adjusting position until the hatch gently bumped the external airlock door. Another quick tweak of the controls, and she had mated the envelope with the *Orktes'* airlock. Then she initiated a small force field dome about the envelope, ensuring no other ship could come in to dock, thereby destroying her only way to escape the *Orktes*. If anyone tried, it would certainly reveal the presence of the escape envelope, but that was a risk she had to take.

She moved to the hatch, pressed her hand against the flexible polymer skin of the envelope until it just contacted the external emergency-ingress panel beside the hatch, and pressed the button sequence corresponding to 8-5-2-6-5-4. There was a hiss, and the hatch opened, the envelope releasing some of its atmosphere through the hatch and into the airlock, even as the airlock emergency-pressurized. Omega leaped in as the hatch quickly closed and the airlock fully pressurized, and moments later an extra 'Dabanoran' was inside the Cortian ship.

* * *

Even as Fox deactivated the tractor beam, he could see on the viewscreen—which Cast had quietly activated so that everyone else could readily see Omega's progress, just visible to the *Genesis* as they were both inside the cloaking field—that Omega was adjusting the positioning and orientation of the emergency envelope, aligning it with the airlock hatch of the Cortian vessel. Moments later, he saw it mate with the hatch, and Fox called, "Sail! NOW!"

"*Genesis* to escorts, NOW!" Sail announced into his headset.

* * *

(The Dabanoran delegation has arrived, sir,) the comm officer told Captain Incke.

(Very good,) Incke noted. (We will be ready soon. You have sent someone to escort them to the auction room?)

(I have, sir.)

(Excellent.)

(CAPTAIN!) the helmsman shouted, pointing at the forward screen. (LOOK!)

Three tiny spacecraft abruptly dropped warp bubbles some ten kilometers or so off the *Orktes'* port side. The trio drifted forward, their momentum carrying them; then all three came to a sudden halt, and seemed to sit there in space, almost as if their occupants were gaping in surprise at the presence of the big grouping of different makes of ships of the line, just off the brown dwarf orbiting the tiny red dwarf star.

Moments later, and before the weapons master on the bridge of the *Orktes* could react, the three small corvettes had spun about their vertical axes and darted back in the direction they had come; seconds later, all three had raised warp bubbles and vanished, running away from the group of ships.

(Shall we follow them, sir?) the helm officer wondered. (We could take them all out...)

Incke pondered for a few seconds.

(No, I think not. Most likely they were using this system as a way marker, and the presence of such a large show of force frightened them away...which likely means they were up to no good. They will cause us no further trouble. However, if we break to follow at this juncture, it could antagonize our honored guests on board, whose ship crews may assume that we are taking them prisoner for our own purposes...which we are not. At least, not yet. This could result in our losing the only benefit left to us of our current resource in the holding cell. And we will all be away from here, our business concluded, before those tiny ships can bring the 'authorities' to this location. Which, if I am correct in my surmise of their intentions, they are unlikely to do, in any case.)

(Very well, sir.)

(Escort reports that the Dabanorans have been welcomed, and are being taken to the auction room, sir,) the comm officer reported. (Several of the other spacecraft are sending small shuttles to land in our hangar hold.)

(Excellent. For once, all is proceeding according to plan,) the captain decided.

* * *

Omega entered the corridor inside the airlock, glancing

about her as if she were lost...which, to an extent, she was. Just then, she heard Qq'k'l in her head, *Turn right. Progress some thirty feet down the corridor, nodding at the Cortian you will pass, then duck into the alcove on the left, and activate your sensor scrambler.*

Omega did as she had been instructed, nodding in a friendly fashion at the Cortian, keeping a smile pasted on her face, and trying to maintain control of her anger. But instead of the Cortian passing by, he stopped and turned to her.

Oh shit, she thought. *An' I don't know a word of Cortian.*

But I do not have to, Qq'k'l pointed out. *Stay calm. Let him KNOW you do not know Cortian. You are not Omega, you are a member of the Dabanoran crime syndicate.*

"N'ga tla apap to?" the yellow-plumed avian asked.

Are you lost? Qq'k'l translated for her quickly. *He wants to know if you are lost.*

"Er, dag twing a pop chik," Omega replied in fluent Dabanoran.

"Uhn," the Cortian grunted, confused, then responded in Cortian. "Tla obob a w'oo. Uhh...Englishes?"

"Ah," Omega said. "Yes, speak some Englishes I."

"Uh, good is. Lost you?"

No, Qq'k'l instructed her. *I stayed behind to check the airlock. I go straight, correct?*

"No, is lost not," Omega offered in broken English. "Airlock check I, others go. Security is. Know you how it be."

"Oh, is sense make," the Cortian said, bobbing his head. "Not to bother."

"Is not bother," she said with a smile. "Is straight go, yes?" She pointed ahead.

"Yes, is straight go, two corridor, turn...uh..." Evidently the correct word escaped the Cortian, and he turned to face the way he had come, then waved a clawed hand to the left. "Is turn this. Go end corridor, room there."

"Is got," Omega said with a nod. "You thanking."

"Is good."

And the Cortian continued on his way.

Omega drew a deep breath, and headed onward. *This is gonna be a looong little stroll, isn't it?* she wondered.

Not as long as you think it will be. And you will be invisible to them soon. Ten more feet. Do you see the alcove?

Yeah, thank the good Lord. Omega subtly checked the corridor, then darted into the alcove and activated the little kluged sensor scrambler on her belt. *Here's hoping it works.*

Do you have any reason to think it will not?

No, but shit happens sometimes, anyway.

Keep going. You still have your disguise.

Yeah, but as soon as I get off the beaten path, if anybody sees me, I'll be in hot water.

No. You simply tell them you had instructions from Keeth Dikman—that is the Dabanoran group leader—to find the prisoner and examine him, to ensure he is in suitable, or at least satisfactory, condition.

Eh. I need to settle; I should have thought of that myself.

You are doing fine. Do not denigrate yourself so, young-ling. You are under great stress; that is why we are here 'with' you. Let us continue.

Okay, hang on oooone sec; I have one other thing I wanna do, just so we'll have some future data. With that, she produced a tiny device from a warp pocket, opened it, and it released a small swarm of micro-drones. A few keystroke commands to the device's tiny keypad, and the drones all darted away in different directions, disappearing from her ability to see them when they were mere feet from her. *There,* she said. *Now we'll have intel on 'em in future. Make sure the comm officer on the bridge gets that info; I told Sail I'd do that.*

I shall...done. Now, step into the corridor and go back the way you came. You will take the first corridor to the right, then the next corridor to the right, and travel down it to its end...

* * *

By the time Omega reached the end of that corridor, she had passed four more Cortians, none of whom saw her. Nor did they hear or smell her, as she had been careful to use a scent neutralizer while changing into the clothing Fox had selected, and she was treading very lightly, using an Apache technique that Echo had taught her during their training sessions. The biggest problem she had was passing them without bumping anything in the narrow passageways.

Good. You have navigated that little mobile roadblock, Qq'k'l told her with gentle amusement, causing her to smile. *There we go; that is better. Now at the next corridor junction, turn left, go ten feet, and turn right. There should be a hatch that will take you down to the next deck.*

Omega eased her way to the next corridor junction, turned left...

And stopped cold, staring at a blank wall.

It's a dead end, she said in dismay. *There's two doors opening to the left and right, but I can't go forward.*

Mm, that is not good, Qq'k'l noted. *Does the wall before you seem to be of newer make, perhaps, than the rest of it?*

Huh. Now you mention it, it has a little less corrosion, abrasion, and shit like that on it, than the rest of the plating around here, Omega decided. *What, you think this is a 'Wups, we had a problem here, we needed to rework the space' kinda thing?*

It would appear to be, yes. Find a spot where you will be out of the way and unlikely to be accidentally encountered, and let us study the schematics for a moment. We should be able to find a way around...whatever they have done, here.

You're looking for a detour route.

Precisely.

Omega moved to the very end of the corridor and stood there; it extended some meter or so past the last doors along it, apparently to allow for crew members to do what she termed 'do-si-do'ing' in the cramped space, so it served her current need rather well. Then she crouched down and waited.

* * *

On the *Genesis* bridge, Fox sat at the helm, anxiously drumming his fingers on the console. The others monitored their stations, but as the big ship was operating nominally, there was little to do except sit and wait.

"Do you suppose she's been captured?" Zero worried.

"No," Fox declared. "The Deltiri would know if she had, and Zz'r'p would have contacted me immediately."

"How long has it been?" Sail wondered. Fox glanced at the master chronometer in front of Übermut.

"Thirty-two minutes, thirteen point six seconds," Fox noted, then added in wry whimsy, "and counting."

A soft sigh went around the room.

* * *

Omega crouched in her narrow cul-de-sac, watching the occasional passage of a Cortian crew member, for long, tense minutes, waiting for the Deltiri team to figure out a possible detour in her effort to reach Echo. Finally she got a response.

Omega, do you see a maintenance hatch along the corridor, back near where it joins the main corridor?

Yeah, Qq'k'l, she said. *Oh, don't TELL me I gotta go through THAT thing.*

I am afraid that looks like your quickest route to Echo, right now, Qq'k'l averred.

Now, you KNOW that if he's unconscious, we're not getting OUT that way, right? she snapped. *It's gonna be way the hell too narrow and tight.*

Omega, this is Zz'r'p, the ambassador interrupted. *Settle, youngling. I know this is exceedingly tense for you, in many, many ways. But we felt that reaching Echo as quickly as possible was important, rather than having you sit in one place indefinitely, where you may be detected by accident, while we work out a likely path. This way, you are out of contact of the crew of that vessel regardless of what may happen, for we have verified beyond doubt that currently there is no crew whatsoever in the maintenance tunnels; you reach Echo soon, you keep moving, and while you are preparing him for his escape, we are studying the schematics, and detecting the ebb and flow of minds around the, ah, the 'roadblock,' thereby mapping out its extent. It buys us time to figure out a workaround.*

Oh, Omega said, chastened. *I'm sorry. I didn't mean to be...I mean...*

Hush, child, Zz'r'p soothed. *We know that. No one is offended; after all, YOU are the one in harm's way, here, and you are the one whose mate has been grievously wounded, and who is dealing with that on many levels, including the nd't'lq bond. We are simply working hard to try to determine what the current layout is, and direct you through it...and we know you cannot see that, from where you are. Now, the question is, can you manage to slip into that maintenance hatch without being detected? Just because they cannot see you does not mean they cannot see an open hatch where there should not be one.*

Maybe, Omega said, cautious, as she eased over to the hatch, which was on the near side of the proper door out of the truncated corridor. She examined the latch, then extracted several items from her warp pockets, including the electronic lockpick. *Yeah, it may take a bit to get it unlocked, but I think I can squeeze into it, and do so pretty fast. You'll have to direct me once I'm in there, though.*

Of course.

Omega set to the task, working quickly, and surveying the readouts on her instruments, while keeping an ear peeled for the oddly-ticking sound of clawed boots on the deck of the main corridor; the Deltiri helped in this by providing warning of approaching beings' mental activity. Whenever footsteps came too near the closed-off passage in which she labored, she paused her work and crouched down, placing one sensor-scrambled hand over the latch indicators to help obscure them from a casual glance, then resumed work when the crew member passed on. Fortunately, she seemed to be in a little-frequented part of the ship. *Which,* she considered, *is either the reason they could rework this area, or because they reworked the area.*

Most likely, one way or the other, Qq'k'l agreed. *How is it progressing? Try to hurry; someone is coming.*

Hang on...I've almost unlocked it, she noted—just as the latch clicked softly. *There it is!* she said, easing the hatch open and slipping inside, pulling it closed behind herself...

...Just as a crewman turned into the short hallway and ducked through the door opposite the hatch.

* * *

"That was close," Jj'k'k observed, as the Deltiri clustered in Zz'r'p's stateroom on the *Genesis*.

"It was, indeed," Qq'k'l agreed. "But as long as she was not detected—and she was not—then a miss and a near miss are effectively indistinguishable."

"True," Zz'r'p averred. "How is the determination of a new route progressing?"

"I may have something for you to work with," Bb'y'x said, studying the schematics on a table nearby; in the corner,

Mm'l'n sat with closed eyes and frowning forehead, working on keeping Echo free of pain and unconscious, with some assistance from the multi-tasking Jj'k'k. "I am trying to ascertain the movements of the crew through the area to confirm it. I may have to adjust a few places, but I think I have a general plan now."

"Good," Zz'r'p decreed. "Keep working, and we shall notify you when she is ready to depart with Echo."

"Oh, I hope to have something definitive and ready to use by then," Bb'y'x declared. "I will show you as soon as I have verified it."

"Excellent," Qq'k'l decided.

"Indeed," Zz'r'p agreed.

* * *

Inside the cramped maintenance tunnel, Omega crouched slightly and glanced about; it roughly paralleled the corridor in which she had been standing, and appeared to continue in the direction she wanted to go...though it was a little cramped, and she would have to stoop. So she turned in that direction.

This way? she asked, pointing ahead.

Yes, Zz'r'p confirmed. *These tunnels will not be straight, like the crew tunnels, but will follow the ship's contours. Follow the curvature of this one as it works around the ship. About fifteen feet from where you now stand, there will be a three-dimensional intersection. By that I mean there will be two cross tunnels, one horizontal to your right and left, and one vertical—be careful, for the vertical maintenance tunnels do not curve; they are straight drops. Take the vertical tunnel— our schematics show there will be a ladder—and go down one deck. When you reach the junction on the lower deck, tell us so we can direct you as to which tunnel to take.*

Copy that, Omega said, and she set off.

* * *

Omega came to the junction; there were multiple ladders, one between each horizontal tunnel opening into the intersection, as well as handholds to allow one to move across to a different horizontal passage. She turned and eased over, onto the ladder, then hung on with her hands, placed her feet on the outside of the side rails, and slid down the ladder until she reached

106

the level of the deck below, which had a similar junction.

Okay, guys, I'm here, she said. *I'm basically facing back the way I came from. Well, not quite; I'm adjacent to the tunnel going that way. Sort of on the wall in between the tunnels.*

Ah, Jj'k'k said. *And I see via your eyes that there are means to access the other tunnels. Excellent. Enter the passage that is currently on your left...*

Omega maneuvered herself across to that tunnel, stepped across the intervening space, and continued on.

* * *

The Deltiri led Omega unerringly over to the next maintenance shaft, whence she was told to descend two more levels. Anxious to speed the trip along and reach Echo as fast as possible, Omega used the same technique she had used earlier, that of pinching the side rails between her feet and sliding, rather than stepping from rung to rung, using her hands on the rungs—and sometimes on the rails—to control the motion.

Omega was sliding hand over hand down the ladder to another level when she discovered how well the Cortians maintained their spacecraft—the ladder broke, one of the rungs snapping in two just as she pushed off it and before she had a full, firm grip on the next rung. She pitched backward down the shaft, falling in the Higgs-field artificial gravity just as she might have fallen down the side of a building on Earth.

OH SHIT! she had just time to think. *THIS is gonna hurt!*

A quick glance over her shoulder revealed that there were many decks below her, so she deliberately spread-eagled her arms and legs, arching her back, to increase air resistance as much as possible and slow her descent, even as she pulled something out of a warp pocket...

...The antigrav belt Fox had given her to use on Echo.

Swiftly she fastened the buckle near the end of the belt, forming a large loop, then she shrugged it over one shoulder and her head, held onto it tightly 'twith her left hand, and hit the activation button on the buckle with the right. Then she flung her right arm out, still holding tight to the belt with her left.

As the counter-field expanded from the small device embedded in the buckle, Omega felt and saw her motion slow; she still fell, but that was largely due to her body's momentum, and

107

atmospheric drag was slowing that. Slowly, slowly, she came to a halt, hovering in mid-air as the belt operated as advertised.

"Well, shit," she grumbled to herself. "Now I gotta make it over to the wall, figure out what level I'm on, and hoist myself to the proper level...which is likely to mean I have to climb UP, now."

You do, came Bb'y'x's voice in her mind. *But not too far, perhaps only a couple of levels. You think fast, my friend. That startled all of us almost too much to react. It is fortunate you had that device.*

Yeah, Omega said. *Fox gave it to me to use on Echo, as being easier than me trying to carry him this whole great way out. And quite aside from saving me from making a big splat at the bottom of this shaft, after seeing how far I have to go just to reach Echo, I'm really glad now that Fox thought of this.*

Perhaps you can use it to 'swim' up the shaft, then.

No, I'd rather not, if I can help it, Omega protested. *The power pack on this thing is necessarily small, in order to fit on and in the belt and buckle, and I don't want to risk running the power supply down before I have to sneak Echo out of this damn place.*

Ah. Understood. Forgive me; I am not an engineer.

Not a problem. It's a good idea, and that's exactly what I'm gonna do to work my way over to the nearest ladder, Omega said, putting the plan into execution as she made swimming motions to move her across the width of the vertical maintenance shaft to the closest ladder.

Her progress was a bit slow; air was not as dense as water, and the propulsion produced by flailing arms and legs was correspondingly weaker. But after a couple of minutes of working at it, Omega grasped the ladder, twisted about, and managed to gain purchases with both hands and both feet. Then she paused for a few moments to catch her breath; between the adrenaline induced by the fall, and the effort required to 'swim' through the air, she needed to slow her respiration, never mind suck in more oxygen than usual.

Are you all right? Jj'k'k asked at that.

Yeah, just a little outta breath, she replied. *Gimme a minute, and then I can set back toward Echo. Though I think I'll be a little more careful to test the rungs before I put any signifi-cant weight on 'em, from now on.*

Good, and that is most likely a well-considered plan; the Cortians seem not to be intensely interested in general main-tenance.

Well, Omega explained, *based on the reports I've seen, they're lucky to be spacefaring at all. The homeworld—the whole home system, I've gathered—isn't very rich in...much of anything, really. It seems to be why they chose piracy and slaving for their cultural center; it proved the easiest way to survive, I guess. Okay, let's get going. How far up do I need to go from here?*

Ah, that is interesting information; thank you. Now, let me see. Oh. You need to climb back up three levels...

* * *

Omega climbed three decks back to the level on which the Deltiri wanted her, then moved to the starboard tunnel and worked her way across two more cross-shafts under their di-rection. On the third cross-shaft, she shifted counter-clockwise by one tunnel and proceeded in the general direction of the ship's aft. Given that the Cortian ships were ovoid—more or less prolate ellipsoids, rather than being saucers or spheres—these directions had SOME meaning when the ship was sta-tionkeeping, but not a lot. And while the crew undoubtedly had a grasp of these directions with respect to their standard direc-tion of flight, bridge location, engine room, and other points of reference, for a stranger to the ship, it was a bit more difficult.

Which just makes it harder for a slave who might free itself to actually find a way off the ship, I guess, Omega decided, as she progressed slowly through the *Orktes.*

Indeed, came Kk'q'r's reply. *I can definitely see where the Cortians would consider that an advantage.*

Ee-zackly my point, Omega noted, as she came to a dead-end tunnel. *All right. Now where do I go?*

I believe this is about as close as we can place you, going through the maintenance tunnels, Qq'k'l decided. *We are go-ing to have to put you back into the standard corridors for the rest of the way...*

* * *

Coming out of the maintenance tunnels, Omega found that the locks automatically unlatched, as it was assumed that if you were inside, you were supposed to be there, and might need to hurry to get out of it. So she found the nearest hatch and waited until the Deltiri gave her the all-clear, then swiftly opened it and emerged into the crew corridor, closing it firmly behind herself.

Okay, I'm here. Which way? she asked then.

Left, Bb'y'x told her. *Then take the first right all the way to the end of the corridor. That will place you in the correct corridor for Echo's cell, we believe.*

All over it, Omega told them.

She turned left, then took a right ten feet later, and picked up the pace.

* * *

As she made her way down the long passage, she passed two Cortian crewmen, and flattened herself against the bulkhead to ensure they passed without contacting her. But just as the lead avian approached, he fluffed his feathers, then scratched his belly. Omega felt her nose tickle, and her eyes widened...even as they began to tear.

Oh shit, she thought in dismay. *Who had any idea I was allergic to Cortians?!*

Quickly she buried her face in the crook of her elbow to try to muffle what was coming, and before the Deltiri contingent could even figure out what her statement meant, she sneezed hard.

The two Cortians, some ten feet behind her by that time, stopped dead and looked at each other.

* * *

As the sound of a muffled, distant explosion reached their tympanic membranes, both Cortians stopped dead, and looked at each other in some concern.

(Did you hear that?) one said to the other.

(Yes, but what was it?) the second wondered.

(It sounded like something blew up. But there should be nothing aboard to do so at the moment, save the drive, and that would have produced more than...THAT. We would, in all likelihood, be dead if it had been the drive.)

(Yes. I felt no vibration, nor any atmospheric concussion, to indicate that it was aboard our craft.)

(Exactly.)

(Perhaps something has happened to one of the vessels of the guests?)

(That is possible, I suppose,) the first considered. (But if that is the case, it is no concern of ours. If we are in danger, the bridge crew will handle it. Should the guests in question require assistance, they will have to pay for it, and only then might it become our concern.)

(True.) The second shrugged. (I suppose we will know when we know.)

(Agreed. In the meanwhile, we had best head to our post as soon as we can, or we shall have punition to pay.)

(And that will not be pleasant,) the second said, as the pair hurried on.

* * *

Omega crouched against the wall, the lower half of her face still buried in the crook of her elbow; her eyes teared as she struggled to stifle any additional sneezes...at least until the pair occupying the corridor with her had departed it. As soon as they disappeared at the far end, turning the corner, she relaxed somewhat...and promptly sneezed once more.

"Ugh," she grumbled in an undertone, then sniffled once or twice. Reaching into a warp pocket, she produced a small pack of tissues and extracted one. Then she mopped her streaming eyes, drying her face, before wiping her nose. About that time, she heard a puzzled Jj'k'k.

What just happened? the Deltiri asked. Omega stifled a laugh, though she was certain it came across in her mental voice.

Could you 'see' what I saw, just as those two crewmen reached me? she asked.

Yes...apparently one of them is not so up on his hygenic practices, I should say, Jj'k'k observed.

And I think I'd agree with you, Omega said with a wry grin. *Anyway, it seems like there's something about their skin, or feathers, or something, that I'm allergic to when it's stirred up. I just let out a monumental sneeze. Fortunately, I managed to bury it in my arm, which muffled the sound, but they still heard it. I dunno what they made of it, but evidently they decided that the invisible sneezing woman doesn't exist.*

Oh! Jj'k'k exclaimed in surprise. *So THAT is what happened! I registered that you had had some sort of physiological reaction or response, but could not tell what; Deltiri do not have a 'sneeze' reflex, and so I could not interpret it.*

Yeah, Omega admitted, finally managing to control her nose and eyes, at least for certain definitions of control. She shoved soggy spent tissues and the remaining pack into different warp pockets, and eased back down the corridor, making her way toward the opposite end from where the Cortians had vanished. *I'd love to know what they made of it, though. Did any of y'all happen to pick up that conversation well enough to translate it?*

As a matter of fact, yes, Qq'k'l noted. *When I realized something had happened to you, I made a point of it, in case they had detected you. But evidently Cortians do not sneeze either, nor have ever seen species that do so. They thought it was a muffled, distant explosion, most likely on one of the other vessels. Never mind the question of how the sound could propagate through the vacuum of space. So I suppose their intellect is in question as much as their hygiene.*

Omega clapped a hand over her mouth and nose, deliberately biting her lip hard to stifle the laughter. *Well,* she decided, *it WAS muffled, and I guess it was kind of an explosion, too; it sure felt like it! I thought I was gonna blow my sinuses out through my nose for a second there! But distant, it most definitely was NOT!*

They all shared a prolonged mental laugh, easing the tension a bit.

Okay, guys, I'm getting close to the end of this corridor, Omega noted then. *What next?*

Turn right, Qq'k'l said. *The next corridor is fairly long, but there is only one door anywhere close along it. And that door is your destination. Echo will be inside.*

Gotcha, Omega said.

* * *

He is behind this door, Qq'k'l told her as she came to a

stop in front of the only door visible on that corridor. *Prepare yourself, Omega; we do not know what you will find beyond.*

That's okay, Qq'k'l, Omega said, stifling a sigh. *I...I think I do. I just dunno how bad it's gonna look. Is he unconscious?*

He is. We would have to do that anyway, if for no other reason than it seems that moving him is likely to cause him intense pain, sufficient to render it impossible for him to remain quiet. Once we pointed that out, he asked us to place him in a fairly deep unconscious state, so as to avoid putting his rescuer at risk; he is still hoping it will be another agent, so that you will not see him in his current condition. And we have assisted YOU by providing a tight telepathic block around you, sufficient to ensure that his unconscious mind cannot receive your reactions to it...to him. Even through the nd't'lq.

Okay, good. Here goes.

She pulled out her electronic lockpick and set to work.

* * *

After several seconds of work on it, the door opened for Omega, and she slipped inside, careful to close it behind herself so no one would be able to see within, or even notice anything different. Then she turned...

...And immediately became rooted to the deck in shock.

Echo hung, naked, on the opposite wall, slumped and unconscious, held up only by five shackles—one around each arm, one around each leg, and one about his waist. Before him on the floor lay an oblong puddle of drying urine, in front of a small pile of feces, and his body was covered in a sheen of sweat. The tiny cell reeked of sweat, ammonia, and bodily waste.

But it was the condition of his body that appalled her.

His right leg simply ended a couple of inches below his knee, unevenly truncated to judge by the contours, and swathed in a crudely-wrapped and very bloody compression bandage and tourniquet.

His left hand was missing, the arm ending bluntly just above the wrist, and the stump likewise wrapped in an extremely bloody compression bandage and tourniquet. There was evidence that he had bled through the dressings despite the tourniquet—or perhaps before the tourniquet or bandages were applied—for there were several small puddles of congealing blood on the floor.

But his face was the most terrible. His left eye had been brutally gouged out, the eyelids half-torn away from his face, leaving a raw, ragged socket. Caked blood and bits of tissue covered that side of his face, running down from the open socket. What looked to be tearstains streaked his other cheek, and a deeply shocked Omega dimly realized that the pain must have been—and probably still was—overwhelming, at least when no one was helping him by telepathically suppressing that pain. It did not occur to her that Echo might also have wept at the thought of her horror and revulsion at seeing him in this state. Horror she indeed felt, and anguish, as well as furious, implacable anger at his captors, but revulsion did not touch her thoughts, nor even occur to her.

Finally freed from her temporary paralysis, Omega turned away, biting her lip until it bled in her efforts at controlling her roiling emotions. Only then did she see what was in the corner—a hand, still wearing its wedding ring, which item had apparently been overlooked by the Cortians; and most of a lower leg and foot, the severed edges jagged, irregular and raw. *Oh dear God,* she thought then, in something approaching utter, relentless fury; were anyone there to see, her body would have seemed to swell in size, in righteous outrage. *They just threw what was left of 'em in the corner. Like they were so much trash. Mm. I dunno if that device Fox gave me will burn those, they're so...no, I can't do that. I just can't. They belong to ECHO. MY Echo. I brought the bags, just in case, anyway.*

Omega drew out two large poly forensics bags, then moved to the corner and picked up Echo's hand and wrist, placing it carefully into the smaller of the two bags without taking time to remove the ring; that could be dealt with later. Then she picked up his foot and shin, putting it into the larger bag, before sealing each. Next, she delicately eased both, in turn, into a warp pocket. It took a bit of doing to fit the entire severed leg through the pocket's opening, but with some wiggling things around, she managed it.

There, she thought. *That's taken care of, at least. Maybe... maybe Zebra can figure out how to reattach 'em, if they're still viable at all. They don't LOOK it, but...I dunno. That's not my field of expertise, but I can take 'em to her, in any case.*

She turned to the mutilated man, still shackled to the wall, unconscious. The stumps of arm and leg were, at least, covered by those dreadfully crude but effective compression bandages, though the eye socket had been left raw and open. At least, that way, he was still alive, she decided; had the limb stumps not been so tightly wrapped—a process which, with no anesthesia, had likely been excruciating, in itself—Echo would have died when he bled out from the ulnar artery in his wrist, and the tibial and peroneal arteries in the lower leg.

I'm glad I prepared for the worst, Omega thought, trying to numb her emotions, and grateful when she felt Zz'r'p's gentle touch on a certain portion of her mind, helping her to do just that. *Lemme pull out the emergency medikit I brought; there should be something I can use to bandage what's left of that eye in there.*

Two minutes later, Echo's ravaged face had been gently cleaned of the worst of the caked blood, and the raw, empty socket was tenderly covered with a special bandage. Omega extracted the antigrav belt and slipped it behind the small of Echo's back, working around the wall restraint already there, buckling the belt around his waist and activating it. The strain on Echo's arms and legs, where he dangled from his bonds, instantly eased as his body drifted upward ever so slightly, and she winced as she saw the abrasions and cuts on his skin from the edges of the hard metal.

A special spray bottle came out, and she gently misted the contents over his body; as badly as the room reeked—and judging by the old blood stains in other parts of the room, much of it wasn't even from Echo's ordeal—she could not risk the stench carrying outside this room once they left it. And the spray would help ensure that it did not; it was the same odor-neutralizing chemical she had used on her own body before leaving the *Genesis*...and would apply to herself again before leaving this room, just in case.

Then she extracted several more items of equipment; this included a small padded basket equipped with a tiny antigrav generator. This she placed against Echo's left foot and drew her principal blaster, cinched the beam down as tight as it would go, and carefully aimed at the hinge of the shackle around his left ankle. Wielding the blaster with all the delicacy of a scalpel, she sliced through the hinge, then the lock, and the shackle fell away, landing noiselessly in the basket...all without harming Echo's remaining ankle.

Omega removed the cut manacle from the basket and laid it on the floor before she turned to the right thigh; once the slave supervisor had hacked off most of Echo's lower leg, he had apparently moved the adjustable shackle higher on what remained of that limb in order to ensure the prisoner could not escape. *Like he could manage to do that on his own anyhow, after what those damn sons of bitches did to him,* she raged mentally, wishing briefly for a Cortian neck in her hands. Split-seconds later, that shackle succumbed to the deftly-wielded blaster beam, and seconds after that, the right wrist and left arm were free. Finally she cut off the thick bar imprisoning his waist, and Echo drifted forward, filthy, blood-spattered, naked body limp, into Omega's arms.

Omega held him close for long moments, heedless of the sweat and blood, breathing deep of his innate scent underneath the other, less pleasant odors, and tucking her face into the curve of his shoulder. Then she raised her head.

"It's okay now, honey," she told the unconscious form, murmuring into his ear, in the off chance his subconscious could hear. "I've gotcha, and I'm never letting you go. I'm taking you home."

The blaster went back into its holster; the antigrav basket was deactivated and shoved unceremoniously back into a warp pocket. From another warp pocket came a terrycloth wrap with a hook-and-loop closure; this went around Echo's waist and covered his privates, to provide for modesty once he arrived back aboard the *Genesis*—Echo worked hard to stay in shape and had a powerful, attractive physique, but he was still reserved when it came to displaying his body before others. Omega then tethered Echo's no-longer-QUITE-naked body close to her own by hooking a short cable from his antigrav belt to the back of her own belt—which was, in this case, not leather, but a sort of body armor, the rest of which had, at Fox's insistence, been donned under the black trousers and blouse—then strapped his upper torso and head into a special harness, shrugging the backpack-style straps onto her own shoulders. This would keep Echo's body and head in line, to avoid injuring his back and neck. Then she punched a special code into the tiny keypad of her personal sensor scrambler, ensuring that Echo would be included in its field as they made to exit the spacecraft.

"And now, one last thing," she muttered, intensely angry. "A little gift for this misbegotten asshole ship full of jackasses. Which, given the torture chamber has no sensors or monitors for the convenience of the 'jailers,'" she scowled, "is very convenient for me now." She extracted the modified flare Fox had given her, set the timer for 29 minutes and 59 seconds, then sat it at the base of the wall, on top of the worst of the blood and bodily waste Echo had left in his extremis. "And may it burn the damned place down...once we're out of it."

Then she added, *Hey guys? I have Echo, and I'm ready to go. Is there anyone in the corridor?*

Not at the moment, Qq'k'l averred. *Go now, before anyone shows up.*

Omega opened the cell door and slipped into the corridor, closing it behind them and ensuring it latched and locked, all while feeling the slight tug on her waist and shoulders that was Echo's inertia, as she gently towed him behind herself...

...Headed back to the *Genesis*, as fast as she could go.

Chapter 5

All right, here we go, Omega thought to the Deltiri team as she looked around and oriented herself; Echo floated gently behind her, his body limp—Fox had set the antigrav belt's field strength to a level that was just high enough for Omega to readily tow the unconscious man behind her, while still allowing the local artificial-gravity field to pull his limbs down, out of the way.

Excellent. We still see no sign of sentient life on your corridor, so you will make it well away before anyone can possibly detect you.

Okay, she said. *Which way?*

Left, toward the next intersection; turn right when you reach it.

She headed off.

* * *

Omega had made it up two decks, towing Echo, when she noticed a clump of Cortian crew members headed her way at speed.

Huh, she thought. *I wonder what that's about.*

Some sort of concern about their 'guests,' Jj'k'k noted. *You have stopped. What is the problem? Keep going.*

There's too many of 'em, and the corridor isn't wide enough, Omega explained. *They're wall to wall. Even with Echo an' me invisible, they'll run into us—literally.*

Ah, I see. Yes, that IS a problem. Can you double back about ten feet and turn right, into the cross passage?

No, there isn't a cross passage. Is this area part of the 'interior redecorating' they did?

Ohhh, it is, Qq'k'l confirmed then. *Double back and find the nearest cross passage, then, and head down it as far as you need, to be out of possible contact. You can always come back to this point, and we will continue.*

Okay, Omega agreed, and turned, careful not to go so fast

that she flung the floating Echo into the bulkhead. Once she had reversed direction, she picked up speed, jogging soundlessly in the Apache style Echo had taught her.

She headed back the way she had come for nearly twenty feet, until she reached the next intersection, then turned left.

But the group of Cortians also turned left, into that corridor, so Omega hurried ahead of them, ducking around a dogleg turn, took a right into a cross-corridor, then turned left into a fourth corridor. This final turn proved the trick, as she went a goodly ten feet into this side passage while the Cortians kept going straight.

Whew, she thought, wiping a drop of sweat from her temple. *Finally! Okay. They've gone, y'all. Where do I need to go from here?*

No answer.

Um, guys? Is anybody there?

Omega got no response.

Oh shit. Guys?! GUYS!! Where are you? Where'd you go?

Mental silence.

Just then, another group of Cortians hurried along the corridor she had been traversing moments before, followed seconds later by a third group. *Oh shit,* she thought. *Something big must be going down. Which means I can't possibly go back the way I came, or I have the original problem all over again, and we'll be caught. Damn. Hm,* she considered. *Echo? Honey, can YOU hear me?*

The slightest flutter of thought drifted back to her. It sounded vaguely like, *'M here, b'by.*

Are you in pain, hon? she wondered, quickly locating the pain-relief center and applying pressure, as Mm'l'n had showed her.

Nope.

Okay, Ace, good. I was just checking. Go on back to sleep, she told him. Omega had the impression of a mental nod, and her partner and husband was out of it once more.

And likely won't even remember it, by the way it felt. All right, she decided. *There's nothing the matter with what little telepathy I have, or I wouldn't 'a been able to reach Echo, nd't'lq or no. And the fact that he's still pretty much out of it argues that the Deltiri are still doing SOMEthing to keep him that way. Though the fact that he woke up at all, with most of 'em workin' on him one way or another, says something is prob'ly interfering with their ability, which means I gotta stay on top of that, and try to ensure he stays pain-free and out of it. Except I can't do it by myself, especially not and concentrate on working through this labyrinth. So either I wander around in here and hope that I can find my own way out without Echo waking up and starting to moan in pain, which will give us away; hope I can connect back up with Zz'r'p And Company, again before their efforts wear off and Echo wakes up; or figure out what the hell is going on, here. The first two sound a helluva lot more like last resorts to me, so time to break out the scientist to help the Agent, and see what I can see.*

So Omega began to study her environment in more detail, comparing and contrasting it to her memory of the corridor she had been in before having to take the 'detour,' looking for anything different or unusual in her environment.

Oh, she thought, suddenly noticing the bulkhead material. *That's different. This stuff is way shinier than the original alloy they used when they built this thing. But the metal has a slightly yellow undertone to it, rather than a shade of silver or flat gray. Which argues there's sulfur or a sulfur compound in the metal...which means they didn't have a way to fully purify it.* She shrugged to herself. *Not that that makes any difference, I expect. It would probably take a big ol' wall made out of at LEAST electron-degenerate matter to block the Deltiri's telepathy!* she decided, then paused, as a memory suddenly floated into her mind.

* * *

It had been last Halloween, and Alpha One was chasing a Glu'g'ik suspect that had been giving them fits, let alone refusing to stay in custody, thanks to her ability to manipulate the quantum foam of her own—and others'—bodies. They had finally managed to capture her for good and all, using a set of modified force cuffs designed to randomly move through the Higgs phasing frequencies in such a fashion that the Glu'g'ik suspect could not anticipate them. Unfortunately that hadn't stopped her from attempting to kill Omega by rearranging the atomic structure of her guts. She walked over to the Zeta Reticulan and got right down in the shorter alien's face.

"If you EVER try that again, you will NOT like the consequences," Omega had declared, intensely annoyed and still in some pain from the thwarted murder attempt.

"And just what do you propose to do about it?" Gla'd's had asked, insolent.

Omega had reached around to the small of her back, beneath her Suit jacket—as Echo watched AND maintained a bead on the Glu'g'ik's head with both blasters. She had produced a shiny silver packet and unfolded it...

...Then shoved the triangular, 'tin-foil' hat down on the alien's head.

Gla'd's had let out a shriek of pain and tried to clutch at her head with tightly manacled hands for a moment, then sighed and slumped in on herself.

"You win," she had murmured. "I could not attack if I wanted to, now."

* * *

Aluminum, Omega remembered. *For some reason, the Glu'gu'ik quantum foam abilities can't go past the atomic structure of metallic aluminum. I wonder if...*

She yanked out her cell phone—which actually was anything but an ordinary Earth cell phone, given the galactic tech contained within it—and activated it, then initiated a particular app which she had helped to build. It was a variant and upgrade on the scanner app Echo had showed her last spring, when they went on her first space training mission—when they were exploring Borscht. She raised the phone and used it to scan the odd alloy that the Cortians had used to restructure and rearrange the interior of the vessel, then studied the readouts.

"Hm," she breathed to herself. "Cobalt...a little chromium...lotta nickel...molybdenum...manganese...carbon, and iron. Plenty of iron. Holy shit. It's a variant on koboldalloy. But the abundances of isotopes for each element are comparable to those from cosmological sources...which means they probably scavenged and mined a few asteroids; say, one a standard nickel-iron body, and the other...maybe several 'others'...from a differentiated debris field with heavier and rarer elements. Interesti— what the hell is THAT?!" Omega stared at the screen in surprise, pinched-and-pulled to enlarge the readout, then chewed her lip. "Ohmigosh. Flerovium? Tell me that's not flerovium," she murmured. "NATURAL flerovium! Isotope 298 should have the longest half-life for that element, but it shouldn't be THIS long! Of course, some of those other elements have a fair amount of unstable isotopes, too, especially in the cosmological sources. But they don't generally occur all in the same asteroidal material...which, again, argues for multiple asteroidal bodies, but..."

She stood and pondered, still looking at the readouts, tapping the screen from time to time to toggle displays.

Now that's awful damn interesting, she thought. *Aaand I bet that explains it, too. This...I'll call it 'flerokoboldalloy'...it's a metallic alloy, so it has the whole conductive electron 'sea' thing going...but there's something weird about it, and I bet it's at least partly due to the flerovium. And while there's nano-pockets of impurity that have formed in the metal where the elemental flerovium gas has collected, there looks to be flerovium sulfate in the crystalline substrate, too. Which, given the flerovium as part of the composition, isn't surprising; there's metal sulfates and sulfides through the whole thing...and that's not uncommon with ores. Never mind a freakin' trans-actinide element in the mix, what I AM surprised about is why the Cortians didn't purify this shit a little better before using it. Well, then again, given what they're used to in their home system, maybe not. Or maybe they flat-out didn't have the resources left to do it, an' just hunted until they found material pure enough to be suitable. But whatever is going on here, there's some sort of an odd field being set up by the interaction of elements and isotopes in the crystalline matrix, and the way the various particles are interacting...it's almost like some sort of bosonic field is setting up inside it. I need to record this so I can study it later. If we can figure out how to artificially reproduce it— 'cause I seriously doubt we're gonna find asteroids like what these guys appear to have found—it might be damn useful in any of several ways I can think of, right off the top of my head. But flerovium—oy, as Fox would say!*

Omega hit several virtual buttons on the screen, ensuring

all of the data was recorded and filed in the device's memory, took a couple of photos of the material in the bulkhead, then pondered a bit longer.

Okay, I'm laying money...not to mention my and Echo's life...on that being what's blockin' Zz'r'p an' his buddies from contacting me. So I think what I need to do is to keep moving forward, she finally concluded, *and pay attention to the alloy, both eyeballing it, and periodically scanning it with this thing.* Absently, she waggled the cell phone in her hand. *We already know that the construction was limited in extent, so I have to come out of it sooner or later, and then the Deltiri can tell me where I am, and how to go back to the escape envelope. I know they gotta be freakin' by now, about not being able to reach me.*

Omega turned and headed toward the far end of the corridor.

* * *

"WHAT?!" Fox almost shouted, as he sat in the command chair on the bridge and waited until he was needed at the helm controls again. "You LOST them?? How the HELL could you lose them?"

"We are unsure, my friend," Zz'r'p explained over the intercom. "One moment we 'saw' Omega, communicated with her just fine, the next instant she—and Echo—were gone. We are continuing to monitor; we have never experienced it before, but it is just possible she has entered some sort of 'shadow' that blocks our mental sense of them. Whether that is deliberate, and the Cortians have managed to develop a device to do this, or whether there is some other mysterious factor we have encountered, we do not know, as yet."

"Damnation, shit, merde, cachu, khro, glagaram, abdab, and gronk!" Fox cursed. "Keep me posted. I want to know as soon as YOU know."

"We will, my friend. And believe me, I am as upset as you are. And my team is not far behind the two of us in that, either."

"I understand," Fox said, calming himself with an effort. "Please know that I'm not upset with any of you. This has just... it's been far more complex than I—than any of us—expected."

"I know. But we are, all of us, doing our best."

"Yes, we are. It's just...it's personal for me, this time."

"I understand. As well as I know Omega by now, I feel the same. Try to stay calm, as much as you can, my old friend. They will need you soon...once we locate them and extract them. And rest assured, we WILL."

"Yes, you will, and they will. Which, I suppose, makes for a good thing for me to hang onto. Fox out."

"Zz'r'p out."

The already-tense bridge crew stared at each other in heightened anxiety.

* * *

Omega tried to traverse as much distance as she could without turning to the right or left, or changing decks; she had decided that she stood the best chance of quickly coming out of the 'anti-telepathy field,' as she thought of it, by doing so.

It took over five minutes of walking, and intently studying the walls around her, but eventually she noticed an abrupt change of metal color and texture at a corridor junction, and realized that she had probably managed to bring Echo through the modified area. This was immediately confirmed by an agitated exclamation in her head.

OMEGA! Zz'r'p's mental voice cried. *THERE you are, my nn'chn, my niece! What in the name of the Maker happened?!*

Long story, Omega told him. *For now, let's say that the materials they used for their new construction seem to have some weird properties, and let it go at that. I'm gonna have to sit down and look at the data I recorded before I can tell you more than that, anyway. Meantime, let's get the HELL outta this damn ship. Where am I, and where do I need to go from here?*

You need to cut hard left, as soon as you can, Zz'r'p informed her. *You are nearly on the opposite side of the ship from your escape envelope.*

All right, I have a cross-corridor right here; I can do that, Omega declared, turning left. *Let's go.*

* * *

FOX! We have them! Zz'r'p told him.

"HALLELUJAH!" Fox exclaimed aloud, and the bridge crew sat up straight, keeping close attention on their Admiral Director. "Are they all right?"

They are fine. It seems it was as I theorized, though Omega promises she will debrief us later on, once she has had time to work out some details. She did record a good bit of data, however. To manage to escape the shadow area, she had to work over nearly to the far side of the Orktes, *but we are bringing her as nearly straight across as we dare, now.*

"Very good," Fox said out loud once more, having become aware of his bridge crew kibitzing on his end of the conversation. "Let me know when they are ready to return."

Will do. We shall speak in a bit.

Go, Fox added mentally. *Bring 'em home to us.*

As fast as we can.

* * *

As they rounded the next turn, Omega stopped dead, absently feeling Echo's unconscious, limp form bump lightly against her back.

Ahead, the corridor was blocked at the next intersection by at least three dozen beings, more than half of whom were NOT Cortians, but were any of at least a dozen different alien races—Dabanorans, Teludals, Reptoids, Ke!endarians, Veldorn, and more.

All from groups that Ace has managed to piss off by taking 'em into custody for their crimes, she thought. *I dunno whether to be more worried or proud—*

She broke off the thought suddenly when she spotted a tall blue being with a fish-like face in the crowd. Omega quickly ducked back around the corner, pressing herself and Echo against the corridor wall in deep alarm.

Oh SHIT! she cried, trying to lock-send to Zz'r'p. *There's a Deltiri here, Zz'r'p! They've got 'em a telepath! And I dunno if I've had a strong enough block up to hide...*

Hush, youngling, and calm yourself, Zz'r'p responded. *Everything is all right. Even if you did not have a strong enough block erected, WE did. We have been shielding you both, as well as the entire* Genesis *crew to a lesser extent, from virtually the moment we arrived at the rendezvous site. As we worked on tracking Echo, we had considered the possibility that one or more of the groups congregating for the auction might have telepaths of their own in their employ, and we have acted upon that probability. Our advantage in such an instance is that we know that you and Echo have an nd't'lq link, and they would not. But so far, we have only detected the one—about the same time you did—and HE has NOT detected any of US.*

Oh, Omega thought in titanic relief. *I thought we were dead meat, for a few seconds, there. Echo an' me, I mean.*

No, no. Not at all. Bb'y'x knows him, however, and she is telling us that he is not nearly as trained as the lot of us. He chose a more...mm, 'everyday'...kind of profession, one that only uses our innate telepathy in standard communication. What you would call 'chit-chat.' One fact about him that is important, however, is that he IS Tt'l'k's cousin...which is likely why he is there. Can you possibly tell the reason for the gathering?

Oh HELL yes, Omega replied, irony heavy. *Some of 'em are all but screaming; I can hear 'em all the way down here, around the corner. Apparently they want to actually SEE Echo, to verify it's really him that the Cortians have captive. It seems that there have been others claiming to have caught Echo before, but either they were trying to defraud the crime bosses, or it was flatly a case of mistaken identity. So they want to KNOW it's him before they'll consent to the auction contract.*

Then we cannot afford to wait until they disperse, Qq'k'l observed, interjecting into the mental conversation. *We must detour around them, and quickly. Else they shall discover that—what is that Earth saying? Ah—'the bird has flown the coop,' and then we shall have no time left.*

Good choice of metaphor, Omega chuckled grimly, *though in this case, the human has flown the birds' coop, I think. Just tell me where to go and I'll go.*

You take the lead on it, Qq'k'l, Zz'r'p ordered. *You have the plans and schematics in front of you.*

Very well, Qq'k'l said. *Instead of turning right here, go back to the previous junction and turn left. Well, right as per your new direction, I suppose.*

There, Omega said, silently scampering in the direction she had come, obeying the direction as she ducked right around the corner, into a new corridor. *Now what?*

Good. Find the stairway hatch—third door on the left—

and go UP two decks...

* * *

The detour route was long and convoluted in an already long and complex journey, but at least for the time, it seemed relatively uncrowded. Apparently a significant portion of the crew was under orders to move swiftly to corral the crime bosses and their minions, lest a kind of controlled riot break out aboard the ship—and this movement had been what had forced Alpha One into the odd new-construction section of the ship, to begin with, causing the telepaths to lose track of them for a brief period. Still, the Deltiri team decided Omega was making good time with Echo through the Cortian vessel despite the long detour.

"Zz'r'p, do you have a moment to discuss a matter?" Bb'y'x wondered.

"Is it important, Bb'y'x? Will it not wait?" the ambassador asked, mildly distracted. "We have rather urgent matters to attend, here..."

"Potentially yes, sir, very important," she noted. "It is about the Deltiri Omega saw on the *Orktes*. As I said at the time, I know him, and this behavior is not like him; frankly, I believe he may be misinformed...possibly by Tt'l'k himself. You see, I was considering attempting to communicate with him in private, to try to rectify matters. I think perhaps if we explain to him what really happened, he may go from enemy to ally. Or at least, to a noncombatant of sorts."

"Mm," Zz'r'p considered the matter, looking around his stateroom as he did so—Qq'k'l, Kk'q'r, and Jj'k'k were all studying the schematics of the Cortian ship to help provide direction to Omega, with Qq'k'l relaying the specific route determined thereby; Mm'l'n still sat in a corner with her eyes closed and her forehead creased in concentration as she continued to neutralize Echo's pain and ensure he remained in an unconscious state...though the ambassador knew that the powerful Jj'k'k was splitting his time between directing Omega and helping Mm'l'n. "Well, the others have matters well in hand, it appears, so we have a few moments. But it is a dangerous notion, Bb'y'x," he warned. "Should you be unable to convince him, he could betray us to the others, which would—or at least could—be tantamount to killing Echo AND Omega. Never mind if he discovers you are not on Earth, but on the Division One flagship, and quite nearby."

"I understand the danger," Bb'y'x averred. "But that is why I come to you now; you will be my backup. You see, I did not jest when I said that we are truly far more skilled in the nuances of telepathy than Xx'q'z is; he owns a shop on Deltir, and that is all he does. And you still know the forgetfulness technique, do you not?"

"Ah. Now I see," Zz'r'p realized. "I 'piggyback' the conversation without his awareness, and if he refuses to see reason, I cause him to forget the entire communication..."

"Precisely," Bb'y'x declared. "And potentially, his entire vendetta, into the bargain. I hate to do it, but I believe this is one of the circumstances that falls under the legal use of the technique, if memory serves..."

"It is," Zz'r'p confirmed. "And it would be done in order to prevent bloodshed between Deltiri...and their allies. It should be an acceptable and legal use of the technique." He considered, then added, "In fact, it would likely be encouraged, given the circumstances."

"Yes," Bb'y'x agreed. "Are you willing to try? At worst, it changes nothing. At best, we may have gained an ally."

* * *

Aa'v'u? Zz'r'p reached out to the Deltiri head of Diplomatic Services on his homeworld, Aa'v'u ag Dnn'tucc. *Aa'v'u, are you there?*

Zz'r'p, is that you? came the reply after a moment. *Forgive me, I had my mind on a personal family matter.*

Do I interrupt?

No, not at all. You must have a 'situation,' as you like to put it, for you do not normally contact me in this fashion unless it is urgent, youngling.

Well, I do. Let me explain... and he laid out the matter of Bb'y'x's friend for her.

* * *

Ah, I see, she said after he had explained. *And you need me to deliver a quick approval or disapproval of your intent to interfere with his mind and memories.*

128

Yes, Zz'r'p said with a sigh. I am loath to do it, but frankly, I suspect that tampering may already have occurred.

What reason do you have to think so?

He is the relatively near kinsman of Tt'l'k ob Nnor'vvii, my former envoy.

Ohhh. The one with Mr'd'k-P'rr'l syndrome, who in his ill hubris, tried to program the Division One Agent?

He did not merely try. He DID program her. And it was nearly her undoing. We were beginning to fear for her sanity, and possibly even her life, before the matter was resolved, and the 'program module' removed.

And you suspect that this kinsman may have visited Tt'l'k, and Tt'l'k may have inserted somewhat in his mind, as well? Would that not be too difficult? If Tt'l'k's family is as highly-trained as he...

But they are not. This cousin, in particular, Bb'y'x declares is a 'nice guy,' as the humans would say, but not very trained in matters such as you and I are. He is a simple shopkeeper, not a diplomat, or an interrogator, or an inter-species relations expert...

Ah. I begin to see. Mm. And you are in a delicate, and very dangerous, position, which if your operation is successful, should uncover the plot...

Precisely. And if matters are as I suspect, this poor Deltiri shopkeeper does not even belong here.

Very well. Make sure you have at least one witness to what you do, then have Qq'k'l ob Sii'stek properly interrogate you after, and deliver a report. I believe you are correct, and it would be a very moral, as well as legal, use of the technique.

So I have permission?

Indeed. Do it. And make haste. You may be able to save a Deltiri life in the doing. In many senses of the word.

Thank you, madam.

You are welcome, old friend. Come by and say hello next time you are on Deltir.

I shall.

* * *

"Mm. Let us see what happens, then," Zz'r'p decided. "I have just pinged the diplomatic head on Deltir, and she confirms it is indeed a legal use, and urged me to try to prevent a Deltiri from being involved on the wrong side of this unpleasant little...imbroglio."

"Oh, good," Bb'y'x murmured.

"It is my considered opinion that it may be worth knowing if there are other telepaths on board the *Orktes*, as well. And he should, at least, know that," Zz'r'p pointed out.

"Very good," Bb'y'x said with a smile.

* * *

Xx'q'z? This is Bb'y'x. Bb'y'x ag Ogg'nii. Do you remember me? came the voice in the head of the Deltiri who waited on board the *Orktes*. He tried not to jump in startlement, or glance around to see if anyone else had noticed...not that they were paying much attention to him, in any case, given the concern over ascertaining that the Cortians really did have the true Agent Echo.

Oh! Hello, Bb'y'x! the other Deltiri replied then, relaxing a little. *Yes, I remember you. I enjoyed our little 'dates' as some planets term them. And I hated it when you were transferred to Earth. I have missed you.*

Yes, we had fun together. Listen, do you have time to talk for a few moments?

Well, I am a bit busy with something of importance...

Yes, I know, Bb'y'x noted. *That is what I want to talk to you about.*

Huh? What do you mean, 'you know'?

I know you are about to participate in an auction for a Division One Agent named Echo, Xx'q'z. You must not; he is innocent, which cannot be said for those around you. And she showed him a quick montage of the bloodthirsty thoughts around him, as well as the criminal record of the more 'important.'

Innocent? Xx'q'z declared, incensed...and ignoring the montage. *How do you know?! Do you know what Echo has done?? What he did to my kinsman, Tt'l'k? That og'dm'n arg'driyk deserves to die! And I intend to see to it that he DOES! Preferably slowly and agonizingly!*

Echo did nothing to Tt'l'k, Xx'q'z. But Tt'l'k mind-raped him AND his partner, and psychically attacked both of them...

on multiple occasions.

What?! Who told you THAT lot of lies?

Ambassador Zz'r'p. He's right here, beside me. Would you like HIM to tell you?

Wait. Zz'r'p ob Tii'rkin? The famous diplomat?

The same.

Oh og'dm'n, Xx'q'z murmured blankly. *But I thought Tt'l'k was his right-hand being? Almost a brother?*

* * *

I see you have been listening to the tales of my former assistant, Zz'r'p interjected drily. *Yes, he was my envoy. No, he was not my 'right-hand being,' nor did I ever consider him family. Unlike, let me add, Omega and Echo.*

But...but he said...

He has said—and done—many things, Zz'r'p noted, *many of which were biased, untrue, or outrightly illegal. Largely, we believe, as a result of his illness.*

Yes, Xx'q'z snarled. *The one that was CAUSED by Agent Omega attacking him! At Echo's instigation and urging! Those two nearly destroyed him!*

NO, Zz'r'p declared, calm and firm. *Tt'l'k was already ill with Mr'd'k-P'rr'l syndrome, a deteriorative mental disorder. We believe this deterioration is what has resulted in his aberrant behavior, and forced us to send him back to Deltir. And yes, Omega did attack him, but NOT because Echo encouraged it. In point of fact, Echo could not have done, because he was already unconscious...due to a completely unprovoked attack on him BY Tt'l'k.*

NO! You are LYING!

No, I am not, Zz'r'p averred, still calm. *Check my memories, my intent, and you will see I speak the truth. More, this attack by Tt'l'k and retaliation by Omega occurred after Tt'l'k mind-raped both Omega and Echo a few weeks earlier. And the reason Omega attacked was because she had no choice— Tt'l'k was about to kill Echo; Omega stopped him. Here is the memory of the event; I and my embassy were her advisors, and remained 'with' her through the event.* And he laid the memory bare to the younger male.

Oh...oh, no... Xx'q'z murmured, confused almost to the

131

point of disorientation. *This...this cannot be...he said...*

Yes, it can be, and is, Zz'r'p confirmed. *I speak the truth, and you know it. More, Tt'l'k attempted to control Omega by means of a kind of 'brainwashing' program he inserted into her mind. Given that Bb'y'x staunchly asserts that this blood thirst you have to kill Echo—and I can see in your mind, you want to do it bare-handed, slowly, and brutally—is very unlike you, and does not fit your personality at all, at least as she knew you not so long ago, it occurred to me, Xx'q'z, to check YOUR psyche for a program...and you indeed have a 'subroutine' inserted, as well. It is apparently intended to induce you to exact Tt'l'k's revenge on Echo and Omega...precisely as you are now attempting to do.*

Oh no, Bb'y'x murmured, deeply concerned. *Can you fix it, Zz'r'p? Can you remove it? Xx'q'z is a good male; he would not truly want this!*

Wait...what, now? Xx'q'z wondered, patently confused. *Tt'l'k stuck something in me? In...in my head?*

Indeed, Zz'r'p confirmed. *Can you not sense it?...Here?* He indicated a place deep in the other male's mind.

He...what? But...og'dm'n! Xx'q'z exclaimed then. *What in the name of O'sh'n is THAT thing?! Get it out! Get it out! Get it out!*

Calm down, Xx'q'z! Bb'y'x cried. *Zz'r'p, what is wrong?*

He sees the subroutine within his mind, Zz'r'p explained, *but he apparently perceives it as a...as an alien entity, a bizarre creature attacking his brain, possibly even feeding off it. Which, in a way, it is, except it does not have a life outside of his mind.*

Get it OUT! Xx'q'z nearly shrieked.

Hush, youngling! Stay calm, lest you give away this conversation to those around you, and give me a moment, Zz'r'p ordered. Xx'q'z silenced, though his tension and fear could still be felt. Finally Zz'r'p said, *There. That should have done it. How do you feel now, Xx'q'z?*

Um...confused... came the response. *Really, really...confused.*

All right. Let me check you for any more peripheral subroutines...aha. And...there. Better?

Oh yes, thank you! I...what? Xx'q'z said then, his befuddlement and disorientation obvious to the other two Deltiri. *What am I doing here? Where IS 'here'?*

You are aboard a Cortian pirate and slaver vessel, Bb'y'x explained, *with a group of interstellar criminals, prepared to purchase Division One Agent Echo at auction...to kill him.*

Oh great Maker, the other Deltiri exclaimed, horrified. *I remember now! How did I even see my way through to this point? How did I make it so far with this horrid scheme?*

That would be the programming that Tt'l'k placed in you, Zz'r'p explained. *This one was rather elaborate; he may be learning. I should probably contact the medical center where he is being treated and warn them to check the staff treating him.*

Um... Xx'q'z began, *do you think anyone would notice if I just slipped away and left?*

Have you signed anything? Zz'r'p asked.

What?

Have you SIGNED anything? the ambassador pressed. *While aboard the Cortian spacecraft? Any contracts, anything of that nature?*

No. No, I haven't. Though... Xx'q'z broke off, then added, *...I think I was about to...*

Good. Then they cannot hold you there. Go. Just leave. If anyone questions you about it, tell them you realized that you did not have sufficient funds to bid against such worthy competitors, and you trust that they will take care of matters for you, as well as themselves.

Uhn...a-all right.

Bb'y'x and Zz'r'p sensed Xx'q'z start to ease away from the group of crime lords still gathered in the corridor junction. They carefully monitored him as he made steady progress toward the hangar bay in the lower aft portion of the large ship.

Wow, he said a few minutes later, as he neared the hangar. *This might actually work.*

Xx'q'z? Zz'r'p said.

Yes?

Now that you are safely away from the others, did you happen to notice any other telepathic races in the group you just left, perchance? Any gastropoids, for instance?

Mmm, let me think, Xx'q'z said, as they sensed him enter the hangar and approach his small personal spacecraft. *Not offhand, no. I do not think so.*

But you do not know for certain.

No, I am afraid I do not. But I was not looking very hard for THAT. I...I was focused on...killing Echo. The pair sensed his shame.

No, YOU were not, Zz'r'p corrected gently. *Tt'l'k's programming within you was.*

How do you feel now, Xx'q'z? Bb'y'x asked.

Like I have awakened from what promised to be a very dreadful nightmare, just before it all turned horribly bad, Xx'q'z said with a sigh, as he boarded his craft and prepped for takeoff. *I gather you two are really very busy right now, but...later, could you please explain to me what just happened?*

* * *

In the stateroom on the *Genesis*, Zz'r'p and Bb'y'x exchanged a meaningful glance. Bb'y'x answered.

We would be happy to do so, Xx'q'z, she said. *For now, just get out of there.*

I am already in my ship, with leave to depart, he said. *And... there. I just passed through their hangar bay doors into space. I have promised them—the Cortian guards in the hangar—that I would tell no one of this; it was the price of my release from the auction and the hangar. Nor shall I tell ANYone; I am too ashamed. That the two of you already know was NOT asked, and I did not tell.*

Good. Do NOT visit your cousin Tt'l'k in the mental hospital until AFTER you have talked with us again, when this is all over, Zz'r'p said. *There are many matters we need to explain. It may prove much too dangerous for any of Tt'l'k's family to visit him, at least until the physicians have made more headway on his illness. Assuming they do, or can. Let alone what influence he may try to make on them.*

All right, Xx'q'z declared. *I suddenly find I have little desire to visit Tt'l'k after this little incident, in any case.*

That is good, then, Zz'r'p averred. *Until we next speak.*

Later, Xx'q'z said.

And he was gone, his spacecraft raising a warp bubble and disappearing into deep space.

* * *

"That...worked surprisingly well," Bb'y'x decided. "You helped him escape, did you not?"

"Perhaps a bit," Zz'r'p noted with a slight smirk.

"But then why are you not helping Omega in the same fashion?"

"What makes you think I have not?" Zz'r'p wondered. "Qq'k'l and I are rather skilled at such things, and we are doing our best to ensure that, for instance, a passing Cortian is occupied with other matters, or looking in a different direction, or such like. But the situation is very different for her; your friend was anonymous to the Cortians, but Omega is not. Nor is Echo. It only took a bit of, mm, let us call it nudging, from a mental perspective, to cause the Cortians whom Xx'q'z encountered to take little to no notice of him, because they were already so inclined. It would require MUCH more mental intervention to produce such a response to Omega in a Cortian, and unlike Xx'q'z, they would NOT forget."

"Oh. I...think I see," Bb'y'x murmured, thoughtful. "Is there any chance I can learn this, too?"

"I expect so, with enough time and practice. But first, there is an Earth film you should watch some time, youngling," Zz'r'p told her with some humor. "The key phrase in this instance was, 'This is not the being for whom you are watching.' Though I believe it is phrased a bit differently in the film."

Bb'y'x looked puzzled.

Zz'r'p laughed.

* * *

In the end, one of the lesser members of the Gu'ursh tem al Ke!thas was sent with a 'volunteered' Cortian crew member to visit Echo's cell, while the rest of the various contingents repaired to the auditorium once more; this particular Ke!endarian could personally identify Echo and come back to verify his presence to the others, regardless of affiliation. Given that both beings—Cortian, and Ke!endarian—were of the Avian morphology and not that different from each other aside from plumage colorations, they were reasonably content

135

in each other's company—more so, at least, than one of the Opdip races would have been with the Cortian.

"Awk dirr?" the Cortian tried.

"Prriik ac!ern," the Ke!endarian responded in its own language. "Um, Enklish?"

"Englishes mean you?"

"Englishes mean, yes."

"Is Englishes little, yes," the Cortian agreed. "Much not, but is."

"Much not either, but we do. Echo Agent has you?"

"Yes, Echo slave is has we. Is you show, I." The Cortian turned. "Come. Follow."

They headed down the corridor, then entered a hatch, taking a set of stairs down to the next deck.

"Is no elewator?" the Ke!endarian asked, following the Cortian down the tight, narrow stairway.

"Know not. 'Elewator' what is?" the Cortian wondered.

"Box is, up-down go, cable or antigrav," the Ke!endarian explained. "Us carry it."

"Eh. Them is," the Cortian grunted. "Not is here. Stairs cheap, stairs safe. Not power need."

"Ah. Feature safety."

"Yes."

They came out on the deck below, which was darker and more dimly lit, without many of the 'amenities' to be found on higher decks, such as paint or corrosion resistance.

"Is prisoners hold, deck this?" the Ke!endarian wondered.

"Yes, is prisoners, is slaves, is what need." The Cortian shrugged. "Not fancy need. Is waste."

"Understand I."

"What is do him with? Echo slave, mean I."

"Oh, slow will kill, him." It was the Ke!endarian's turn to shrug, callous and uncaring. "Is him do as do him leader old our. Kre Meorn us lead he. Kill dead. So Echo-him kill dead. Is Omega partner killing we, day one, too. Her was, actual shoot. But him was train her, order do."

They went down one corridor, turned right into another, then took a dog-leg and stopped before a lone door on a dead-end passage.

"Is here," the Cortian declared, then entered a code on the keypad beside the door. The door clicked and hissed as the latch released, and he opened it and entered, gesturing the Ke!endarian through and into the small cell before closing it carefully behind them.

Then they looked up.

The wall facing them was empty, save for numerous blood smears and spatters of various ages, several of the most recent of which had run down to the floor, where they puddled around some brown waste and yellow liquid and congealed. Five heavy manacles had been deftly sliced from the wall, and their remains lay in the assorted puddles, heedlessly abandoned.

"Aitrrk! Awwk trrp!" the Cortian cursed in his own language. "Where it be? Happen what here?"

"This what is?" the Ke!endarian wondered, picking up a small metallic device that was lying beside the puddles of bodily fluids.

"Know not," the Cortian replied. "Not ours is."

"Shit oh!" the Ke!endarian exclaimed, throwing the device back where he had found it, and both avians spun for the door...

...Just as the flare ignited in blinding, blue-white light.

Ke!endarian and Cortian both screamed as all their feathers ignited at once, and their flesh began to burn—

—But no one could hear them outside the soundproofed torture chamber.

* * *

Damn, is there a shift change going on, or something? Omega wondered, as she surreptitiously maneuvered herself and her incapacitated partner through the narrow corridors of the Cortian ship. *There's more Cortians in that one group ahead than I saw in the whole time I spent trying to REACH Echo's cell! What gives?*

That is exactly what is occurring, Omega, Qq'k'l observed. *According to a quick scan of several Cortians, this is one of three regular shift changes that occurs on the* Orktes *each day. It seems to be rendered worse by the breaking up of the gathering of crime lords you saw earlier; all of the Cortian crew members who had been involved in controlling that are now either changing shifts, or returning to their regular duty stations...and they were relatively close to you, to begin with, because of that gathering. We are attempting to keep your path as short as possible, detour notwithstanding. So you are not that far from where it was.*

Shit. Should I maybe find a good spot and me an' Echo hole up for a while, until things clear out a bit?

While not optimal, that might be a good—oh og'd'mn!

What's wrong?! Omega asked, urgent. *What's happened? Do I need to find shelter right now??*

No, there is no time to shelter until the crowds thin, Omega! Qq'k'l declared. *The flare you left in Echo's cell went off scant seconds ago...just as a Cortian crew member led one of the Gu'ursh tem al Ke!thas to view Echo and prove that they really had him!*

Oh SHIT! Omega exclaimed. *So they're pretty much toast now, huh?*

Very much so; their feathers ignited almost instantly, and... well, let us simply say it was a quick but horrible death. And it is, therefore, only a matter of time before someone goes looking for a missing Ke!endarian and a missing Cortian crewman. If they find any remains of either being in Echo's otherwise empty cell, they will begin a most thorough—and likely very angry—search.

And we need to be offa this ship when that happens, Omega decreed. *Help me out here. We gotta move FAST now.*

All over it, as Agent Romeo would say, Qq'k'l offered. *Be prepared; we are about to 'pull out all the stops,' as you put it, and take some risks. It will exhaust us, but there will be time to rest later. There! Cut to the right, directly between these two crewmen...do not fear if you bump them; we will divert them into thinking they bumped each other; just hurry...*

* * *

It took some doing, and intense concentration upon the part of Omega and all the Deltiri helping her, but within another half-hour, Omega had dodged, detoured around, or otherwise avoided all of the moving roadblocks between her and escape. At last, she found herself, with Echo, back at the airlock through which she had entered the *Orktes*. But she wasn't done quite yet; she still had to slip through the airlock, into

138

the escape envelope, and away, with Echo, withOUT alerting anyone.

So the first thing she did was to extract her anti-bugging device from a warp pocket and adjust it to a particular setting, before aiming it at the airlock and activating it. This would ensure that no 'open airlock' signal would register on any security or bridge control panel, anywhere aboard the ship; she would have preferred to use it when she had entered the *Orktes*, but the location of the circuitry in question had precluded her doing so—hence Fox's carefully orchestrated distraction. Then she put that tool away and produced her electronic lockpick, letting it scan the airlock, hack the access code, and activate it.

Moments later, Alpha One was within the airlock, with the inner hatch closed. Omega moved to the control panel and adjusted the atmosphere controls to a positive-pressure setting to allow for mating with another ship without 'contamination,' then opened the outer hatch and carefully eased through it, towing her badly injured partner behind herself. She turned and closed the *Orktes* hatch, then the emergency egress envelope's hatch, deactivated the force field, and detached from the Cortian craft.

Zz'r'p or Qq'k'l or whoever's listening, she sent, *please let Fox know that we're ready to be brought back over to the* Genesis.

Consider it done, my dear young friend, Qq'k'l averred.

* * *

Fox, came the mental communique from the Deltiri ambassador, *Omega just told Qq'k'l that she is ready to return to the* Genesis. *And yes, Echo is on board with her. Please begin the tractor beam withdrawal.*

Copy that, it's wonderful news, and we're preparing to begin tractor beam withdrawal now, Fox replied, as he moved to the helm console, seated himself, and woke the appropriate instrumentation, then looked up at the bridge crew.

"Here we go," Fox told them, activating the tractor beam and pulling the egress envelope back toward the *Genesis*. The linkage to the various cloaking systems was still active, so as he did so, the envelope remained within the extension of those fields, which gradually retracted as the envelope neared the

139

Genesis.

"Is Echo with her? Are they both in the envelope?" Boy wondered.

"Yes, they are indeed both in there, according to Ambassador Zz'r'p," Fox confirmed, and a soft exclamation of relief went around the bridge. "Nothing was said about their condition, however," he added, and they all sobered.

Wielding the tractor beam controls like a virtuoso, Fox eased the escape envelope away from the *Orktes*, careful not to do anything sudden, lest the envelope rupture and kill both members of Alpha One in the vacuum of space. As they pulled away from the *Orktes*, however, he sped up the motion, anxious to bring them back aboard the *Genesis*, planning to reverse the acceleration as the envelope grew close to the flagship.

"FOX!" Cast shouted. "Zargothian escort ship at one o' clock low, approaching at an angle and moving up! Their trajectory will intersect the tractor beam in six seconds!"

"Khro, abdab, and gronk!" Fox cursed, immediately killing the tractor beam. "There! Is the envelope in danger?!"

* * *

Omega felt the gentle tug of the tractor beam as it towed the relatively fragile envelope back toward the *Genesis*. The thing was tougher than it looked, of course, and designed for exactly this kind of maneuvering...though not for precisely this reason. Still, she was glad that whoever operated the tractor beam was being gingerly; too rough a motion could risk the envelope tearing open from its own inertia, and that would end matters very quickly for both Omega and Echo.

Abruptly the entire envelope lurched, as a small fighter-style vessel came flying up from their port side, and she felt her feet leave the bottom of the envelope as it drifted, its momentum carrying it forward. The fighter zipped past, missing the envelope by only a few tens of meters, even as Omega struggled to regain control of her—and Echo's—momentum, and avoid falling or otherwise smacking into a side of the envelope—lest one or both of them be injured, or worse, the envelope be damaged.

Seconds after the fighter cleared the space, the envelope gave another small lurch, then resumed moving toward the

Genesis. Omega landed relatively smoothly on the new 'floor' of the envelope, taking one step back to help stabilize herself and the limp body that floated behind her, then she spread her legs and shifted into a shallow horse stance to help control any further unexpected shifts in momentum.

* * *

"SHIT, that was close!" Cast exclaimed then. "No, the envelope is intact, Fox—though the Zargothian craft didn't miss it by much more than, say, fifteen or twenty yards, if that. I take it, you brought the cloak and sensor scrambler in with the tractor?"

"Yes; I didn't have much choice," Fox noted. "I had 'em all tied together, and there wasn't time to decouple. When I had to kill the tractor beam, the cloaking fields reverted to the standard configuration. The fighter hasn't seen Alpha One, has it?"

"All indications are that it did not," Cast decided, studying his instruments. "It's continuing along its same trajectory, banking around the Cortian spaceship to link up with its...'squadron,' I guess we'll call it...on the far side. Er." He looked up with a sheepish grin. "Wow, did my Air Force background just come out. It didn't bank at all, it just turned. You know what I mean."

"Yes, zun, I know," Fox said with a slightly shaky chuckle. "I've worked with various Earth military units in my past, as well; I understand how old terminology sometimes crops up. Is it safe to resume bringing the envelope back?"

Cast spent a moment in careful scrutiny of his sensors' readout of the space around them. Finally he looked up.

"Yes sir. Go for it," he noted. "But maybe we need to make this kinda quick, before another hotshot pilot does something like that again."

"Agreed," Fox said. "Programming in an acceleration/deceleration protocol. Please monitor and warn of approaching craft."

"Copy. Wilco."

* * *

Omega noticed that the envelope now seemed to be approaching the *Genesis* with rather more speed than it had before, and, judging by the fact that she had to adopt a one-foot-

141

forward, one-foot-back stance, with her weight on the rear foot to compensate for the forces, the envelope was accelerating at a smooth clip. Once it came within a hundred meters of the big flagship, however, she found her weight shifting into the front foot; Fox was ensuring the envelope decelerated smoothly and gently.

When they were within some twenty-five meters of the hull, the tractor beam eased off, then vanished, and Omega moved to the little control panel to maneuver the envelope into position and transit the last few meters to the airlock hatch.

Chapter 6

The emergency egress envelope docked smoothly with the *Genesis* airlock, and when the inner hatch opened, an impassive Omega stood in it. Nothing was visible behind her, as she somehow spread out enough to fill the hatch.

"There they are!" Romeo said, relieved, as he and India moved to the hatch to assist. "C'mon, pretty lady, let's take Echo t' th' sick bay an' seen to."

"Where is he?" India wondered. "Meg?! You did get him, didn't you? He was, was alive, wasn't he?"

"Yes, he was and is alive," Omega murmured, "and yes, I have him. He's unconscious, wearing an antigrav belt, and tethered behind me. Are you sure you're ready for his condition?"

"That bad, huh?" Romeo queried.

"Every bit," came Omega's grim reply.

"Come on, honey, we need to take him to the sick bay, so Zebra and I can start work on him," India urged. "Quit playing games and let's put him onto the gurney and moving."

"Games? Hardly. I'm not sure what you can do for him right now," Omega noted. "Not until we get him home, anyway. And maybe not even then. I...I hope, but..." She broke off, staring at their expectant faces. "Okay, y'all asked for it."

Omega stepped forward, towing the unconscious Echo, floating silently in mid-air, behind her. India and Romeo both gasped, their darker skin turning ashen as they paled in horrified shock as soon as they realized that his eye, hand, and almost half of one leg were all missing.

"Told ya," Omega said, succinct, as she started to remove the harness that had allowed her to pull Echo behind her without needing her hands to do so. "Help me lift him onto the gurney. Antigrav belt or no, he's still got inertia."

A stunned Alpha Two silently obeyed the order, unsure what to say.

* * *

Fox and Zebra awaited them in sick bay, along with Yorker; all three blanched when they got a look at Echo's condition. Fox, in particular, turned nearly gray—even his lips went pale—and he staggered for a moment. Zebra and Yorker steadied him and insisted that he sit down for at least a few minutes; Zebra even pulled medical rank on him, ordering him to do so. Then, once he was sitting in the nearest chair, India joined them at the side of the gurney to perform a quick evaluation exam on Echo, while Omega and Romeo went to flank Fox, standing next to his chair.

Little was said; no one seemed to know what to say, and the mood was bleak, discouraging of conversation. Even the normally-loquacious Romeo remained silent. Yorker obeyed gestures from the two physicians, who mostly communicated via finger points, hums, nods, and the occasional grunt. Finally Zebra looked up.

"Okay," she said. "Yorker, take him next door to the prep room, and you and the rest of the team see about getting him cleaned up a bit; don't worry too much about it until after we have him stabilized a little better, though. And that's your more immediate task—get him hooked up to the vitals monitors, which means you WILL have to clean him up enough that things like the stickum for the cardiac leads actually stick— and let me consult real quick with India on what meds to use, at least to start with, then we'll come in and place an IV with the appropriate shit dripping into him."

"Right," Yorker said, grabbing the handles on the antigrav gurney and pushing it toward the door.

"Guys," Zebra addressed Fox, Omega, and Romeo, "if you could go in there," she pointed at another door on the opposite side of the room, "India and I'll be in to discuss matters after we have Echo stabilized better and a few things going, like pain meds, antipathogens, and the like."

The two physicians headed after the gurney containing their patient, as the three non-medical family members moved into the consultation room.

* * *

Fifteen minutes later, India and Zebra arrived in the tiny

consultation room off the exam room, to find Fox, Omega, and Romeo were standing around the table, rather than sitting. Before they could broach the matter, an antsy Omega spoke.

"So...do you, I mean...can you," Omega tried, apparently having trouble gathering her thoughts, let alone coming up with the words to express them, "can you fix him?"

"...I don't know yet, honey," Zebra murmured, overwhelmed. "We'll do the best we can."

The group was silent for a long moment; Omega's face fell, and nearly-palpable disappointment hung in the air.

"Um, there's one more thing," a nearly-white Omega said then, biting her lip almost bloody. India and Zebra automatically reached for her face, brows furrowing in concern, but she waved them back. "I dunno if this'll help y'all or not, but I couldn't just leave 'em behind to...to burn. The bastards had simply tossed 'em into a corner." And she pulled out the forensics bags containing Echo's missing hand and foot.

A gasp filled the room, and the others paled again.

"I-I know they're probably not viable any more," Omega continued, beginning to stammer while laying the bags reverently on the nearby table, "but I thought maybe...and I couldn't leave...I mean, I-I just couldn't..."

Finally at the end of her metaphorical rope, abruptly Omega crumpled, burying her face in her hands with a gut-wrenching sob as she bent slightly at the waist and her shoulders curled forward. Fox leaped to catch her in case her knees buckled, and pulled her into a hug. Immediately Omega turned into his chest, buried her face in his shirt-front, and began to cry.

"I'm sorry, Fox! I'm SORRY! I know you told me to bring him back in one piece, but I couldn't HELP it! They already DID IT! I'm so sorry! Oh, Abba, I dunno what to do!" she sobbed, practically wailing the apology. "They butchered him! They BUTCHERED him! At least Slug, damn him, put ME back together! They hacked Echo half to pieces! What do I do? What do WE do?! I—"

"Hush, hush, meyn zis kind," he murmured, patting her back and stroking her hair, as the others watched, worried. "Sssh now, hush, hush, there now. Take a deep breath, beibi maydele; there we go, now. Ssh. Calm down. Calm down. I know this has been hard, and it isn't over yet. But he's ALIVE, meyn tekhter! And he's going to stay that way. Even if Zebra and the entire medlab cannot repair the damage, it isn't the end of the world. We have access to technology that the rest of Earth doesn't have, so don't think all is lost, my dear, dear girl. There's cloning technology, and cybernetics, and all kinds of ways we can make Echo whole again. And rest assured, I will see that whatever is needed for him is done!"

"But it won't be the same," Omega murmured, deeply downcast, as she finally raised her head slightly and pushed away a bit, mopping at her tear-wet face with one hand. "I know, f'r instance, that, that the cybernetics doesn't have the ability to 'feel' like a real hand could. I mean, the touch sensation just isn't anywhere near being able to do that. And a cyber eye doesn't have the resolution of a real one. I know, because I ran across all that research while I was working on the design for Uncle Pul's wing. I dunno so much about the cloning, I'll admit..."

"It's okay, Meg," India said, coming close and laying a light hand on the other woman's shoulder. "If we have to develop new technology to make this work for Echo, then that's what we'll do. You KNOW Madrid and his Weapons Development department will help us, never mind R & D—they'll do everything they can to help us. Echo is a personal friend to too many people in BOTH departments, never mind Medical, or Alpha Line! We'll fix him back somehow, I swear to you we will."

"Meg," Zebra said, looking up; she had pulled a medscanner and begun examining the amputated limbs. "I think this might help, yes. I mean, no, the soft tissues aren't really viable any longer...but I think the bones still are. And if...well, it's kinda gory, and you've already had a bellyful of that, by the sound...but we might be able to use the bones as a framework to re-grow the limbs, if we can put him into a regen bath fast enough, and figure out how to attach 'em properly." She shrugged. "I don't have to have 'em to regrow the limbs, but he stands a much better chance of having them regrow more properly, more like the originals, WITH them."

"Oh, thank God," Omega whispered, turning her face back into Fox's chest. "I did something right. I just guessed, but..."

"Don't start crying again, meyn tekhter," Fox warned in a gentle tone, then teased, "it'll mess up my shirt. Worse."

That elicited a wobbly, watery laugh from her.

"That's better," he said, hugging her again. "And I hope you know I don't really care about the damn shirt right now. Bubeleh, can you spare thirty seconds to come here? One of our daughters desperately needs to know she is loved and not alone, I think. And that we will all do everything we can to repair what has been done to her partner and spouse. Who is also much loved by us."

"Well, of course we will, and we do," Zebra said, laying the medscanner aside and coming to join the embrace. "How 'bout our other daughter, India? Wanna join us, sweetie?"

"You bet, 'Mom an' Sis,'" India told them, sliding into the cluster. "Romeo, get over here, honey. You're the remaining son, here."

"Group hug," Romeo said as he moved out of the corner and joined in.

"We have one meshuggah family," Fox decided, "what with our 'daughters' married to our 'sons.' I suppose it's good it's not a GENETIC family."

"Ain't that the truth," Zebra snickered, and they all chuckled.

"Thank You, God, for family to lean on," Omega breathed then, "even if they're NOT genetic."

"Amein," Fox pronounced the benediction.

* * *

Seeing all of the 'special visitors' to the *Orktes* roaming about, the slave supervisor—one Acktrr, by name—decided it behooved him to go back and visit the slave who had garnered such interest, and make sure he was dealing well with his wounds. A bit of water might not come amiss, either, he decided; after all, the slave needed to stay alive long enough to be purchased and then executed...in whatever manner the buyer preferred. Still and all, alive was essential. Conscious was also good, as every one of the bidders was an enemy of the slave, and wanted to acquire him for the sake of vengeance; therefore, for the slave to be able to see his fate coming exacted that much more revenge.

So Acktrr the slave supervisor—and torture expert—made his way to the cell containing the slave called Echo. He punched the special code into the electronic lock outside the door, waited until it beeped softly, then opened the door...

...On a room that had been so thoroughly 'sanitized' that the spacefaring-alloy walls shone like polished, new metal. It was doubtful that the room had been so clean since it was first put to use. In the area where the prisoner had been shackled to the wall, a few blobs of cooling molten metal, both puddled on the floor and protruding from the bulkhead, dribbling down the wall in shiny rivulets, were all that marked the remains of those shackles. Heat still radiated from the highly-insulated interior, and the atmosphere was so full of carbon combustion products that it was unbreathable; he dared not enter.

There was nothing else to be seen.

"Aitrrk! Awwk trrp!" the Cortian cursed; to a human, it would have sounded like angry birds squawking.

Then he spun and ran to find Captain Incke.

* * *

(Where is it?) the Ke!endarian called Kla!kut kre Nutheer, formerly a member of the H!nar kre Naese!en!Re cult, and the designated successor of Throtlama kre Meorn as head of the Gu'ursh tem al Ke!thas crime syndicate, demanded of the commander of the Cortian vessel. (I want to know where my deputy is! It went off with YOUR crew member, designated by YOU, and it has not returned! What have you done with it?)

(What? What I have done with it?!) Incke retorted. (Tell me what YOUR right-hand being has done with MY crew member! He is a trusted member of my personal guard staff, and I have not seen him since he took YOUR being to see the captured slave! Explain THAT, if you please!)

(YOU are the race who captures and sells other beings as slaves!) kre Nutheer pointed out. (What have you done with it? My most trusted subordinate! If you have taken it as a slave, you will regret it, I can assure you!)

(I have not, nor would not!) Incke declared, lying through his teeth on the addendum, at least. In point of fact, he had wondered what kind of price he could obtain from taking a number of these beings as slaves, and whether or not the Pan-

Galactic Coalition would be willing to purchase them in order to punish them appropriately, given they were lawbreakers according to that same Coalition. No Cortian accepted the Pan-Galactic Coalition government—or any other government than their own, really—as legitimate, but they were not averse to playing both ends against the middle, if there was a monetary advantage to be gained by doing so.

(Then what do you claim became of them?) a deeply incensed kre Nutheer demanded.

(I know not,) Incke said with a shrug. (It is, perhaps, that neither of them was as worthy of our trust as we had thought, and they have fled together.)

(Oh! Are any ships missing?) kre Nutheer wondered, surprised at the idea.

(I do not yet know,) Incke said. (I had only just realized my bodyguard was missing when you arrived, and your accusation was the first news I had had that your deputy was also missing. I will contact my slave supervisor and verify whether or not they came by to examine slave Echo, and then I will proceed from there. All I know at this point is that my bodyguard did not show up at his post when he was expected, and now, that your assistant did not return. I assure you, I shall look into it. And if something untoward has happened, my bodyguard will pay the price.)

(That...may be acceptable,) kre Nutheer decided. (But if my assistant has been harmed, I shall want reparations, as well.)

(In action, or in monetary consideration?) Incke asked.

(That may depend upon the nature of the harm done, I think,) kre Nutheer said.

(That is understandable. Then perhaps you could take a double turn at the lash for the bodyguard, or a five percent discount off the purchase price of slave Echo, should you be the winning bidder,) Incke suggested.

(Ah. Those would do nicely, I think,) kre Nutheer agreed. (I can trust you to locate my missing assistant?)

(Certainly. If it is still aboard my vessel, we will find it. But if it has done somewhat amiss, I may claim it as property.)

(What? Explain what you mean by 'somewhat amiss.')

(If it has, say, managed to kill my bodyguard, or injured the slave, or damaged my ship,) Incke elaborated, (it will be my turn for reparations. And that will take the form of claiming your subordinate as my new slave, to do with as I will.)

(That...is fair.) Kre Nutheer shook his head. (I will be very surprised if it has done anything of the sort.)

(No doubt. Then we have a deal.)

(Very good then. I shall return to the auditorium to await the auction.)

(By all means. I will let you know as soon as I have heard anything.)

* * *

(NO!) Incke practically howled in frustrated fury, when the slave supervisor had located him in his cabin off the bridge, a scant ten minutes later. (It cannot be! Tell me this is nothing but a sick joke!)

(I fear not, sir,) the slave supervisor said, kneeling before the captain and trying not to tremble in fear. (I do not know what he did, nor where he found the ability or means, but not only is he gone, the cell is...sterilized. Bare walls, molten shackles, and the bulkheads, deck, and overhead are...shiny.)

(What?)

(The metal, milord. It is...shiny. It has been...scoured, or perhaps sublimated...down to fresh, unoxidized carbon tungs-to-steel.)

(That is impossible!)

(Nevertheless, sir. And it was...hot. It still radiated with heat so great, I could not enter. And the air was...very bad.)

(Why did not the fire alert sound?!)

(Remember, that is the special interrogation chamber, sir.)

(Oh. Of course. I am not thinking.) Incke performed the Cortian equivalent of a face palm, careful to avoid raking his talons across his own face. (It has no such sensors, so that we may best be able to interrogate the prisoners as we see fit.)

(Yes sir. And that is why it is also made of carbon tungsto-steel for the bulkheads, deck, and overhead, with insulating materials separating it from the rest of the ship, including a small vacuum space,) the slave supervisor reminded him. (The designers wished us to be able to use any and all means of in-terrogation without putting the rest of the ship at risk. We are fortunate, in this instance, else we might now have a serious situation on our claws.)

(Yes, yes. I am not thinking.) A thought suddenly popped to the forefront of Incke's thoughts. (Was there any sign of the Ke!endarian visitor, or the bodyguard I assigned to escort him? They are missing. Do you know if they reached the cell before...) Incke broke off, his beady red eyes dilating in shock. (Oh no. They would have been in the cell when...whatever happened, happened.)

(To my knowledge, sir, that is likely,) the slave supervisor agreed. (I know that your bodyguard came by my station—alone—to ascertain the keycode for that room some little time prior, yes. And the timing is likely right. I can go back and try to look for any remains if you wish it, for I did have sense to purge the bad air overboard before I closed the cell and came straight here...)

(Mmph. Any device capable of melting the shackles is not likely to have left much, if anything, in the way of remains to identify.) Incke drummed his talons on his desk in an intensely annoyed, but thoughtful gesture. (Give me a moment to consider this matter.)

They were silent for long moments. The slave supervisor still knelt in fear—it was well within the captain's right to have him executed for this, and there would be no recourse and no appeal—though neither Echo nor Omega would have immediately recognized the position as kneeling; as avians, the Cortian's lower legs properly descended from the ankle-equivalent, and thus bent backward. The Cortian thigh was extremely short, and the true knee was therefore largely hidden in the body feathers under the uniform.

(All right,) Incke decided, still staring at his desktop, (go fetch the head of security and bring him to me. Brief him about what has happened as you go. I want a search begun for our prisoner as soon as possible. Based on what you told me you did to extract information he apparently did not possess, he cannot have gotten far. Not missing a foot. And no one aboard would aid the son of a bitch! Damnation, he is nothing but trouble, that one.)

(I...I...) the slave supervisor tried, surprised.

(Hm, what?) Incke said, glancing up. (Oh. No, no. Get up. Something odd has happened here, but it is likely not your fault. I have always thought you were a bird after my own hearts, after all. Though if I find you were negligent, I shall be very displeased. But no, in all likelihood, the annoying bastard somehow managed to conceal some diabolical device he then produced and used to escape. It is just possible he used it to commit suicide, but I have hopes otherwise. If he has, then we shall see no benefit at all from his capture, damn the creature! Now go fetch Security.)

(Y-yes sir! Thank you, sir!) the slave supervisor said, and hastened out, before Incke could change his mind.

* * *

Within ten minutes, the Cortians had begun a thorough sweep of their ship, looking for an escaped prisoner. They were subtle, however; they did not want to upset their 'guests,' let alone tip them off to the fact that the reason those guests had arrived was now missing. Nor did they want to reveal the probable fate of the missing Ke!endarian; the captain had his own plans for that explanation.

Twenty minutes after the search commenced, the slave supervisor was back in the captain's cabin with the chief of security of the *Orktes*.

(...Nowhere to be found?) Incke repeated, when they had concluded their report.

(No sir,) the security chief reiterated. (Not so far. We are continuing to search with diligence, but we see no sign of him. There is some indication in the ship's internal records that the door may have opened and closed, which might indicate that he freed himself—or it may indicate that your bodyguard and the Ke!endarian were inside when...whatever happened, happened—but the data give no more than that, and we have not yet searched the records in detail, as that is even more labor-intensive than the full volumetric search of the ship.)

(Get on it as soon as possible,) Incke ordered. (It may provide some clue where he has hidden. He cannot have gotten off the ship, so he must be holed up somewhere within it. And hopefully you will find the missing crewman and visitor into the bargain. Perhaps he holds them prisoner, somehow. They may be functioning as his missing limbs for him.)

(Aye, sir.)

The pair left to see about beginning a search of the ship's housekeeping data records.

(And that leaves me to convince our guests that this delay is quite normal,) Incke sighed to himself. (Never mind whatever has happened to the damned Ke!endarian 'guest.' It sounds like it is probably dead, along with my favorite bodyguard. Never mind that he served me well in my mate's absence, since she is imprisoned at home on Corta; I shall miss that, and him. AND...we aborted a promising raid in order to go to my agent's assistance and recapture the slave! Damn the creature to the depths of perdition! I wish I had not laid eyes upon its very image! He has been nothing but trouble from the moment I heard he had been spotted! NOTHING!)

He rose and headed for the onboard auditorium, where their 'honored guests' were gathered, mulling what he could do to stall...and how long he could get away with it before they started becoming suspicious.

* * *

Several quick discussions between Zebra, India, Omega, and the Deltiri team ascertained that, given the severity of Echo's wounds, no one medication was apt to free him from pain...especially once the doctors began the process of cleaning and debriding the wounds. Nothing, whether telepathic or pharmaceutical, was going to completely eliminate the pain from that.

"And I'm in a position to know," Omega averred.

"Yes, you are," India agreed.

"However," Zebra pointed out, "we can't afford to drug him up too much anyway; he's really shocky, and the condition he's in, I don't want to risk crashing his vitals. That could kill him, as surely as the Cortians would have...or whoever those bidders were, I guess. But put together, the telepathic and pharmaceutical techniques ought to do the trick. And from what Meg has told me, you guys could probably use a bit of a break anyhow," she told Zz'r'p. "Or at least, the assistance that the pharmaceutical add-ons will provide."

"Well, that is admittedly true," the Deltiri ambassador replied. "We few have been very busy in recent hours, and while we are now keeping a shift schedule, we were not, originally. And we have not only been keeping Echo free of pain, we have been leading the *Genesis* to him, determining his exact location within the Cortian craft, directing Omega to him within the Cortian ship, helping her stay calm, helping her maintain her cover..."

"Wait, wait. Helping Meg stay CALM?" Zebra jumped on the statement, then she spun on the Agent, irritated. "You didn't take your meds, did you?"

"Stop, Zebra, stop," Mm'l'n declared, holding up a staying hand before Omega could react. "Do not condemn her. She HAS been taking them. In the maximum dosage, let me add. We Deltiri all know this, because we could...feel...their effects...and it helped her considerably. But she has also been mentally connected to Echo, who has been..." She broke off. "Omega, I need to ask you something, my friend. It is something we all wondered—even surmised—prior to your rescue of your spouse, but had not had opportunity to find out. So... did you already know, or at least suspect, what wounds, what KIND of wounds, Echo had?"

"Yeah," Omega said in a low voice. "I was hoping like hell I was wrong, but...yeah, I knew."

Zebra and India both gaped in astonishment.

"You felt it, did you not?" Mm'l'n continued. "Both when they were inflicted, and once he dropped the telepathic block?"

"Um, yeah. Not...not like he did, not anywhere close. But yeah, I could feel it. It's what woke me up—that, and Echo screaming with the pain."

"I thought so!" Qq'k'l suddenly said. "You tended to favor your right foot, you kept unconsciously massaging your left hand, and you had twinges of pain behind your left eye, for you kept rubbing at it. I suspected, but I had not fully realized the import of those gestures until just now, thinking on Echo's injuries."

Omega gave a shrug, then a wry, lopsided, humorless grin, and simply nodded. Zebra and India gasped in horror.

"Oh, holy shit, Meg," India whispered, deeply shocked, and Omega sobered, expression somber. "YOU felt it?! You

FELT it?? Along with Echo?? And you didn't tell anybody?!"

"She DID tell someone, India," Zz'r'p pointed out. "She issued an emergency contact to Fox immediately, requesting I attend with him, and told us that things had 'gone south' as she and Echo both are wont to put such things. And when she finally convinced Echo to drop his telepathic block and let her in—and by extension, my team—the pain SHE felt ramped up so much that her body trembled violently, and she collapsed. Fortunately, we saw it coming and Jj'k'k was close enough to catch her in a well-padded chair, lest she land on the deck with some force. But, now that I think back," Zz'r'p recalled, "it was that right leg that gave way. The same one Echo...lost."

The other Deltiri pondered for a moment, then nodded; Omega sighed.

"But she didn't tell us what they DID to Echo!" India cried. "Why didn't you tell us, honey? Tell us YOU could feel it? Maybe we could have helped!"

"I...was afraid to, India," a downcast Omega sighed. "I was hopin' and prayin' I was wrong, an' well..." Her shoulders slumped. "But I wasn't wrong."

"No, no, no," an astonished and dismayed Zebra finally murmured. "I'm so sorry, honey. Please forgive my sharp tongue. I had...no idea."

"I guess there's good points an' bad points to an nd't'lq bond," Omega tried, the crooked grin returning and growing a bit wider, and Zz'r'p gave a rueful, rather bleak chuckle.

"Indeed, youngling. It is a wonderful, intimate bond between spouses, but when something goes wrong, the pain can be...incredible. I still recall 'feeling' my wife's death all too vividly, decades ago though it has been, now. At least you knew he was still alive."

"True," Omega admitted, rubbing both hands over her face. "So Zebra an' India, you're gonna dope Ace to the gills, and the Deltiri team and I are gonna take it the rest of the way?"

"Not...quite," Zz'r'p noted. "I am still your counselor, my dear girl, and you have done a great deal for him already—including risking your life to fetch him back to the *Genesis*. And you are very tired and still highly stressed. I think that the thing you are best suited for, at this point, is to rest, sit with him, let him 'feel' you near, and let US take care of the last of his pain."

"But I," Omega began.

"NO," eight voices—all six Deltiri, plus Zebra and India—chorused. "You need to do what Zz'r'p said, honey, and that's a medical order at this point," Zebra issued the addendum. "Just because you're not helping suppress his pain any more doesn't mean you're not helping at all. Echo's subconscious will know you're there with him, and that'll go a long way toward helping us keep him settled. You know how he tends to become agitated during stuff like this."

"And it has another benefit to him—making sure he knows you accept him, regardless," Mm'l'n pointed out. "Remember, Zz'r'p told you of his asking Fox to send another agent, lest you see him in his current state. And that is understandable—he has gone from a prime specimen of a strong, confident human male, in peak condition, to a battered, maimed being, with several missing body parts, taken from him while he was completely helpless to stop it. You have only recently been introduced—as his spouse, in the most intimate fashion of knowing—to him, to his body, in that peak condition...and now..."

"Oh," Omega murmured, reminded of the incident. "I'd forgotten about that. Yeah. Okay, I get it."

"Um. Good," a still-shaken India noted, pulling herself back together with an effort. "Now that that's all understood and taken care of, should we set to work? What do you want to do first, Zebra?"

"I think we need to clean things and start a good broad-spectrum antipathogenic going into him," Zebra decided. "I didn't like the looks of those compression bandages at all; they looked downright damn nasty. We have that IV in him, but after seeing the bandages up close, the more I think about it, the more I want to use metafloxin, instead of the pentaflexin we started with; it's faster-acting, hits a lot more of the interstellar buggums, and I think it's a lot stronger. Never mind continuing to rehydrate him and also put some nutrients in there—near as I can tell, the bastards didn't give him ANY food or water, the whole time he was in their power. But I'd rather wait to begin debridement until we're ready to dunk him, once we're back at Headquarters. That way, the raw tissues stay viable for the regen procedure. I only wanna have to do THAT just once."

"Fair enough," India agreed. "Call the medtechs, let's dope him up, and you and me get started."

"Are you guys up for this?" Zebra asked the Deltiri team.

"We are," Bb'y'x insisted, and the others nodded.

"I will assist Omega in keeping Echo settled and relaxed through the nd't'lq," Kk'q'r offered.

"Much appreciated," Omega said with a nod. "Because... yeah, I have to admit, at this point I'm pretty damn tired. Sneaking in and out of the Cortian ship was a blasted obstacle course, all by itself. It just went on and on! An' no opportunity to let my guard down for a second."

"Zz'r'p, if you have no objections, I think it would be wise if I kept an eye on activities aboard the Cortian ship," Qq'k'l suggested.

"Ah; you make a good point, my friend. I think that is an excellent idea," Zz'r'p concurred.

* * *

"How do you wanna do this, Zee?" India asked her superior in the Medical chain of command. "I gather you're wanting to work on the amputated limbs, too. What, debride 'em until you have viable tissues, then preserve 'em until we can use 'em as a framework for regrowth?"

"Exactly," Zebra noted, "but I'm not quite sure what needs doing. I need to do some research, maybe contact Zar back home. Maybe even consult Doron about the best way to go about it."

"Mm. That's a lot," India said, considering.

"Yeah, I know. But if I don't manage to remove the dying and dead tissue soon, and do it the right way, it could poison the remaining tissues and the bones, and then..." She shook her head. "But in the end, I might have to see about preserving 'em, 'cause I'm not sure I have what I need to do it all, here. That's why I'm thinking about consulting with Zar and Doron."

"But if we don't get Echo's wounds cleaned and properly bandaged, they could become infected," India pointed out. "And then we REALLY have a mess. And we might lose him."

"I know. Decisions, decisions," Zebra remarked with dark,

157

sardonic humor. The smile she offered her colleague was more than a little rueful.

"Okay, let's do it like this," India suggested. "You know more about the procedure you want to do with the limbs. I'm used to working ER. I'll treat Echo and change out those dressings, and you go see about what to do with the hand and leg the damned Cortians chopped off."

"That should work," Zebra decided. "You can have all the medtechs, for now. I'll need to figure out exactly what I'm doing before I can actually DO it, IF I do it, and I won't need a medtech to help until then. And I'm betting you'll be done by that point, anyway."

"All over it," India said. "Okay, Yorker, round up your team. You guys are with me, for now."

And the majority of the staff headed for the operating room, as Zebra headed for the physician's office.

* * *

India managed, with some difficulty, to pull the tourniquet and compression bandage, caked and clotted with dried blood, off Echo's leg stump, having to wield a scalpel and surgical scissors from time to time; the bandage had stuck badly in several places, and did not want to release from the wound. The right leg had been severed just a couple of inches below the knee, in what looked to her like at least two strokes, possibly as many as three or four, if the visible planes of cleavage were anything to go by. *Which means,* she thought, trying not to cringe as she and the medtechs quickly clamped off bleeders, *they literally hacked it off. One of my best friends is lying here, deliberately chopped up by those evil, destructive sons of bitches.* Even with the light anesthesia Yorker pumped into the IV and with the Deltiri telepathically treating his pain, Echo still squirmed a bit as she peeled the bandage from the raw wound...which was just beginning to fester.

"Are the Deltiri still helping suppress his pain?" India wondered, pausing in her work, as the medtechs tried to hold the injured man's leg still enough to work on it.

We are, Mm'l'n's mental voice told her. *In fact, I am completing scrubbing and gowning, preparatory to entering the treatment room to assist where I may. He is simply in a good bit of pain from the procedure—the clotting is all throughout the bandage, and you are having to pull it free from raw tissue, cutting it loose in places—and since the pain changes moment to moment as you work on him, we are constantly adjusting. It is...hard.*

Just then, the gowned Deltiri came into the room.

"Here I am," she said aloud. "Agent Yorker, might you possibly increase the anesthesia upon Agent Echo?"

"I can, but given his poor condition, we don't want to use TOO much," Yorker replied, adjusting the drip as he spoke. "He's lost a lot of blood, and he's a little shocky—okay, a lot shocky—and I'd rather not suppress his vitals any more than we can help, or we could have a lot more serious problem on our hands. There. Hopefully that'll do it. I've barely got him under, to begin with, and I really don't wanna have to use a stronger anesthetic, either, but damn."

"I will do my best, as well," Mm'l'n said. "I had hoped to assist the procedure, but all things considered, it may be better if I focus my attention upon Echo's pain, and suppressing it."

"I think that's a plan," India said, nodding. "I can handle this, as long as he's not actively reacting to it. This is the biggest wound, and I've done this sort of thing lots of times before."

"Then that is what I shall do," the Deltiri said, and moved to the corner. One of the medtechs pointed at a stool near the prep table, and Mm'l'n sat on it, then closed her eyes and concentrated, wrinkling her blue forehead in the process.

Moments later, Echo settled, and the medical team resumed work. Within a few minutes, the leg was thoroughly cleaned, treated with antipathogenics, sprayed with a special sealant which Doron had developed for the regeneration process which would close off further bleeding and protect from contamination, and carefully covered with a fresh compression dressing, with new padding and a bandage designed not to stick to the wound.

Doron had developed and intended the sealant for this express purpose—it would stop the bleeding of even the largest vessels and stay on the raw wound until the regenerating tissues grew through it, to prevent any risk of bleed-out, infection, or debris contamination, and then it would gradually dissolve—it was specifically designed to dissolve only in the basic carrier liquid of the regeneration fluid, under the influence of regrowth of tissues. That said, everyone there knew that this particular layer would be removed during debridement back in the med-lab on Earth...but then it would be reapplied just prior to Echo being 'dunked' in the regen pod, so all would function as need-ed, without further risk to him. And it worked very, very well.

India next began work on his arm. But that limb had been severed just above the wrist, and the hand had many more sen-sory-oriented nerves than the foot, with a correspondingly large supportive nervous system in the arm, and Echo responded ac-cordingly, beginning to thrash a bit in reaction. India blanched slightly and stepped back, as the medtechs reluctantly strapped down his legs and remaining arm, then carefully held that arm still. Meanwhile Yorker adjusted the medications in the drip for a second time; Mm'l'n's forehead creased deeper as she fought to block the maimed Agent's pain. Eventually Echo was still, and India resumed work, cutting away the clotted bandage and clamping off bleeders, thoroughly irrigating and cleaning away any debris or sign of infection, and applying antipathogenic medications, before thoroughly sealing the stump and bandag-ing the wound once more, again using materials intended to be 'non-stick.'

Then she stepped away for several minutes, moving into a corner of the room and turning her back to the others. The medtechs glanced at each other in concern, then Yorker stood and moved to her side.

"What's wrong, India?" he murmured, laying a gentle hand on her shoulder.

"Oh," she said, giving a wobbly laugh, "I'm just dreading working on his eye. If the leg and arm hurt that much, how much is his face gonna hurt?"

"He's unconscious, honey," Yorker soothed. "His body is reacting, yeah, but he's not feelin' it."

"I just hope you're right," India replied with an anxious sigh. "Double-check his vitals for me, especially the EEG, and let's make sure he's well and truly out, before I start on that eye."

"Can do," Yorker said, surveying the vitals readouts with a practiced gaze. "Looks solid out, to me."

* * *

"I can verify," Mm'l'n said. She opened her eyes once more and focused her gaze on the physician, sensing the other female's emotional turmoil. "Yes, Echo's body hurts, and yes, it is reacting in reflex, but we are keeping those sensations from reaching his mind. He is effectively in a state somewhere between sleep and..." she broke off, looking for words to describe something beyond the range of human experience or understanding. "Not a coma, precisely. It is a deep unconscious state that telepaths can create in our patients, but that also often occurs during full anesthesia. So he essentially is under a full general anesthesia without the need to use such strong drugs. Which, in his depleted condition, is safer, as it does not decrease his vital signs and risk crashing him."

"And you're sure?" India wanted verification.

"I am positive," Mm'l'n said with confidence. "I have done this sort of thing before, numerous times. It is hard, and I will be tired later. But we have this. Come, my friend; let us finish, make him comfortable and safe from infection, and be done."

Firming her jaw, India pushed away from the corner.

"All right, let's get this over with," she said, using forceps to reach for the bandage Omega had placed over Echo's missing eye.

* * *

When it was done, India left the medtechs to clean up the operating room, make Echo comfortable and place him into a proper hospital bed, and headed into the scrub room herself. There, she pulled off her gloves, mask, and gown—smeared with Echo's blood—throwing them angrily in a corner, before plopping down on a stool by the far counter. She folded her arms on the countertop, rested her forehead on them, and within moments, the tears were overflowing despite her best efforts.

Seconds later, Mm'l'n, with Yorker in tow, burst through the door from the operating room and came straight to India.

"There, there, my friend," Mm'l'n said, peeling off the unused gloves on her hands and laying them aside, then gesturing to Yorker, lock-sending the message, *Fetch Zebra at once*, to him. Then she eased gentle arms around the distressed physician, even as Yorker left the room at speed. "I know he is a dear friend, someone you consider as family. I know you are worried for him, and for Omega, and for their relationship, and I know you are projecting your fears for Romeo onto this matter. A situation like this exposes and attacks many fears. But it is all right, my friend—and you are MY friend, too, though we do not yet know each other so well as the others—you did excellently, and now Echo is safe from infection. All that is left is to see about regrowing the missing parts. And you ensured he can survive to do so, and that all will be viable and ready for that."

* * *

"...And so that's sort of the situation we have," Zebra finished explaining to the other two physicians on the video conference...which conference was VERY carefully ciphered, with the relay to Doron running through the Headquarters comm system, to avoid the communiqué from the *Genesis* being detected by the motley collection of criminals, cutthroats and slavers that sat all too close to their position. Once Alpha One was back aboard, Fox had even moved the *Genesis* well away from the rest of the ships in the otherwise-uninhabited system, the bridge crew having managed to locate a satellite of the brown dwarf that had fallen into a synchronous orbit; the *Genesis* was currently lurking near—or just slightly behind— the satellite's limb as viewed from the grouping of spacecraft about the *Orktes*. "Echo's a hacked-up mess, but Omega not only brought him back as intact as she found him, she also brought back the hand and the lower leg the damn rat-bastard Cortians cut off him. The soft tissues are pretty much gone, but the bones look to be still viable, and MAYBE the tendons, too; I can't really tell yet."

"Mm," Doron hummed, frowning. "They are not nice beings at all. I have known this personally for many annums, but this..."

"Indeed," Zarnix agreed, scowling. "This was far outside the bounds of anything remotely approximating acceptable, civilized behavior."

"No argument there at all," Zebra practically snarled, then forced herself to regain a semblance of calm. "So, okay, what do I need to do with the severed limbs, guys, to ensure that we have SOMEthing to work with, when I carry him back to Earth and put him into a regen pod?"

"Doron is the expert, here," Zarnix said, "but I would suggest cleaning them thoroughly, then bathing them in an antipathogen; perhaps even place them into a solution containing a goodly concentration of antipathogen, and then into a stasis field. I suspect that debridement down to viable tissue will need to occur only very shortly before reattaching the bones and whatever else of the soft tissues we might rescue. Is that your assessment, Doron?"

"It is," the diminutive red being agreed, his large yellow eyes half-closed in consideration. "You will probably not be able to save many of the tendons, if any at all, but the bones should remain viable for a time yet, provided you prevent infection from setting in on the severed ends. That is why I should prefer to see the parts placed in an antipathogen bath, rather than a simple wash. And those bones will make excellent scaffolding for the regrowth of those limbs."

"Got it," Zebra said, taking notes. "Special attention to the cut edges, and put 'em in a bath."

"Then transport them to Earth alongside Echo, where they will be prepared at the same time he is prepared for the regeneration process," Doron instructed. "You will want to attach them only moments before placing him into the regeneration bath, as Zarnix suspected."

"Right, then," Zarnix said, also taking notes. "But how do we attach them? If the tendons and ligaments and such must be removed via debridement, how do we even hold them together? There are many small bones of the hand and foot..."

"You have what is sometimes called 'three-dimensional printing' technology, do you not?" Doron queried.

"We do," Zarnix averred. "Rather finely detailed, at that."

"Excellent," Doron declared. "I will send you the formula for the protein you will use to replace the connective tissues."

"Oh, I see," Zarnix said, countenance lightening. "We'll create a framework to hold them together, and then the tissues developing from the stem cells will fill in and absorb the protein..."

"Yes, yes," Doron said with a smile. "The regeneration fluid simply helps the body know what to do to heal itself, after all."

"Yes, but..." Zarnix broke off.

"But what?"

"But how do we attach them?"

"That, I will show you when I arrive," Doron pronounced. "It will take more of that same protein, but it is not as difficult as you may think. We can do it together, and I will show you how, and you can learn it, in case another agent loses a limb in injury."

"Oh, thank God, you're coming to help," Zebra murmured. "We're gonna need all the expertise we can get to return Echo to some semblance of his old self, guys. Doron, THANK you."

"He and Omega are my friends," Doron explained. "I have nothing urgent on my schedule, and as soon as we end this communication, I will see about obtaining an emergency transport from Edeptis to Earth; I think Lady Teela will be of help there. It will take a while, since the transport will first have to come TO Edeptis, so you may well reach Earth before I do, Zebra. But I am coming! As fast as I may! I will not leave my friends in trouble when I may help! And that includes the two of you, and Lord Levy as well. For I know that you are all a family of sorts, and I am a friend of that family. I am coming! I will help my friends!"

"Thank the Maker for that," Zarnix agreed. "We shall be glad to have you at our side, showing us what to do, Doron."

"It is..." the Edeptan broke off, chewing his lower lip. "I could not stay here," he admitted then. "They are FRIENDS. MY friends. I cannot stay. I must be there. You understand, I am certain."

Zebra and Zarnix nodded. The three were silent for a long moment. Finally Zebra, whose eyes were moist, commented.

"Um, okay," she murmured, then cleared her throat. "So I clean 'em like I would a wound, treat the severed edges, then dunk 'em in an antipathogen solution. What concentration?"

"Only you know how much you have," Doron pointed out, "but I would like to see the same concentration that you typically use in an intravenous solution? Perhaps just a little bit stronger?”

"Oh, that's not a problem, then," Zebra declared. "We have lotsa that on board; we came with the notion that we might have to board the bastards' spacecraft and fight our way through to Echo. I got bags an' bags of that shit. I'll just put 'em in sterile containers, then empty the bags over 'em until they're submerged..."

"Very good," Doron agreed.

"And then put 'em in a medical stasis field?" she finished.

"That is excellent," Doron asserted.

Just then, someone fairly banged on the closed office door.

"Zebra!" Yorker's voice called. "We got a situation. India's having a little bit of a meltdown, and Mm'l'n told me to come fetch you as soon as you could get there!"

"Oh shit," Zebra said, worried, as she ran a hand over her hair. "Guys, you two work out any additional details, and I'll get back with you in a bit. Zar, if I have all I need to know until I reach Earth, just ping me, and I'll see that we transport Echo, his hand, and his leg all back there in hopefully-useful shape."

"I understand, Zee," the chief of staff affirmed. "Go take care of whatever is happening, before things become worse."

"All over THAT one," Zebra said, killing the vidcomm feed and heading for the door.

* * *

Mm'l'n had paused long enough to telepathically analyze India's mental and emotional state. "Would you like me to help you, India?" she offered then. "I could, perhaps, soften the memories a bit..."

"N-no," India sobbed her answer to Mm'l'n, even as Zebra entered with Yorker. "No, I just wanna go back to my quarters and hug Romeo as hard as I can."

"India, honey, are you okay?" Zebra said, coming to her other side and joining Mm'l'n's embrace. "Did it not go well?"

"It went fine," Yorker said then, keeping his voice low and quiet. "I think that, given her patient was Echo, getting the procedures done was a little rougher than she realized it would be." Just then, the other medtechs peeked through the operating room door. "Huh? What is it, Gig?"

"We have Agent Echo ready to transport to his room, Yorker," Gig replied, very soft. "We just wanted to know if it was okay, or if we needed to wait a bit."

India waved her hand in a *go, go* gesture without raising her head, and Yorker and Zebra both nodded their permission. Zebra took a quick look at the wounded Agent as the gurney went past, then nodded to herself.

"He looks pretty good, considering, honey," she told India then. "You done good. Real good. I think it's time for a break for you. You were there at the airlock when Omega left for the Cortian ship, you stayed there until she brought Echo back to the *Genesis*, you've been here through stabilizing him, and you cleaned all the wounds. You've done your part and then some, and I definitely think it's time for that break, girl." She looked up at the Deltiri woman. "Mm'l'n, do you have any sense of where Romeo is right now, or if he's busy? I think maybe, unless Fox has him doing something damn important, he just needs to come here and take India back to their cabin, maybe spend some quality couples time with her. She needs plenty of opportunity to settle, and I think he's the best one to do that."

"I think that to be an excellent idea, and I should be happy to locate him and ascertain matters," Mm'l'n agreed, then her eyes defocused. Within seconds they resumed a present light, and she said, "I have contacted him; he is not busy with anything especially important, and he is on his way."

"Good. Then let's you and me stay here and keep India company until he gets here," Zebra decided, gently stroking India's hair. "I should have helped her with this. I knew it would be difficult. I just had my head full of panicky, *how do I keep the limbs going until we need 'em* thoughts, and..." She hugged India tighter. "I let my other stepdaughter down. I'm so sorry, honey."

"N-no," India hiccupped, "it's okay, Zee. Not your fault. I vol-volunteered. Yorker was right. I just...didn't think about..."

"How hard it would be," Yorker murmured, wrapping his long arms around the trio of females. "It wasn't easy for me, either, and I don't know him as well as you guys do."

The four stood like that, as India tried to regain her objectivity and perspective, tried to put aside memories of raw, bloody flesh and severed bone on one of her dearest friends...

with only moderate success. Five minutes later, Romeo entered at a swift walk, just shy of a jog.

"Whassup?" he demanded. "Mm'l'n said India was— India!" he exclaimed, and suddenly India was pushing through the protective huddle around her, to fling her arms around her husband and partner.

"Oh, Romeo!" she said, beginning to cry again. "Oh, honey, you have to—I mean, we need to...we gotta be careful! Echo was...he was...it was bad." She buried her face in his chest, choking slightly as she struggled to control the weeping.

"Take her back to your cabin, Romeo," Zebra ordered in a gentle voice. "Carry her if you need to, and she'll let you. Calm her down as much as you can, and spend some private time with her, just the two of you. Whatever you need to do to calm her down, do it; that's between the two of you. All things considered, and with the 'there but for the grace of God' kind of feeling we all have right now, I think that's my prescription for her. If you can't settle her, call me, and I'll send over the same prescription we're giving Meg, only at the lower dose."

"Is Echo gonna be all right?" a worried Romeo wondered then, holding India, who was still crying despite all she could do.

"He's in better shape now, thanks to India's excellent work, than he was before," Zebra averred. "Mm'l'n just mentally showed me a quick rundown of the procedures on his leg, arm, and eye, and India did brilliantly; you're a really skilled emergency room physician, honey. And while there was some infection trying to set up, it's all cleaned out, everything's dressed and bandaged and ready for regen prep, we've added a stronger antipathogen to his IV, and he'll survive long enough for us to put him in a regen pod. After that, I'm still not sure, but we're gonna give it our damnedest."

"Yes," Mm'l'n agreed. "India is very, very good; I have worked in emergency rooms before, myself, so I speak from personal knowledge on that. She simply had difficulty maintaining her objectivity, given the closeness of the patient to her personally. And I would be in a similar condition, were it one of my dearest friends, so it is no reflection upon her as a physician."

"We all would. That's why it's generally a thing that doctors try not to work on relatives or close friends, in the outside world at home," Zebra pointed out. "Or at least, try not to be the principal physician working on 'em. Unfortunately, given that the Agency is a relatively small fraction of a percent of the total population, and nobody else is supposed to know about it, us Agency medics don't really have much choice in that regard."

"Oh," Romeo said, understanding. "An' it sounds like maybe she's kinda projectin' some there, huh, India? Like, what if that hadda been me?" he asked the woman in his arms, who nodded, but could not speak. "Well, I c'n get that. Alla that. Ever' time somethin' happens t' Meg, I have th' same kinda reaction, if I'm honest with ya. Let's go back t' th' cabin we got assigned, an' I'll give ya a glass o' somethin' to settle ya, an' maybe a neck rub, then some cuddles."

"O-okay," India agreed with a sniff. "T-that sounds good. Let's go. I...I'm sorry, Zebra..."

"Hush that, and get on with you," Zebra said with a slight, soft smile.

They left.

Chapter 7

Half an hour later, Echo was clean all over; in the course of cleaning the grime off his body, the medtech team discovered quite a few bruises, scrapes, and contusions of various sizes, indicating that the 'interrogation' the Cortians had performed had included a certain amount of beating, as well as the more acute severing of limbs and gouging of eye. They did quick checks of his other eye, both ears, and his mouth—as well as more private regions—to ensure nothing had been done there that Omega had somehow missed, but found no sign of damage to those bodily parts.

Soon the male Agent was not only clean, but swabbed down with Rejuvic and lying in a hospital bed with a fresh osmotic-cannula IV running into his good arm. Said IV contained a low dose of a hefty painkiller, the very broad-spectrum antipathogenic Zebra had mandated, and sufficient nutrients to help sustain Echo's current needs, in addition to simple fluid and electrolyte replacement; he had indeed been rather badly dehydrated when Omega had rescued him, let alone unfed for the whole time he had been in the hands of the Cortians. Once the IV had been established, and certain exit pathways duly intubated, Yorker eased a special version of the medical jumpsuit onto Echo's body—basically a pair of loose-fitting shorts with the same hook-and-loop, wrap-around, multi-flap design, intended to avoid contact with all of Echo's injured areas—then he took a swab saturated with Rejuvic to the various bruises and abrasions produced by the manacles, ensuring they were treated a second time, thereby preventing them from becoming infected.

Echo had regained consciousness briefly, after being settled in a hospital bed in sick bay, to find Omega standing at his bedside.

"Hey, baby," he murmured, managing to focus on her with his one remaining eye for a few moments before it slid shut again. "I guess I'm on a PGLEIA ship 'r something...?"

"You're on board the *Genesis*, Fox's flagship, Ace," Omega told him, taking his hand in hers and lacing her fingers with his. He instantly tightened his fingers around her hand and held on as best he could, given his weakened state. "The medics an' medtechs gotcha all cleaned up and bandaged, and slapped your behind in a nice soft bed. The 'immediate family' is all here, and you're safe, honey. The Cortians an' all their damn 'guests' will be in custody pretty quick, I hope. We're gonna be headed home as fast as the *Genesis'* engines will let us, real soon now, and when we get there, we're gonna see about putting you in a regen pod as fast as we can."

"All right. Sorry I'm such a mess..."

"Hush that. I never wanna hear you apologizing for what those bastards did to you!" Omega declared, angry and hurting for him.

* * *

He blinked in surprise at the strength of her reaction, then opened his eye and looked at her again, seeing the anger, pain— and love—written on her face, then nodded, ever so slightly.

"Hokay," he agreed, "provided you do somethin' f'r me."

"Anything, sweetheart. Whatcha need?"

"You gotta do th' same thing...where Slug's concerned."

"Huh?"

"You gotta stop blamin' yourself f'r what he did to ya," he told her. "An' 'en I'll stop apol'gizin' f'r how I look now. 'R how I'm gonna look, I s'pose."

* * *

Omega pondered that for a long moment.

"Mm. Okay, I see your point," she decided. "An' not only will I try, I'll talk to Zz'r'p about this conversation. Maybe he can show me how to see what I'm doing, 'cause I guess I don't always see it...though if that's the case, now I'm starting to understand some of your reactions to things, when we're talkin' about it. You might have to be patient with me for a bit, though, while I figure things out and...replace habits, I guess."

"I c'n do that," he agreed. "F'r you, yeah."

"Okay. Then I guess you have a deal, honey."

"Awright, baby. What, um...I guess I need to..."

"Nothing," she told him, picking up on his question and mild confusion. "You don't need to do anything. Just lie there an' relax, sweetheart. You're safe, we're gonna keep you as pain-free as we know how, and we'll have you patched up as soon as we get home. Everything else is being taken care of."

"You sure?"

"I'm sure."

"'Kay."

"I'm gonna be spending most of my time here, beside you," Omega added. "And even when I'm not here, just reach through the nd't'lq and I'll be right there."

"Gonna do more o' that mind-cuddle stuff?"

"Did you like it?"

Echo tried to raise a wobbly head and look around, hampered by the fact that he only had one eye with which to do so, and not much in the way of strength left in the rest of him.

"No no," Omega said, placing her hand on his forehead and gently nudging his head back to the pillow. "You stay put. What do you want?"

"Wanted t' see if anybody else 'uz in here..." he tried. "You said th' fam'ly was here..."

"Oh. No, I meant they're all on board the *Genesis* with us; it's just you an' me in the room—for right now, anyhow. I think Fox is on the bridge; I expect Zebra and India are prob'ly off working on how best to treat you, 'cause I haven't seen 'em in a little while, and..." Omega threw up her hands and grinned briefly, "I dunno where the hell Romeo got to. Probably talkin' to the fighter pilots or something."

"Okay," Echo said. "Then...yeah, I liked it. Th' mind-cuddle shit, I mean."

Omega smiled.

"Then I think it goes into the regular rotation," she concluded, rubbing her thumb across the back of his hand. "I agree with ya. Mental snuggles ain't half bad."

"Nope." He turned his head to look at her with his one eye, which developed an oddly mischievous glint, before he added, "Not quite 's much fun as bedroom stuff run through th' nd't'lq, but not half bad."

Omega clapped her free hand over her mouth to stifle the

guffaw that escaped at the unexpectedly ribald remark, then grinned at him.

"All right there, behave," she told him.

"Aw. Do I gotta?"

"Do you really wanna say something like that to me just as Zebra comes around the corner and into the room? You KNOW how SHE'LL react to it. We'd never hear the end of it. So, do ya?"

"...Uh, no."

"Okay, then. Behave. You go on to sleep, now," she said, squeezing his hand gently. "You need lotsa rest to start to recover and heal. I'll be here, on and off, and always here," she lightly tapped his right temple. "The more you try to rest, the less pain you'll feel, and the easier we can get you back up to snuff."

"Hokay. Goin' t' sleep now."

"You do that, honey."

And he was out.

* * *

(Captain,) the security chief of the *Orktes* reported, after Incke had managed to divert the various criminal buyers aboard his craft—via plying them with a considerable amount of the best of the food and drink stores of the vessel, reserves he had counted on to take the crew through the next lunation; it was not fancy, but it was good, and it at least appeared reasonably plentiful, and what their guests did not know would not hurt them. Though, he considered, it was apt to come back to bite HIM in the cloaca, if he was unable to find replacement foodstuffs fast enough to provide for his crew. But at least he had gotten Kla!kut kre Nutheer drunk enough to temporarily forget his missing assistant. Abruptly he came back to the present, and looked up at his chief of security.

(Go ahead, Security; give me your report,) Incke said, stifling a sigh. At the moment and after the fast talking he had managed in the auditorium, he could not have recalled the security chief's name if his life had depended upon it, and he did not even feel like bothering. He simply sat down rather heavily in his desk chair and waited for the other being to deliver his report.

(We have not found the prisoner anywhere, nor yet determined any evidence for how he did what he did,) the Cortian officer reported. (There are a few spurious indications of doors and hatches opening and closing rather as if by magic, but without corresponding passage of beings...save for one, and that was indeed the missing Ke!endarian and your bodyguard, who entered the cell...but did not come out.)

(Ah. So they are almost certainly dead, then.)

(And their bodies obliterated in...whatever happened in there, yes. That is my conclusion.)

(Damnation.)

(Also I suspect, based on the report of one of the crew, that a few of our invited guests have chosen to wander the halls without our authorization—the rationale given was a security check, which is understandable, I suppose—but none of them are apt to free our prisoner without our knowing.)

(Well, possibly to avoid the sale price,) a jaded Incke noted in deep irony. (But they would not then remain here, demanding to see the slave, when once they had him in their possession. They would return to their ship and leave straight away. And we would thereby know who had him.)

(Exactly, sir.)

(And no one has left?)

(No sir. There was some discussion that a lone Deltiri was here and left when he realized he would be outclassed in the bidding, but no one seems to be able to confirm that, so I do not put much stock in it.)

(Mm. And slave Echo is positively not on the ship?)

(No sir. We have swept it three times physically, and four more times via sensor suite. All life forms are accounted for. We are beginning to conclude that either he did, in fact, commit suicide by means unknown, or he has managed to escape the *Orktes* altogether, also by means unknown.)

(You are saying we do not have a slave to auction,) a grim Incke noted. (After packing an auction room full of what the locals consider criminal gangsters, all waiting eagerly to bid on that one slave. So they might kill him. All of them bloodthirsty and ready for death.)

(I am afraid so, sir. As I said, we still have not determined how the slave managed to do whatever he did, nor yet whether he is himself alive or dead.)

(Why am I not surprised?) Incke wondered, blasé. (And that, after all the stories I just heard from our guests about how resourceful that one was. We went up against a wizard in that one...and it appears we have lost.) He broke off, and the cabin was silent for a long moment. (Well. What do you recommend?)

(Find a way to urge the guests off the *Orktes*, raise a warp bubble, and disappear, sir,) the security chief suggested.

(Mm. Let me consider the matter, then, I suppose,) Incke sighed. (No sell price, no new technology, no genetics harvested, and most of our food stores for the next month gone to pacify the 'guests.' Never mind my favorite bodyguard, dead. This has been a debacle. A complete and total debacle.) He waved a talon at the security chief. (Go. I will find a way to see to this. Bring me answers as to what he did, and how he did it. I will not have it happen again.)

The security chief left, and Incke slumped at his desk, wondering what to do next.

* * *

Zz'r'p, Qq'k'l called from his cabin, *we have a situation developing, and fairly swiftly.*

What is it? Zz'r'p asked, from the bed in his stateroom, where he was resting, now that Echo was safe aboard the *Genesis.*

The Cortians know Echo is gone, though they do not know where, or how. They have realized, however, that he is no longer aboard their ship. They are preparing to eject the crime syndicates that came to bid on Echo, and then they will ALL likely flee.

Meaning they will all escape, to try again another day, Zz'r'p realized.

Exactly. What shall we do? Should we not do SOMEthing to protect Echo and Omega, going forward?

Stand by, and let me consult a knowledgeable party on the matter, Zz'r'p said, rising from his bed and donning a tunic.

* * *

Omega? This is Zz'r'p, my dear girl. Are you busy?

Not particularly, she replied, leaning forward in her visitor chair to check on her partner/spouse. *Just sitting here with Echo.*

And how is he doing?

Okay, considering. He's sound asleep. Barely even a peep out of him through the bond. Between y'all and the pain meds, I think he's not hurting, at least.

That is...good, under the circumstances.

Yeah.

Might I take a few moments of your time, then? Could you come to my stateroom for a conclave?

Sure, Zz'r'p. What's up? she asked as she stood and slipped out of the semi-darkened room.

Well, as Qq'k'l put it to me, we have a situation developing, and rapidly.

Hm; okay. On my way.

* * *

"Huh," Omega pondered, as the Deltiri team—less Mm'l'n, who was still in the medlab helping block Echo's pain—watched her thoughtful response to the news. "Yeah, that won't do at all. But we're not in a position to really DO anything about it yet..."

"Has not Fox called for backup and support?" Bb'y'x asked.

"Yeah, he has, but they're not here, and won't be, for at least another hour or two, I'd estimate," Omega pointed out. "And that leaves...just us. And while we're not running a skeleton crew, the ship is still pretty understaffed, given my emergency summons."

"Precisely," Zz'r'p agreed. "We are one ship at half-strength, with a few fighter escorts. Granted, the *Genesis* is not just any battleship, and we have the advantage of surprise, since they are still unaware that we are here. But once we reveal ourselves, we are outnumbered. Fox may know more of our abilities than you or I, granted. But it seems foolhardy to risk the Division flagship, the crew, the Director, the man we came to rescue..."

"I hear you," Omega said, then her eyes brightened. "But I have an idea. See what y'all think of this..."

* * *

"Hm. That...would work," Qq'k'l averred five minutes later, after Omega finished explaining.

"It would," Zz'r'p agreed. "I am concerned for other matters secondary to the plan, but it would indeed solve the immediate problem." He eyed Omega. "It could put you into serious trouble, however."

"I'm willing to risk it, if it means keeping Echo safe from here on out," Omega declared. "Are YOU?"

"That is not the topic in question," Zz'r'p tried.

"Yes, it is. I'm willing to do this, regardless of consequences, because frankly, I don't see any other choice for me or for Echo, going forward. The question is, are y'all willing to go along with me and help me out with it?" Omega wondered. "If you're not, say so now. I understand, and I won't be mad, if the answer is no."

"Since Mm'l'n is not here, perhaps you should poll us as a team," Bb'y'x suggested.

"I think I shall," Zz'r'p agreed. "Stand by, Omega, while I do that."

"I ain't goin' anywhere," Omega pointed out.

* * *

"Fox?" Zz'r'p contacted the Director through the standard ship's intercom, a short time later.

Fox leaned over his desk and thumbed the intercom switch, glad for the diversion from interminable paperwork...especially in the wake of the successful rescue of his Assistant Director. *Which position,* he thought, *I am EXTREMELY glad the Cortians don't seem to know about. There'd be nothing left of him but a torso and a head by the time they were done, if they had.* Then he added aloud, "Go, alter khaver. I thought you were resting."

"I was. Something has come up."

"That doesn't sound good."

Zz'r'p's sigh was audible. "Do you have a moment for me to speak with you in person...and in private?"

"Of course. Can you come here? I'm in my office off the bridge."

"I shall be there shortly."

"I'll be waiting. Fox out."

"Zz'r'p out."

* * *

"Have a seat, my friend," Fox said, waving his hand at a visitor's chair as the Deltiri ambassador entered the captain's cabin. Fox moved to the door as Zz'r'p seated himself, glanced out, and caught Zero's eye. When that worthy focused on him, Fox gave him a subtle hand signal that said, *Don't interrupt unless it's an emergency,* and Zero nodded. Fox closed the door, moved to his desk chair, and sat. "There we are. Now we won't be interrupted. What's on your mind, Zz'r'p? Is everything all right with Echo, or is it something else?"

"It...is rather something else."

"Tell me, and if I can help, I will."

"Fox," Zz'r'p told the Director, "be aware that Omega has...plans...for the Cortians and the various crime 'bosses,' I believe she called them. And they are not good ones."

"What do you mean?" Fox wondered.

"I believe all I need to say is, 'They hurt Echo,' and you will understand," Zz'r'p said. "Remember what happened to Tt'l'k...but more...permanent. And terminal."

"Oy gevalt!" Fox exclaimed, shocked. "I mean, on one level I understand, but...we have them, dead to rights! All of them! The case is open and shut! There's no need for her to take justice into her own hands!"

"Is it truly open and shut?" Zz'r'p pondered, bland. "Is there no reason to act swiftly? We are one undermanned ship with at most a few small escorts, Fox, and there are two Cortian fleet vessels out there, ships of the line, and not to be scorned— plus easily half a dozen or more flagships of the various crime syndicates, also not small, and all with significant fighter escort squadrons as well. You KNOW the danger, or you would not have the *Genesis* so thoroughly cloaked and hidden. Yes, we have Echo onboard now, and yes, we now know what they did, and have several telepathic interrogators aboard, who have already begun our reports. But that is a long way from having them all in custody."

"We have backup en route."

"But by the time they get here, this lot may have all dispersed. They have been desperately searching for Echo for some time already, with considerable energy, and are beginning to realize he is not on the *Orktes*; they have tight-beamed a request to search the *Ramtum* also, but so far that search is, of course, fruitless as well...because Echo is NOT on either ship. Currently, they do not seem to realize that Echo had help in his escape; should they reach that conclusion, they will be looking for an infiltrator. More, the Cortians believe it unlikely that the various and sundry crime syndicates are responsible for his disappearance, in light of their behavior—it would logically be expected that, if one of those had acquired him, they would promptly withdraw and depart, post-haste. Since none of them have done so, the Cortians rightfully believe they are not responsible."

"Which, in turn, means somebody else took Echo," Fox realized.

"Precisely. So if they do not find Echo aboard the Cortian vessels, they may well 'hightail it outta here,' as Omega put it to me—ALL of them, Cortians, syndicates, and all. But were they to detect the *Genesis*, and recognize that the infiltrator likely came from us...well. We are greatly outnumbered. Even for all you have done with this very special vessel, it may not be enough, alone against a force of some ten battleships and very many more fighters."

"That's unlikely," Fox retorted. "We took on several times that number during the Battle of the Orion Nebula."

"I do not dispute it—though let me remind you that you had an entire fleet backing you up then—and you are probably right, though I do maintain that this dangerous possibility exists. And we both know that you do not have the manpower aboard now that you had then, so you cannot possibly run all battle systems at full capability...and Omega knows this; she is nothing if not strategically savvy, for Echo taught her very well. But the Cortians and their 'guests' are far more likely to flee, spreading out and taking different directions, and then we shall never find them." Zz'r'p shook his head. "And then, they may try this exact same tactic in future...against Echo AND Omega. No, Omega feels this must be done, and soon, or all is lost. And that...she will not tolerate."

"She's really that angry?"

"Every bit."

"Is it safe to talk to her?" Fox queried. "I mean, she shouldn't be angry at ME, but..."

"Yes, I think it will be safe for you, friend Fox," Zz'r'p noted. "You are, after all, 'Abba Fox' to her. But listen carefully to her, do not press too hard, and above all, think prudently and deeply about the being to whom you will be speaking."

A worried Fox nodded acquiescence.

"Take me to her," the Director ordered.

"Come with me," the Ambassador from Deltir replied.

* * *

Omega was in the sick bay of the *Genesis*, as Fox had expected, sitting at Echo's bedside. His wounds had been treated and bandaged, and he was unconscious from pain medication—as well as the Deltiri team's telepathic aid in relieving his pain through the nd't'lq, via a method known to them, but which she had discovered by accident while the Alpha One partnership had been stranded in a crashed spacecraft, the previous spring—but she held Echo's remaining hand and studied his injured face with a mingling of love, agony, and raw anger in her expression.

"Omega, tekhter, it's me," Fox said in a soft voice after a few moments. She looked up.

"Oh, hi, Fox," she murmured; then, seeing Zz'r'p behind the Director, added, "Oh. I guess Zz'r'p told you, huh?"

"Yes, he did. May I discuss it with you, tekhter?"

"You can, Fox, but my mind is made up," Omega noted, voice rising in volume even as her expression hardened.

"Tekhter, we have reinforcements coming swiftly," Fox pointed out. "They will be here in an hour, two at most."

"And you know what this lot can do in that length of time, if they decide that they've lost Echo," a calm Omega observed, cool. "By the time reinforcements can arrive, they'll have faded back into the damned shadows they came out of. And taken the *Genesis* out into the bargain, if they can find us. But if they don't find us now, then they'll just keep coming, and coming, and sooner or later, they'll off us, Echo an' me." She shook her head. "No. This has to be done, Fox."

"But Omega—"

"Fox, do you trust me?"

"Implicitly, meyn kind. As Echo would say, 'With my life,' were it needful," Fox said immediately. "You proved yourself to me long, long ago. Last Christmas, in fact, though I trusted you long before that. But I wonder if you are thinking quite clearly at the moment..."

"Then I need you to trust me, Fox. Trust me, and keep trusting me."

"But you cannot do that all by yourself, tekhter. You are skilled, and you are strong, and you have been 'enhanced'... but you are not QUITE superhuman. And I am not in a position to be able to help you, if you will not tell me your plans. And what I have heard of them second-hand does not put me in a good position to do so. Let alone to defend your actions in the aftermath." Fox shook his head. "We would all be either brain-bleached and ejected from the PGLEIA, or in your case, imprisoned, likely for the rest of your natural life."

"She will not be acting alone," Zz'r'p observed from behind Fox. "The entire Deltiri contingent aboard the *Genesis* is behind her, and will provide all the support she needs." He gave Omega a meaningful glance. "It will be...difficult, but we believe we can help her do this."

"You're HELPING her?!" Fox exclaimed, shocked. "But... it's illegal, meyn khaver!"

"TRUST me, Fox," Omega said, calm, meeting the anxious hazel eyes with a serene sapphire gaze.

"What did you do to 'convince' all the Deltiri, meyn kind?" he wondered, concerned.

"I 'talked' to them," she said, putting air quotes around the word with her fingers. "And they 'listened.' And went along. Because they saw my point, what I was trying to do...and agreed with it." She paused, then sighed. "Fox, you have my word, when I'm finished—when WE'RE finished—I'll turn myself over to you to handle as you deem fit in the aftermath. But we ARE going through with this."

"I can't talk you out of it?"

"No."

"Not even for Echo's sake?"

"This IS for Echo's sake."

"Then my hands are tied," Fox sighed. "You are not putting Echo in a happy position, daughter."

"Echo isn't in a happy position now, Fox." Omega gestured at the bandaged stumps, the big patch of gauze over the ruined eye socket.

"All right," the Director said with another sigh. "Do as you will. I have no real means to stop you, anyway, given I'm not a telepath."

"No, you're not, and yes, you're right."

A worried Fox glanced at Echo's motionless, battered, mangled form, and left the sick bay, headed for the bridge.

* * *

Omega, Zz'r'p, Mm'l'n, and Qq'k'l entered the bridge about ten minutes later. Fox started in surprise, then motioned for Sail to place a chair for the ambassador next to his command chair.

"Zz'r'p, if you please, my friend," Fox said. "I am afraid there is only one spare chair on the bridge, or I would provide for all of you."

"No need, friend Fox," Zz'r'p noted, waving Omega to the seat provided. "I think Omega will need it more than I or any of my contingent. The strain, after all, will be hers to bear."

"Where are the others?"

"In my quarters, preparing," Zz'r'p said. "Except for Bb'y'x, who just handed over with Mm'l'n. So she is now in sick bay, helping to remove Echo's pain."

"Why are you even here?" Fox wondered, deeply distressed.

"Because I wanted all of you to 'hear' what I'm about to do," Omega noted then, taking the chair. "And see what happens as a result."

Concerned glances shot around the bridge crew, and Fox closed his eyes, drawing a long, deep breath. Then he opened his eyes and met the clear sapphire gaze once more.

"Omega, my daughter in every way but blood, please stop this," he murmured.

"Trust me, Fox," she responded in kind, her demeanor peaceful and composed. "You KNOW me. THINK."

Fox paused, considering, for long moments, then he quirked an eyebrow. Omega returned the gesture, tilting her head to one side in a quizzical fashion, and he nodded very thoughtfully. Omega turned to the Ambassador.

"Zz'r'p, are you and your people ready?"

Zz'r'p hesitated for a moment with a distant gaze, evidently consulting his team telepathically. Finally he nodded.

"Yes, Omega, we are. Give the command, and we will obey."

"The command is given," Omega declared. Seconds later, everyone on the bridge heard her telepathic announcement, boosted with the help of the Deltiri.

This is Agent Omega of the Alpha One partnership, assistant chief of the Alpha Line special forces department of Division One. You are surrounded. My partner...and MATE, Agent Echo, chief of Alpha Line, is in my custody and being cared for medically. For the torture and maiming they inflicted upon him, the Cortians' lives are forfeit. They have three minutes to make peace with whatever deities they possess.

Those of you who came to purchase my partner-mate for your own heinous purposes, stand down now and surrender to PGLEIA forces, and you will be treated fairly. Refuse, stand with the Cortians, and I swear to you upon everything I deem holy, you will suffer their fate. You have fifteen minutes to decide. The Cortians...have two minutes.

The bridge crew spun to stare at her in shocked comprehension. Zero, the security chief and sometime captain for the *D1 Genesis*, went for his blaster, but Qq'k'l held up a hand in a *halt!* gesture, and Zero froze where he stood, unable to move, as the Deltiri locked up his voluntary nervous system.

You will not be allowed to interfere, Zz'r'p declared mentally to the bridge crew. *There is no time to argue. They already know that Echo is no longer aboard the Cortian vessel, anywhere; it is potentially a matter of minutes before the 'bidders' begin to flee, and the Cortians likewise. And then they will simply come back after Alpha One, again and again and again. It MUST be done now, or all is lost.*

"Pull up the video from the bugs I planted," Omega ordered, waving a hand at Sail, the communications officer. Sail threw a desperate look at Fox, who nodded confirmation.

"Pull it up, Sail," Fox verified the order in a tired voice, "and put it on the main screen."

"There are six bugs," Sail noted. "Split screen?"

"Split screen, meyn khaver."

* * *

Seconds later, the big, slightly-curved viewscreen at the front of the oval bridge depicted six different scenes, all from the Cortian ship which had held Echo:

The bridge of the *Orktes*, complete with captain and full bridge complement, several of whom seemed bewildered. The captain, however, had the equivalent of a scowl on his birdlike, hawk-beaked face.

The slave barracks, empty of all beings save a few guards, who were milling about in a confused, anxious fashion.

The brig, complete with guards and quite a few imprisoned—and angry/upset—crew members.

The ship's mess, which was full of perturbed crew members who had stopped eating.

The weapons banks, where grim Cortians were preparing to do battle...with they knew not what.

The hangar deck, where numerous now-frightened crime syndicate members were trying to escape in their personal shuttles...but no one could find the controls to the hangar doors, apparently thanks to a bit of 'assistance' from the Deltiri.

* * *

(Honored captain, what shall we do?) the Cortian helmsman wondered.

(Nothing,) Incke declared, waving a dismissive hand. (She is bluffing. This is the disgusting female escaped slave and possible consort to the captured prisoner. Likely the formal mate, back on the Tiniken planet, summoned her for assistance. She can do nothing to us.)

(With all due respect, sir, she is speaking in our minds.)

(I know this, fool,) the captain snapped. (Division One has many amazing technologies. But they cannot work miracles. She bluffs, hoping we will panic and surrender the *Orktes* and all its crew without a fight, when in all likelihood, she sits alone with the chopped meat that we made of her partner, in some carefully-hidden little ship, a goodly way off.) He shook his head. (No. She is helpless. We are absolutely certain that slave Echo is no longer aboard the ship?)

The helmsman murmured something into his headset mic, then listened for an answer.

(No sir, he is not. Of that, the security team is certain.)

(Then she may somehow have found her way aboard along with the proper guests and effected his rescue. The shields are up?)

(They are, honored captain. This has been prepared since the time when it was reported to me that slave Echo was missing, and I initiated it within moments of the female slave's message just now. If I had a target, I could already be firing, as well.)

(Good. Keep a watchful eye out for any target, but be careful not to fire upon our 'guests.' Oh, and have Acktrr the slave master placed in one of his own cells; there is no way the slave could have escaped, even with the help of his partner, without his treasonous participation. I will see to Acktrr later. Then plot a course to take us out of the galactic plane, in the general direction of Corta, and prepare to raise the warp bubble at my command.)

(What about our sister ship? What about the *Ramtum*?)

(It can see to itself, even as we do. It has served nothing more than escort duty on this mission, in any case. And that in a most perfunctory fashion. So I care not.)

(As you wish, honored captain.)

The Cortian captain sat back in his chair, lightly clacking his beak in thought, as he wondered how the escaped slave Omega had managed to free her consort, and what Acktrr had accepted as a bribe to assist.

* * *

Ready? Omega's mental voice came then, audible to the entire *Genesis* bridge crew. She checked her wrist chronometer. The tension on the bridge was palpable.

We are, Zz'r'p responded in like fashion, calm. Omega's eyes stayed focused on her chronometer for long seconds.

NOW, Omega abruptly declared...

...And suddenly every Cortian visible in any of the video

images dropped to the deck and lay, deadly still.

A gasp went up from the bridge crew, even as criminals of several species, still visible in the hangar deck video, began to panic. Omega 'spoke' to them again.

Members of the Rrgllbrrgll, Children of Ashdug, the Family Thing, and Gu'ursh tem al Ke!thas, you now have... she glanced back at her wrist chronometer, *twelve minutes to surrender, or you will meet the same fate.*

The *Genesis* bridge crew stared at each other in horror.

* * *

Moments later, Sail turned to Omega and Fox.

"Sir, ma'am, the Rrgllbrrgll have surrendered. Unconditionally. To a being. AND apologize profusely...for violating their oath to Lord Entiyti. Whatever that means. But they sure sound damn upset about it." His eyes widened, and he held up a finger in a *hold it!* gesture, putting the other hand to his headset earpiece, listening for long moments before murmuring a soft acknowledgement. He turned back to the two humans in charge. "Add the Family Thing into that. Except for the oath part, I guess."

"What about the Children of Ashdug, and the Gu'ursh tem al Ke!thas?" Omega pressed.

"There is a lot of comm traffic going back and forth between the *Orktes* and those organizations' flagships, but there has been no official surrender statement as yet," Sail noted.

"The *Ramtum* is starting to drift..." Cast observed.

"See if you can steady it with a tractor beam, without giving away our position," Fox ordered. "We don't want it drifting into another ship, but we don't want the lot of 'em to turn on us at this point, either."

"On it, sir," Boy responded, suiting action to word.

Omega glanced at her chronometer, then made a slight gesture at Zz'r'p, who nodded.

This is Agent Omega, she mentally broadcast once more. *Members of the Family Thing and the Rrgllbrrgll, your surrenders are graciously accepted, and you have my word, you will be treated well. Stand by to be boarded and taken into custody. Children of Ashdug, Gu'ursh tem al Ke!thas, you have six minutes left. Choose wisely.*

Seconds after that, Sail looked up.

"The Children of Ashdug have surrendered," he announced. "But Gu'ursh tem al Ke!thas is all but screaming defiance."

Omega nodded.

Gu'ursh tem al Ke!thas, she declared, *for your defiance, you now have only two minutes before you meet the doom of the Cortians. Consider your fate, and make the wise choice.*

She looked across the bridge at Sail, who listened intently to his earpiece.

"No ma'am," he responded. "Still defiance."

Omega looked at Zz'r'p, who quickly glanced at Mm'l'n and Qq'k'l , both of whom shook their heads.

"No, Omega," Zz'r'p said then. "They are firm. They will die rather than surrender."

"All right. May their wish be granted." Omega glanced at her wrist chronometer, then announced, "Thirty seconds. Twenty-five...fifteen...ten...five, four, three, two..." Omega looked back up at Zz'r'p, who nodded.

The bridge crew watched as all of the members of Gu'ursh tem al Ke!thas visible in the *Orktes* hangar bay dropped, motionless, to the deck. Omega turned to Fox.

"Sir, might I respectfully request that you prepare boarding parties suitable to taking into custody several rather meek crime lords and their entourages?"

Fox sighed.

"Zero, prepare the boarding parties," Fox ordered. Zero, finally released from his paralysis, eased his weapon back into its holster, stretched surreptitiously, and nodded.

"Sir," he added, "shall I prepare another large team for recovery, with a copious supply of body bags?"

Omega and Zz'r'p exchanged a glance, and the Deltiri nodded.

"Oh, that won't be necessary, Fox, Zero," Omega noted then, with a smirk. "Nobody's dead. Either on the *Orktes*, the *Ramtum*, or the Gu'ursh tem al Ke!thas ship."

Everyone on the bridge started in surprise, and even Fox blinked. Zero stared blankly at Omega and the Deltiri team.

"Tekhter?" Fox wondered.

"I told you to trust me, Abba Fox," she murmured in response, sobering. "With a great deal of help from the Deltiri team—who only agreed when I explained my non-lethal solution—all of the Cortians and the Gu'ursh tem al Ke!thas have been put into what amounts to telepathic comas. It just LOOKS like they're dead...to the other criminals on board. Once they're in custody, we'll wake 'em all up."

"It required a tremendous effort," Zz'r'p admitted, rubbing his temple with long fingers as if a headache loomed, "as well as the long-distance assistance of most of the embassy staff on Earth, simply because of the number of beings we had to affect. But it was done, and done well, and served the intended purpose of ensuring that the perpetrators could be taken into custody without bloodshed, and before anyone could flee."

"Please forgive the deception, all of you—especially you, Director Fox," Mm'l'n added, "but after discovering a rogue Deltiri aboard the *Orktes*—"

"He was a cousin of Tt'l'k's, and had evidently visited his cousin in the mental hospital, during which time Tt'l'k apparently 'programmed' him to take revenge upon Alpha One," Zz'r'p interjected, "save that Bb'y'x and I were able to 'deprogram' him..."

"...We could not be certain that none of the vessels had telepaths of their own on board, who would be reading the *Genesis* crew, even as we read them," Mm'l'n continued. "And if there were 'enemy' telepaths, we desired that they should 'read' what we wanted them to read, not what was actually about to occur. We lot," she indicated the Deltiri team and Omega, "had powerful telepathic blocks erected, but the rest of you did not, nor could not. And that was deliberate on our part, so that they might get the wrong impression. At this point in time, however, the bridge crew is shielded under a joint telepathic block, so that any telepaths working for the criminals will not know the real sequence of events, and thereby consider contravening the surrenders."

"More," Qq'k'l appended, "the 'dead bodies' will continue to appear dead to those who have surrendered, until such time as all are in custody. AND they are under the impression that Omega did all of it...without help."

"Which, we hope, will frighten the lot of them into letting

her and Echo alone, in future," Zz'r'p supplemented.

"Lotsa mind games," Omega noted with a wry, rather mischievous grin. "Layer upon layer. Serious damn game of telepathic poker."

"But your bluff was successful, youngling," Zz'r'p told her.

"Oh, by the Name," Fox breathed, eyes widening. "Omega, my dear girl? That was BRILLIANT."

"It was," Mm'l'n agreed.

"And here comes the PGLEIA backup we requested, dropping out of warp at full battle stations and ready for action," Sail noted, looking up from his comm console. "I've just informed them to stand down from general quarters and assist with taking everyone into custody. Other than a bit of surprise at finding matters well in hand, they've agreed to assist however we need it."

"Excellent," Fox said. "Zero, let me leave you to arrange the boarding parties exclusively from those backup reinforcements; we'll be headed to Earth as a medical emergency transport in just a few minutes—about as soon as you can set all that up, in fact. Well, as soon as that, and I hand over command to Wux. THEN we'll go."

"Very good, sir," Zero acknowledged. "And...Agent Omega? Your Excellency Zz'r'p? I...apologize. I should have known better."

Omega nodded; she and Zz'r'p exchanged another glance.

"No apologies are necessary, Agent Zero," Zz'r'p said. "We anticipated such an action, in any case. By your lights, and given the information you had, you acted appropriately."

"Thank you, sir."

"Sail, get Chief Wuxullian on the horn—he's in the lead ship of the reinforcement task force, right?" Fox ordered, and Sail nodded. "Good—and pipe it straight through to my office cabin, please. Ciphered maximum secure link, if you would be so kind. Omega, if you and Zz'r'p would attend? Yes, Zz'r'p, the rest of your contingent—on the bridge and in their state rooms—may stand down and rest as soon as the entire group of spacecraft is under control, and I promise I won't keep you long, either. Nor you, tekhter, but I need you both to explain your stratagem to Wux."

"All over it, sir," Omega agreed. "But let's hurry, please? I want to see Echo home and into a regen pod as soon as possible, before something messes up with all that."

"Right, and so do I," Fox averred. "So let's go."

* * *

Ten minutes later, PGLEIA Chief Wuxullian was duly apprised of matters.

"That was excellently done, my dear girl," Wuxullian observed. "And not so unlike the stratagem you and I devised to take in the leader of what would have been a formidable Veldorn crime syndicate, just recently."

"True, sir," Omega admitted. "But I kinda turned it a little wrong-side out, this time."

"Whatever works, youngling, whatever works," Wuxullian chuckled. "I can see where your bridge crew was likely quite perturbed, however, Fox."

"Well, they were," Fox admitted. "Zero even tried to draw down on them."

"He DID?! No one was hurt, I hope? What in the name of the Maker came of that??"

"Qq'k'l ob Sii'stek came of it," Zz'r'p noted. "He transferred to Division One recently, considering that we might need the assistance of another interrogator in our ranks to help ferret out any of Aggum's leftover plants, and there were indeed a few in the civilian offworld population...though no longer. So when I asked for volunteers from the embassy staff to attend me after Omega's plea for help, Qq'k'l was one of those. You may know that, unlike some species of telepaths, Deltiri have the ability to lock up the nervous system of another being without causing lasting harm to that being. And he is highly trained and particularly skilled at it."

"Ah. And he did that?"

"He did. Because we brainstormed the possible reactions before putting the plan into operation, and we expected that someone would do so. Given what we knew of the bridge staffing, it was likely to be Zero, as head of security for the vessel. So no one was shot, and the plan executed as intended."

"What about you, Fox?" Wuxullian wondered.

"What do you mean, Wux?"

"Did you know what was about to happen? Were you part of the plan?"

"No, I didn't," Fox admitted, "and at first I was worried, because I knew how angry Omega was, and is, at what was done to Echo, and I know how much she cares for him. But I consider those two as among the nearest thing I have any more to close family, and I know her. As she and the Deltiri team executed the plan, I began to suspect what was really happening...though I kept it to myself..."

"Save for mentally contacting me," Zz'r'p amended, "so that I might put a block around him, for the same reason we came to the bridge to execute it—in case they had other telepaths that could monitor us. Obviously prior to that, they had had no idea we were there...but as soon as Omega 'broadcast' her threat, that would change."

"So you figured it out?" Omega wondered, looking at Fox. "I have to admit, I was hoping you would. I told Zz'r'p to please watch for that, just in case."

"Which he did, and yes, I did," Fox admitted, laying a hand on her shoulder. "I didn't understand the full scope of the plan until afterward, but you were too calm to do what you were claiming to be doing, too...'zen,' I think Zebra would call it. I might have believed that you would kill them in righteous anger, but not in cold blood, tekhter. I've seen you play with children, both human and alien, and that was the face I saw before me on the bridge—not the face of fury, nor even the face of determined, grit-your-teeth-and-do-it for the greater good...but the face of someone who was at peace with what she was doing. And that, therefore, meant you were not killing. ANYone."

Omega gave him a slight, pleased smile, and Fox grinned.

"I know my tekhters," he observed. "Both of them. And that was one helluva good plan, tekhter. Some bluff, too."

"It was, indeed. And now we're mopping up the aftermath of your excellently-conducted operation," Wuxullian agreed. "So I believe you need to hasten back to Earth to see about having Echo patched up, right?"

"We do, sir," Fox confirmed. "The Cortians were none too gentle with him, and he will literally need some reassembly after this. Yes, Echo needs a bit of...putting back together, I'm afraid.”

“What? What do you mean?”

“I...whoa!” Fox began, then spun swiftly toward Omega, who had paled and wobbled. He grabbed her shoulders, steadying her. “Do you need to sit down, tekhter?”

“M-maybe,” the female Agent breathed. “I’m...just a little tired, and, and stressed, I guess.” She waved a hand in a vague fashion. “When you...started to explain, I...I remembered... finding Echo...”

“Ah. Allow me, Fox,” Zz’r’p murmured, as Fox saw Omega seated in a visitor chair before her knees buckled. “Omega, with your permission...?”

Omega simply nodded.

“Chief Wuxullian, let me show you the image in Omega’s mind of the moment she found Echo,” the Deltiri said.

Fractions of a second later, the Erikian let out a horrified, high-pitched squeak—almost an uncharacteristic scream—of dismay.

“Oh, great Maker,” he breathed, after a moment to halfway compose himself. “Putting back together, indeed.” He glanced down, then waved a hand. “Go. GO. I have matters in hand here. How is it you humans say—go put Dumpty Humpty back together again. If you cannot, then I am beginning to think it cannot be done anywhere.”

* * *

With that, Fox officially handed over the entire operation to him, and Fox, Zz’r’p, and Omega stepped back onto the bridge.

“Sir! Custody teams are in action as we speak,” Zero reported. “All from the other PGLEIA ships.”

“Excellent. And I have handed over control of the action to Chief Wux. Cast, set a course for Earth. Übermut, as soon as you see it come up in the navcomp menu, move out, and as soon as we’re clear of the task force, raise a warp bubble and take us home, at maximum emergency cruising. Sail, put your head together with Übermut, then notify the medlab at Headquarters of our ETA. Zero, you’re in charge; I’m heading with Omega down to the sick bay to check on Echo.”

“Roger that, sir,” came the acknowledgements from several voices.

"C'mon, Zz'r'p," Fox said, waving the Deltiri along with Omega to the doorway. "We'll drop you off at your stateroom along the way."

* * *

Fox and Omega followed behind Zz'r'p as that worthy entered his stateroom; within, the rest of the Deltiri awaited, save Bb'y'x, who had been—and was still—in the sick bay, on her shift of helping to keep Echo free of pain, and therefore was not allowed to be a part of the Cortian 'death' ruse.

"Thanks, guys," Omega murmured, intensely grateful. "That worked like a charm, an' everybody's pleased, including Chief Wux."

"That is very good, Omega," Jj'k'k said, offering her the Deltiri equivalent of a smile, as his eyes tilted up at the corners. "We are all pleased, as well."

"Hey, you were the anchor man," Omega told the Deltiri. "You have some serious brain power, there."

"He was indeed, and he does," Zz'r'p agreed. "That is why I was VERY glad when he volunteered to come with us. Finesse is excellent in its place, and certainly Jj'k'k can do that when required; but there is a time and place for sheer power, and he is the most powerful telepath I know, of any species. He is, indeed, what you call our anchor man."

"Well, it's done, and done damn excellently, and now you can all take some rest," Fox noted. "And thank you from myself, as well—and Chief Wuxullian sends his appreciation, also."

"Where are you going from here?" Mm'l'n asked then.

"We are headed to Earth, as fast as the *Genesis* can take us there," Fox said. "We want to put Echo into a regen bath while all the appropriate tissues remain viable or before anything becomes infected, and that means the *Genesis* is moving at emergency accelerations once more." He sighed. "I am seriously thinking we do need to put a red cross on it and just designate it a kind of interstellar ambulance, at this rate. Damnation, shit, merde, and farkakte."

"And that is good, but I meant, where are the two of you going right this moment," Mm'l'n clarified. "For if I am not mistaken, Omega is at least as weary as any of us."

Fox turned to his Agent.

"I'm awful tired, yeah," Omega confessed. "But I don't think I'm going to get much rest until we put Echo into a regen pod, Fox."

"You have hardly been in your cabin since you came aboard, meyn kind," Fox reprimanded, but gently.

"I know," she murmured, dropping her gaze to the floor in embarrassment. "I'm sorta gettin' afraid to go to sleep a little bit, if I'm honest. I'm asleep, Echo gets kidnapped. I'm asleep, he gets his hand and foot whacked off, and his eye gouged out. What happens the next time?"

"No, no, that will not do," Zz'r'p said in a soft voice. "You know that is not a reasonable thought, youngling."

"I know it, but that doesn't stop that little voice in the back of my head from asking it anyway," Omega pointed out.

"Omega," Fox said, considering, "would the two of you— you and Echo, I mean—like to leave off doing field work? Especially now that you're married? I can bring Echo into the directorship work a good deal more than I have, as yet; I might even take up Pul on his recent offer to return to my old position, and bring Zebra with me. That would leave Echo in charge of the Division. And you can then take over running the department...from your desk. And that, in turn, would keep you both safer."

"Hold onto that thought, Fox," Omega said, running a lightly-trembling hand over her face. "I don't WANT to leave field work, and I know Echo wouldn't want that either, not yet, anyway. But I'm afraid it might not end up being a case of what we WANT to do. Let's just, just wait and see...how the regen turns out."

"Point made," Fox said, nodding in sympathy and under-standing. "All right. But I'll work something up to that effect in the way of a plan to move forward, and we can have it in our hip pockets, just in case. Will that do?"

"I think that's a good idea," Omega agreed. "But...don't take this the wrong way...I hope we don't have to pull it out. At least not at this point in our careers."

"Understood, and no offense taken," Fox said, laying a light hand on her shoulder. "The two of you are my best Agents, my two top Agents in fact—though no one heard me say that; I don't want to discourage the others, or seem to play favorites, and it's almost a toss-up anyway, the top three or maybe four teams are so close in skill—but I know you and Echo better, and I like having you to lean on when the going becomes complicated. If you two leave field work, that means that Alpha Two and Four have to seriously step up to the plate. Not that they don't already. But you know what I mean."

"Yeah," Omega said. "It's the difference between three top teams, and just two."

"Exactly."

"And she has managed to divert all of us," Zz'r'p noted then. "When are you going to rest, Omega?"

"When I get so tired that I simply can't stand up any more, or keep my eyes open any longer," Omega declared. "But for now, I thought I'd just go sit with Echo. I'll feel better there anyhow, rather than in an empty cabin."

All right, Zz'r'p told her. *But if you need me, CALL.*

You're tired, too, Omega protested. In the background, Fox raised an eyebrow as he became aware that the counselor was conversing privately with his patient.

Not as tired as you are, Zz'r'p pointed out. *I have not been bearing Echo's pain or his presence—his personal angst, if you will—continually. You have.*

Not all the time, not full-on.

No. But it is in the background of your thoughts continually; HE is in the background continually. I can sense that. And while he is unconscious, his subconscious is still connected to you, still depicting his personal anxieties and fears to you.

I'm dealing. I'm fine.

For now. But you will not be for long, if you do not REST.

It's okay. I figured on a little psychic cuddle time, she told him. *That...seems to be good for him AND me.*

Ah. That is better. Very well. That will do, for now. It is a soothing, calming means of 'being' together, when it is all pared down to the essentials. And that is restful, in itself.

I thought so, yeah.

But you still need to sleep at some point.

I know, and I will, I promise. I just...have to, kinda, be ready for it. If you understand me.

"Yes, I do. Off with you, then," Zz'r'p declared aloud. "You have but to call if you need me. You know that."

"Okay," Omega capitulated.

"Let's go, yung froy," Fox said, and they headed for the sick bay together.

* * *

After they left, the five Deltiri shared mental notes for a moment in a kind of rapid debrief, then headed out for their own quarters aboard the big spacecraft. Mm'l'n stayed behind for a few minutes.

She is exhausted, is she not? she wondered. *Omega, I mean?*

She is, Zz'r'p said. *And while she is admittedly a little afraid to sleep, for the reasons she stated, she KNOWS she is tired—'bone-tired,' as she puts it—and is beginning to welcome the thought of rest. I think, when she is ready, she will sleep, and do so willingly. She may need to burn off a bit of adrenaline and excess energy first, but sooner or later, she will sleep. I also think that being here, aboard the ship, with her friends and 'family' around her and Echo beside her, protected and safe, will help ease her into that relaxed state where sleep will come more easily.*

I hope you are right. She can, and has, gone for long periods without sleep. Like her mate, she has great willpower. But that does not mean it is good for her.

No, it is not, Zz'r'p told his assistant. *But I have just had an idea. Stand by one moment while I pass it to Zebra; she can, perhaps, have it enacted before Omega and Fox reach sick bay.*

Mm'l'n waited for a few minutes, then Zz'r'p 'returned' to the discussion.

All right, he told her. *That is taken care of. She has at least gone looking to see if such a thing exists.*

What? Mm'l'n wondered, and Zz'r'p showed her a mental picture. *AH!* she said, delighted. *YES! It is perfect!*

They began to laugh.

Chapter 8

When Fox and Omega reached Echo's room in the med-lab, they found him resting peacefully...in a considerably larger bed.

"What the hell?" Fox wondered, as he and Omega moved to Echo's side, and Zebra came in with Yorker.

"Oh good, we finished it just in time," Yorker said with a grin.

"What's going on?" Omega wondered. "Why is Echo in such an oversized bed? I know he's tall, but he's not WIDE!"

"No, but Zz'r'p contacted me with an idea just a few minutes ago, and it was a good one, I thought," Zebra said, matching Yorker's grin. "Because THIS bed is just big enough for TWO bodies, not one."

"We know you've been having trouble settling enough to sleep, Omega," Yorker said, voice quiet, attitude respectful. "And the good Lord knows, you have every right, given the... shit...that's gone down on you two. But we all thought that, if you could rest next to Echo, knowing that you're both safe here, with all of us looking after things FOR you, for a change, you might be able to relax and rest."

"And that...is a capital idea," Fox pronounced. "And I do solemnly and officially approve it."

"Good! From the Admiral, no less, so it's now officially legal on the *Genesis*. And we thought so, too, when Zz'r'p recommended it," Zebra agreed. "So Yorker and I set out to dig through the medical stowage to find one of the beds for the larger species of sentients, and maneuvered it in here, made it up, and transferred Echo into it, just before you got here. I even fetched a set of some of the nice, stretchy scrubs for you to use as pajamas, Meg, because I know you're reserved and modest that way, and there'll be medtechs coming and going to tend to Echo. No, no," she said, holding up a staying hand as Omega started to protest. "You don't have to climb in the bed right now. You need to wind down a bit, anyway, and I totally understand that. We just want to have things ready for when you do finally run out of steam, girl! In the meantime, I had one of the other medtechs bring in a nice comfy chair, rather than that ol' straight-backed visitor chair, and put it over there, where you can sit beside the bed and hold Echo's hand if you want to. It's not a recliner like I could make it be in the medlab, 'cause this is a spacecraft, and the chairs have to lock to the deck. But it's way more comfortable than the regular chair."

"So sit there an' unwind," Yorker tag-teamed Zebra, "and then, when you just can't sit up any more, climb into bed next to your hubby, there, and get some shut-eye."

"But put on the scrubs before you're to the point of falling over," Zebra said with a grin. "I don't wanna have to put stitches in your face just 'cause you got tangled up in the pants and fell down."

Omega snorted in amusement.

"Okay," she agreed, to everyone's surprise. "I'll have to be a little careful not to whack any of his injuries once I go to bed, but..."

"Nope," Zebra said, grin growing wider still. "Done thought of that. We put splint-things on the, um, the stubs, and you'll note his face is padded real good. Unless you kidney-punch him or something, you can't hurt him."

"So tekhter, matters are taken care of," Fox declared. "You and Echo are both safe. Can you trust the rest of us to look after you both for a few hours?"

Omega looked up into Fox's eyes; hazel gaze met sapphire. Abruptly that sapphire gaze sparkled far more than usual.

"I think that would be great, Abba Fox," she whispered in a wobbly voice, biting her lip to maintain control. "Thanks, y'all. You have no idea how much that appeals, right now."

"Good. Then that is what we'll do. Now, set that little tuchus of yours down in the chair, there." Fox pointed, and Omega obeyed. "Zebra, bubeleh, wherever you've stashed those scrubs, please lay them across the foot of the bed so our adoptive daughter can find them easily, and...where did India go?"

"I sent her off to spend some time with Romeo, a while back," Zebra said. "She did the bulk of the wound cleaning and rebandaging, and it..." She broke off.

"What?"

"I should have helped, instead of going off to see what needed doing about the hand and leg bones," Zebra said, contrite. "She didn't have quite the objectivity needed to work on one of her best buddies like that. It was rough on her."

"Yeah," Yorker confirmed. "She took it hard."

"Aw," Omega murmured, sympathetic and concerned. "Is she all right?"

"I think she will be," Zebra noted. "But I knew better; that's why she didn't take part in your debridement after the Cortians burned you. I was just..." She raked a hand over her face. "I'm not exactly unaffected, either, if I'm honest. I was about frantic to figure out how to best keep the bones viable and use 'em as a framework to help reconstruct Echo's hand and leg. And in the doing, I...let her down."

"No," Omega said, rising, coming over and taking the physician's hand in both of hers. "Sometimes you have to let us do what we gotta do, Zebra, hon. She didn't ask for help, did she?"

"No. In fact, she told me that the best division of our effort was what we did. I know more about the regen procedure, see, and she used to be an ER physician, so we thought it made sense..."

"Which is correct," Fox averred. "It's possible she didn't realize it would upset her like it did."

"I was there," Yorker observed, "and I think that's exactly what happened, Fox."

"What did she do?"

"She broke down and cried afterward," Zebra admitted. "Like, hard. Which was when I sent for Romeo—he had been down with Weapons Control, making sure everyone knew how to take out a Cortian ship, if it came to that—and told him to take her off to their cabin and make her relax. Whatever it took, just make her relax."

"Like what you're doing for me, now," Omega observed.

"Yup," Zebra agreed. "And to be honest, I'm really regretting that we don't have a third physician aboard. Because I'm starting to need a little down time, too."

Omega pursed her lips and stared thoughtfully into space. Fox, Zebra, and Yorker glanced at each other.

"Is she...?" Yorker wondered.

"Looks like it," Zebra agreed.

* * *

Mm'l'n, are you there? Omega wondered.

Yes, Omega. Is everything all right?

It is. I was just wondering something.

What?

Didn't you say at some point that you used to work in a hospital?

I did. Before I entered the diplomatic service, I was a physician. In fact, I was a diplomatic physician before I became a diplomat, proper.

Do you have any experience working on humans, or at least humanoids? Opdips?

A bit. Why?

Because India's wiped, and Zebra's getting that way fast, and we could use a third shift in sick bay. And don't have one.

Ah. I see. Well, if you will give me a few hours to rest, I will come down and see about lending a hand. That is easier than telepathic broadcast OR pain reduction, anyway.

That'd be great! Omega declared. *Thank you.*

You are very welcome. I know what it is to work long emergency shifts, and I will be glad to help.

* * *

"Okay, you have a shift relief coming in a few hours," Omega told the others. "Mm'l'n used to be a doctor, and she's had some experience treating humans. If you can hold out until she can catch a couple hours' snoozing—what with their mental abilities, Deltiri don't need nearly as much sleep as humans—she'll be in here."

"That works," Zebra declared. "Thanks, honey."

"I think that's my line, to all of you," Omega decided.

"Why don't you wait on that until we have Echo patched up," Zebra said, suddenly uncertain.

Omega sighed.

* * *

"What surprises me," Fox observed, as he sat with the Deltiri ambassador in his captain's cabin several hours later, after Zz'r'p had had a chance to sleep a bit; the two were discussing matters in private, even as the *Genesis* rushed for Earth, "is how calm Omega is over all this. I mean, given how she feels about Echo, you can see why, for a bit there, I expected the plan you lot executed to be...real."

"Indeed," Zz'r'p agreed.

"In fact, during the ruse, she was as calm as I've ever seen her. Yet I know, because I've talked to Zebra, that the anxiety medication Omega has been taking is not THAT strong," Fox continued. "It isn't a full-on tranquilizer, just something to help her settle on her own. Are you helping her to stay calm? What's keeping her from wanting to kill something?"

"I am helping," Zz'r'p admitted. "At her own request, let me note. But even that is insufficient. She is FIERCELY angry at what was done to Echo. I think it was very wise of you to assign prisoner duty to our backup craft, while we take Echo home."

"Because it keeps her away from the Cortians?" a shrewd Fox noted. "Yes, I thought about that. It was one of several reasons why I did it that way. Frankly, it kept ALL of us away from the Cortians. Too many people on this ship know Echo quite well, and are NOT happy with the crew of the *Orktes*. Not at all. For instance, I shudder to think what Romeo might have done, but if we'd participated in the mop-up, he'd have insisted. It was...simply the best way."

"Yes. And that was wise, all of it. But Omega? I think we may need to watch out for the anger manifesting, at some point."

"Understood."

* * *

About an hour later, Fox was alone in his captain's cabin, working on a formal report of events to PGLEIA Chief Wuxullian, when he felt the touch of a familiar mind.

Fox, Zz'r'p notified him, *do you have access to the ship's security videos?*

I do, Fox replied. *Why? What's going down that I need to see?*

Anger management, I suspect, came the answer. *I have*

200

been quietly, ah, 'monitoring' matters, in my capacity as counselor, and I think it is coming to a head. Pull up the video on the ship's fitness center. I expect you will eventually want the dojo room, if I am reading matters correctly, but for now, the main gymnasium should do.

Roger that, Fox agreed, and punched several buttons on his virtual desktop, even as a wall screen lit. A few more keystrokes, and two desktop speakers extruded, allowing for him to hear what was going on as well, though he kept the volume low, in deference to a certain Agent's privacy and the bridge crew just outside his office.

* * *

Omega entered the fitness and training center aboard the *Genesis* and headed straight for the manager's office.

"Hey, Chain," she addressed the buff, muscular manager of the onboard gym and training center. The fact that this facility kept agents honed and prepped for battle meant that Chain tried to ensure he was along for every mission of the *Genesis*, in order to help the agents aboard stay ready for anything that was thrown at them. He was currently attired in black shorts, black perforated t-shirt, and black high-top athletic shoes with white socks, though a full Suit—with shoulder holster for a proto-cyclotron blaster—hung from a couple of hooks on the wall of his tiny office; Chain was anything but a gym rat.

"Hey, Omega," the manager responded with a slight smile. "Um, how's Echo?"

"The same—a mangled wreck," she sighed, and Chain winced. "At least we have him pretty much outta pain right now. We're headed back to Earth at speed, to try to put him into a regen bath as fast as we can; Zebra thinks we can regrow the missing parts without too much residual damage. She hopes, anyhow. Listen, um, speaking of which..."

"Yeah, whatcha need, hon?"

"Is anybody in the dojo room?"

"No, not right now."

"Good. I want it for the next...let's say two hours, and if it's shorter than that, I'll let you know when I'm done. Can do?"

"Ohhh-kay," Chain murmured, studying, then annotating, the electronic scheduling tablet. "I don't have any reservations on it, so yeah, that oughta do..."

"All right. It's mine for two hours."

"Okay, got it. What else you need, anything?"

"I don't have my gi; how strict are y'all about...?"

"Won't be a problem," Chain said, waving a hand in dismissal. "Sometimes we have aerobics classes in there. And if you don't have workout wear, I can provide that, too."

"Great. Lemme have a set of workout wear, then," Omega decided, "and...do you have any, like, OLD pads and bags and whatnot, for kickboxing and general martial arts?"

"What do you mean, 'old'?" Chain wondered.

"I mean stuff that you were gonna trash, that it won't hurt if it gets damaged."

"Mmph," Chain grunted. "Somebody needs to vent a little, huh?"

"Oh HELL yes." Omega's face hardened momentarily.

"Yeah, I can drag out some old stuff," Chain agreed, sympathetic. "We just got in the replacements shortly before Fox took the *Genesis* out to help you find Echo, and I set 'em up while we were en route and stuff. But I can pull out the old stuff from storage—I was gonna trash 'em once we got back to Earth—and you can whale away at it, if you really just want to. You're welcome to use the new stuff, though. It's better."

"No, trust me. Put out the old stuff," Omega maintained. "You'll be sorry if you don't."

"Ha! If you say so," Chain laughed.

* * *

Ten minutes later, Omega emerged from the small locker room, attired in leggings and t-shirt; her feet were bare. She gave Chain a thumbs-up to let him know that it all fit, and he returned it.

"Everything's set for you, just like you wanted it, Omega," he said from the reception desk. "Go blow off some steam. I'm sure you could use it, gal."

"All over it," Omega noted, face hardening once again.

She turned and entered the martial arts room.

* * *

The first thing she did was to survey the equipment, planning her 'workout.'

There were three floor-standing heavy bags, a fourth that was a human-shaped torso bag, and one hanging heavy bag, scattered in a loose circle around the room. In the far corner hung a speed bag. To her wry, bleak amusement, Chain had even gone so far as to spray-paint the 'head' of each bag in a bright canary yellow, quick-dry paint; a few crude swipes with a fat black marker had provided reasonable facsimiles of Cortian faces.

At least Chain got the idea, I guess. Mm, she thought, considering. *It's all pretty much standard boxing and kickboxing stuff. Wish at least one of those was a heavy-duty muay thai bag. This 'workout' might not last as long as I'd hoped.*

She moved to the center of the room and prepared for her workout.

* * *

Omega stood silent in the center of the padded floor, and bowed at the mirror along the back wall. Pulling her body into a slight horse stance, arms cocked near her waist, hands loosely fisted, she began to practice katas, starting with the white belt katas and going slowly, moving without pause from one form to the next, and working through higher and higher belt levels, gradually increasing her speed as she warmed up and loosened taut, tense muscles. Given she had had a black belt years before encountering Echo and being sucked into the Agency, this did not require great thought, but she concentrated on the moves anyway, letting her mind and body flow through the movements, and only increasing the speed when she felt that flow.

But by the time she reached the brown belt katas, her hands and feet were beginning to blur with the speed of their motion, as she struggled to vent all the pain and sheer, raw fury she held inside. Tears trickled down her cheeks, borne of mingled hurt and anger over what had been done to her beloved's body. But she was not consciously aware of that physical expression of her emotions; the sapphire eyes were focused on something far away, and she deliberately blanked out all reasoned knowledge of recent events as she placed her entire focus on the movements of her body...and the excess energy and emotion she desired to release.

By the time she reached the katas reserved for black belts,

Omega moved with all the efficient, fluid grace and agility of a professional ballet dancer—save for the fact that every movement was precise, finely honed...and VERY lethal.

* * *

Fox watched the video, vaguely aware that Zz'r'p was, with his permission, also viewing the scene through the Director's eyes and mind.

"Well, this is interesting," he decided, as he watched Omega warm up, gradually increasing the speed of her movements as she did so. "And rather impressive; I think I see what Echo means when he says it can be a little bit like watching a science fiction movie. I don't think I've ever seen her do a solo martial-arts workout bef— oh shit!"

* * *

Suddenly Omega let out a bloodcurdling scream, simultaneously unleashing a powerful heel kick at the closest kickboxing stand. The battered, worn, and half-rotten vinyl of the pad's cover split under the force of the impact, and the stand itself, despite being heavily weighted, skidded several feet across the floor of the gym, rocking slightly under the impact of the kick's spinning motion. Two more carefully-timed kicks and a punch exacerbated the wobble of the stand, and moments later, and with one more powerful high kick near its top, it overbalanced and fell over with a loud thud.

Seconds later, the door to the room burst open, and an alarmed Chain stood in it, drawn by the sound of the scream followed mere seconds later by the stand falling, and worried Omega had been hurt. He stood and watched in amazement as Omega, unaware of the observer—either in the room, or monitoring the security video—continued her internal and external battle.

Omega then spun into a furious fighting routine, throwing a flurry of kicks, punches and knife hand strikes at the various heavy bags as she advanced steadily around the room.

The old torso bag went next, as a large split appeared in the side of the vaguely-humanoid form with her first blow, which was a powerful, chambered straight punch, thrown with the mass of most of her body behind it. The bag was designed to be taken down like a standard biped, so it was not as heavily weighted in the base as the first bag, and she threw a snap kick to the head, then twisted and hit the floor, kicking the base in the opposite direction, effectively taking its 'legs' from beneath it. It toppled onto its side, spinning away across the floor, the side of the dummy head stoven inward. Omega kipped to her feet and kept going.

* * *

Holy shit, Fox thought. *Zz'r'p, are you SEEING this?*

I am, friend Fox, the Deltiri responded, *thanks to your courtesy in allowing me to 'use your eyes,' as Omega would say. This is...most impressive.*

And that's an understatement.

You do understand that what you are seeing is NOT all her 'enhancements,' yes?

It's not? What, then, the adrenaline and anger?

Most definitely. In fact, it is MOSTLY adrenaline at this point. She is choosing a private means of venting, and she IS venting...unleashing everything, all the anger and pain, all the tension and pent-up stress and adrenaline, all at once, as best she can. And there is a lot of 'all of it.' Especially after recent months.

But I don't think she knows anyone is watching.

No, I can confirm that. If she knew, she would stop immediately, rather than let someone see her 'operating at maximum,' as I have heard Echo put it. She is not even aware of the gymnasium manager in the doorway. She is only aware of the pain, the anger, and the...targets. And in her mind's eye, each of them is a yellow-plumed avian. In fact, Zz'r'p corrected himself, *let me see...yes. It does not require more than a cursory surface scan to discover that it is the SAME Cortian face each time. I expect this was probably Echo's keeper, an identity she likely gleaned from him through the nd't'lq, and thus the being responsible for his current condition...*

And the Deltiri mentally showed Fox a Cortian face.

Mm, Fox hummed to himself, and the sound was almost a growl. *Zz'r'p, can you reach Chief Wux from here?*

Quite probably. Why? You wish me to ensure he watches out for this particular Cortian?

Exactly. That and any of its associates.

I can do that.

The two were silent, as Omega continued her fierce workout onscreen. Moments later, Zz'r'p spoke again.

All right. Chief Wuxullian is apprised of the identity of that particular Cortian, and will ensure it is telepathically interrogated VERY thoroughly, and consequent to that, if the interrogation verifies that it is, in fact, personally responsible for the torture of Echo, it—and any colleagues involved, as well as the captain of the Orktes*—will be tried for barbarous and heinous crimes against Agent Echo. There is some discussion under way as to whether to include the captain of the* Ramtum *in those charges, but that is none of my concern, so I left it be.*

Excellent. Now we have something to tell Omega later, which might make her feel a bit better.

True. You are aware she was debating about asking to participate in the execution of sentencing on the prisoners?

No, I wasn't, Fox replied, worried. *Have YOU discussed it with her?*

I have. For she approached me as her counselor, asking for advice. I advised against it, for her own sake. I told her that, while it might give her a sense of satisfaction in the short term, it would do her no good in the long run. And might eventually cause her objectivity to suffer.

What did she say to that?

It will likely please you to know that I only confirmed her own conclusions. She has decided NOT to be involved. In fact, she is not sure she even wants to give testimony at the trials, because she does not want to even SEE those sadistic creatures. For which I cannot say that I blame her. And certainly Echo will not be able to do so; he will likely still be under medical care, even as the tribunals convene. Which means Omega needs to be at his side, to provide a legal voice for him, for his care.

True.

So I offered to provide their testimonies as telepathic interrogation reports, and she has accepted this offer, for herself and for Echo, as his duly-appointed spokesbeing while he is under medical care.

Good. So after she finishes this meshuginah little 'work-

out,' Fox jerked a thumb at the viewscreen, which still showed Omega taking out bag after bag, while Chain gaped, *she should feel better, eh?*

Only marginally.

But...

Stop and think, Fox. How would YOU feel if what was done to Echo had been done to Zebra instead? How do you feel about the specific Nazis who killed your genetic family? How do you feel about the Nazis in general?

Fox's thoughts came to a dead halt, as a slow blaze of fierce anger welled up at the notions the Deltiri had just presented.

And that is my point, Zz'r'p noted, interrupting and derailing that particular train of Fox's memory, much to his private relief. *Omega's beloved mate and partner was tortured at their hands, Fox. And she was the only one of us capable of mentally 'sticking with him,' as she put it, of handling the pain that he was experiencing...and she was also the one who went in and brought him out. SHE was the one who discovered his true, full condition, Fox. Not any of the rest of us. You have not seen the image seared into her mind...but I have, and I showed it to Chief Wuxullian; remember his reaction? The hardened, seen-it-all head of the PGLEIA...cried out in horror. Now, think about how that would make YOU feel, in Omega's shoes. Then tell me: do you think one session of 'tearing up jacks' as she calls it, is going to relieve those emotions?*

...No. No, it won't. Because it took me YEARS to deal with what I saw in the concentration camps.

Exactly. Unfortunately, you did not have a telepathic counselor working with you, but I believe I can help her work through it a bit faster than you did. And with your assistance and experience—via a caring, trusted shoulder for her to discuss matters, compare reactions, and the like—factored into her recovery, possibly faster still. But it will not be immediate, or anywhere close. Perhaps months. If all goes well. And then there is Echo's reaction to his ordeal...

Mmph. Right. Do everything you can for 'em, alter khaver.

I plan to, and I am.

Good male.

Thank you. I do my best.

And it shows.

* * *

Chain finally gained control of his astonishment and slipped back out of the dojo, quietly closing the door behind himself, before Omega could become aware of him. He went back to his office and sat down in his desk chair, still staring off into space in a kind of awe at what he had just seen. Just then, the ship's intercom bleeped. He hit the mic button.

"Fitness center. Chain here."

"Chain, this is Fox."

"Hello, sir. What can I do for you?"

"When Omega is finished with her, ah, 'workout,' please put the equipment back into storage, and be prepared to transfer it to the gym at Headquarters, if you would."

"Ah, uh, you, um...you're watching?"

"I am. Through the security system video. She is, after all, one of my top Agents, the assistant head of Alpha Line, and her everyday skills are pretty damn high-level. But right now, I think...well, you know I gave Omega away at her wedding to Echo?"

"Yes sir. Everyone realizes she views you as a kind of father figure. I gather she doesn't have a family of her own, outside the Agency?"

"No, she does not, and yes, I am. And I am fond of her as well; she and Echo, as well as several other agent teams... well, the whole Agency, really, but that handful, especially... somehow Omega managed to put together a little family for us within the Agency. So...I'm trying to watch out for her, as best I can, at any rate. Echo was not merely captured by the Cortians, you see; he was tortured by them...and she...well. I'm making sure she has help handling it. I can well imagine, based on some things in my own past, what she is feeling right now, and the levels of adrenaline she needs to work off. And...you know what feats adrenaline can enable us to do, let alone what havoc it can wreak within the body if not adequately burned off."

"Oh. So THAT explains it. Damn. That's some serious stress burning in there, then. And...so, what—you want the old, battered equipment for her to beat up on, back at HQ?"

"Exactly. It's only going to be worse battered by the time she's finished with it, anyway. And I can say from personal experience that there is a certain satisfaction to actually managing to split a seam on a heavy bag, or knock over a weighted kickboxing stand. Satisfaction that she needs, and is feeling right now—let alone the exertion, the burning off of all that stress which you rightly note...except that stress isn't going to go away any time soon. So that's how I'm approaching it with her. Let her tear it up completely, if it helps her, then we can throw it out when she's done."

"Good point. Yeah, I can do that. Make sure the agent running the gym at HQ knows it's coming, otherwise he or she is gonna be pissed at me for givin' 'em junk."

Fox laughed.

"I'll do that, Chain, don't worry. I've been in communication with her counselor, and he wants her to have that as an outlet, so it'll be done formally. We might even put in a private little workout room for this very thing, via the space warp, so she doesn't feel self-conscious; she can go in there all by herself, 'kill' a few pretend bad guys bare-handed, bash hell out of the bags for an hour or so, and generally work out her anger, at those times when it's getting to be a bit too much for her to handle otherwise. Come to think on it, Echo might want it, too, when all is said and done, and he's able to do such workouts again. So...yes, it'll be done formally. No problem there, zun."

"Okay, good. I'll have it ready after we arrive back on Earth; meantime, I'll leave it all set up, in case she needs to come back down and blow off steam again, before we get there."

"That sounds like a very good idea, and I approve. Fox out."

"Chain out."

* * *

Omega went through all of the heavy bags, even deliberately managing to knock the hanging bag off its hook, though that took some doing, and several coordinated, sequential kicks and punches at specific angles. With an effort—there was a REASON they were called 'heavy bags'—she reset everything, and went through the entire circuit again, with similar

209

results. When she was done, the old, heavy bags were indeed rather decidedly the worse for wear.

Then she battered the speed bag in the corner until it split an already-frayed seam, and called the workout at an end.

She grabbed the towel she had left on the rack by the door and mopped her sweaty, dripping face, then exited the dojo. Chain was waiting nearby.

"Um, hi," she murmured. "I, uh, I'm afraid I did do a little bit of damage to the bags, Chain. But no mirrors were broken." Omega gave him a crooked, slightly sheepish smile.

"Oh, that's impossible," the gym manager noted, returning the smile with one that was more open. "There's a soft force field about an inch and a half in front of 'em for just that purpose. You couldn't break one if you tried, 'cause you can't REACH it. Um, I guess you really had some adrenaline up, huh? I heard a couple 'a REALLY loud thuds..."

"Oh HELL yes," Omega declared, succinct and decided. "But really, don't freak out when you see what I did. See, several of the seams were badly frayed, an' the vinyl covers on a couple of the bags were kinda rotten. So it wasn't really that hard to create the damage I did. To tell the truth, it felt pretty damn good, actually seein' the bags take damage; they don't, usually. I mean, it's not like," she chuckled, rueful, "I have super powers or anything."

Chain opened his mouth to say something, then evidently thought better of it and shut it again.

"Right," he agreed. "Be aware that, um, when Fox found out you were blowin' off some steam in here, he recommended I have the old equipment transferred to your gym at HQ, so you could bust 'em up real good. He thought it might do you some benefit, havin' stuff to break for a while, I guess."

"That's...a fairly decent idea, to tell the truth," she decided. "Oh, and I loved the decorations you put on 'em. That was perfect."

"Fit pretty good, huh?" Chain grinned. "Gave you some incentive to really get into the workout?"

"Oh, you have NO idea."

"Want me to fire up the hot tub for a quick soak, after all that? I mean, like I said, I heard a couple thuds and whatnot,"

Chain tried. "It might help with any residual soreness. And you need to be able to look after Echo, not go hobbling around because you put a hitch in your gitalong, trying to vent."

"Eh, good point," Omega considered. "But I can't take long. I need to head back to the medlab. I just," she shook her head and then sighed. "I needed...They want me to rest and all, but I...I had too much going on inside, and...I mean, I sat there beside the bed for as long as I could, but I didn't want to pace in Echo's hospital room, not with him there, needing to rest an' not be disturbed..."

"No, I understand it," Chain murmured, daring to lay a light, sympathetic hand on her shoulder. "Don't feel like you have to explain anything to me. Fox already...told me a little. If I were in your shoes, I'd need a soundproof room just to yell an' scream an' all that shit."

Omega offered him a rueful grin.

"You have one 'a those aboard?" she wondered.

"Nope, sorry."

"Then yeah, lemme go shower an' get cleaned up, then I'll soak in the Jacuzzi for maybe twenty, thirty minutes, before I dress and head on back."

"I'll go rev it up while you clean up. It'll be hot and clean, 'cause I just did the maintenance this morning, but the jets need to rev up an' stuff."

"Thanks, Chain."

"No prob, Omega."

* * *

By the time Omega returned to the sick bay from the gym, the energy expended in the workout and the soothing effects of the soak in the hot tub were making themselves known, rather to her secret relief; the fact that a thoughtful Chain had added a lavender spa soak to the tub had helped considerably, as well. She entered Echo's room and sat down heavily—decidedly more heavily than she intended, if the truth be known; it was almost a thud, and she was glad for the more thickly-padded chair—with a sound that was half-grunt, half-sigh.

"Oomph," she muttered. "That mighta finally gotten to me." She eyed the scrubs Zebra had left for her to use as pajamas, and which were currently draped across one corner of the

211

bed at its foot. "And that'll be more comfortable to sit around in, anyhow."

She got up and ducked into the little head, where she changed into the scrubs. True to Zebra's description, they were soft, stretchy, just loose enough to move well on the body, and very comfortable. A pair of slip-on shoes that were somewhere between sneakers and slippers completed her bedtime ensemble.

Omega came back out and carefully hung her Suit items—including three full holsters—on a set of hooks on the wall behind the door, placed her dress shoes on the floor beneath them, then sat back down in the chair and took Echo's hand, holding it in a gentle grip. She sighed, brought his hand to her lips and deposited a kiss on the back, then lightly rubbed it against her cheek.

Oh, dear God, she prayed, *thank You so much for bringing him back to me, even if he isn't quite the way he left me. And please help all the doctors and medtechs to return him to as close as they can manage to the way he left...for HIS sake. Because I'll love him regardless, but he'll be devastated if he's not...the way he was, or close to it.*

Then she kissed the back of his hand again. She closed her eyes and reached inward and outward at the same time, finding the nd't'lq connection and moving through it, locating the mind of her drowsing husband and 'cuddling' with it as the Deltiri had taught her.

Mmph, Echo sighed, in response to the gentle mental contact. *Mm. Meg?*

Right here, she told him. *Literally beside you. Needed to cuddle. Getting pretty tired.*

Lie down an' snuggle up, then, he told her, groggy. *I need 'a move over? They put me inna bigger bed; fig'r'd it 'uz t' make room f'r you...*

No, you're fine, and yes, they did, she told him, finally giving in to temptation and climbing into the larger hospital bed. She slid under the covers, eased carefully into his side, being careful to avoid his injuries despite Zebra's reassurances, and settled down.

Pu'y'r head on m' shou'der, he slurred, as he drifted back into drug-induced—and Deltiri-aided—somnolence.

Okay, she agreed, shifting until her head tucked into his shoulder, not quite willing to put the whole weight on him, but allowing him to feel the contact; she let the top of her head sink into the pillow beside his head, with her cheek on top of his bare shoulder.

Echo gave one more sigh, seeming content at the touch, and drifted back into full sleep.

Omega sighed as well, hugging his good arm to her chest.

Fifteen minutes later, Yorker came in to check Echo's vitals and found them curled up together, sound asleep.

* * *

The *Genesis* arrived at the Lunar Farside Drydocks a few hours later. A space-based ambulance-type shuttle was waiting; it docked with the sick bay airlock on the *Genesis*, and the medical staff loaded Echo aboard, along with Omega, Mm'l'n, Zebra, India, and half the medtechs, then headed for Earth at breakneck speeds. Fox and the rest of the Headquarters-based crew would come along later.

Echo was rushed to the medlab via emergency maglev, and taken straight through to a treatment room. Omega hung back, and India paused with her.

"You okay, honey?" she wondered.

"Yeah," Omega sighed. "I was just thinkin', it hasn't been that long since we did this."

"Ooo," India hummed agreement. "Good point."

"Run on in there," Omega said, waving her on. "Y'all see what you can do about putting him back together again."

"All right, hon," India said, giving her a brief hug before disappearing through the door marked STAFF ONLY.

* * *

"...And so Doron recommended using the bones as scaffolding, as you thought, Zee," Zarnix told the team of physicians and medtechs assembled to work on the maimed Agent, as the chief of staff briefed them in the main medical conference room. "He said to remove the tissue surrounding them, as that was unlikely to still be viable..."

Everyone winced, but Zebra nodded.

"It's not," she confirmed. "I have 'em soaking in a strong

solution of broad-spectrum antipathogen, and I managed to put 'em into a small but powerful stasis field, so they haven't deteriorated further, but there's no salvaging the soft tissues. By the time Meg found 'em, it was already too late for that."

"Right," Zarnix said. "And judging by how you and India both paled a little when I said something about it, I think I should be the one doing that."

"I won't argue," India said in a low voice.

"Me neither," Zebra agreed with a sigh. "Debriding is gonna be hard, too."

"Why don't you let me and Rglfrz handle that, then?" Whiskey volunteered. "We're not as close to him as you two. You guys are family, after all, even if you're not genetically related." He laid a hand on Zebra's shoulder. "And I'm sorry I wasn't available when you were getting together the team to go fetch him back. If I'd been here, I'd have gone with, and glad to help."

"We both would," Rglfrz agreed. "But we were helping to transfer a patient from the Geneva Office. And yes, I will definitely help Whiskey with this. Echo's family members, non-genetic though they may be, do not need to be assisting with THAT."

"I know, and I appreciate it, both of you," Zebra said with a tired smile, "but we managed. It turns out that Mm'l'n here is a physician in her own right, and has some knowledge of working on humans, so she filled in for us on the return jaunt, and gave us both a chance to rest and recover from the...mental strain, I guess we'll call it. And that's why she's here now; she's volunteered to help provide extra hands and a brain. I'm seriously considering asking her to be an adjunct to the Medical department. Maybe some sort of consultant or something."

"That is good, all of it, and we thank you," Zarnix noted, "but are you not tired now?"

"I am," Mm'l'n confessed, "for the Deltiri team was VERY busy during this little excursion, but I should very much like to be involved in helping Echo recover. And so I am here to see what the plan is. I would simply request that you do not assign me a duty right away, but allow me to go back to my quarters for a full sleep shift before I start. I think that will be best for me AND our patient."

"That sounds great," Zebra said, "and thank you again, and we'll do that."

"And so to get straight to that plan," Zarnix began. "After you left the vidcall to go tend to things, Zebra, I continued to consult with Doron, and we ended up having a very long discussion of the matter. He has indeed contacted Lady Teela, who arranged for expedited—not quite emergency, but not far off—transport for him to Earth; I expect him here within the next, oh, six to eight hours or so. It seems he became quite fond of the Alpha One team during the time he worked on Omega, let alone when they escorted him back to his homeworld, and he was delighted to be invited to their wedding in addition, so he greatly wants to help."

"Aw," several voices murmured.

"So once he arrives—which will give everyone who hasn't had enough rest the time to catch up," here Zarnix paused and stared hard and meaningfully at Zebra, India, Mm'l'n, and Yorker, "then we will set about doing several things in parallel. One, I will remove the dead tissue from the severed limbs, exposing the bones, and clean them well, ensuring the cut ends are viable and they are free of any pathogens. Two, Whiskey and Rglfrz will begin prepping Echo for the regeneration bath, and three, the regen bath will be prepared. Once one and two are complete, we will then lightly tack the bones into their correct positioning, using a special 3-D printed protein matrix to hold them together in lieu of tendons, which tendons should grow in around the matrix and absorb it, after we put him into the regen pod. Once THAT is complete, we dunk him. ONLY after he has been placed in the regen pod will we contact Dihl, down at the Ranch, and summon her. In the meanwhile, I want NO ONE to tell her of any of this. This entire plan regarding Dihl was per Omega's considered request; she believes that Echo's full, current condition—especially so soon after the space plane incident—would be unduly distressing to her."

"Well, hell yeah," Whiskey muttered. Dihl was a highly-skilled medtech, but she was also Echo's birth mother, recruited to the Agency the previous summer after years of believing her only son dead; Echo's father had died in a ranch accident a few years prior to his joining the Agency. This had left Nalin Iyaaye Bryant alone for many years, and she had been utterly shocked and delighted to 'get her son back,' as she was wont to say—along with that son's partner, who was now her daughter-in-law. All of this was, however, classified information, lest Dihl be targeted by one of Echo's old enemies, even as he and Omega had been; only recently, Whiskey and Rglfrz had figured out the secret, though the 'family' already knew.

"What's Doron's ETA?" India wondered. Zarnix glanced at his wrist chronometer.

"Mm. About six, six and a half, hours," he estimated. "Probably closer to the latter. And he'll want a bit of time to examine our patient, after he arrives here. SO. Here are your instructions. I want everyone who just arrived to scurry off to your quarters and sleep. That includes ALL of the Deltiri, so please let them know, Mm'l'n. The embassy staff has been apprised of the technique for managing Echo's pain levels, and will handle matters for now, though I expect you may have to double up when we reach the point of debriding his wounds. Those of us who have remained here for the duration of the search will see to caring for him while the rest of you get some sleep, because I expressly planned shifts for that intent. We'll reconvene here not earlier than eight hours from now...mark."

Everyone set alarms on their cell phones or wrist chronometers.

"Now, as our much-loved patient Echo would say, 'Git!'" Zarnix said with an encouraging smile.

They got.

* * *

While the others rested or prepped for the big push, Zarnix went to one of the labs and pulled out the hand and leg, carefully packaged in a nutrient/antipathogen bath—it was, in fact, an IV solution, as Zebra had originally said—and preserved in a stasis field, in order to study them with some intensity. After some ten minutes of scrutiny, he considered.

"Mm. Zee was right. None of the soft tissues are anywhere close to viable at this point," he decided. "But the bones still look good. It will take some time to do this the way it needs to be done; perhaps I had best start now. I was really hoping to rescue at least some of the tendons, and keep everything tied together that way, but it looks like I shall have to do this the hard way, after all. Echo, my friend, it will be a miracle if we can put you back to anywhere close to what you were. Which is a damn shame.”

He dug in various cabinets and drawers; extracted and laid out packages containing sterile forceps and a selection of scalpels, as well as a container for the dead tissue, then went to scrub up.

* * *

Whiskey entered the hospital room where Echo lay, motionless and unconscious; Omega sat by the bedside, pale and tired. Dark blue-black circles stained the light skin under her eyes, which were mildly bloodshot.

“Hey, Omega,” the physician said softly as he entered. “How’s he doin’?”

“’Bout the same, I guess,” Omega murmured. “He’s pretty out of it, but he knows I’m here through the bond; the Deltiri and the pain meds are keeping him from hurtin’ too much, if at all.”

“Well, that’s good,” Whiskey decided. “How are YOU? You look dead tired, but I had it to understand that you slept on the way to Earth...?”

“Yeah, but other than that, an’ a couple hours when India an’ Zebra knocked me out—an’ I woke up from THAT when the damn Cortian slave keeper, or jailer, or whatever you wanna call ‘im, started whackin’ off Echo’s body parts—I haven’t really slept since...since before we left Tiniken,” Omega revealed. “You know...the Eden planet. And that was after the Cortians captured Echo...which thing also woke me up.”

“Oh damn, hon,” Whiskey said, sympathetic, as he ran a quick check of Echo’s vitals, and felt his pulse. “And worrying that whole time! No wonder you look like you’re sleepwalking. Is there anything I can do?”

“I dunno,” she sighed, despondent. “I’m not sure I’m gonna be able to do much until I know what’s gonna happen with him,” she gestured at the bed by way of antecedent. “I could go home, I guess...but I think that’d be worse.”

“Why?”

217

"Because by now, they're gonna have our quarters merged, an' it's gonna be bigger than my quarters alone were...except those were lonely enough when Echo wasn't there, I mean like next door, what with us mostly keepin' the back door open all the time," she explained. "I think that a BIGGER place, an' him not there, would just be that much worse. Never mind that I don't feel right taking possession without Echo beside me."

"Ooo. Good points, all," Whiskey considered, thinking hard. "Well, I have an idea. It might at least help..."

"Let's hear it," Omega declared.

"See, when us doctors are on shift, but the medlab is quiet, we have some rooms in a corner of the department, expressly reserved for getting a little shut-eye," he told her. "They're not big, just barely large enough for a cot an' a nightstand an' a little wardrobe—there's a shared, multi-stall bathroom with showers at the end of the hall, kinda like you'd find in a gym— and each of us has one that's effectively ours, so we can keep, oh, toothbrushes and combs and hairbrushes and shit like that in 'em. Also changes of underwear an' stuff. You know, over-night things an' personal stuff. We call 'em 'down rooms.' But there are about four extras, for when we have visiting staff. But we don't HAVE any visiting staff right now, so they're unused. Would you like me to assign you one of those? I can contact Supplies and Laundry an' have 'em bring around some stuff for you—say, a couple changes of clothes, a standard women's overnight kit, and anything else you might want or need, and put 'em all in there. Then you can go lie down and get some shut-eye, but it's not your quarters—old OR new—and it's tiny, so it might feel, I dunno, more cozy? And, you know, temporary?"

"Oh," Omega said, sitting upright to ponder the offer. "Ac-tually, you know what? That sounds like a really good idea. Because I'm about to fall over sitting here, but I didn't know what else to do. I know what they did for me on board the ship is against regs here, so..."

"Oh, Zebra told me about that—you mean bringing in the bed big enough for both of you? Yeah, I'm afraid so, girl. I really don't know WHY, because we do have situations like yours every once in a while. I suspect maybe it might go back to the founding of the Agency proper, maybe; things were a little more reserved back then, 'cause nobody had realized about the marriage omission in the charter. But I think I might suggest that particular regulation be revisited," Whiskey decided. "It's a little too prim and proper for the modern agents. Never mind now we finally HAVE a marriage provision in the charter. Okay, lemme go look at the room roster, and I'll contact Supplies and Laundry and explain what's going on. Is there anything in particular you want 'em to make sure to bring?"

"No, other than sleepwear, not that I can think of. I grabbed my kit when I left the *Genesis*, so I have a few things." She pointed at the small travel bag in the corner, against the wall. "Well, maybe a change or two of clothes, and some undies."

"Okay, I'll go with standard stuff, then. They should have something there in about ten, maybe fifteen minutes. Then I'll come back and fetch you and show you where it is. After that, it's your call when you're here, and when you're there."

"THANK you, Whiskey," Omega said, grateful. Then she jumped slightly, eyes widening in surprise.

"What?" Whiskey wondered.

"Oh, apparently Echo woke up for a bit, an' he's been listening in, only I was too tired to realize it," she said with a rueful grin. "So he just said to tell you HE said thanks, too. Only I wasn't expecting him to 'say' anything, and it startled me."

"Heh," Whiskey chuckled. "That's good to know. An' you're both welcome. Tell him I asked if he's doing okay, or if he needs anything."

Omega paused, looking at the resting form of her partner and mate, then returned her attention to Whiskey.

"He's pretty groggy," she noted. "He just said, 'Nope,' and went back on out again. He's asleep now."

"No pain?"

"Not that I could sense. He wasn't really awake long enough for me to ask."

"Good. How are the lesser wounds doing? The bruises and abrasions from being..." Whiskey broke off, not sure how to say it, and finally ended by wrapping one hand around the other wrist, to indicate the manacles.

"Oh! No, those are almost gone, I think," Omega said.

"Once they got him cleaned up—he hadn't had any care given him except the basics required to keep him from bleeding out, and that only 'cause they intended to sell him off, and needed him alive so whichever old enemy won the bidding could kill him—I think Yorker all but bathed him in Rejuvic. 'Cause apparently there were some contusions from where they beat on him, too."

"BEAT?! Wait, cleaned up? No care? What do you...?"

Omega shook her head, loath to revisit the mental imagery.

"The place reeked like a charnel house, and for about the same reasons. He was fairly splattered with his own blood and tissue," she elaborated, "the room was hot, so he had been dripping sweat, and there was, um, waste...on the floor under him."

"Number one or two...?"

Omega quirked her face.

"Both," she said, succinct. "Near as I could tell, he just had nowhere else to go."

"So it wasn't that he, um, lost it, when they started...?"

"No, didn't look like it." Omega shrugged. "I expect he hadda dump sometime before they started in on him, and at that point, since he hadn't eaten since the night before he was captured, there wouldn't have been anything much else left there to get rid of, anyway."

"Oh," Whiskey said, casting a sympathetic glance at the unconscious Agent. "Damn. Poor guy. That whole thing musta been hell."

"You have no idea."

"And frankly, and no offense, I don't want one," Whiskey acknowledged. "Not like that." He patted her on the shoulder. "Okay, lemme get my ass in gear and see about arranging that down room for you, before you fall over sitting here, with me yakking at you."

"Thanks," she called softly as he headed out the door, and he threw up an acknowledging hand, just before he disappeared down the hall.

* * *

Fox led the first non-emergency team to debark from the *Genesis*. Captain Du'ven'de piloted the cloaked *Exodus* long-range shuttle—crammed full of Deltiri and Alpha Line teams;

the Field and Security teams had stood back and encouraged it, given Echo headed Alpha Line—from the *Genesis* down to Penn Station, and Fox and the others hopped a special maglev train into Grand Central Station. Zebra awaited them there.

The Alpha Line Agents thoughtfully found other things to look at while the Director greeted his wife with an embrace and a tender kiss. Meanwhile, the Deltiri, having already been apprised of things by Mm'l'n in a telepathic communication, slipped away, headed to the embassy, thence to their own quarters. So when the Director and the Assistant Chief of Staff of Medical finally stepped back from their embrace, the remaining group's attention returned to the Assistant Chief of Staff.

"So, bubeleh, what's the word?" Fox wanted to know. The Alpha Line Agents—including Romeo, who had not come down with India, preferring to allow a medtech to have the available space on the emergency shuttle, in case Echo experienced problems—leaned forward to listen.

"We have him stabilized further, free of pain, and established in a room in the medlab," Zebra reported. "Zarnix has been consulting in depth with Doron of Edeptis, who is en route to Earth to assist us in treating Echo."

A pleased, "Ooo," went around the small assembly as Fox added, "Oh, now there is a bit of assistance and good news. The inventor of the technique is going to help you, then?"

"He is," she affirmed. "I think he's too fond of Echo and Meg not to want to help out; if I understood correctly, those three have been keeping up a kind of intermittent interstellar correspondence, ever since he treated Meg. So anyway, best I understood it from Zar, he contacted Lady Teela and arranged for a transport to be sent to Edeptis, to bring him here as soon as reasonably possible, without QUITE traveling at breakneck emergency speeds."

"Tha's good," Romeo contended. "Tha's REAL good. Damn if Echo done gone an' got all messed up—DAMN those rat-bastard yella-feathered birds!—an' this time 'e might not come out of it th' way he went into it. So we'll take alla th' help folks 'll give us, puttin' him back t' some semblance o' normal. Ain't no offense intended t' th' reg'lar med staff, neither," he added, "it's just Echo's awful messed up, this go."

"Ain't that the truth," Love commented. "Shit."

"Yes, it is good; yes, Echo's pretty messed up; and we're all really glad Doron's coming," Zebra noted. "We're all gonna give it our best on Echo, but having the master of the technique in your corner is a nice trump card to play. It's a bit convoluted, so I'm not sure of the details, but apparently after Doron contacted her, Teela called Pulgey, who then called Zarnix, and... well, all things considered, Doron may soon have a kind of emergency medical transport permanently assigned to him, complete with a small flight crew and medical staff, to ensure he reaches all the various places in the galaxy where he goes to help out, and does so fast enough to respond in a timely fashion to emergency situations."

"Good, and even better. What else, meyn froy?" Fox pressed.

"Well, India and I have been designated 'family,' and told to go home and rest," Zebra added. "Zar, Whiskey, and Rglfrz are gonna take it from here, and Mm'l'n is going to help after SHE obtains some additional rest...which is probably where all the Deltiri went, too. And of course Doron is gonna throw his weight in, once he arrives here."

"So India done gone home?" Romeo wondered.

"I think so," Zebra said. "I'd lay money on it. She said something about going on home and fixing dinner for the two of you, so it would be ready by the time you came home."

"Right," Romeo said. "I'll head straight there from here, then. Unless you need me t' do somethin', Fox?"

"No, zun, run home and have dinner with India," Fox decided. "We could all use some rest, I think. I'll be taking Zebra home as soon as she finishes briefing us all, myself. When we handed over to Wux, that pretty much took care of anything bureaucratic that won't wait until later. We can all do our debrief reports when we come up for air, and keep 'em sketchy, since everybody who's gonna see 'em already knows what's in 'em, anyhow."

"Good," the general murmur of relief went through the group.

"I do want to thank all of you for volunteering to staff our potential boarding forces, though," Fox insisted. "I'm just glad we didn't have to do things that way."

"Kinda felt like we mostly just took up space," Monkey said, "but hey, we were there and ready if you'd needed us."

"Exactly," Fox agreed. "You were all on alert and standby for heavy action. And to that end, all of you stand down for a standard sleep shift, and come back on duty when you're rested. Zebra? Anything else?"

"Not really," she decided. "Doron arrives in a little over five hours or so. We're all supposed to report back to the medlab in..." she checked her wrist chronometer, "around seven, seven and a half hours from now, to start coordinating things on treating Echo—which gives Doron a chance to get here, catch his breath, and come up to speed on Echo's condition—but right now we're good. The Deltiri embassy staff—those that didn't go with us, I mean; the ones who came with us are also supposed to be resting—so the remaining embassy staff are handling Echo's pain, with the aid of some more sophisticated anesthesia and pain shit than I had aboard the *Genesis*."

"Did we forget something when we headed out, bubeleh?" Fox wondered.

"No, there's just not room for me to take the medlab's entire pharmaceutical with us," Zebra said with a rueful grin, "and I guessed wrong."

"Right, then," Fox said with a nod of understanding. "Let's head home, everyone. We have to make room at the gate for the next load from the *Genesis*, anyway."

The group headed for the main concourse and the elevators up to the agents' quarters.

* * *

Half an hour later, and about the time that the last of the *Genesis* crew made it to Grand Central Station, Omega was curled up in the cot of her own down room, with the intent of taking a brief sleep, and being up and about by the time Doron was ready to begin procedures on Echo. Supplies had brought a complete spare hygiene kit, intended for female agents, and Laundry had brought two full changes of casual clothing, a fresh Suit, half a dozen spare bras and panties, and a set of comfy pajamas with matching slipper-socks. Omega had promptly changed into these latter, padded down the hall to the joint bathroom to brush her teeth and wash her face, then she came back and crawled into the cot.

Huh, she thought, scootching around and settling into the one-person bed with a sigh. *It's more comfortable than I'd have expected. Even the Agency cots are better than regular ones.*

O' course, she heard Echo slur in her head; Omega had concluded that these communiqués were done while he was in a kind of dream-state, for he never seemed to remember them from occurrence to occurrence. *We go 'th' tech. Get s'me sleep, baby.*

All over that one, Ace.

Good. 'Night.

Ni-ni, hon. I love you.

Love you too.

And moments later, she was sleeping the sleep of exhaustion.

Chapter 9

A couple of hours later, and while Omega was still asleep, Doron arrived, somewhat ahead of schedule; several of the flight crew for his transport knew Echo, as it turned out, and they poured on the juice to bring the little healer there as fast as possible. Notified of the early arrival, Zarnix met him at the emergency entrance and took him straight through to see Echo.

"But where is Omega?" the little physician wondered in some surprise, as he entered the room to see Whiskey checking vitals once more, standing beside an empty chair.

"I sent her off to get some sleep," Whiskey noted. "She was wiped. She's barely slept in days."

"Ah," Doron said, knowing. "Yes, that was good, then."

"Yes, it was," Zarnix agreed. "Did you have to fight her to get her to do it?"

"No, actually not," Whiskey told them. "She was about to drop in her tracks, and she knew it. When I offered to set her up in a down room, she jumped at the chance."

Zarnix raised both eyebrows.

"She IS tired, then," he decided.

"Oh, yeah. And stressed. And she knows it. But," he added, thoughtful, "I think she also knows that she can't afford to let herself get too run down. Echo needs her at this point, and going forward, he's gonna need her just as much, but in different ways. So she knows, now that he's safe in the medlab, she can tag-team with the rest of us, in order to keep herself going...for his sake. And the down room is close, and we know where she is if she's needed."

"That...is wise, on many levels," Zarnix decided.

"Yes, it is, and it is good to hear. Well, let me see to Echo," Doron declared, and Whiskey courteously and without comment lowered the bed so the diminutive Edeptan physician—the tallest Edeptan was only about four and a half feet tall, and Doron was not even of average height—could easily reach his patient. With a nod of appreciation, he toddled over to the bed and commenced his examination.

Gentle fingers on a red-skinned hand slid over human skin, palpating and feeling for abnormalities, as Zarnix arranged for fresh dressing material to be brought into the room. Sharp, alert yellow eyes scanned the injuries as Zarnix and Whiskey carefully removed the old bandaging where Echo's eye, hand, and lower leg used to be, leaving the special sealant on the wounds. Doron chewed his lower lip, considering, then nodded.

"Ah, my poor friend; how cruel sentients can be! Yes, this can be done, though it will be difficult," he concluded. "I cannot say it is certain that he will be completely as he was before, but we can definitely make him functional again." Doron turned to Zarnix. "Have you begun work on the severed bones?"

"Yes, I have, per your instructions," Zarnix said. "I have most of the tissues removed already except for the tendons, and I have already begun replacing out the tendons with the printed protein framework as you recommended, though I may be going slower than is truly necessary, to ensure I do it properly. Do you want to see? I should like to ask you, anyway, about the best way of attaching..."

"Yes, yes, show me," Doron said, and toddled along as Zarnix headed for the door. Abruptly the chief of staff paused and turned back to Whiskey.

"No problem, Chief," Whiskey told Zarnix, before the other male could say anything. "Send Gig to me straight off, and she and I will bandage him back up, just fine. It was time to change the dressings anyway."

"Right," Zarnix said, offering a thumbs-up, and he and Doron were off.

* * *

The Edeptan and the Chesharilzi doctor put their heads together on the protein matrix, and soon both hand and lower leg were in a state that Doron considered, "Excellent, excellent. This should do him nicely. The hand is especially well done, and should therefore cause him no dexterity problems."

"It is the leg I am most worried about, actually," Zarnix noted. "The cuts were not clean, the tibia partly shattered on one of the blows and I fear I am not sure I managed to find, let alone salvage, all the pieces and chips. I am not even sure all the pieces were there! It was like what the humans call a jigsaw puzzle, and a damned difficult one, at that. So I am worried it is not going to reattach properly." He paused, then considered, "But yes. The hand has to be just about perfect, or he is going to lose a lot of dexterity. Fortunately, he is right-handed, but I know he fights and wields his weapons with both hands, so..." Zarnix frowned, anxious.

"Hush, hush," Doron said, soothing the worried physician. "You have done a truly outstanding job, and I have now added to it. I made a point to review the most recent research on this as I rode here, and I believe I can say without reservation that, with the technology we currently have, it could not be done better."

"Then we will just have to live with however it turns out, I suppose," Zarnix said with a sigh.

"Well, no," Doron pointed out. "ECHO will have to live with it."

Zarnix sighed again.

* * *

Moments later, Zarnix called a meeting of all of the physicians he considered suited to the gory work that was about to commence: himself, Doron, Whiskey, and Rglfrz.

"All right," he began, "now comes the hard part. Doron and I will begin the debrid—"

"No, you won't, Boss-man," Whiskey declared, interrupting. "Rglfrz and I have already discussed this. You're too close to your patient, and so is Doron, at this point. Rglfrz and I will do the debriding."

Zarnix blinked, staring at them in surprise for several seconds. Doron nudged his leg.

"They are right, my friend," he murmured. "They have our best interests at heart; I heard about what happened to India. Do as they say. You and I will finish preparing the 'scaffolding' for reattachment. When that is done, we will begin preparing the formulation of the fluid in the pod, so that it will be ready to receive Echo when they are finished."

"That...works," Zarnix decided. "If Doron and I can have... let me see...one or two medtechs as extra hands and feet—I already know that tacking the bones in place takes far more hands than I have—you two can have the rest to help you."

"Done," Rglfrz agreed.

"Does somebody need to go wake up Omega?" Whiskey wondered.

"Mm," Zarnix hummed, thoughtful. "That is a consideration..."

"Why?" Rglfrz wondered, in the characteristically blunt fashion of Kardorians; their resemblance to Earthly velociraptors was more than merely physical, though they were generally gentle and caring of others, and the longer arms made them far more functional than a velociraptor possessed of a comparable brain. Rglfrz had a better bedside manner than most Kardorians, however, and generally worked well with his patients, though he did not always understand some humans' emotional considerations. "She is finally asleep; she has needed that for some time. Leave her be."

"I agree," Doron averred. "I know how she is, how she becomes, when she is upset. And Echo is much like her, and I saw how hard he drove himself when SHE was injured. Let her sleep. We can have this over and done, and Echo within the regeneration pod, before she wakes."

"I dunno, guys," Whiskey said, doubtful. "Do we know who it is that's on duty for pain relief among the Deltiri?"

Zarnix pulled up the information on his 'outboard brain' and studied the display for a moment. "It looks to be Dd'n'l ag Boo'nnh," he concluded. "He is a fairly strong telepath, with some previous volunteer work in assisting patients in a hospital. It should be good, but I will notify him to be prepared, and perhaps to have backup."

"Good plan," Whiskey agreed.

"Now remember, my friends—we require clean, smooth scalpel cuts," Doron reminded them, "exposing fresh, blood-filled tissue. If you are in any doubt as to the viability of the tissue, it is best to remove it."

"Sharp debridement," Whiskey murmured.

"Yes," Doron verified. "If it bleeds, it is viable."

"Shall we contour the surfaces of the wounds?" Rglfrz asked. "Omega's were contoured, according to the case study I read, in preparation for this procedure..."

"Ah, that is right; you were not here as yet," Doron remembered.

"No, I arrived some two lunations after she was released," Rglfrz explained.

"I have been debating about that," Zarnix noted. "I think perhaps a LITTLE bit of contouring would be appropriate, but not too much. He has already lost a lot of tissue, and will lose more in this process before it can be regrown. We do not want to overdo."

"'If it ain't broke, don't fix it,'" Whiskey quoted the aphorism. "We don't wanna risk trying to do too much, and end up by making matters worse."

"I suppose that is true," Rglfrz conceded. "All right. Let us not waste any more time. The sooner we put Echo into the regeneration capsule, the better off he will be."

"Go," Zarnix said. "Call if you need assistance."

"You know it," Whiskey acknowledged.

* * *

In short order, Echo's unconscious form was brought into the operating room nearest Lab B, where the regeneration facilities were housed; he was gently and carefully stripped, his naked form draped in a sheet for modesty, and his leg stump uncovered. The scrubbed, masked, and gowned debridement team metaphorically flexed, in preparation for the procedure.

"How's the anesthesia, Yorker?" Whiskey wondered.

"He's as deep as I'm comfortable putting him," Yorker replied. "We gotta trust to the Deltiri for the rest, I think."

"Do they know?" Rglfrz wondered. "The Deltiri?"

"Yes, I checked with Zar right before we scrubbed up," Whiskey averred. "He notified Zz'r'p, who immediately notified that Dd'n'l being."

"Good."

"All right, guys," Whiskey said; as the more senior physician, he would be in charge, and Rglfrz would assist. "Everybody take a deep breath."

The medtechs obeyed; even Rglfrz followed that instruction.

"Aaaand...go," Whiskey said, holding out his hand. "Number 15 blade scalpel..."

"Number 15 blade," Gig said, placing the sharp instrument carefully into his gloved, outstretched hand. "Lavage ready."

"Rglfrz, stand by with the curette, when we're ready to fine-tune a bit," Whiskey said, bending over what remained of Echo's leg.

* * *

As the blade bit into his flesh, Echo abruptly roused partway from his unconscious state, brought to that level of awareness by the acute pain of finding his body being cut on once more.

AIIAARRGGH! he thought, finding himself unable to scream aloud. *Did I pass out? Did I just hallucinate being with Meg? On the* Genesis? *Or—oh, dear God—did the Cortians capture her, too? And the others! Fox! India an' Romeo! What's happened? Meg?! MEG!! WHERE ARE YOU?!*

* * *

Omega was sound asleep and dreaming peacefully of a picnic with Echo among the flowers, when his panicked, confused mental shout cut through into her conscious awareness. The next thing she knew, she was sitting bolt upright in bed, eyes wide, staring into the faint orange gloom, as a sharp, biting pain cut into her right calf.

I'm here, honey, I'm here, she told him. *Calm down, everything's fine.*

No, it isn't! They've captured me again, Meg! They're cutting again! Are you safe? They don't have you, too, do they?

No, Ace, I swear, the Cortians don't have me. We're on Earth, sweetheart. You're safe.

Then why am I being cut on again??

I dunno, but I sure as hell aim to find out!

The next instant, she was standing beside the bed...

...And the next, she was out the door of the down room, and running down the hall.

* * *

"Ah! I think I am beginning to get the hang of this, as Zee says!" Zarnix decided, as he and Doron finished rebuilding the bones of Echo's severed foot, carefully attaching them with tiny printed scaffolding of a special protein that would encourage connective-tissue growth along its framework. They were in the small workroom just off Lab B; only a few minutes before, they had finished the initial formulation of the regeneration fluid in one of the new, specially-built pods, and it was now ready to receive Echo, once his body had been prepped for the process.

"Yes, you are doing very well with it," Doron noted as he watched. "I will have to list you with the galactic medical board as an expert in the procedure by the time we are finished. I think—"

The door burst open, and Omega stormed through.

"What the HELL are y'all doin' to Echo, and WHY in damnation is he AWAKE through it?!" she demanded to know.

* * *

"No, no, no," Zarnix exclaimed into his cell phone, as he, Doron, and Omega hurried toward the operating room down the hall, where Echo was being prepped. "I know, Zz'r'p, I know. But Omega is right here, and she says that he contacted her through the nd't'lq, in a panic because he thought you had all been captured by the Cortians and were being tortured—which is apparently what he thinks is happening to him, AGAIN, because he can FEEL it. And he was NOT in a good mental state, according to Omega."

Omega, all three suddenly heard the mental voice, *Cc't'i was monitoring you, and says you became upset while dreaming. Are you certain Echo is truly awake?*

I'm POSITIVE, Omega declared, firm and unmoved by the suggestion. *I didn't grow upset until AFTER he woke me up, mentally shouting! I think he even came close to screaming again, but I'm not sure, because I WAS asleep. And yes, I was dreaming. Have YOU ever been woken up, straight from a dream state, by someone you loved screaming and yelling? I promise you, Uncle Zz'r'p, you become upset pretty damn fast.*

Oh dear. All right; stand by.

* * *

Zz'r'p burst from his office into the main reception area of the Deltiri embassy in Headquarters, slamming through the door and running into the large room. The various staffers manning the facility leaped to their feet in alarm.

Friend Zz'r'p, what is wrong? one of the junior envoys asked.

Dd'n'l! the ambassador called. *Dd'n'l, are you all right?*

I am, Zz'r'p, the reply came, *but I am overwhelmed by the sudden force of Agent Echo's will! I need assistance, please! He has awakened, and I cannot return him to the peaceful state! I was just about to call for help!*

Jj'k'k! To me! Zz'r'p ordered, and suddenly the big Deltiri emerged from another office.

Here, Zz'r'p! he answered, as two more familiar figures stood just inside the door from which he had emerged. *Qq'k'l and Kk'q'r are here, as well.*

Good. Let us assist Dd'n'l, and calm Echo. They are debriding him, and the pain and panicked confusion were evidently sharper than the scalpel, for it cut through the anesthesia AND Dd'n'l's efforts to keep him calm and unconscious.

We are right beside you, my friend, Qq'k'l said as he came out of the same room from which Jj'k'k had emerged, with Kk'q'r right behind him.

Zz'r'p led them toward the private meditation room where Dd'n'l strove to ease Echo's pain and distress.

* * *

Scant moments later, Omega, Doron, and Zarnix entered the scrub room; Zarnix quickly threw on a gown, gloves, and surgical mask, while Doron turned to Omega.

"You should stay here, my friend," he told her. "He would not wish you to see..."

"He stood by me while y'all were doing the same thing to me, last winter," Omega pointed out. "And we weren't even an item then. Now we're married. Do you really think you can convince me NOT to go in there?"

Doron looked up at her, surveying her determined expression, the hardness of her eyes and the truculent set of her jaw; then he sighed.

"Very well," he concluded. "You have a point. Help me find a surgical gown that will fit me..."

* * *

Moments later the trio banged through the door of the operating room. Whiskey and Rglfrz had stepped back, while the medtechs attempted to hold Echo's reflexively thrashing form down on the table; one was trying to strap down his arms and legs to hold him still, even as Yorker adjusted the anesthesia.

"No! STOP!" Omega ordered, flinging out a hand, and everyone in the room stopped dead, looking up at her in confusion.

"Oh, no! What are you guys DOING here?! Meg, you need to clear out," Whiskey said. "All of you do. You don't need to be seeing this."

"No, you do not understand," Zarnix explained. "We are here because Echo is at least partly CONSCIOUS, and FEELING the debridement. It woke Omega...as you and I feared... when he called out to her through the nd't'lq bond, in pain and confused. He thought he was back in the hands of the Cortians."

"Or else had only hallucinated that he'd ever been out of their hands," Omega said in a low voice. "If you strap him down, in the semi-conscious, confused state he's in, he'll think he's back in the manacles they used to fasten him to the wall..."

"Oh shit," Whiskey and Yorker said simultaneously, even as Rglfrz murmured something in Kardorian that had a similar tone.

"But how do we keep him from falling off the table?" Gig wondered, as the medtechs quickly released the strong hook-and-loop straps, but continued holding his body on the table, keeping their grip as gentle as they could; his thrashing had diminished, however, as the scalpel and curette had stopped cutting into his leg.

"Leave that to me and the Deltiri," Omega said, coming to the table and taking Echo's lone hand in her gloved one.

* * *

Ace, honey? she thought at him. *Are you still awake? I'm right beside you. Can you feel my hand holding yours?*

Yeah, sorta, came the response. *I'm 'wake, but not; I can't seem t' quite move, least not 'cordin' t' the way I wanna, an' everything's...muddled. Wha's happenin'? You said I wasn't still on th' Cortian ship...*

You're not, I swear you're not, Ace. You're in Headquarters on Earth, in the medlab. In the operating room, specifi-

cally. The docs are prepping you, making you ready to go into the regen bath.

Oh shit. Now I get it. Whadda they call it... 'debridement' or something. Like they did t' you.

That's it. And there should be Deltiri listening in by now. Evidently the pain, combined with the knee-jerk of, 'Oh no, the Cortians got me again!' overcame both the anesthetic AND their attempts to block your pain.

That is correct, Omega, Zz'r'p's mental voice answered. *We do apologize to you both. It seems that, when the first twinges of pain slipped through everything, Echo's reaction was so strong, it overpowered our friend Dd'n'l, who was helping to care for that pain, and did not expect such an intense response. He called for help only moments after Omega notified us that something was wrong, and 'the cavalry has arrived,' as you are wont to put it, Echo. Qq'k'l, Kk'q'r, Jj'k'k and I will now be assisting Dd'n'l to suppress your pain through the procedure. The medical personnel do not want to give you too much anesthesia because of the unwanted side effects upon your already-much-abused body, so we will be here to help.*

So will I, Omega declared.

For the moment, Zz'r'p agreed. *But you should go back to bed soon, nn'chn. You need rest, too.*

I know. But...

Baby, lissen to 'im, a groggy Echo said. *I'm sorry I woke you. I just...when I felt the knife, it...I mean, I thought...I thought you'd been...I thought they got both of us...*

No, I get it, Ace, she told him. *It's only that...*

That what?

Everything happens when I go to sleep, dammit, she fussed. *I go to sleep, you get kidnapped. I go to sleep, you get tortured. I go to sleep, the medics start cutting on you and trigger a knee-jerk from the torture. I...I don't WANNA go to sleep! Bad things happen when I sleep, dammit!*

Aw shit, Echo grumbled.

Hush, hush, Zz'r'p offered. *Let us take care of Echo for the moment, and then I will personally help you to relax and go back to sleep, nn'chn. And you will finish your sleep with no more unpleasant incidents, if I have to personally sit beside your bed and watch over you to ensure it.*

Omega sighed.

Do it, baby, Echo said. *F'r me?*

All right. For you, Omega said, stifling another sigh. *But right now, you need to relax and let us put you back under the anesthetic, so the docs can finish and put you in the regen pod. That way, we'll get you all healed up.*

I'm not holdin' m' breaf on 'at. Omega noted his mental voice was already starting to slur, as the medications combined with the telepathic work gradually took effect.

Hey, they're good, hon. It's okay. Just...let us do this.

Hokay. Do it.

And within moments, the combined mental efforts of one semi-telepathic human, five telepathic Deltiri, and one medtech anesthetist, had Echo unconscious, relaxed, and still.

* * *

"Whoa, that's a relief," Yorker murmured, as Echo slid back into full unconsciousness and his body relaxed on the table. "I was startin' to become a little worried, there."

"You an' me both, pal," Whiskey agreed. "An' now I see why India had such a bad reaction, too. Damn! Okay. Now, why don't you three," he addressed the most recent arrivals, "clear out, while we finish this? Then we can dunk him into the regen pod and get him on the way to being whole again."

Zarnix shot a glance at Omega, who shook her head.

"Y'all go on," she told them. "You have stuff you're doing. I'm gonna stay here for him, like he did for me."

"Omega, you need to rest," Zarnix protested.

"I will...when he's in the regen pod," Omega said, calm... and very firm.

Zarnix and Doron exchanged glances. Doron cocked his head, and Zarnix sighed.

"Let her stay," the chief of staff told Whiskey and Rglfrz, "but someone help her scrub up properly."

"Right," Gig said, stepping forward. "Omega, please come with me."

* * *

In the end, a properly-scrubbed and -gowned Omega sat beside the table, staying very still, and held Echo's remaining hand, occasionally stroking its back with a gloved fingertip, all while avoiding looking at what the doctors were doing, and thankful that neither she nor Echo could feel it any longer. She suspected that, had the patient been someone other than Echo, she could have dared to watch, but she cringed inside at the thought of watching them cut away his flesh. *I know it has to be done,* she thought, *and I know they're helping, but...* She stifled a sigh that would have been at least half a groan of sympathetic pain.

At long last, it was done. Zarnix and Doron were summoned, and they came in with two trays and a very special kind of 'glue gun,' intended to deposit small beads of the protein they had been using to attach the bones. Together, and with the help of the other staff, they attached the hand skeleton to the bones protruding from Echo's arm stump. Then they did the same to his leg.

"There," Doron proclaimed. "It is done. Now we must seal the wounds and hurry to put him into the bath."

"Consider it done," Whiskey said, as he nodded at Gig, who began removing the clamps on the blood vessels, one at a time, as Whiskey wielded the special sealant spray, fairly hosing the main blood vessels to prevent Echo bleeding out on the table.

Moments later, the blood flow had ceased, and the wounds were properly protected; Omega vaguely recalled that Doron had not yet developed that particular sealant treatment when she had been so badly injured the previous winter.

No, they had to spray me down with the regen fluid, then drape a sheet soaked in the stuff over the raw tissues, she remembered. *Good thing that the burns basically cauterized all the blood vessels in the whole damn area. But DAMN, did all that hurt. Never mind that they didn't dare knock me out, 'cause I'd have crashed and not lived long enough to go into the regen bath.* She shook her head slightly. *I suppose there are up sides to an alien psychopath beefing up your pain tolerance for his own ends. But shit.*

"All right, transfer him to a gurney and let us head to Lab B," Zarnix decreed. "Gig, if you would see to Omega, and summon the rest of the 'family,' we will be in there shortly to—"

Whiskey cleared his throat. Loudly.

Zarnix stopped dead and stared at him, then glanced down.

"Um," Zarnix tried again, "what I meant to say is that WHISKEY will be in there shortly to give everyone a rundown on how it has gone."

"Right," Whiskey said. "Meg, chin up, gal. Run along with Gig, and I'll be in there in a moment. Doron, you're with me. Zarnix, I'll see you in the waiting room."

"Very well," the chief of staff said with a sigh, as Gig led Omega out of the operating room.

* * *

As the 'family' waited for Whiskey and Doron to come in and brief them, Zarnix turned to Omega.

"Oh, before I forget, I have something you need to hold on to for Echo," he said, and pulled the wedding ring out of his pocket; it had been duly cleaned of blood and debris, and the alien precious-metal alloy shone silver-gold in the light. "Here." He took Omega's hand and opened it, then placed the ring in her outstretched palm. "I took it from the finger of the severed hand while I was working on it. It's been cleaned and polished."

"The Cortians didn't take it?" Fox wondered, surprised.

"No," Omega murmured, staring down at it, thoughtful. "I don't know why. It was on the hand that they'd thrown in the corner." She glanced up at the others. "I didn't take the time to try to get it off; I just left it on his hand and shoved it all in the forensics bag, then got all of it into a warp pocket. I figured I'd worry about it later, but by the time we made it outta the Cortian ship and got to sick bay, I'd forgotten..."

"Well, that's understandable, honey," India soothed. "And getting him taken care of was more important at that point, anyway."

"True...but I still don't understand why they didn't touch it," Omega noted, looking back down at the circle of precious metal in her palm.

"I think I do, because Doron explained it," Zarnix said. "The Cortians have plagued the Edeptans for at least a couple of Earth centuries, and they have a fair amount of knowledge of the sons of bitches. Unwanted knowledge, but still."

"Tell us, meyn khaver," Fox urged.

"It seems there is some sort of belief in Cortian culture," Zarnix explained. "Since they have very little in the way of metals at all, even something simple like copper or brass or iron is extremely valuable to them, and rarely used for ornamentation...and when it is, it is considered IMPORTANT. The rarer the metal, the more important the object. And it seems that there was a suntan shadow under the ring, showing that Echo wore it all the time..."

"Okay," Romeo muttered. "So? I mean, that's jus' a weddin' ring."

"Cortians do not use wedding rings, at least for the fingers, and Cortian males do not use nuptial jewelry of any kind," Zarnix added. "But they DO use rings for special rituals, notably for protection and such matters. A kind of talisman."

"But...a ring isn't protective," India observed, confused.

"No...unless in the believer's mind, it has had a very special ritual performed on it, laying a curse upon whoever harms it...or its wearer," Zarnix pointed out. "And that is the nature of the special Cortian ritual. The ring is then worn continuously by the possessor until death. They therefore likely assumed that the ring Echo wore had a similar purpose. But since he was 'only a slave' to them, obviously whatever entity that was invoked was not considered as strong as the entities they invoke..."

"Aw shit," Romeo cursed.

"Indeed," Zarnix agreed. "However, according to Doron, it is likely to have resulted in them choosing that hand to remove, since they would want to get the ring away from his body as quickly as possible, with the notion that the lesser deity invoked could be hoodwinked into not knowing what became of him..."

"Which also explains why they dumped the hand and leg in the corner, relatively intact," Omega realized. "They didn't wanna mess with a 'cursed' object."

"That was my understanding, yes."

Omega sighed.

"Well, at least I got one answer for all the questions," she decided, "even if it was kinda gory and weird."

The others nodded.

"What about the heirloom cross you told me about, Meg?" India wondered, as Omega unbuttoned her collar.

"Echo had been careful not to wear it into the ocean," Omega explained, fishing something out of her shirt, "because he didn't want to damage it—the ring won't tarnish, but the silver of the cross and chain will, and salt water can corrode it; I remember Daddy used to do the same thing, when the family vacationed at the beach—and we'd gone for a moonlight swim the night before, AND planned to go back to the beach after breakfast that morning, so he hadn't put it back on yet." She pulled the antique silver cross pendant from inside her shirt. "It was still in his things in the room. Here it is. I'll give it all back to him when...when he's able."

Omega slipped the necklace off, added the ring to the cross on the chain, then put it back on, tucking it back into her shirt.

"Occasionally small things come back to thank us, I suppose," Fox noted, and the others nodded in silence.

* * *

"Okay, he's in the regen pod, and everything's set and running," Whiskey said some half an hour later, coming in to the nearby waiting room, where Omega, Alpha Two, Zarnix, Fox and Zebra stood. "Shall we call Dihl now?"

"How does he look?" Omega wondered.

"Not too bad, all in all," Whiskey noted. "I know you didn't watch what we were doing, and I understand why, so hey. Because of the way the pod is designed, you can't see his body at all, so the hand and leg are effectively invisible. And his face doesn't really look bad at all, though it's a little puffy. I mean, you can tell there's something wrong with that eye, but we had to kinda loosely tack the lids back into place with some dissolving suture so they'd reattach properly anyway, and since most of his face is still bruised to hell and back, what with the resulting edema, it isn't too noticeable."

Omega bit her lip, considering.

"Honey, I know you're trying to protect her," Zebra said quietly, "but you can't delay any longer. We can always explain that it was an emergency and we didn't have time to call her until we put him into the pod...which is sorta true, but not...

but if you wait any longer now, she's not going to be happy about it...with us, or with you. And frankly, I wouldn't blame her."

"Yeah, you're right," Omega murmured with a deep sigh. "So yeah, let's call her. But if she gets upset, blame it on me. Tell her, flat out, that I didn't want her to have to see him in the shape he was in, so soon after the last little incident. And, um, that I was ashamed for not taking better care of him."

"Oh HELL no!" India exclaimed. "Like ANY of what went down was YOUR fault!"

"Easy, India," Omega said, her face twisting into a pained, almost sardonic expression. "I didn't say it was. If it helps for her to THINK that, though, I'm okay with it. Not happy about it, but okay with it. But I do feel like, somehow, I shoulda done something, seen something, to prevent what went down. See, Zz'r'p warned us both, after Echo came outta the telepathic coma after being 'mostly dead,' that he might have some temporary problems with situational awareness, and that he should stick close to me, so that I could handle watchin' out for shit, for BOTH of us. And I didn't catch this. Well, at least I didn't catch it like I guess I shoulda done." While the others took in that information, she added, "Besides, if my mom-in-law is gonna get mad at me, it might as well be for something big."

Several snorts emerged from various 'family' members.

"Well, you make a good point about that," Fox decided. "But I don't think she's going to be angry, tekhter. Upset, certainly, but if we call her now, and someone OTHER THAN YOU explains to her not only what condition he was in, but what YOU saw, what you did to return him safely to us all...I cannot see that she can possibly be angry. At anyone. In my considered opinion and experience, Dihl is eminently sensible, and she should understand that we may possibly have delayed contacting her out of a desire to protect her."

The others watched as Omega chewed her lower lip, considering the matter at length. Finally she nodded.

"Yeah, that's good," she declared. "Go ahead and call her. And bring her up here as soon as you can."

"All over it," Whiskey said, heading for his office.

"And I will arrange for the emergency transport," Fox determined, pulling his ubiquitous tablet from a warp pocket.

* * *

But when Dihl arrived in the medlab a couple of hours later, she was in uncommonly high dudgeon. Omega, who was sitting in Lab B with the regen pod containing Echo's silent form, trying not to slump over from exhaustion, heard her raised voice through the closed door. She rose and went into the adjacent holding area, where the others tried to calm the unusually-agitated Apache medtech, who was—metaphorically, at least—on the warpath. As Omega entered, a wide-eyed and obviously uncomfortable Doron slipped out the far door.

"And just WHY did NO one tell me of all this?!" she demanded, as soon as she arrived. "You ALL know who I am, what I am to him! Zebra! Fox! You could have told me he had been kidnapped! And there you are, Omega! Why did YOU, my shich'ee'ké, not tell me when it happened?!"

"Stop, Dihl," Fox ordered, holding up a hand. "Calm down, my dear lady; apparently you only have part of the story. For one thing, Omega was still trying hard to figure out what had happened, and the local police were not only no help, they threatened to arrest HER when she reported Echo missing, claiming she was filing a false report! She had to call me, and I ended up having to go around the police to the appropriate Division chief to get anything done! By the time we knew for certain what had happened, we had to chase after him—and his Cortian kidnappers—to have any hope of bringing him back at ALL." He paused, as Dihl stared at him in a kind of astonishment. "Then Omega performed one of the bravest things I have ever seen anyone do: she entered the Cortian ship where Echo was being held, alone save for the mental direction of a handful of telepaths sequestered on MY ship, helping lead her to him. There, she freed him, and brought his unconscious body safely out of the enemy vessel without being caught."

"Oh, great Creator," Dihl breathed, shocked. "She did WHAT?? Surely I did not just hear..."

"You did," Fox confirmed, and the room was silent for long moments.

* * *

"There's two reasons why we only just contacted you a

little while ago, Dihl, hon," Zebra said then. "We've either been going hell bent for leather, or dropping in our tracks, and tag-teaming each other, to try to get everything done and Echo safely home and into the regen pod to heal."

"So...you either had no time, or no energy, to do so," Dihl murmured, beginning to understand.

* * *

"Exactly," Fox said. "But also..." He broke off, looking for the words to explain to the mother what had happened to the son.

"The Cortians hacked him up, Dihl," a distressed Omega blurted, before Fox could gather the words. "I mean, literally hacked him up. I...when I found...and then he...and they..." She put her face in her hands, and a worried Fox immediately moved to her side, easing an arm around her in case her knees tried to buckle again. "I didn't know that they...I mean...it was my fault," she confessed. "I didn't want you to see him until..."

A wide-eyed Dihl stared at her daughter-in-law. "It...it was...that bad?" she whispered then.

"Every bit," Omega choked out.

"And Omega was the one to find him, meyn khaverte," Fox added, guiding Omega to the nearest chair and urging her to sit. "Zebra, would you or Zarnix, or one of the other physicians, like to take Dihl in hand and brief her on the medical aspect of what was done to Echo?"

"I have it, Fox," Zarnix volunteered. "Whiskey, what was your message, my friend?"

"I didn't want to upset her too much, what with a couple of hours' ride ahead of her," Whiskey explained, "so I only told her he was badly injured, we'd just dunked him, and she needed to come on up as soon as she could." He pulled a face. "I thought we could explain all the rest once she got here; I didn't think about her gettin' mad BEFORE she got here."

"Which I did anyway," Dihl said with a sigh. "Become upset, I mean. And he was right in his assumption; I would likely have worried far too much. So..." she broke off, then glanced at Omega, concerned. "What constitutes 'hacking,' in this instance?"

"He is missing his left eye, his left hand just above the

wrist, and the right lower leg from a few inches below the knee," Zarnix said, very quiet. "He was also beaten somewhat, though much of that has been tended already."

"Oh, dear God!" Dihl exclaimed in horror, clapping her hands over the lower half of her face as she paled. "My boy! They...Omega? You found...?"

Omega simply nodded, as tears welled in the blue eyes and overflowed.

"No one knows what she saw, save the telepaths who were helping her, and the head of the PGLEIA, to whom she gave those telepaths permission to show," Fox said softly. "And the head of the PGLEIA, one of the toughest beings I know who is not a professional soldier...all but screamed in shock when he 'saw.'"

* * *

Abruptly Dihl rushed to stand before Omega. She dropped to her knees on the floor, then leaned forward, reaching out to take the younger woman in her arms, gathering her to her breast and pulling Omega's head to her shoulder.

"Oh, my dear shich'ee'ké," she whispered, holding her as Omega cried quietly, "and you cannot forget..."

"N-no," Omega sniffled. "Kinda wish I could. For his sake, if not mine."

"But you saved him, shich'ee'ké. You SAVED him."

"No, I snuck him out," Omega corrected her. "If the doctors can't fix him, then I dunno how he's gonna react. That's the real saving part, I think."

"Meg," India said then, "remember, I told you, we'll do whatever we have to, develop whatever new technologies we need to, to bring him back to normal again."

"I kn-know," Omega sighed, hiccupping once through her tears. "But that could take a long, long time."

The room was silent except for Omega's soft sniffling sobs. Moments later, Dihl tucked her head into Omega's shoulder and began to cry quietly as well.

* * *

The others stood watching for long moments. Whiskey and Rglfrz, along with most of the medtechs, left first, slipping out and leaving the 'family' in privacy. A quick, gestured exchange between Zarnix, Zebra, and India ended with India bending over Omega and Dihl.

"Hey guys?" she breathed, not wanting to upset the pair any further, let alone startle them. "Is there anything we can do? What do you need from us? We're here, and we wanna help..."

"T-there's...there's nothing you can do, not for us," Omega said in a wobbly voice, hiccupping a few more times. "Ju-just do ev-everything you can t-to fix Echo!"

"That," Dihl agreed. "And...I am so sorry I was angry; I didn't understand. I, I'm sorry. I didn't understand."

"It's okay, honey," Zebra said, crouching nearby and laying a gentle hand on Dihl's shoulder. "We know you didn't. We're sorry, too; we didn't want to keep it from you, but after seeing how Omega reacted, and how every blessed one of us reacted when we saw his condition, too...we only wanted to save you that level of emotional distress."

"I know," Dihl moaned softly. "It is all right. I—"

* * *

"Oh shit," Omega said then, snapping upright in her chair.

"What?" came the chorus of voices.

"Echo's awake, sort of," she said. "And he knows his mom's here, and that his mom AND his wife are both crying... about him."

"Oh shit," India reiterated, worried. "How coherent is he?"

"Sort of, but not a lot," Omega decided after a few moments to consider. "It's sort of a subconscious thing, but not quite. Where's Mm'l'n?"

Just then the Deltiri physician stuck her head in the door.

"It is all right, Omega; I 'heard,'" the alien woman said, tapping her temple, "and I am already taking care of it; Dd'n'l has gone to rest after the debridement procedure. Echo is not truly awake, as you realized, and he is unlikely to remember any of this little interlude. The mental state in which we have been keeping him—for the most part, at least," she added, rueful, "has been designed to ensure he does not remember the pain or the trauma that must be inflicted to ensure successful treatment, because doing that avoids creating mental distresses which would be layered atop the trauma of the original attack on his body. We will have to deal with the latter eventually, but we felt it best to try to eliminate the former, whenever possible." She closed her eyes for a moment, then opened them and looked at Omega with a slight smile. "There. He is unconscious again, and calm."

"Oh, thank You, Lord," Omega whispered, "and thank you, too, Mm'l'n."

"I like to think I can be Maker's hand, from time to time," Mm'l'n replied, "so I thank you for the realization of that hope. I will be near if you need me." She slipped back out.

* * *

"C'mon," Zebra said, laying a hand on Dihl's shoulder. "Let's go brief you about exactly what happened, what we've done, what needs doing, and the prognosis."

"All right," Dihl said, reluctantly releasing Omega and standing.

Omega made to stand and follow, but Fox dropped his hand on her shoulder, applying sufficient force to prevent her from rising.

"Wha?" she said, looking up at the Director.

"No, that's good, Fox," Zebra asserted, seeing what he was doing. "If she's in there with us, she'll rehash the whole thing in her head, second-guess herself out the wazoo, remember all the worst parts, and be in a state fit to break something by the time we're done. Keep her here, or...oh!" she said, as an idea struck. "Why don't you take her and Romeo back into Lab B and the three of you sit with Echo and chat? About anything BUT what's happened, preferably."

"A capital idea, bubeleh," Fox agreed. "Tekhter, zun, shall we?"

"I think it's a plan, Fox," Romeo agreed.

"Okay," Omega said simply, as Fox allowed her to stand once more.

They turned and headed into Lab B as Zarnix, Zebra, and India escorted Dihl into the consultation room across the way.

* * *

Once Dihl was filled in on the full details of what had happened and what was being attempted on her son, she entered Lab B with India and Zebra, came straight to Omega, and

245

hugged her tightly. Then she hugged every other member of the 'immediate family' in turn, whispering her thanks.

"No, no," Fox murmured, patting her back in a soothing fashion. "There is no need for thanks, meyn teyere; he is dear to us, too. Just because he is not truly my son does not mean I don't care for him as one. And we have talked, you and I; you know he is my oldest human friend still living. The others have similar feelings for him. We could not—no, we WOULD not—lose him."

"What he said," Romeo avouched. "Dude's my buddy, my former partner, an' th' nearest thing I got to a big brother. I got a question on shit, I go t' Echo, more often 'an not."

"A lotta that," India agreed. "I've seen him do it, and I've done the same sorta thing myself."

"I didn't know Echo that well until Fox and I started seeing each other," Zebra admitted. "But as I started to see the way Fox treated him, and began to grasp that they were close in many ways, I started to seriously respect Echo—because Fox doesn't give his full trust, let alone his close friendship, to just anybody. Then Omega came along, and I saw how Echo treated Meg...and then Meg kinda put together this little family, which I became a part of when Fox and I settled down together, and...well. Yeah, all of that. What they said."

Just then, Doron entered the lab, apparently intent on checking on Echo, but he stopped dead at the cluster of people in the room, then, spotting Dihl, made to slip out again. But Omega put out a hand.

"It's okay, Doron," she said with a smile. "C'mon in here. There's someone you need to meet, anyway. But you gotta promise to keep who she is a secret."

"What?" Doron said, moving somewhat hesitantly to Omega and taking her hand. "Why? What secret?"

"See this lady here?" Omega said, indicating Dihl. "This is Echo's mom. His real mom."

"Ohhh," the little Edeptan murmured, eyes growing wide. "This is his lifebearer? The female who had the cancer, for which Zebra consulted me last summer?"

"Ah!" Dihl exclaimed in delight. "So this is the famous healer Doron, who helped you all treat my pancreatic cancer?"

"The very one," Zebra said with a smile. "Doron, meet Dihl. Dihl, meet Doron."

"I am VERY pleased to meet you," Dihl said then, sitting so as to be closer to the Edeptan's height. She held out a hand, and they shook. "I have wanted to thank you, very much, for what you helped to do for me. And now you're helping my son, as well. And I already know about how you saved Omega's life."

"I am always happy to help save a life," Doron said simply. "It is what I do, heal."

"It's what Dihl does, too," Omega said with a grin. "She's a nurse, or a medtech, however you wanna call it. And she's a GOOD one. She even has a doctorate in it."

"And I am an herbalist healer as well," Dihl noted quietly. "I find that often the old and the new ways can be made to work together rather well, if one is only willing to try."

"Ooo," Doron said again, yellow eyes widening. "You work with herbs as well? We may have much to discuss, you and I."

"That sounds lovely, and I would like that very much," Dihl agreed immediately.

"And now I understand why you were so upset earlier," Doron admitted. "You are his lifebearer, and you had not been told. But truthfully, Dihl, I was in agreement with not bringing you in until he was in here," he laid a light hand on the pod in which Echo floated. "Omega was VERY much upset, and so would you have been. She had to fetch him out of the Cortians' spaceship, so she HAD to see; you did not."

"No, I understand now," Dihl said, calm, quiet, and regretful. "Please forgive my earlier anger. It was...uncalled-for. I know that now."

"But I can comprehend it, nevertheless," Doron said, with a slight smile. "You love your son, and you were upset. It is a lifebearer's prerogative. It is all right." He pattered over to the monitoring instruments to check Echo's status. "Now let me see what needs to be done for this son of yours, so that we can do as much for him as we possibly can..."

* * *

Two comfortable chairs, both recliners, were brought into

Lab B, one for Omega and one for Dihl, as well as a small end table with shelving underneath to place between them and hold a reading lamp, drinks, blankets, and books—anything they needed to remain calm and stay properly hydrated. Zebra made arrangements for meals to be served to them when food was brought around for the other hospitalized patients.

"And I want you two to make sure you have some sleep," Zebra ordered. "BOTH of you. If you want to work out, say, overlapping shifts, so that you spend some time together, but also so that one of you is here in case we need a voice for Echo, that's fine. But Omega, in particular, needs to rest when she grows tired. After all, she's also bearing Echo's subconscious reactions, never mind having already borne his pain. Am I understood?" Zebra stared at the Agent.

"Yes, ma'am," Omega said meekly, and Dihl chuckled, then nodded.

"Yes, Zebra, you are indeed understood," she noted, "but I am also looking after my daughter-in-law, in the best way I know how."

"And that's understood, too, honey," Zebra agreed with a smile. "If either of you wanna stretch out in the recliner and take a nap at any time, feel free; if there's not blankets in the cabinet over here," she walked to the corner of the room and checked, "yeah, there we go. But if I need to order more, I can and will; just tell me. I can also send for whatever kind of pillows you'd prefer to use..."

"No, we're good," Omega said. "Whiskey set me up with a 'down room,' so I can stay close."

"Commendations to Whiskey, then," a pleased Zebra said with a smirk. "Dihl, I assume you'll just run to your own quarters when you need to sleep?"

"Most likely," the medtech asserted. "Omega and I will discuss the matter and work something out."

"Yeah, it's cool," Omega confirmed.

"There's gonna be docs and medtechs coming and going to check on things," Zebra reminded them. "You both know how this works. We'll try and be quiet and not disturb you, especially if we see you're napping or something, but shit happens. I'm the world's worst for finding something to trip over, or drop, when I'm trying my damnedest to be quiet. And if you don't believe me, ask Fox!"

The three women giggled.

* * *

Fifteen minutes later, the door to the lab opened; a tall blue Deltiri stood in it, scowling.

"Hi, Zz'r'p," Omega said, offering him a smile that tried to be happy, but was not, quite. "What's up?"

"I should be asking you that," he replied. "Hello, Dihl. Are you well?"

"I am, Zz'r'p," Dihl confirmed. "Thank you. I would be better were it not necessary for me to be here, but other than that, I am fine."

"Good. Can you sit with Echo for a few hours, alone?"

"I can; why?"

"Because Omega was asleep, and was startled awake when Echo partly woke during the debridement procedure and called her through the nd't'lq," Zz'r'p explained. "It seems the pain reached him rather unexpectedly, despite the anesthesia and our volunteer's best efforts, and he was temporarily confused, thinking himself back on the Cortian spacecraft..."

* * *

"Ohhhh my," Dihl hummed, suddenly understanding, as she stared at Omega's attire...which was still suspiciously paja-ma-like, though Gig had found her some enclosed shoes suited to work in an OR. "And someone never went back to bed after matters settled?"

"Not. At. All," the Deltiri decreed. Then he fixed Omega with a stern gaze. "So. I said you would sleep, and sleep well, if I had to sit by your bedside to ensure it. I did not mean in order to ENFORCE it, but I will if need be."

"Okay, okay," Omega groused, rising and heading for the door. "I'll be back in a few hours, Dihl."

"Sleep well, shich'ee'ké," Dihl said, as Zz'r'p escorted the female Agent out the door. "Echo and I will be right here when you wake."

Omega waved without turning around, and disappeared down the hall.

* * *

Omega slept another four hours or so, with Zz'r'p himself keeping more than half a telepathic eye on her from his office, just to make sure nothing disturbed her. Then she rose, padded down the hall to the communal bathroom and showered, returned to the down room to dress in casual, off-duty clothing, and headed straight for Lab B.

The first day with Echo in the regen pod was the busiest; all the doctors were coming and going roughly every hour, sometimes every half-hour, in order to check the readouts and adjust the formulation of the fluid in the pod, to ensure he healed as well as they could possibly manage. This duty largely fell to Zarnix and Doron, though Rglfrz and Whiskey often accompanied them, and sometimes Zebra and India insisted on helping, even though they had been designated 'family,' and instructed not to participate on this patient.

"But ONLY for today," Zarnix ordered. "After things settle, I want you both to rest, and become 'family.' The rest of us will take care of matters."

India, who was still rather traumatized from cleaning Echo's wounds aboard the ship, agreed immediately; Zebra took more persuasion, but was eventually convinced to take a well-earned break, once matters settled down.

* * *

"How is it coming?" Omega asked toward the end of the day, when Doron came in to check on matters.

"Oh, fairly well, fairly well," the little healer asserted. "Without doubt, we will be able to recover his functionality; of this, I am confident. It is a little soon, so I cannot yet say how close to his previous condition he will be, but I am pleased with how matters are progressing to this point."

"It's okay," Omega said, voice low. "I'm not holding my breath that he'll come out the way he was before the Cortians grabbed hold of him. But if you can bring him back to the point where he can live a normal life, I'll be grateful, even if he can't go back out in the field. Fox and I have plans for what to do for that."

Doron cocked his head to one side and gazed at her for a long moment.

"Patience, my friend," he said. "Look in the mirror. Then

250

realize that Echo was just as concerned for how you would come out."

"He...he was?" Omega said, surprised. "But...but that was before...I mean, he didn't, not yet...did he?"

"What did he feel for you at that time?" Doron filled in for her, as Dihl watched. "I cannot say for certain, of course; I am not a telepath like friend Zz'r'p. But I remember becoming convinced during the journey to Earth that he loved you... save for the fact that he did not wish you to know. I concluded that either he had something to hide, which given his honor and his determination to risk all for you, I considered highly improbable; or he was uncertain what your reaction would be to discovering the depth of his feelings for you. I considered the latter to be more likely, all things taken together. And later, a discussion with Fox revealed that I had been right."

"Yeah, he told me that Fox actually figured out how he felt before HE did," Omega said, shooting a sheepish, slightly embarrassed grin at Dihl, who returned it.

"And I am not surprised," Dihl added, unperturbed. "His feelings are real, and deep, and always have been, but even as a boy he was more, mm, a person of action, and prone to missing things like that, because he was simply too busy to see. And yes," she added, "he loved working with you, but because by that point you were talking past each other on the matter, he was uncertain if you would accept him as a would-be lover. Yet he valued your friendship, your partnership, your presence at his side, far too much to risk losing all of it if you did not desire him in that way."

"You knew, too?"

"I know my son," Dihl said with a shrug. "Even after being separated from him for so long. I recognized it in him, and basically told him to 'fess up,' as his father used to put it. And to me, he did." She paused, then added, "And I urged him to take action, when it began to look like you might have an interest in him. And he did." She chuckled. "It didn't take much urging."

"Aw," Omega murmured, touched. "I'm glad he did. I... well, given what I am, I...didn't think...I mean, well, I just wasn't sure," she confessed. "I didn't even know if it had occurred to him that we could. And if he hadn't, I kinda wondered if I should even suggest it, because was it really fair to him to let him become involved with me, given what's been done to me? I...still worry about it."

"I do not think he minds any of that," Doron observed. "He only wants you with him, beside him, as his mate and partner. Nothing else is important. So, regardless of how he emerges from the regeneration process, if you love him and stand by him, he will do well."

"That's not even in question," Omega declared. "It doesn't even factor into the slightest worry. I love him so much it hurts. I only want HIM to be happy."

"Then we will make this work," Doron averred.

He smiled at her, then began reviewing the instrumentation readouts, and making small adjustments here and there to the fluid composition.

Chapter 10

Very late in the shift—it had been well over twenty hours since Zz'r'p had escorted her off to rest—an exhausted Omega finally went back to her down room, intent on a full night's uninterrupted sleep. She changed into fresh pajamas, then collapsed into the cot without bothering to do anything else. She was asleep within moments.

Unfortunately, her mind remained active.

* * *

Zarnix was passing by the down-room corridor, considering retiring to his own down room to rest, when a sudden, bloodcurdling scream emanated from it. Startled and shocked, he ran to the nearest wall comm panel—they were all over the medlab, for just this purpose—and slammed a hand down on it.

"Emergency in the down rooms! I think it is Omega! All available personnel, including medical security, respond stat!" he ordered, then headed for the down room at the end of the hall, from which the screams still emanated.

* * *

He fairly exploded through the door and into the room, with Dihl, Mm'l'n, and Whiskey close behind, to find Omega sitting in the cot, scooted all the way to the head of the bed, her back pressed against it, body curled into a fetal position, as she continued to scream. The blue eyes were dilated and unfocused, and her face wore an expression of horror. As Zarnix reached for the bedside lamp and switched it on, Dihl went straight to her and sat down on the bedside, pulling Omega into her arms—or trying to do so; Omega fought and pushed the older woman away, screaming even louder.

Zarnix grabbed his medscanner from a lab coat pocket and ran it over the Agent, then shook his head, adjusted the scanner, and tried again.

"Damnation," he declared. "She is asleep, in REM state, and evidently having a dreadful nightmare...but she is not waking?? Is she under telepathic attack?"

"Asleep, yes; under attack, no. But I think, from what I picked up, she may be experiencing a flashback of sorts within that dream," Mm'l'n observed. "I contacted Zz'r'p and headed across the medlab as soon as I picked up her distress...which was perhaps a couple of minutes before she began screaming...because, frankly, he and I discussed something like this happening, and I have been watching her with one part of my mind, just in case. I suspect he has, as well. Hopefully he, as her counselor, will know what to do."

Seconds later, Zz'r'p entered the room at a run, shoving his way past the medical security team, barely slowing until he reached the bedside, where Omega still screamed. Then he crouched in front of her, held his hands over her head, and closed his eyes. Omega gasped, choked, and finally stopped screaming; she slumped, almost doubling over herself, and Zz'r'p finally laid his hands directly on her head.

"Here," he murmured then, reaching for Dihl with one hand while maintaining contact with Omega's head with the other. "Come and hold her. Zarnix, you may dismiss the security team; they will not be needed now."

Dihl, who had moved aside to make room for Zz'r'p, sat back down and drew Omega's limp form into her lap, holding her like a child and rocking gently, as Zarnix stuck his head out of the open door and murmured orders to the security team lead, who nodded and motioned to her team to depart. After several moments, Omega stirred, blinked, then lifted her head, opening her eyes and looking around. Those eyes, Zarnix noted, were still dilated, her face pale.

"Wh-what...?" she breathed, confused. "I...I was..."

* * *

"Hush," Zz'r'p said, soothing, as he lightly rubbed her head with long, sensitive blue fingers. "All is well, my adoptive niece. Nothing of what you dreamed has happened in reality. And yes, it was a dream, wrapped around a flashback," he explained. "Based on what I saw in your mind, a particularly nasty one, too."

"Uh, um, yeah," Omega murmured. "Slug, an' the first encounter with th' Cortians, an' Wright tryin' to rape me, an' the

254

Cortians torturing Echo...”

“Oh, DAMN!” Whiskey exclaimed, shocked. “All at once?”

“All at once,” Zz’r’p confirmed, even as Omega nodded affirmation. “She is connected to Echo’s memories of his torture through the nd’t’lq, and it is feeding into her own PTSD, exacerbating it.”

“Oh shit!” Omega exclaimed, trying to sit up, even as Dihl and Zz’r’p restrained her. “ECHO! Did that come from him?! Did HE have a flashback??”

“No, no,” Mm’l’n noted. “Not only was the dream ‘all yours,’ as soon as I realized there were about to be...problems...with it, I contacted Jj’k’k, who is off-duty and resting but awake, and told him to contact whoever was easing Echo’s pain and erect the strongest telepathic block possible, strong enough to prevent nd’t’lq backflow, and he is telling me now that not only did he do as I ask, he personally helped to boost that block. So while I did not know how to stop your flashback—I am still training on certain counseling techniques, and Zz’r’p is far more experienced, which is why I summoned him—I could, and did, arrange for Echo to remain unaffected by it.”

“Oh, thank the good Lord for that,” Omega whispered, then she turned into Dihl’s shoulder and began to cry again; the small group had seen her cry more in recent weeks than in the whole time they had known her in the Agency, as she flatly reached the end of her endurance. “I am SO messed up, guys.”

“Hush, hush,” Dihl said, tightening her hold and beginning to rock again. “Shush, my dear shich’ee’ké, the love of my son’s life. We love you, and we are here to help. You are not alone, nor is he.”

“No, you are not, and yes, we are,” Zz’r’p said. “Omega, will you let me soothe this for you? You need not suffer from this dream. And for you to experience such an horrific blending of attacks upon yourself AND Echo, with both of you being dismembered and disemboweled...” A gasp went up around the room. “No, my dear. We must do something about this, and now, else you will add this trauma to your fears from being awakened by Echo’s kidnapping, his torture, the debridement...and it can only end in psychosis for you, when you are no longer able to sleep because you are too afraid."

"Wh-what do you want to do?" Omega wondered, her voice low.

"Not a great deal," Zz'r'p explained. "I have the ability to...to soften the memory, I think you would express it. We already know, for you and I have tried, that I cannot make you forget any more than the brain bleacher can do so..."

"Damnation," Zarnix grumbled. "I had been considering asking you about that. So you have already tried, in her counseling sessions?"

"We have," Zz'r'p admitted. "What I had hoped to do was to help her deal with her emotions and responses, then help her to forget each event as we dealt with it. But it did not work, for the same reason that the brain bleacher does not work—Azeln evidently intended to ensure that she would be and remain his tool, with no possible outside interference. I am still attempting to ferret out how he did it, but so far have not been able to circumvent THAT. He never expected anyone to develop a technique for erasing his programming, however."

"Lucky for me and Echo," Omega murmured.

"Indeed. He seems not to have known that much about the other telepathic races in the galaxy," Zz'r'p concluded. "Not that there are many of us. But the deliberate isolation of his homeworld told against him in that." He caught and held Omega's gaze. "So, nn'chn, niece of my heart and mind, if not my genetics or my species, will you let me at least soften the memory, so it will not tear at you so?"

"I...yes, I think that'd be...awfully good," Omega whispered, resting her head against Dihl's shoulder. "I'm so tired. That's not the first dream I've had, but it was far and away the worst."

"That is because it was tied into a flashback," Zz'r'p explained.

"Yeah, I think I remember you said that a minute ago," Omega recalled. "Y'all please excuse me; I'm still a little confused an' disoriented."

"Quite understandable, nn'chn," Zz'r'p averred.

"This makes sense, this 'flashback within a dream,'" Zarnix

decided. "Your eyes were wide open, and you were screaming, but we could not wake you. Dihl tried to help, to hug you, but you fought her off as if she were a monster."

"Oh no," Omega said in dismay, looking up at Dihl with a contrite expression. "I didn't hurt you, did I? I'm so sorry. I would never have..."

"No, no, it is all right," Dihl soothed. "I am not injured, and I am not offended, dear one. We knew you were not awake—your eyes were not even focused. As soon as Mm'l'n suggested you were having a flashback, and Zarnix confirmed you were in REM sleep, I understood you weren't awake, weren't seeing ME. I expect you saw a Cortian trying to capture you, or the like."

"I...I'm not sure where that woulda been in the whole mess," Omega said, "but yeah, probably. There were damn sure enough of 'em in there."

"All right, let me see what I can do," Zz'r'p said. "Try to relax, nn'chn."

Omega closed her eyes, and Zz'r'p laid both hands back on her head, careful to make his touch light and gentle. Then he closed his own eyes. Within seconds, the others saw Omega's entire body relax. A few moments later, she and Zz'r'p opened their eyes.

"There. Is that better?" the Deltiri ambassador asked.

"Mm. Yeah. Yeah, it is," Omega attested, then she slumped in weary relief, still in Dihl's embrace. "Wow, am I tired."

"Then you should try to obtain a little more sleep," Zarnix ordered, but gently.

* * *

"Ooo. Not quite," Mm'l'n interjected then.

"Huh? What's up?" Omega wondered.

"Echo," Mm'l'n noted, succinct. "It seems that the lack of the feedback through your bond woke him, and he is concerned, wondering where you are and if you are all right. I think it may be a kind of follow-on to his confusion during the debridement. He is not fully awake...yet...but waking fully inside the regeneration pod would likely not be good."

"No, that is true," Zarnix said. "We have refined the pod design, and had a few built expressly for the purpose, so they are rather closer-fitting than the old hyperbaric chamber we were using, in order to conserve the chemicals used in the regen fluid. Even Echo might find himself a bit claustrophobic in it, were he to fully awaken."

"So I need to 'talk' to him, settle him down, before I crash again myself?" Omega wondered.

"It would likely be advisable," Mm'l'n recommended. "Jj'k'k and Cc't'i have dropped the block that prevented him from sensing you through the nd't'lq, so you can contact him now."

"Okay, hang on," Omega said, closing her eyes and scrunching her forehead a bit.

* * *

Ace, honey? Can you hear me? she asked. *Are you there?*

Yeah, 'm here, he slurred groggily. *Where'd ya go? You awright? Th' bond jus' kinda...stopped. I 'uz afraid somethin' 'uz wrong.*

I think I'm okay, yeah. I just had a bad dream, is all.

Aw. Ni'mare?

Yup. Pretty bad one, if I'm honest. I gather that the Deltiri picked up on it as it was...mm, as it was beginning but before it turned completely nightmare, I guess you could say, and they stopped it reaching you, so YOU wouldn't get upset, too.

Aw, he said again. *Wish they hadn't 'a done. Maybe I coulda helped.*

Well, you're in one of the new regen pods, Omega tried to explain—and divert—without going into the details of the dream. *It's pretty snug-fitting, 'cause that means they don't need as much regen fluid, and I think they don't wanna risk your waking up in a tight space like that, in case you get claustrophobic or something.*

Eh. Never had a probl'm wi' that, he said with a kind of mental shrug, unworried. *Jus' wanna help you, baby.*

I'm good, honey, she told him. *Zz'r'p was waiting when, um, it woke me up, and he helped me deal with the nasty imagery.*

You sure you're okay? Echo pressed.

Hon, I was already dealing with PTSD before this all went down, Omega pointed out. *So no, I'm not really okay, but I'm gonna be. Our family is helping me, just like they're helping you. I don't want you worrying about me. I'm safe, and I have people right here with me, right now. Just work on gettin' all healed up, all right?*

Awright. 'F you're sure.

I'm sure. Just relax and go on back to sleep.

Hokay, honey. Love ya. G'night.

I love you too, Ace, so much. Good night.

And he drifted back into the pain-free, fully unconscious state that the medications and the Deltiri, combined, were providing.

* * *

Omega opened her eyes.

"Okay, that's taken care of," she declared to the room's inhabitants. "I explained just enough to Echo to settle him and reassure him that I'm okay without actually telling him what the dream was about."

"Great," Whiskey said. "We don't need him becoming all upset, waking up, and thrashing around inside that thing. That'd be apt to injure him worse before we could get him out."

"No, I explained that, too," Omega said. "He's not claustrophobic at all, so he wasn't too worried about that, I gathered. He mostly wanted to try to comfort me after a nightmare, I think."

"Next time you talk to him, tell him his mother had matters under control on that," Dihl said with a smile. Omega hugged her.

"You did, at that," she agreed, then eased out of the older woman's lap. "There. I bet your legs were about to go to sleep, holding me like that!"

"I had not noticed, no," Dihl said with her patented pert grin. "But finding where to put YOUR legs was a bit of a challenge! You are some bigger than my son was when I last rocked him to sleep as a little boy..."

"Oh, now THERE'S a mental image," Whiskey said with a smile. "Echo as a little kid, being rocked to sleep by Dihl."

"Don't you dare let on about it, either," Omega said, throwing the physician a semi-serious glare.

259

"Nah, it's cool," Whiskey said, gentle smile widening. "It's just, he's a big, intimidating guy when he wants to be, and that sorta humanizes him for me, you know?"

"Yeah, I get it," Omega said, expression softening. "I understand that, really good. It's one of the things I like talking to Dihl about—what he was like when he was little. An' she even has photos to show me!"

"Well, enough chit-chat, I think—let us all clear out, so Omega can take a proper rest this time," Zarnix ordered.

"Um, what if I have another dream like that one?" she asked, brow furrowing in concern.

"Now that we know you are having them, we will add a bit of monitoring to your sleep times, if you will let us know when you are considering a nap, or going to bed for the 'night,'" Zz'r'p offered. "If we see another nightmare developing, with your permission we can see about 'nudging' it in a different direction. I cannot guarantee you will have no more nightmares, but we should be able to prevent one of that magnitude, at least. Not indefinitely; you will have to learn to deal with them, youngling. But for now, you have the embassy's help every bit as much as your spouse does."

"Zz'r'p, might I ask something?" Dihl wondered.

"Of course." The Deltiri rose to his feet, nodding at the medtech.

"Why does the embassy help them so much?" Dihl asked. "Why do YOU help them so much? My son and my daughter-in-law?"

"I help them because we have become dear friends," Zz'r'p explained. "When the attack by the gastropoid criminal occurred, relatively early in Omega's tenure as an Agent, I was the one who worked with her and tried to show her the mental techniques she needed to stay alive...which she learned with some aplomb despite the situation, let me add. And when we discovered she had had the ability for a certain amount of telepathic-type activity 'spliced in,' as she puts it, I decided it behooved me to assist her by training her in her budding abilities—there were very few Deltiri in the embassy at that time, and NO other telepathic-race embassies, so there were few other options for her, and I felt it imperative that her abilities be honed, for very many reasons. But those two have performed some small favors for the embassy, as well, quietly uncovering a thief in our midst most recently, and among other things."

"But I have heard nothing of this!" Dihl exclaimed in surprise. "Neither they, nor Fox, have said a word!"

"Fox doesn't know, an' it wasn't any big deal," Omega said, staring at the floor as her cheeks turned a rosy pink. "Zz'r'p came to me with the situation, and Echo and I just kinda discreetly looked into it around our official duties. When we discovered a couple of the staffers' kids—if memory serves, there were, like, four kids, across three families—were a little too rambunctious and mischievous for anybody's good, Ace an' I realized that if we reported it and made it formal, the kids would have juvie records...and they really weren't stealing to be malicious, or for the money. Half the stuff wasn't even valuable, you know? Just trinkets or memorabilia. The kids were trying to tease folks they liked, and they didn't understand the ramifications or repercussions of what they were doing; they were too young." She shrugged. "So we handled it ourselves, by sitting down with all of the appropriate adults and explaining what was really going on. Then we brought the kids in and gave 'em a little scare, then told 'em why it was wrong, an' what they were really doing."

"And it worked?" an interested Whiskey asked.

"Oh yeah," Omega said with a grin. "'Cause we've had to handle REAL juvenile delinquents in our jobs, so we could mentally show them what was in store if we caught 'em again. Especially after we took the time to sit down with 'em and counsel 'em this time. And to the best of my knowledge, they've behaved ever since."

"They have," Mm'l'n confirmed.

"Oh my," Dihl said blankly.

"Exactly," Zz'r'p said. "And that is only one example of how this pair has quietly and largely anonymously served our embassy, all without fanfare or reward. Just because they could."

"Little things, for the most part," Omega noted. "Nothing really big. Just...hey, when we can help, we do, you know what I mean? That's what I'm all about, and it always has been. And

Echo's pretty much the same way. He wants to help people, that's all. It's just that sometimes helping the good people involves taking the bad ones off the streets...or the spaceways, as the case may be." She offered a lopsided grin. "And sometimes it means sitting down with kids and explaining to 'em how what they thought was a joke...wasn't."

"So it is a give and take relationship," Zarnix realized. "They help the two of you, and you help them."

"Not because we feel obligated," Zz'r'p insisted. "But because they have earned our respect and friendship, and our lives would be poorer without them."

"And the feeling's mutual," Omega contended. "So, as Ace would say, 'We're good.'"

"We are, indeed," Zz'r'p agreed. "Now, it is time for you to obtain some more sleep, youngling."

"Yes sir," she said meekly, as the others slipped out. Omega crawled back between the sheets and settled down. She took a deep breath and let it out slowly, then relaxed into the mattress and let herself drift back into slumber...all the while aware of her partner and husband, through the bond they shared.

* * *

The next few days were anxious and restless, and Omega was thankful for the help of the Deltiri in enabling her to sleep nightmare-free, during the somewhat scant times she chose for rest. In general, unless she was about to fall over, she simply didn't bother.

Dihl tag-teamed with her, allowing both of them to have some rest and down time, while ensuring that someone was with Echo most of the time. This also enabled them to keep each other company, as Echo's unconscious form in the regen pod was rather less than loquacious.

But Zz'r'p notified Fox of the flashback-nightmare one-two combo.

* * *

"...And so I was wondering how the plan to create the special workout room, so that she might vent, is progressing," the Deltiri ambassador asked, after finishing a quick debrief to Fox.

"Oh," Fox said, sitting up and activating his virtual keyboard desktop. "I need to find out about that. I know that my gym manager on the *Genesis* has already sent the old equipment down to the training center here in Headquarters, and of course I explained what was going on to the center manager, but the last I knew, the training center and Facilities were trying to work out the best place to put it within the center. I recommended someplace on the outskirts, maybe even where Omega doesn't have to go through a busy training center, and all the staring eyes, to get to it—though it needs a door into the training center for them to perform maintenance, certainly..." He typed a quick message, then hit the <enter> key. "There. I should hear something back in a few minutes."

"This sounds promising," Zz'r'p noted.

"I hope so," Fox decided. "It surely sounds like meyn tekhter needs the chance to blow off some anxiety and anger."

"I would agree."

Moments later a soft *ding!* sounded, and Fox pulled up the response.

"Okay," he said, scanning the message. "It's definitely in work. They took into consideration what was going on, and my recommendations, and they are indeed putting two entrances on it—one inside the training center, the other outside, both pass-coded—and it should be ready for use within the next day or two."

"Oh, very good, then," Zz'r'p decided, satisfied. "I will say nothing; that news should come from you. But I thought you should know of the incident, and perhaps speed the matter toward completion, if necessary."

"Thank you for the heads-up, alter khaver," Fox said. "And I will definitely light a small extra fire under them to complete it as soon as possible."

"Providing you the knowledge was not a problem, friend Fox. I am about to end my shift and go home to rest in any case, so I thought I would make the opportunity to speak with you about it. If I know Omega, I suspect she would likely not tell you herself."

"So I'll keep my mouth shut about it," Fox decided. "It sounds like enough people heard it go down; she might not appreciate the notion it could have been gossiped about. Not that we are, but still."

"I did not take away the impression anyone there WOULD," Zz'r'p considered, "but you are right—that does not mean SHE might not have that impression, were you to mention it."

"Exactly."

* * *

Omega, came the telepathic summons two days later, *is all well?*

I guess so, Zz'r'p, she said, immediately recognizing the mental voice. *Echo's just sorta floatin' here in the regen pod, an' Dihl and I are sittin' here reading. What's up?*

I was just contacted by Chief Wuxullian, Zz'r'p said. *The tribunals for the Cortians and their 'guests' will begin soon, and they will need your and Echo's testimonies for those, and he wanted to let me know so that I might have it ready in time. I already have all the various Deltiri testimonies prepared and ready to append to it. Oh, and we have taken care of matters of Tt'l'k's kin, while I am thinking of it.*

Oh geez, she sighed. *I don't really wanna do this.*

It will not be as difficult for you as you think, my dear youngling, the Deltiri noted kindly. *Not all interrogations are performed on criminals or suspected perpetrators. Many times we encounter situations like yours and Echo's, where either one of the witnesses or victims is unable to testify in person for various reasons, or is even traumatized and unwilling to face the accused. There are protocols that can be invoked that, if followed, render the telepathic report as the court's equivalent to the being's testimony—a deposition or affidavit, it is sometimes called, here on Earth. And we are gentle and understanding with such, and have developed techniques for accessing the memories without your needing to deliberately recall them.*

What about Echo?

We will access his memories in the same fashion, but through the nd't'lq. If you will come to my office in about half an hour, we can have this over with and done with a minimum of fuss and unpleasantness. And then you need not face it in this way, ever again, either of you.

Omega turned to Dihl, who sat quietly beside her, reading a book; together with the regeneration pod as the base, the two women formed the top vertices of a rough square. Sensing the younger woman's gaze, Echo's mother looked up at her.

"Is something wrong, shich'ee'ké?" she wondered.

"Um, yes and no," Omega murmured. "I need to run up to the Deltiri embassy so I can give them my and Echo's testimony on what happened, so it can be used in the trials. I'm not looking forward to it, but it's gotta be done. Would you mind sitting alone with Echo, while I go do that?"

"Not at all, child," Dihl noted, putting aside the book. "Go do as you need to do, and I will be here if anything comes up. Come back here when you are done, and if you need a hug, I can provide it; if you need to lie down, I will be happy to sit here with Alex while you do. Or go with you, if you don't wish to be alone. Whatever is needful, I am here to do, dear."

"Okay, thanks; you have no idea how much I appreciate that," Omega said, giving the older woman a smile of gratitude. *Zz'r'p, I'm on my way,* she added mentally to the ambassador.

I will expect you shortly, then, came the response.

* * *

When Omega arrived in Zz'r'p's office within the Deltiri embassy, two other Deltiri were there with him—Kk'q'r ob Iin'i'rek, the nd't'lq specialist, and Qq'k'l ob Sii'stek, the interrogator. A couch, rather like that in a stereotypical psychiatrist's office, had been placed in a corner, complete with a soft pillow and a fluffy throw blanket.

"Hello, my dear," Zz'r'p said, going to her and taking her hand. "You recall Kk'q'r and Qq'k'l."

"I sure do," Omega said, offering the other two Deltiri a smile. "Good to see you, guys."

"It is good to see you again, as well, Omega," Qq'k'l said, as Kk'q'r nodded.

"Come over here and sit down," Zz'r'p said, leading her to the recumbent couch in the corner and seeing her seated. Then he crouched in front of her, very informal, as he attempted to set her fears at rest. "Here is the way this is going to work, my dear girl. It is required by galactic law that we have at least three telepathic witnesses of repute and certification to corroborate the interrogation, which is why Kk'q'r and Qq'k'l are here. As Qq'k'l and I are both certified interrogators, and Kk'q'r can

265

help us access Echo's memories through the nd't'lq—and who is likewise certified in doing so—this satisfies the requirement. All we want you to do is to lie back and relax, allow us access to your memories, and we will try to help you drowse a bit while we review those memories. Our report will then consist of a written account of what we saw in those memories...which will be what you experienced."

"Yes," Qq'k'l added. "We can sort through and access them in chronological sequence, then go back and revisit any-thing that needs clarification. All without the need for you to consciously show us."

"Oh," Omega murmured, as the tension in her body eased. "That...won't be so bad, then. I thought you were gonna have to ask me about 'em, and I'd have to deliberately show them to you."

"No, no," Qq'k'l demurred. "Not in this instance. You and Echo have both been badly traumatized by your experiences on this little...'adventure.' We are used to dealing with similar situations, and will not require you to do that. We will access them through your subconscious, with your permission."

"Consider it given, then," Omega declared. "What about Echo?"

"You are his legal spokesbeing when he is incapacitated, correct?" Kk'q'r queried.

"Right..."

"And you have his nd't'lq," Kk'q'r pointed out. "If you give us permission to access his memories in the same way, through his nd't'lq, we can do the same for him."

"And as he is already unconscious in the regeneration pod, the matter is taken care of," Zz'r'p noted. "He will neither know, nor remember, that it was done, so it cannot disturb him. You can tell him later how it was accomplished, so that he knows, but he does not have to deal with it."

"Oh," Omega said, eyebrows shooting up. "Hey, that... works pretty damn good."

"It does," Zz'r'p said with a smile. "So, do we have your permission for Echo?"

"You sure do," Omega said, enthused...then she sobered. "But, um...guys?"

"Yes?" Kk'q'r said.

"You DO realize, this ain't gonna be easy for y'all to see or experience, especially Echo's side of things?"

"We do," Zz'r'p confirmed. "But it must be done, youngling. The Council tribunal needs this testimony. Better for us to provide it for you, when we did not experience it, than for either of you to try to do so firsthand."

"Okay," Omega agreed. "Just so you know."

"We do," Qq'k'l averred. "We are as prepared for it as we can be. And we have techniques for dealing with it in the aftermath, developed by telepathic interrogation experts long ago. Now lie back, youngling, and let us begin."

Omega swung her feet onto the foot of the couch, leaned back and adjusted the pillow behind her head, then pulled the throw across her legs. She settled back with a sigh, then looked up at Zz'r'p.

"Okay, guys, whenever you're ready," she said.

* * *

All told, it took a little more than half an hour, nudging toward three-quarters of an hour, to access and properly record the memories of events from first to last, as witnessed by both Omega and Echo; mental communications could occur extremely rapidly, and these three were experienced at the things they were doing. So it did not take long.

When it was over, and the proper recording of both Agents' testimonies had been made and finalized, Omega was allowed to awaken.

"There. How was that?" Zz'r'p asked...though Omega thought he appeared somewhat pale, and his face looked drawn.

"Not bad at all," Omega decided, "at least for me. It was like taking a nap. But," she added, glancing at the other two Deltiri, who appeared much like Zz'r'p, "y'all look like hell."

"It...was not easy, at all," Qq'k'l admitted, "and I have done this for many annums."

"As have I," Zz'r'p agreed, "and this was, perhaps, one of the most difficult interrogations I have ever had to perform."

"I...would not argue that," Qq'k'l admitted. "Kk'q'r, you are not so much trained and experienced at this side of matters. Are you all right, my friend? You look...ill."

"I could...could do with sitting down," a VERY pale Kk'q'r confessed, and Zz'r'p led him straight to his own desk chair, helping him to ease into it, then parked the wastebasket in front of him, just in case.

"Damn," Omega whispered, perturbed. "I'm so sorry, guys."

"The two of you are very brave, youngling," Qq'k'l said. "That was...that was..." He cast a glance at Zz'r'p, seeming to hope that the ambassador could finish the statement.

"I have no words," Zz'r'p said with a shrug. "Though I suppose we shall have to find them, to properly compose the report."

"The words horror, abomination, torture, and incomprehensible cruelty come to mind," Omega said, a hint of a snarl in her voice.

"Well said," Qq'k'l averred, "and we will likely use them, at your recommendation, and with your proper attribution."

"Indeed," Zz'r'p agreed. "Now, Omega, we are done here, and you may go. It is up to us to settle ourselves and compose the report from this point. When we are done, we will send it to the Chief, unless you wish to review it first."

"I probably should, just for the sake of due diligence, but...I'm gonna trust y'all to get it right," Omega decided with a sigh. "I just don't think I can stand to read a report about Echo's torture at those bastards' hands."

"I do not blame you," Kk'q'r said, from where he had buried his face in his forearms on Zz'r'p's desk.

"And that is fine, and the reason why at least THREE telepathic interrogators must be present," Qq'k'l noted. "We are each other's checks and verifications."

"Off with you, now," Zz'r'p said. "Do whatever you need to do next. I will take this information into account when I counsel you and Echo—he will need counseling, without doubt; I assume you would want me to do it?"

"If you would—if you can, after seeing what you just saw—I think that'd be really good," Omega said, putting her hand on his arm. "If you can't handle it, just say so. If you can, great—I'll ask him when he gets outta the medlab, of course, but I really doubt he's gonna say no, on account of what you just proved you were able to do."

"Of course, yes. Do ask him, though. He may possibly prefer a human counselor, and I will understand if he does."

"Okay. Um, y'all...try to take it easy about this, all right?" Omega said, deeply concerned for them. "It's all over now, after all. We just have to get Echo patched back together...at least, as best we can." She bit her lip. "As far as that's concerned, I guess you should know that I'm not under any illusions that he's gonna come out looking like he did on our wedding night." She shrugged. "Or anywhere close, really. I just hope he really WILL be functional enough to take on more in the assistant director role, 'cause I doubt he can come back to Alpha Line. But...it IS over. At least this round. So...try to let it go, if you can."

"We will be all right," Qq'k'l declared. "As Echo might say, 'This ain't our first rodeo.'"

"Oh! That sounded almost exactly like him!" Omega laughed, which brought weak smiles to the faces of the Deltiri.

"That is much better. Go," Zz'r'p said, and Omega took his hand, squeezing it for a moment, then left.

The three Deltiri looked at each other.

"Og'd'mn," Kk'q'r said.

"That," Qq'k'l agreed.

* * *

"Come in and sit down, both of you," Fox invited, as Alpha Two entered his office off the Core. "This is an official chat, but it's more a just-in-case plan for us to have going forward, rather than anything any of us need to act on right now."

"Uh-oh," Romeo said, pulling up the chairs for himself and India, before seeing her seated and taking the remaining seat. "That don't sound good, Boss-man."

"Well, it might not be, zun," Fox admitted. "This is something I discussed with Omega, and I felt like I ought to let you two know what we're planning, because it will involve you, Romeo, directly—and to a lesser extent, you, India."

"Oh boy," India murmured. "I think I can guess what's coming."

"It's 'bout Echo not bein' th' head of Alpha Line no more, iddn' it?" Romeo wondered.

269

"Yes, Romeo, it is," Fox confirmed. "He's been badly wounded, and in my humble and decidedly non-medical opinion, it will take a miracle to return him to a condition in which he is able to go into the field again. And he may not be able to face running the department from a desk, even so, because of the memories of what has happened, and of what he was, once."

"I dunno, Fox; I think we have hopes for a good resolution, down in the medlab," India said, doubtful. "But yeah, I dunno that I can say he'll come out of it as 'top of Alpha Line' good, I'll admit."

"Right. So what I have planned to do is this: Echo will take on a much more active role as the Assistant Director," Fox explained. "I'll give over more of my responsibilities to him, more of my actions and such. Eventually, as he recovers from all this farkakte drek and regains his confidence—because I'm certain having your arm and leg hacked off, and an eye gouged out, while you're helpless to do anything about it or even fight back, has done a number on that confidence—eventually I'll transition ALL of my duties over to him, and he will become the Director. During the aftermath of the assassination attempt, while he was recovering, Pulgey Entiyti made me a magnanimous offer—he has offered me my old job back as his chief bodyguard, as well as a rejuvenation of my own. So I'll take that, and Zebra and I will move our formal residence to Emdali and I'll travel with Pul again, introducing Zebra to the rest of the galaxy in a proper fashion; she'll become his travel physician into the bargain, and work with Werfer Eretigen at his clinic when we aren't traveling. Echo will run Division One. But that leaves Omega to run Alpha Line...with you as the assistant chief, Romeo."

"Ooo," Romeo said, trying not to cringe. "That's better than headin' it up, Fox...but not by a lot. Meg does a LOT for the department, an' I'll haveta pick up th' slack on alla that shit."

"Well, it gets tougher," Fox pointed out, quirking his lips in a wry expression. "Because with Echo in this office and no longer able to go into the field, that means Omega's partner is no longer able to back her up...so SHE can't go into the field, either."

"Oh shit," India exclaimed, amber eyes going wide in realization.

"Right, tekhter. That means that Alpha Two has to step up to the plate, and become the lead field team. Not the backup to the lead, but the LEAD. And Alpha Four steps into your slot as your backup, assuming you've no objection."

"Naw, Fox, they's good; they'll be good backup. But...dayum," Romeo grumbled. "Shit an' more shit, piled higher an' deeper."

"What he said," India agreed. "Great green globs of it. Fox, did you say you'd discussed this with Meg?"

"I have," he confirmed. "She isn't happy about it, because she and Echo both love the field work...but she acknowledges that, if Echo comes out of the medlab incapacitated or severely handicapped despite everyone's best efforts—which he may well do—this is probably the best plan. It preserves his knowledge and his experience, and gives him an honored position which more than adequately makes use of all that, without requiring him to use skills and abilities he may no longer have."

"What if he ain't up t' doin' it?" Romeo wondered. "Let's face it, Boss-man, you're no slouch when ya gotta go ballistic on somebody's ass, y'rself."

"Well, thank you, zun; I do certainly try," Fox acknowledged the compliment with a slight smile. "But that simply happens to be who I am; my personal directorial style, if you will. Oboe was not a combatant, and she was my predecessor in this position. The way she handled it was to keep security guards about her whenever she needed to go...'out,' let us call it." He shrugged. "She kept bodyguards. I'm sure that we could arrange for one or two of the Alpha Line teams to serve in that capacity for Echo, should it become necessary. Perhaps even rotate through the roster, so that all of the Agents who love and respect him so much have an opportunity to guard him. And certainly if they needed to travel as a couple, Omega could be one of those guards for Echo."

"Yeah, she'd be one helluva mama bear," India murmured, and Fox chuckled aloud at the comment. "Huh? What?" India said, puzzled at his reaction.

"Oh, nothing important. It's just—Echo once provided that

very description of Omega to me, himself," he revealed.

"Did he?" India smiled. "I can sure see it. She definitely does not like it when bad guys mess with the people she loves. You did NOT see her face when we released the emergency evacuation envelope from the *Genesis*, Fox. I was half expecting the Cortian ship to blow up as soon as you got them well away from it, after she slipped Echo out."

"That thought occurred to me at the time, tekhter," Fox admitted. "She certainly has the capability and the knowledge. Let alone the cargo capacity!"

"Huh?" India and Romeo said at the same time.

"Never mind," Fox chuckled, sounding grim. "But...she did not, because she also has a very strong moral core and foundation...although I must admit, she gave the *Genesis* bridge crew a goodly scare..."

"I heard 'bout that," Romeo said with a snort. "Damn good game o' poker, sounded like."

"Rather," Fox said, dry. "At any rate, that looks like being the plan we will have in our hip pocket to execute, should Echo be decanted in a physically incapacitated condition. He's alive, and we're all thankful for that. But we need to provide a workaround if he can't do the Alpha Line work any more, something that preserves and makes good use of his body of knowledge, with all of the respect he has earned and is due. Given his marriage to Omega, never mind the nd't'lq bond between them, since she cannot be brain-bleached and 'retired,' he cannot be either—his memories would simply reboot from the nd't'lq, the way they did on Aleancë during the 'Adita's Coup' drek—so we need to ensure he has a way to not only feel, but BE, useful while remaining within the Agency. And I think this is our best shot at that."

"Well, it is what it is," Romeo noted with a sigh. "India an' me, we'll do ev'rything in our power t' do what needs doin', Fox. You know that."

"A whole lotta what he just said," India seconded.

"I know," Fox said with a warm glance. "I just felt that I needed to sit the two of you down and tell you what Omega and I had been discussing behind the scenes. Especially given its ramifications for the two of you. Do you want me to bring in Alpha Four and talk to them, or do you two want to handle that?"

Romeo pursed his lips in thought, while India watched.

"Nah, I think I'll do that," he decided. "Take it down th' chain o' command, as it were."

"That's fine. I'm available for a conclave if you need me, but otherwise, I'll step back and let you handle it, then."

"Right."

"Does Echo know?" India wondered. "About this plan, I mean."

"I don't know," Fox admitted. "Given the mental bond thing, I expect he does, on some level. Though whether that level is conscious or not as yet, I couldn't begin to tell you." He shook his head. "If it comes to it, and frankly I'll be surprised as hell if it doesn't, I guess it'll be Omega and myself telling him. I don't mind telling you, I'm not looking forward to that."

"I don't blame ya," Romeo said.

* * *

Some ten minutes after Alpha Two left Fox's office and headed to the Alpha Line Room, Fox glanced up from his desk, through the bay window, and saw Alpha Four enter their departmental meeting room across the Core from his office. He swiftly hit the controls for the window, changing it to one-way viewing, and rose to stand before it and watch.

There were a couple of viewing windows on either side of the door of the Alpha Line Room, fairly recently added, which could be modified in the same fashion as Fox's bay window, but which were currently transparent. So he watched in silence as Romeo sat Golf and Easy down, with India beside him, and explained matters to them.

Fox watched as their faces blanched, then their expressions fell. Then their jaws fell open, and they both gaped at Romeo in shock. Finally they nodded, squaring their shoulders. Romeo nodded back, then cocked his head toward the door in a gentle dismissal. Alpha Four rose as one, and exited the room, backs ramrod straight, shoulders squared, heads held high. Both wore expressions of grim determination.

"And that takes care of that," Fox murmured.

He sighed, and returned to his desk.

* * *

"Chief Wux," Nargiss Nesh's squeaky little voice came over the intercom, "the Division Seven Director is on line three."

"Thank you, Nargiss," Wuxullian said with a smile. "Hopefully this will be some good news."

"Do you know anything more about Agent Echo's condition?" Nesh wondered. "He seemed like a nice being, and I was just wondering..."

"Not yet, no," Wuxullian said with a sigh. "I am expecting a telepathic deposition and report from the Deltiri embassy on Earth that will provide the testimony and sequence of events from Alpha One very soon, however."

"But I thought Echo was unconscious."

"He is. I promise I will explain how that is possible in just a bit," Wuxullian averred. "Let me contact Yaacrun Elyryqoli on Ryynqitsk and obtain the Division Seven update to find out what news he has, and then I will call you into my office and explain. Remember, though, this information I am going to give you must be kept quiet; it is not classified, but nor should it be bruited about."

"All right," Nesh said cheerfully. "You know I will tell no one, and I will be here when you are ready to explain."

"As usual," Wuxullian said with another smile; the little salamander-like Sluuite had proven a most able assistant, as well as occasionally gently amusing and very affectionate, and he was glad to have her about and helping him with his work... which was all too frequently nigh unto overwhelming. Nargiss made it a little less so...never mind more fun. With that thought, he flipped the switch to connect to the incoming line on which Division Seven Director Yaacrun Elyryqoli waited.

* * *

"...And that is about the size of it, Wux," Elyryqoli told him, after a lengthy discussion. "My assistant director has been VERY busy on Tiniken. I thought you should know right away, and he wants to make certain that Agent Omega is told, as well. If you are too busy to pass on the information to her, I can call Fox directly and brief him...and possibly her, at the same time; I know you have the tribunals for the Cortian ship crews getting under way."

"No, do not trouble yourself, Elyryqoli," Wuxullian said. "I know you have your own hands full, sorting out the Cortian mess on your end. Besides, I got to know Omega a few weeks back, quite well, actually; she was instrumental in solving a cold case—notably, who hired the gastropoid who went on a rampage on Earth nearly two decades ago—and preventing the perpetrator of that case from setting up a full-fledged crime syndicate based on Veldor."

"Ah. I heard somewhat about that," Elyryqoli recalled. "So you want to pass on word personally?"

"Yes, I think I should like to do so, if that does not offend you," Wuxullian decided. "I owe her and her partner somewhat, in any case, after that whole 'Adita's Coup' grig."

"Ah. Right. That did look...bad from the outside, in many ways," Elyryqoli remarked. "I remember being puzzled over Alpha One's apparent behavior during the coup, myself. So I can see that. All right, I will leave you to it. I assume you want the being added to the tribunal docket?"

"Yes, I do," Wuxullian declared. "May I count on you to contact the tribunal manager? I will give her notice to expect it, so she will not be surprised by it."

"Of course," Elyryqoli said. "Then I will see the being is sent your way on a special prisoner transport."

"Good male," Wuxullian said. "Thank you."

"Not a problem. Elyryqoli out."

"Wuxullian out."

Wuxullian flipped the speaker switch back.

"Nargiss," he said, "I have one more thing to do before I can give you your promised explanation. But in the meantime, could you contact Impiir Flibul over in the Hall of Courts and let her know we have another prisoner coming from Tiniken, who is involved in the entire Cortian grig going down? He will have to be added to the docket for the tribunals, and she is the one to do that."

"I will be happy to, Chief Wux," the little being piped back. "I will have it done in a moment."

"You are the best executive assistant I have ever had, Nargiss."

"Aw! You say that to all your assistants!"

They laughed.

* * *

"...And that is the latest, Fox," Wuxullian finished the briefing. "I thought you would want to know, and I know Omega would. Is she available?"

"No, it's my understanding that she's currently in Ambassador Zz'r'p's office right now, providing the depositions for herself and Echo—at least she was, the last I heard," Fox elaborated. "Then I'm sure she'll head straight for the medlab again. She's hardly left Echo's side since she pulled him out of that Cortian hellhole."

"Ah. Oh well. And I cannot blame her."

"What, do you need to talk to her?"

"Need? No," Wuxullian said with a chuckle. "I had only hoped to deliver the news myself."

"Oh," Fox said with a smile. "Omega does have that effect upon those she trusts, and who come to trust her, doesn't she?"

"Well, she does," Wuxullian admitted. "She is virtually fearless where the majority of perpetrators are concerned, yet gentle and thoughtful toward the victims of those same perpetrators. And that is a good thing; I have seen far too many PGLEIA agents become cold, hard and callous, after more than a few months facing the sort of grig she and Echo face."

"Yes, and it probably will not surprise you to know that, while he keeps a well-practiced poker face when on duty, Echo is much the same."

"No, it would no longer surprise me. He loves Omega, so there is an affinity there; they strike me as likely being a lot alike. Omega and I had several deep, almost philosophical discussions together, while planning to take down that Veldorn, last lunation. I picked up a good deal about Echo in the process...which probably will not surprise YOU."

"Nope, I'm not surprised," Fox said. "They have their enemies, of course...as this most recent incident proves. But Omega and Echo are heroes to many."

"Has this incident gotten out to the public at large? Have there been media inquiries?"

"A few. Not many. And I've tried to divert those. Your media office has been getting those forwards."

"Aha. All right; I shall verify they are being handled with an eye to your Agents' privacy. How is Echo?"

"In a regen pod," Fox told him, stifling a sigh. "More than that, I couldn't tell you, because I just don't know. I don't even think the doctors know for sure...but they've become positively close-mouthed since putting him in there, which probably doesn't bode well for the outcome. I am, however, preparing in case I need to pull Echo in full-time as the Assistant Director, while Omega takes over running Alpha Line."

"Grigduzin," Wuxullian cursed with intensity and anger. "Which, in turn, loses both of them from the field work."

"Yep, and yep," Fox avouched.

Just then, a loud alert went off in the Office of the Chief Administrator of the Pan-Galactic Law Enforcement and Immigration Administration, and Wuxullian flinched despite himself.

"Oh grig," he grumbled, "I have to go, Fox. I am being called to testify at one of the tribunals."

"Go, meyn khaver," Fox said. "I'll take care of things on this end."

"Gone. Wux out."

"Fox out."

* * *

When Omega returned to the medlab from her interrogation appointment, she found Fox waiting with Dihl beside the regen pod in Lab B.

"Hey, Abba Fox," she said, coming to him and giving him a brief, heartfelt hug; it caught the director off-guard, and he hugged her tight in return. "What's up? Did you come down to visit Echo?"

"Partly, tekhter, but partly to give you some news, as well," Fox said, releasing her. She moved to her recliner and sat down, and Fox grabbed one of the visitor's chairs, flipping it backward and straddling it, folding his arms on the back as he faced Omega and Dihl. "Chief Wux and the Division Seven people all thought you'd want the info."

"Let's hear it, then," Omega declared.

"That purported Ke!endarian who worked at the hotel on

Tiniken has been taken into custody," Fox said with a grim smile. "He vanished on a 'family emergency' about the same time Echo went missing, and showed up again a couple of days ago...which would mean he left the *Orktes* some six to twelve hours before we caught up to it, by my rough estimate. Given he's the only being of Avian morphology who was in the hotel since at least a month before Alpha One arrived there, and his principal feather color is blue, AND you found that blue feather at Echo's abduction site that turned out to be a dyed Cortian feather, the being was taken into custody and tested," Fox elaborated. "He wasn't at all happy about that—"

"I notice you're saying 'he,' not 'it,'" Omega observed, eyes narrowed.

"Nice catch, tekhter," Fox said, his grim smile deepening.

"Wait, what is the importance of the pronoun?" Dihl wondered. "Why does it matter whether the being is a 'he' or an 'it'?"

"Because," Omega explained, "while Ke!endarians are principally binary-sexed, they don't make a distinction between genders in their own language or culture, and in Earth—or other planets'—languages, they prefer the gender-neutral 'it,' or the equivalent form. They can grow quite incensed over the matter, if you call 'em the wrong thing. But the Cortians have a very male-dominated society, and any Cortian male would be highly offended by being addressed with any other pronoun but 'he' or 'him.' And Fox just—"

"Aha!" Dihl exclaimed in understanding. "Fox just called the being 'he.' It was a Cortian!"

"Exactly," Fox confirmed. "Well done, Dihl. More, Omega, your friend the Division Seven assistant director—"

"Vaea Kilinisi," Omega supplied.

"Ah. Yes. His name escaped me for the moment," Fox said. "So he took the being and had it—and its feathers—extensively tested. Not only do its genetics match the dyed feather you found, the dye chemicals in its feathers are a perfect match, right down to the dye lot. THEN they executed a search warrant on his apartment, and they found...Echo's wallet and *carte noir*."

"They nailed 'im," Omega snarled. "They caught the son

of a bitch."

"They did, tekhter," Fox affirmed. "The wallet had no cash in it, so if Echo was carrying any there, it's gone, likely spent by the undercover Cortian. Apparently he was trying to use the *carte noir* as some sort of additional cover, purporting he was a PGLEIA agent, I suppose; I'm having Accounting review Echo's financial records to ensure the bastard didn't try to drain his account, or buy a bunch of drek with the ID. Kilinisi said to tell you he was sending the wallet, identification, and all other contents back under special courier, and Echo's phone, chronometer, and weapon will be sent back as soon as they've been used as evidence in the tribunals...which basically means the first couple; after that, they'll have been read in as evidence, and the prosecutors will only need to reference 'em. It'll all come in to me, and I'll hand it off to you to keep until Echo is out of the medlab."

"Okay, that'll work. And no, Echo wasn't carrying a lot of cash on him. Just enough for a tip here or there." She shrugged. "If there was more than the Tiniken equivalent of twenty bucks in there, I'd be surprised. He rarely carries a lot of cash on him, because of getting into situations an' shit. Never mind traveling here, there, and everywhere, and currency changes."

"Good. There's more..."

"Out with it, then."

"All right; with the crews of the two Cortian ships in custody," Fox noted, "Wux has ensured that every member of both crews was genetically tested to match the other feathers you found...so they have THOSE crewmen identified as well. Wux said the Deltiri interrogators have confirmed that they—and three or four more—were involved in Echo's kidnapping, but that our Ke!endarian impersonator was giving the orders to the kidnapping team."

"So in the end, his own co-conspirators confirmed his guilt?" Dihl asked.

"Effectively, yes," Fox said. "Not intentionally, but their telepathic interrogations gave corroboration that he was responsible. He is in Division Seven custody as we speak—in their securest facility, if I understood correctly. And he is being added to the court docket on Aleancë for his own tribunal—

which puts him right up there with the captain and the slave supervisor, among others—with extra charges, to include espionage, conspiracy, and kidnapping of a PGLEIA agent. Several of those have mandatory death sentences." Fox paused, then added, "I have a name for him, tekhter, if you're interested..."

"I'm not," she growled. "He can go to hell and be forgotten for all time, as far as I'm concerned." She took a deep breath, calming herself with an effort, then asked, "Anything else?"

"A little bit more, yes," Fox said. "It seems that Kilinisi and his people are now looking into reopening some ten or twelve missing-persons cold cases that originated in that borough of the city in the last six or eight months. So," he added, "if he's convicted—eh, more like when he's convicted; they have him dead to rights—they may still need to hold off a little while on executing the sentences, until the Deltiri interrogators milk him dry of info on the cold cases. But while they're doing that, he'll be held in solitary on Aleancë, with every possible security measure they can bring to bear on him, so not even another disguised Cortian can help him escape. He'll be going nowhere—except to his execution, once they've closed the last of the missing persons cases."

"Oh shit," an incensed Omega grumbled. "The Cortians were running a kidnapping and enslavement ring, right out of the capital city of Tiniken. And we walked right into it. No wonder they were so well-prepared when they nabbed Echo."

"It certainly looks that way," Fox agreed, as a shocked Dihl simply listened. "They now have hopes of being able to find some of the missing persons, because they have the slave sales records aboard the *Orktes* and the *Ramtum*, AND the Deltiri interrogators can pull the crew memories. Though it'll probably also involve arresting some slave holders into the bargain. Which isn't a bad thing, it just extends the process a bit."

"Slavery is illegal throughout the Pan-Galactic Coalition, is it not?" Dihl queried.

"Yes, it is," Fox confirmed. "Though that doesn't mean that there aren't slave-holding planets in the galaxy; they simply aren't members of the Coalition—and won't be, as long as they continue slave-holding. But the Large Magellanic Cloud is a veritable hive of it. And there are places even within the

Coalition, here and there, where slavery used to be common, not so long ago. Sometimes it's still practiced in those places, if the slave owners can convince the authorities to look the other way. There IS a black market in sentient trafficking in the Galaxy, though PGLEIA does our best to keep it beaten down as far as we can." He shrugged. "And more than likely, the Cortians have been a clandestine part of it for a very long time; we just didn't know it until Alpha One revealed 'em for what they were."

Dihl shook her head; Omega growled, deep in her throat. They were all silent for several minutes, while Omega struggled to settle her anger. Finally she broke the silence.

"Keep me posted on those cold cases, Fox," she said. "I can't go help investigate, not while Echo's recuperating...but my brain still works good, and I don't have to be on the scene to use it. I can look at the clues, see if I see anything that they haven't because they're too close to it, and maybe help out that way."

"I'll be sure to pass that word back through channels, meyn teyere, because it's a good idea," Fox agreed. "I expect they'll be glad to have the additional eyes and significant gray matter on the things." He broke off, then added, "So. How is Echo?"

Omega shrugged, then deferred to Dihl.

"Ask the medical person, here. She'd know, better than I would."

"I gather that it is still slow going, as yet," Dihl said, shooting a concerned glance at Omega, and making sure to keep her tone low and soothing; it was obvious to her and to Fox that Omega's ire at the Cortians was still bubbling, barely below the surface. "It will, of course, accelerate as healing progresses, but right now, it is too soon to tell much..."

* * *

"...And so I thought it would be a good idea, tekhter," Fox said, a bit later. "I understand what you're feeling, and that there isn't much else you can do right now except sit here and keep him and Dihl company. But that doesn't allow for any real venting. So I've already arranged with the training center and the Facilities department to add a private room, expressly for Alpha One's use."

"Aw, Fox, you didn't have to do that," Omega murmured. "I can just..."

"Hush, now, and listen to your old abba," Fox said firmly, but with a smile. "You have anger and pain that needs to be worked out, meyn kind. If anyone understands that, it's me. And Echo will have similar feelings later on, possibly—probably—even stronger. So Zz'r'p and I discussed how best to handle this, and he felt that having a private workout room where you—and later, Echo, hopefully—can work out some of that anger and aggression would not only be good for you, but might prevent its emerging at an inappropriate time. Like, say, when you were apprehending a perp that didn't NEED beating to a pulp."

"Oh," Omega said, somewhat blank, as she considered the matter. "Well, I guess you have a point there..."

"Yes, he does," Dihl agreed. "And as I know how private you both are, by doing it as he is setting it up for you to do it, you can scream and shout and cry and generally vent all of those emotions with no one outside the room knowing."

"Correct, because I ensured that it is—well, not a hundred percent, but close—soundproof; if you scream or something, a little might work through the doors, but not much. And also, it does NOT have monitoring devices," Fox said. "Or, well, it doesn't have ACTIVE ones. Given what we are, and what just happened, somehow I didn't feel like not being able to TELL, in an emergency, what was going on in there. But it would ONLY be activated in an emergency. And there's emergency call buttons in there, just in case."

"Mm. Okay, that makes sense," Omega decided. "And... yeah, that would make me feel a little more open about blowing off some serious steam."

"Good. Now, I had the old bags you worked over in the *Genesis* gym transferred to our training center, and told the training manager to move them into that new room. I got the notice via email just before I came down here, and it's all ready. You can go beat holy hell out of those old bags any time you feel like it, tekhter. And if you tear 'em up before Echo gets a chance at 'em, I told the training manager to hang onto any old bags that get replaced, and we'll put THOSE in there, too."

"Where is it in the center?" Omega wondered.

"Offhand, I don't know what Facilities worked out with the training manager," Fox admitted. "But just go down there and ask, and they'll show you. There's an entrance inside the gym, and an entrance outside, both pass-coded, so you'll have to obtain and memorize the code, too."

"Okay. Um," Omega said, tentative, "listen, Fox...thanks. For...for everything."

"I may be the head boss around here, but that doesn't mean I don't have a heart, child," Fox noted, firming his jaw, and Omega realized he was hiding a good deal of emotion himself. "Never mind the fact that I've rather taken to this 'abba' role you've given me. I want to look after my kinder as best I can. Besides..." he added, glancing away for a moment, "I hope you don't mind if I might see my way toward making use of such a private 'venting' facility myself, once in a while."

"Not in the least," Omega declared. "In fact, it might be interesting if you and I—and later, you, me, and Echo—actually tried a few joint takedown sessions in there. After all, you gotta figure, if Echo goes more toward the assistant directorship—which will happen sooner or later, regardless of how all this turns out—when y'all travel, I'll probably be along for most of it. So knowing each others' styles and being able to fight side-by-side ain't a bad notion in the event something goes wonky on one of those trips. Nor is keeping any tactics we work out together...secret."

Fox raised an eyebrow in surprise.

"No, it isn't," he agreed. "It's an excellent one, in fact. Yes, let's do that. No matter what happens."

"Okay," Omega affirmed.

* * *

It took several hours for the three Deltiri to come to terms with what they had experienced in Alpha One's memories, at least sufficient to complete the formal report. "Because I have never in all my annums as an interrogator encountered anything that barbarous," Qq'k'l noted.

"And you are the most experienced of us as a criminal interrogator, so that says considerable," Zz'r'p told him. "And I think that needs to be included in the report."

"I agree," Kk'q'r averred.

"But I have never interrogated a prisoner of war," Qq'k'l pointed out, "only crime victims. Arguably this was a war crime of sorts, I suppose. That may account for the barbarism."

"Possibly, but there is still the contraband aspect of matters," Zz'r'p noted. "The war was effectively over last spring, when Corta was blockaded and surrendered. Though I suppose these may be considered soldiers in the field, who either do not know about, or do not recognize, the surrender."

"I think they just do not care," Kk'q'r decided. "And perhaps all of that needs to go into the report."

"Very well," Qq'k'l said, and added a lengthy annotation to the report to include the discussion they had just had. "There. Is that it?"

"I believe so," Zz'r'p concluded. "We have been over and over it, so I think that it is as good as it can be made. Do you agree? Yea or nay?"

"Yea," Qq'k'l said.

"Yea," Kk'q'r said.

"Send it to Wuxullian," Zz'r'p ordered, and Qq'k'l hit a few keystrokes on the workstation.

Moments later a pop-up window appeared on the screen confirming the documentation had been sent via tight-beam ciphered warp bubble blip. The three leaned over the screen, watching, for several moments before another pop-up acknowledged receipt.

"I pity Chief Wuxullian, reading that," Qq'k'l declared.

"As Omega would say, 'No shit,'" Zz'r'p agreed.

Chapter 11

Omega managed to sit for about an hour after Fox left to head back to his office, but it was an effort, and it was anything but 'sitting still.' Around reading on her tablet, Dihl watched her surreptitiously as the younger woman shifted position yet again, unable to relax or get comfortable. Finally she put down her tablet and turned to her daughter-in-law.

"Omega," she said, firm enough to catch her attention. When Omega focused on her, Dihl continued. "Fox's idea about the special workout room he had created for you—and later, Echo—to blow off steam is a good one. Go."

"Huh?"

"You have been stirred up by the deposition and by the news that Fox brought," Dihl pointed out. "You can barely stand to sit in that chair, my dear daughter, let alone sit still in it. You need to vent. You need to blow off steam and burn adrenaline. Go to that workout room Fox created for you and see if you cannot tear up one of the old bags."

"That's...a really good idea," Omega said, and she rose, headed for the door.

* * *

Omega borrowed a 'loaner' set of workout togs at the Headquarters gym, then slipped inside the private workout room Fox had arranged for her to use to vent her emotions. Fox had given the gym staff a pointed heads-up NOT to disturb Omega—or Echo, should he use it, later—while she was in that room, explaining the emotional vent aspect, as well as her innate reserve, and they all understood and agreed.

So when the guttural—if very muffled—martial screams emerged from behind the door, accompanied by significant and sometimes loud thuds, they glanced at each other in concern, then studiously ignored it.

* * *

Omega basically replicated the workouts she'd executed

on the *Genesis*. Each workout saw one or another of the bags become more dilapidated, but it gave her a feeling of satisfaction every time she tore a bag or split a seam, and she came away dripping sweat, exhausted, appeased, and calmer.

A quick shower, a hot tub soak, and a change of clothes, and she was back at the medlab, better for the very physical break.

* * *

PGLEIA Chief Administrator Gwag Wuxullian finally returned to his office from the tribunal of several rank-and-file Cortian space sailors, to find the expected report from Earth awaiting him on his desktop screen. He made a brief exclamation of satisfaction, then sat down and opened the file to read.

Wuxullian was tall for an Erikian—they were comparable in height to the Edeptans, but otherwise reasonably closely resembled their galactic 'cousins,' the Glu'gu'ik, save for the green skin of the Erikians—and Wux's face was rather more verdant than average, thanks to the hotter, larger star of Aleancë deepening the pigmentation, rather like a tan on a human.

But as he read the report from the Deltiri interrogation team on Earth, it grew more verdant still, as he scowled in increasing anger.

"Grigduzin," he snapped, "ag ogdun rag gargun."

Abruptly, however, he blanched, as the blood drained from his face.

"Doh," he breathed then, growing even paler. "Oh, grig! Doh, doh, doh! They did not!" He paused, reading a bit further, then exclaimed, "They DID! To ECHO! And she knew! Oh, Maker! Grigdu! Doh! His EYE!"

* * *

Suddenly Wuxullian leaped from his chair, sprinting across his office and into the outer office, past a startled Nargiss Nesh sitting on top of her desk going over some paperwork, and into the private restroom just off the outer office.

He slammed the door behind himself, and a concerned Nargiss stared at the closed door for a long moment...before the sounds of gagging, and something splattering into the toilet, reached her hearing membranes. Alarmed, she climbed down from her desktop and scampered across the floor toward the door.

"Chief?" she called. "Chief Wux? Are you all right?"

She got no answer.

"Wux? Wux?! Gwag, answer me!" she cried, worried. "Are you all right, Gwag? What has happened?"

"Just...just a minute, Nargiss," came a wobbly reply...in a voice that barely sounded like the strong, determined Erikian male she knew...and secretly cared for.

After a few more moments, the door opened, and a very pale Wuxullian emerged, wiping a moist disposable cloth across his lips.

"What has happened, Gwag? Are you ill? Do I need to call a healer?" a now-frightened Nesh asked.

"No, no, my dear," he murmured, reaching down and picking her up, moving her to his shoulder, where she hugged his neck...and he permitted it. "I have been reading the report on Division One Agent Echo's abduction by the Cortians." He shook his head. "I must insist that you do NOT read it, dear friend. I have been doing this job for many long annums, and I am tenacious and resilient, used to many of the hard things of the world. But this..." He shook his head again. "This was the work of barbarous captors against a prisoner of war. I am an experienced law enforcement official, and I have seen much of death. But torture is another matter altogether...and they tortured Echo. And Omega felt it."

"Through the...through that bond you told me of?" Nesh wondered. "I forget the term..."

"Just so. I..." he broke off, considering, then added, "I think I am going to take this forward to the chief prosecutor and ask for an addendum, or at least a modification, to the charges. This was a war crime."

"But...I did not think we were any longer at war with the Cortians," Nesh pointed out.

"WE may not consider it so," Wuxullian noted, "but that does not mean that the Cortians agree with us."

* * *

"In the name of the Maker!" Kryunub Corgrese, chief prosecutor for the Aleancë court system, exclaimed, his yellow eyes going wide, even as his short, stubby antennae waved in dismay. "Surely you jest, Wux! WAR crimes?!"

"Precisely, and no, I am deadly serious," Wuxullian affirmed, handing the Zardran a printout of the report. "Read it, Kry. But make sure your stomach is empty when you do, else you WILL purge it." He quirked his lips. "A bit of antiemetic beforehand might not be amiss, as well."

"Damnation," Corgrese murmured, shocked. "That bad?"

"That bad."

"...All right. Let me see what I can do."

"That is all I ask," Wuxullian said.

* * *

Corgrese read the report and reacted more or less as Wuxullian had warned; once he recovered a little, he promptly called in all of the tribunal members and judges slated to sit for the various trials, as well as all of the prosecutors and defense attorneys, having them read the report in a non-public environment, namely the large courtroom devoid of the accused, other witnesses, and the gallery visitors. Then he addressed the judges.

"Honored beings," he said, "this report is comprised of the depositions of the Alpha One team of Division One, as compiled by a team of Deltiri interrogators headed by esteemed Ambassador Zz'r'p ob Tii'rkin. As you will no doubt know, Agent Echo, the senior member of the Alpha One team, was the target of the Cortian kidnapping and attempted slave trade incident, and Agent Omega, his partner recently made spouse as well, was responsible for rescuing him, with considerable help from Director Fox; the crew of the *Genesis*, which is Division One's fleet flagship; Alpha Line, that Division's very unique special forces department; and staff from the Deltiri embassy on Earth. As Agent Echo is understandably still incapacitated by the attack upon him, is in fact unconscious and undergoing serious medical treatment which it is hoped—but not certain— will return him to a semblance of normalcy, and Agent Omega is thereby helping to tend him as his partner and spouse—she is his designated legal 'voice,' with responsibility for decisions made in his stead and with regard to his care, while he is unable to speak for himself—they could not come to the tribunals themselves. But they willingly arranged for these depositions to be presented before you, so that all might know the truth."

"Arniquatug truth," the judge from Ryynqitsk muttered. "Hellacious, as the humans say."

"Indeed. And since we have barely begun the process, which will be a long one given the multiple ships' crews involved, I would like to request that we pause the proceedings in light of these depositions, in order to consider if we are handling the tribunals properly."

"How so, Chief Prosecutor?" M'ssiit Wrrrff, the Bastian chief adjudicator, queried formally.

"It is the considered opinion of the Chief Administrator of the Pan-Galactic Law Enforcement Agency that these acts against Agent Echo and, by extension, his partner Omega, constitute war crimes," Corgrese declared. "And I have contacted the interrogation team on Earth to verify the meaning and intent of certain wording they used, and they are in agreement."

"On grounds what?!" the flabbergasted Hypothenamoid judge demanded to know. "The Coalition not any longer at war with Corta!"

"Chief Wuxullian points out, quite reasonably, that merely because WE are not at war with the Cortians, does NOT mean that the Cortians are not at war with US," Corgrese noted. "The marauder vessels which yet roam our spaceways, while thankfully fewer each lunation thanks to Wuxullian's teams, still manage to wreak untold havoc in the lives of our various peoples. They refuse to recognize our jurisdiction or authority, and they seem set upon causing as much theft and destruction of life, of way of life, and of property as possible, perhaps over and above that induced by their own general culture and manner of operations. If this is the case, if they are effectively attempting to wage asymmetric warfare upon the Coalition, then I submit to you that, as Echo and Omega are, between them, responsible for revealing their true intentions to the Coalition as a whole, they are effectively prime targets of the Cortians. This therefore means that Echo was a de facto prisoner of war, and the atrocious acts perpetrated upon him were, indeed, war crimes."

The large tribunal chamber was silent for long moments.

"We need a bit more information than that, to make such

a judgement call as to rework the nature and order of the tribunals," Wrrrff decided. "But you make several interesting points."

"Might I suggest examining the captains of the two Cortian vessels involved in this altercation?" Corgrese offered. "If they will not speak out, then telepathic interrogators can be provided to obtain their thoughts as we put the questions to them."

"This will work," Wrrrff said. "Can it be arranged within the hour?"

"I believe so, milord," Corgrese agreed.

"Do it," Wrrrff ordered.

* * *

The two Cortian captains were brought in, wrists and legs in force-cuffs, and provided electronic translators, which hung about their necks; several Deltiri investigators also stood by, not only to be used if the accused refused to answer questions, but also to verify that they were telling the truth on anything they chose to verbalize. Seated in their appropriate places around the courtroom were the members of the bar—both prosecution and defense—and the adjudicators, attired in their formal robes as appropriate.

But instead of first bringing up Incke, captain of the *Orktes*, the principal vessel involved in the kidnapping and torture, Corgrese chose to bring the captain of the *Ramtum* for initial interrogation. Corgrese had been watching several of the Cortians—notably those who were being charged with the most serious, the most heinous crimes—since they had arrived on Aleancë, and it had struck him that Incke was the smarter of the two captains, and therefore might prove difficult. And, he considered, if he handled the matter carefully and brought Captain K'ti up for questioning first, the *Ramtum*'s captain might tell them all they needed to know, at least for the current matter under consideration.

"K'ti," Corgrese began, "your recent mission...was it to capture an enemy of the Cortians? Agent Echo?"

"I believe that was the case, yes, though I know of no agents," the captain of the *Ramtum* noted through the translator. "We were there to take an escaped slave back into custody, for he has caused the Cortian Amalgam much trouble. He has been designated Amalgam Enemy Number One for his actions against us. But yes, his name is Echo."

"Agent Echo has never been a slave!" Wrrrff declared. "He is a greatly respected law enforcement agent of the Pan-Galactic Coalition!"

The Cortian captain K'ti shrugged.

"He was an acquisition," he claimed. "He is therefore a slave. He is currently free, therefore he is an escaped slave. It matters not for how long he was in custody, or even if he was ever in custody, for he was our acquisition, and therefore he is our slave until such time as we determine to sell or kill him. As for this coalition you claim, we do not recognize it as a legitimate government."

"What do you consider it, then?" Corgrese pressed, holding up a staying hand as Wrrrff started to interject again.

"It is nothing more than a loose grouping of rebellious slaves, trying to overthrow our rightful place and ownership," K'ti said callously, with another shrug. "Like all such slave rebellions, it is weak. Look at the other renegade slave, Omega—she claimed that she would kill us all, that our lives were forfeit. Yet here we stand. She could not do it. She is weak. YOU are weak, and your rebellion is weak. We will soon crush it, and you will do our bidding."

"Well said, K'ti," Incke murmured from the side, where he waited. "We are being illegally detained by those who should be serving us."

"But you do not have your full armada," Corgrese pointed out. "You are no more than a handful of ships, widely separated and scattered across the Great Spiral by twos and threes."

"True," K'ti agreed. "That is unfortunate, for it would go much faster, so. But it matters not, for the conflict will go on as long as we have breath...and soon or late, we shall win. Then we will force all of you to do our bidding. You would do well to surrender now, while you can."

"But we are many, and you are few," Corgrese pressed.

"Perhaps. But we are the righteous owners; the gods are on our side. You are but slaves, beneath the gods' notice. We will win." K'ti was brazenly presumptuous.

"Listen to him," Incke averred, even more audaciously

complacent than his colleague. "Give yourselves up to us now. It will go easier for you when we finally have complete control, and you will be treated better than the more rebellious slaves."

Wrrrff put his face in his paws.

"Enough," he ordered then. "I have already heard enough. Take them back to their cells."

After the force-shackled prisoners were removed from the room, Corgrese turned to Wrrrff.

"Well?" he said, succinct.

"Have the tribunal manager change all of the Cortian entries on the docket to war crimes, structuring the schedule appropriately," Wrrrff decreed. "Do I hear any dissent to this decision among the judiciary, the prosecutors, or the defense after that little manifesto?" He waved a paw at the witness stand.

No one said anything, not even the defense attorneys... though several made as if to say something, then decided that discretion might be better called for, in the face of such a blatant statement as the Cortian captains had made.

"Very well. Have Impiir make the necessary adjustments to the sitting adjudicators, prosecutors, and defense lawyers as necessary, please." Wrrrff glanced around. "This gathering is dismissed."

He rapped one block on another, and the formally-robed beings rose and dispersed.

* * *

"You're kidding," Omega said, dumbfounded, as she sat in Fox's office with that worthy. "War crimes?"

"No, we are not, youngling," Wuxullian said on one of the wall screens in Fox's office. "The judiciary and the bar brought in the Cortian ships' captains and queried them. And in process of responding, the *Ramtum*'s captain made it plain—and the *Orktes* captain confirmed it—they considered their actions a military response to 'a slave rebellion,' and they intended to put it down, no matter how long it took...as if their paltry few spacecraft could ever do so."

"And that does, indeed, put it in the realm of a military action, a military attack against a key rebel," Fox said, "at least by their lights. Which makes their actions war crimes." He paused, then added, "Which, in turn, ramps up the punishments considerably."

"It does," Wuxullian confirmed. "We have brought in several military leaders and some adjudicators from various military forces, in order to more properly conduct the tribunals, given the different classification. Considering the charges, and the amount of evidence we have against them—most notably, yours and Echo's depositions, Omega, as well as everything that was found when my forces boarded the Cortian spacecraft—all of the principals, to include the captains, the undercover implant, and the torture master, are apt to be convicted and executed via military firing squad. Not, I suppose, that that will make any difference to the other Cortian spacecraft crews out there. They will continue trying to 'put down the slave rebellion' until we have had to destroy every last one of them." Wuxullian let out a deep breath in a sigh. "This is not how I wanted all of this to end. I should much prefer to convince them to end their rampages than to have to wage war against them. But if this is the general attitude of the Cortian pirates, it appears that will not be an option. And," he added, "we have been interrogating the rank and file crew members on this for that very reason, and it appears it IS, indeed, the general attitude. Most unfortunate."

"Are you calling out the militaries?" Omega wondered.

"Lady Teela and Lord Entiyti are discussing that very thing with Lord Guurn and Lady Raiit," Wuxullian attested. "The Corta system is still under a blockade, though they are starting to become a bit more tractable, at least in certain regions of the planet. But I fully expect a specialized statement of galactic emergency—possibly with, or without, a limited, temporary enactment of martial law—that will be tantamount to a kind of declaration of war against the renegade Cortian vessels. It means that we will have to increase armed patrols around our inhabited planets, stations, and shipping lanes, but if that is what it takes to rid ourselves of the plague of these pirating slavers, that is what we must do."

Omega nodded in silence, her countenance thoughtful.

Fox and Wuxullian watched her for a long moment, then Fox said, "If Division One can help with that, Wux, believe me, we have plenty of reason to do so. And we will."

"And that is understood and appreciated, my old friend," Wuxullian agreed, "and we will likely need it. However, I think it would be wise if you did NOT use your top Alpha Line teams in that. You may or may not know, but according to the records aboard the *Orktes*, there seems to have been a confusion of identities between Omega...and Agent India of Alpha Two."

"WHAT?!" Omega cried, incensed. "You mean one of my best friends is threatened by those sons of bitches, TOO??"

"I am afraid so, Omega," Wuxullian confirmed. "I am uncertain how the mistake occurred, but her image was attached to your name, and designated 'Cortian Amalgam Most Wanted: Public Enemy Number Two.' Or Cortian words to that effect."

"Which probably was lucky for Omega, or they'd have taken her, too," Fox observed.

"Indeed."

"Damn," Omega fussed. "We need to make sure Romeo an' India know about THAT. They need to watch their backs even more than usual until this buncha shit is straightened out."

"They do," Wuxullian averred. "And so do you."

"I understand and completely agree," Fox declared. "We don't need Echo and Omega, let alone any of their close colleagues who may ALSO be on the Cortians' list, put in even more harm's way."

"Exactly."

"And don't worry, tekhter," Fox added, "I'll make sure to give Alpha Two a personal heads-up, as soon as we're finished here. It does make me reconsider a couple of pending assignments I was planning on giving them; I think I'll hand those off to some other teams. But I agree: neither you, Echo, Romeo, nor India needs to go into the field, at least off-planet, until this resolves."

"Well, that assumes Echo an' I'll be going back in the field to begin with, I guess," Omega murmured, shoulders slumping, and Wuxullian looked distressed for a moment, then hid it quickly.

"Chin up, tekhter," Fox said, as encouraging as he knew how to be. "Yes, we have that plan in our hip pocket, you and I. But let's hope things turn out better than all that."

"I'm trying, Fox, but I also don't want to have any illusions about how serious this is," Omega said, looking more than a bit downcast. "I dunno how much Zebra's told you, but Zarnix came to me early on—without Dihl, let me note—and explained that he just wasn't sure. See, the leg...well, it took at least two strokes of whatever bladed thing they were using, maybe more, and the big shin bone basically shattered as much as it cut. And he extracted all the bone chips he could find from the pieces I brought back, then he checked Echo's stump for more. But he still doesn't know if he got it all, or how much was lost, or..."

"Oh," Fox murmured, deflating a bit. "So if they didn't put back all of the bone, but they didn't leave enough of a gap for it to grow back...or leave TOO MUCH of a gap..."

"Right," Omega confirmed. "Never mind his eye. If that eye doesn't grow back right, he'll have to leave field work, be disqualified as an aircraft pilot, disqualified as a spacecraft pilot...hell, Fox, he won't even be able to drive the 'Vette."

"Shit, merde, cachu, khro, abdab, and gronk!" Fox cursed. "I hadn't thought of that."

"And grablap, dingor, og'dm'n, grubdrfrutz, grigduzin, and geessht," Wuxullian added.

"Lotsa that," Omega sighed. "Alla that. Unfortunately, I don't know much of anything at this point. When I ask now, the docs are kinda tap-dancing around everything, and not actually giving me an answer."

"Would you like me to see what I can find out?" Fox wondered.

"That..." Omega broke off, and rubbed her face.

"What's wrong, tekhter?" Fox asked, concerned. "If you don't want me to, I won't."

"I don't know what to answer," Omega admitted then. "Part of me really needs to know, because I need to be able to plan, to know what to do, how to react when he comes out. To know how to HELP him. But the other part of me is afraid to find out."

"Ah," both males, the human and the Erikian, said in unison. "Well, then I will ask for myself," Fox decided. "And if you like, you can come to me later and I'll tell you what I found out."

"That might work," Omega considered. "Okay."

An alert went off on Wuxullian's end of the vidcomm.

"And that is my signal to go," he sighed. "Yet more courtroom drama, I fear. Keep me posted on what is happening there, both of you, please?"

"Of course," Fox said, nodding. "And please do likewise, especially with regard to the whole Cortian situation. I'm sure Omega would love to hear how the trial of Echo's especial captor goes."

"Damn straight," Omega snarled. Fox raised a concerned eyebrow; Wuxullian furrowed his brow.

"By all means," Wuxullian agreed smoothly, pretending not to have heard Omega's comment...or at least, to consider it in a more natural, less vengeful light than her tone of voice would indicate. "I may need your and your people's help with taking down more of them, after all."

"And you'll have it," Fox noted. "Now run see what you're needed for, alter khaver."

"Right," Wuxullian said with a chuckle. "Later, Fox. Take care, Omega. Wuxullian out."

"Fox...and Omega...out," the Director pronounced.

The screen went dark.

* * *

"Are you all right, tekhter?" Fox wondered after a few moments of silence; Omega sat in her chair, gaze unfocused, countenance thoughtful, saying nothing. But at that query, Omega visibly roused herself from her reverie, literally shaking herself for a second or two.

"I guess so, Fox," she murmured, trying not to sigh and failing. "I just keep...I wonder what Echo's reaction is gonna be, when he comes out of the regen pod and, and can't..."

"Can't go back to what he was before?"

"Yeah. He LOVES to fly, Fox! Every bit as much as I do! If it flies, he can pilot it, and loves doing it! That's why I nicknamed him 'Ace.' But with only one functional eye..." She looked up at him, an almost pleading expression on her face. "I guess I'm still thinking of all the potential ramifications, I suppose. And I keep being blindsided by—" Omega broke off, and winced. "And if this doesn't work, he really WILL have a blind

296

side. I just...I can't..." She slumped in despair, and buried her face in her hands, but did not cry. "I don't know how I'm going to help him, Fox. I've gone from, 'I'm a mess, I need counseling,' to 'How the hell am I gonna help my husband, who's been tortured and maimed by means so horrible I can't even begin to think of all the ways it's gonna affect his life?' And I have no answers for that." She shook her head. "I love him so much I'd gladly die in his place. But I'm completely helpless on this one, as near as I can figure out."

"We all are, tekhter," Fox offered, coming around from behind his desk and sitting in the empty visitor chair beside her... the one where normally Echo would be sitting. He took one of her hands in his and held it, patting gently before squeezing it lightly. "Other than the medlab staff—and even they are limited, because they aren't miracle-workers—there is little that any of us can do for Echo now. We jointly took him out of that hellhole, and we prevented his being killed, slaughtered like a wild animal killed by savages. And now you and the Deltiri are keeping him free from pain. The rest of us? We have to sit back and watch, helpless to do more than pray for the two of you."

"Two?" Omega wondered in a very low voice, looking up at him. Fox could see the pain in the blue eyes, as well as the mild confusion, and explained.

"Don't think we don't all know how much you mean to each other, Omega. Or how happy you were to be married. And now it looks rather as if the life you had planned together has fallen apart at the seams just as it was getting started, thanks to vindictive old enemies who literally don't know when they're beaten, and will evidently have to be hounded into the grave to stop. And don't think we're all so focused on what's happened to Echo that we can't see how it's affecting YOU. Because you'd be very, very wrong, dear girl. The only problem is, other than being here, being a shoulder to cry on and an ear to listen, there's not a lot any of us can do for you, either. What I DO know, because he's let me know, is that Whiskey has taken it upon himself to see that you are cared-for, as well as the medlab can do it."

"Yeah, he is," Omega admitted. "I didn't know he'd made it one of his duties, though. That's too much; I'll tell him to—"

"Don't you dare," Fox ordered, firm. "You couldn't, anyway. Not only would he be apt to refuse, he told Zarnix and me at the same time what he was doing—seeing that you ate regularly, something about a cot to sleep in, and notifying Wardrobe and Supplies to bring you changes of clothes when you need them as well as an overnight kit, never mind him ensuring you take your anxiety medication—and both of us, Zarnix and myself, formalized that with an order, tekhter. That is now officially PART of Whiskey's job, for the duration of Echo's stay in the medlab."

"Oh," Omega murmured. "It...it's not, I dunno, too much...?"

"No, I have been assured it is not. You aren't difficult to care for, meyn teyere, unless you are TRYING to be difficult to care for. And not only does the medlab have plenty of staff, Zarnix has even called in some physicians from the southern hemisphere offices to help take care of the Harrnakian influenza patients, which number, I gather, is finally starting to ramp up since we're getting deeper into flu season up here, so that the main Headquarters physician staff can focus on Echo. And it isn't going to do Echo any favors to come out of the regen process and find you piled up in a hospital bed of your own, anyway. No matter WHAT condition he turns out in."

"Well, no, but..."

"Have you been venting in that special workout room I had ginned up for you?"

"Yeah, I've already had a damn good workout in there," Omega confessed. "Dihl told me I was bein' antsy an' needed to go hit it up, so I did. I think it's gonna work really good for blowing off steam an' venting emotions, never mind wearing me out enough that I can get some sleep, especially since I took to soaking in the hot tub after, to help relax and not be so sore later on, back on the *Genesis*. And I'm keeping up that...'protocol,' I guess we'll call it."

"That...is very good, then."

"Um, Fox?"

"Yes?"

"Have you...you haven't taken a look at the bags, have you?"

"Actually, I have. I'm thinking you appreciate the paint job that Chain did on 'em?"

"Heh. Yeah," Omega chuckled, but the sound was grim. "Every time I manage to split a seam a little further on one of 'em, I..." She shook her head. "No. I probably shouldn't admit to that."

"You imagine you've just done the same to the Cortian who tortured Echo?" Fox offered the shrewd guess. "Broken a bone, split his skin open, cracked his skull, maybe even disemboweled him?"

"Um," Omega murmured, wide-eyed. "You...I mean, do you think..."

"That you are a terrible person for that? No," Fox told her, squeezing her hand again before patting it lightly. "Youngling—as the galactics say—I've been around the block quite a few more times than you have, by this point in my life. In reality, I'm old enough to be at least your grandfather; possibly old enough to be your GREAT-grandfather. And I traveled the galaxy for several decades, and saw plenty of...shit. Never mind the Nazis and their ilk before that. I know what it is to be furious, to feel genuine righteous anger at what has been done to someone you love dearly and deeply. But I also know that it is one thing to vent that anger and pain in the way you are doing it, and quite another to do so against the actual being. The one is healing, or it can be, if you let it; the other tends to damage the soul in ways that I think might be nigh unto irreparable. At least in this life."

"You know I considered asking to be part of the execution squad...?"

"Actually, I do," Fox confessed. "A certain Deltiri thought I should be prepared for the anger he saw in you, and wanted to ask me to find a way to help you vent. When I heard you'd gone to the gym to bust up a few old punching bags, I decided you'd found your own way before I'd had a chance to come up with anything...but I decided that I COULD ensure you could keep doing it."

"Oh. Okay."

"You don't mind that Zz'r'p told me?"

"No. I'd told him, early on, that if he saw something that

might make me unfit for duty, or that for whatever reason you or Echo needed to know about, he SHOULD tell you. Not necessarily anybody ELSE, because I trust you two; but...yeah."

"Well, I appreciate that, tekhter; it shows your innate wisdom, I think. And, for what it's worth, normally he keeps your counseling sessions sacrosanct," Fox told her. "I suppose he thought this WAS something I needed to know, and for just the reason I told you. And no, other than maybe Zebra—who, after all, is your personal physician—I'll tell no one else."

"And it works," Omega said with a shrug and a slight smile. "I'm...I'm really glad you don't think bad of me for it, though."

"Oh, meyn tekhter," Fox sighed, "if you had any idea what I wanted to do to the Nazi guards..." He shook his head. "No, I can't possibly think badly of you for this, because I came very close to actually killing one of those guards when I was a teen, shortly after I was liberated and the war ended. Fortunately a rather special friend I'd made in one of the Allied military units managed to convince me the scum wasn't worth having his blood on my hands."

"Oh," Omega said. She wrapped her fingers around his and squeezed gently. "Yeah, I can completely understand that."

"I thought you might. All right. Now that we understand each other, is there anything I can do to help you deal? Or shall I just walk you down to the medlab? I can have Alpha Two waiting for me when I come back, for that little heads-up."

"I dunno of anything you can do, Abba Fox," Omega decided, shoulders slumping. "I do appreciate the thought. But yeah, a friendly face beside me, while I walk back to the medlab, might be nice. If you have time."

"For this, I'll MAKE time, tekhter."

"Okay. Let's go?"

"Let's go."

* * *

"No, Omega explained the concern with Echo's leg pretty well, it sounds like," Zarnix confirmed, a little while later in his private office within the medlab. "The wrist was a much cleaner cut, because it has a smaller cross-section and required less force; it went in one blow, and probably the first blow at that. Whereas Doron and I estimated it took at least two, and

300

possibly as many as four, swings of the blade to sever the leg."

"Damnation," Fox grumbled, finally allowing himself to be worried, upset, and angry. "The bastard who did it deserves to find out what it feels like."

"I am not sure I can argue with that sentiment overmuch, physician though I am," Zarnix admitted. "The cold-blooded barbarism of the act tops anything I have seen, and I am not inexperienced in either emergency room or battlefield medicine." He shrugged. "There is the carnage that takes place in warfare, certainly...but which is, to some degree, mindless, as explosives blow and the like. It is almost always...'anonymous,' as it were; rare is the soldier who sees the enemy as individuals, because the psychological strain is too great. To be a soldier, and to continue to be a SANE soldier, tends to mean distancing oneself from the killing, as much as the situation allows. This...this was calculated and deliberate and targeted. This was done...BECAUSE he is ECHO. Because he is, as Omega says, 'The most badass agent in the whole galaxy,' and they wanted to take advantage of every part of that reputation, including his knowledge base...and then kill him. Or allow him to be killed, is perhaps more accurate. All to prove they could, I assume."

"That's what it sounds like to me," Fox agreed. "And I rather understood that Chief Wux and essentially all of the adjudicators and the bar came to the same conclusion. So...you're uncertain of how the leg is going to turn out?"

"Exactly. And I am sorry, but right now I cannot offer you more information, because I do not yet have it."

"What about the hand and the eye?" Fox wondered.

"The hand, as nearly as we can tell, looks to be healing reasonably well," Zarnix said. "I know this sounds like an oxymoron, but the fact that it was cut off relatively cleanly means it suffered far less trauma. I cannot speak to what kind of dexterity he will have when it has regrown, however. It is a HAND, after all—one of the most delicate and fine-tuned structures of the human body. Optimally, if he awakens and is able to flex the hand of his own volition, then we can re-train the dexterity through physical therapy. But if there are problems in doing so, then there may be permanent damage to the nervous structure.

In which case, he could never regain full use."

Fox winced.

"As for the eye, Omega's fears are precisely on target," Zarnix continued. "In many respects, the eye is the most sensitive and complex of the body's sensory organs. And the Cortians pretty much destroyed it. There was little left but some shreds of tissue. Fortunately the bastards did not reach the brain through the back of the eye socket, or he might not have lived long enough to be rescued."

"Do you think they knew that?"

"I suspect so; Omega tells me that Echo has vague recollections of a medical examination before he finally woke in what she has taken to calling the torture chamber, so I am certain they learned what to—"

"Adonai have mercy!" Fox exclaimed. "EXAMINATION?! What did they do to him? Did they obtain tissue samples? What—"

"Calm down, Fox," Zarnix said, soothing, as he raised both hands, palms outward. "I understand your concerns, and they are valid. But for one thing, both Cortian vessels are in PGLEIA custody, are they not?"

"True, true," Fox said, settling. "Meaning there is no chance of cloning, or *in vitro* 'harvesting of genetics,' whatever they may have done." He shook his head. "I'm afraid I'm tired and stressed, worrying about him. And so I didn't think. Sorry."

"Right, and I understand. And for another thing, evidently the medical examination was relatively automated; they barely even touched him, according to his recollection. They stripped him, then ran him through something that looked vaguely like an MRI, but was not; he knows, because it was not as NOISY as an MRI! He was groggy, but remembers the physicians discussing what this or that organ was, and what functions each one served." He shrugged. "Apparently when the Cortians take on an entire group of prisoners to enslave, they process them through at a great rate for maximum efficiency. And this device seems to be something akin to a larger version of one of our medscanners, but without the need for a physician to scan each being individually."

"What, they run 'em through on a conveyor belt?" Fox

wondered, wry.

"Something like, yes."

"So Echo wasn't raped, and he wasn't sexually assaulted, and he didn't have tissue removed for cloning or the like," Fox decided. "He was just tortured in the most inhumane—well, in the most...mmph. I can't come up with a comparable, non-species-centric word in English," he fussed. "Barbaric, I suppose."

"That will do, and I take no offense," Zarnix maintained with a grim chuckle. "I know what you are trying to say."

"So you honestly don't know about his eye?"

"Not at this point, no. And we may not, until he is decanted. I have hopes; Doron and I concentrated on that, once we had the bone scaffolding attached to his arm and leg. But no. I cannot say for certain." Zarnix nibbled his lower lip, then confided, "In fact, I am frankly a little worried."

"Why?"

"The eyelids were ripped partway off, and we tacked them back in place, and those appear to have healed rather well already," Zarnix divulged. "But they should normally have a convex shape, because the eyeball is directly underneath. Only they—"

"Don't," Fox finished for him. "They're still sunken in, because there ISN'T an eyeball under 'em."

"That...is my fear, yes."

"Farkakte, verdammt, merde, glagaram, and argdun!"

"Patience, Fox, patience. It may simply be that it is taking its own time in healing; as I said, it IS a very complex structure. Even if it does not work, I have a few options left," Zarnix said. "I have made two contacts—one to the top cloning expert in the galaxy, and the other to the best cybernetics expert... other than Omega and Madrid, that is. Though I have pinged Madrid on the matter; he says that a cybernetic wing, being more a mechanical construct, is a very different device than a cybernetic eye, so he fears he cannot help. But should the regeneration process not properly regrow a functioning eye, I intend to attempt to either clone one, or build a photonic one, and then insert it surgically. It simply means it will take longer to bring him back up to speed...assuming it works."

"Back on the *Genesis*, Omega said that the current state of cybernetic sensors was inferior to human sensory abilities," Fox pointed out.

"And she was correct in that, as well. But if we have to forge new techniques, develop new hardware, then by the Maker, Fox, we shall! This is our colleague, our friend, and our family member of whom we speak," Zarnix declared, his blue-tinged skin flushing slightly bluer; his orange eyes fairly blazed with the passion of his intent. "If it is my last living act in this existence, I WILL see Echo back to a close semblance of his old self!"

"But it could take years," Fox surmised. Zarnix sighed, seeming to collapse in on himself.

"Yes," the physician confessed. "It could take years."

"Shit," Fox breathed.

* * *

As the days passed, Echo's body began to slowly grow back the damaged limbs, though Omega and Dihl could not see that for the opaque pod around his body. Only a special viewing window over his face allowed them to see him at all, but they watched with care and anxiety as the damage and bruising around his left eye gradually smoothed away.

"But I can't tell if that eye is developing properly or not, just by looking," Zebra admitted to her husband one night, "and since I'm family, Zar is being hard-nosed and refusing to let me in on much, just yet."

"Which means he still isn't sure either," Fox realized. "Which...is probably not the news we wanted to hear. You remember what I told you of the conversation I had with him the other day. When was it? A week ago?"

"Yeah, it was. And yeah, that's what I'm afraid of, too," Zebra fretted. "But he hasn't said a word to any of us about it since then, in any substantive fashion. At some point, I'm gonna go in there and DEMAND he let me in on what's going on; I've helped with enough of it all that he owes me that much."

"I'll pull rank on him, if it'll help," Fox offered, "because frankly, I agree with you, bubeleh."

"When do you have free time to hit him up?" Zebra wondered, giving her mate a mischievous grin.

304

"Just make certain you really want to know first, meyn gelibte," Fox warned.

"Yeah, I hear you," Zebra sighed.

* * *

Several floors away in Headquarters, a similar conversation was taking place at the same time.

"How do you think he's coming along, Dihl?" Omega wondered. "You're the one with the medical degrees."

"I...am not sure, shich'ee'ké," a troubled Dihl admitted. "The rest of the staff is keeping me almost as much in the dark as they are you, in terms of details. But I gather that the hand and the leg are growing back, from a few odd comments that Whiskey and Zarnix have made to each other in my hearing— I've learned to listen for their conversations outside the room, in the hall! I cannot tell how WELL they are growing back, but they are growing back."

"That's good, then," Omega decided. "What about his eye?"

"I have heard very little about that," Dihl noted, biting her lip and pondering for a moment. Finally she ventured, "Omega? I would like your opinion on something."

"Okay, shoot."

"Well, it is about his eye. Do you think the eyelids are..." Dihl bit her lip again and thought for a moment.

"What's wrong?"

"Oh, I'm just trying to figure out wording, dear," Dihl said, shooting her a slight smile. "All right. You know how closed eyelids are convex, curving around the eye beneath them?"

"Yeah?"

"I am very pleased with how his eyelids appear to have healed...but do you think that they do indeed have that curved profile? On the damaged one, I mean?"

Omega's eyebrows shot up, and she stood, walked over to the pod, and bent, staring down into it through the viewing window.

"Huh," she grunted then. "I can't really tell. It isn't like it's LIT inside there, and there's several inches of rather viscous fluid between the window and his face..."

"Exactly," Dihl grumbled. "I cannot tell either. But it troubles me."

"Because if it isn't starting to curve back out, the eye isn't healing right? Or maybe healing at all?"

"That is my fear, yes, shich'ee'ké. And that will have serious ramifications to his future life, as you and I have already discussed."

"Yeah, I know," Omega said with a sigh, returning to her seat.

The two women sat there for long moments, staring at the side of the regeneration pod containing the man they both loved—as son to one, and as spouse to the other. Abruptly Omega stood.

"I'm...gonna run down to the gym for a workout," she declared. "Do you want me to grab anything for you on the way back? I can run by your quarters if you need me to."

"No, I don't think so," Dihl sighed. "But do pay attention to the time, Omega. The staff will be bringing dinner around in just over two hours. Try to be back before they bring our meals, please. I can have them leave a tray, but it will be better if you keep regular meals, dear one." Dihl nibbled her lip. "I worry for you."

"I know," Omega said with a matching sigh. "An' I'm sorry. You have enough to worry about with Echo, without worryin' about me."

"Nonsense. You are Alex's very heart, my dear. Looking after you IS looking after my son."

"All right," Omega promised then. "I'll come back in about an hour and a half, after a good solid workout and a soak in the hot tub to help me relax. Then we'll eat together, and I'll even consider going to the down room for a little nap after we finish. How 'bout that?"

"I think that is an excellent schedule plan, shich'ee'ké," Dihl said with a pleased smile. "After all, I slept in this morning, and took a nap after second lunch today, here in the recliner. But you...you stayed up with him most of the night, didn't you?"

"I wasn't sleepy," Omega confessed. "I'm used to lots of physical activity, but he's mostly unconscious, and there's nothing for me to do but just sit here and read, or stare at the pod, or think. And frankly, thinking's not good for me right now."

"Are you taking your anxiety medication?"

"Yeah," Omega said with a shrug. "But that doesn't do anything for sheer, raw fury. An' trust me, I have a lotta that, right now."

"All right. Go to the gym and kill some mock Cortians," Dihl declared. "For that matter, kill an extra one for me, if you would. I have no martial arts skills such as you and he have," she gestured at the pod, "so you must do it for me!"

"Ha! I'll do that," Omega said with a chuckle. "And, um, thanks for letting me know it isn't just me."

"Oh no, dear," Dihl said, face growing dark with anger. "It is NOT just you. It is me, it is Fox, it is Zebra, it is India and Romeo, it is most of Alpha Line..." She shook her head. "I have even heard Zarnix raise his voice on the matter, so he is not happy, either." She waved her hand in the direction of the door. "Go. I will be here when you get back."

"Gone," Omega declared, headed out.

* * *

A few minutes later, Whiskey came in to check and adjust the regeneration fluid bathing Echo's ravaged body. He looked around and saw the empty chair, with no sign of its usual occupant. So he turned to Dihl.

"Where's Meg?" Whiskey wondered.

"She went down to the gym to 'blow off steam,' as she puts it," Dihl told him, as he resumed checking the instrumentation read-outs on the pod. "After she finishes, she is going to come back for dinner, and she has promised me that she will then spend some time sleeping in the down room, since she did not, last night."

"Aw shit," Whiskey murmured, going to the cabinet along the wall and pulling out specific pharmaceutical packs, then coming over to the pod and hooking them into the circulation system. "There. That ought to do for Echo. So...what? I need to start shooing her off to bed at a particular hour, do you think?"

"I'm not certain it would do a great deal of good," Dihl admitted. "She has a good many negative emotions inside that are rather churning. So while you might shoo her off to

307

bed, that does not mean she would get any real sleep, or even rest. She might only have another flashback nightmare, which would not be good...for anyone. More, she and my son are very action-oriented. They are used to plenty of physical activity... and while HE is in the regeneration pod, SHE gets none. I think that is another reason she does these workouts; it not only relieves stress and burns away adrenaline and anger, it tires her enough so that she CAN sleep. I do not know what she does, exactly, but she ends each session with a hot tub soak, partly to help her keep from becoming sore, and partly to help her relax, as she has told me."

"Mm. At her level of conditioning, she shouldn't NEED to soak to prevent soreness...unless she's goin' over the top with the training, or doing something radically different from what she usually does...which, given the sort of wide-ranging training Alpha Line uses, is a little hard for me to believe. What KIND of thing is she doing?"

"Fox has set up a special room for her, with old punching bags of various sorts," Dihl explained. "So she goes in there and 'kills' something." She quirked her fingers around the word in air-quotes. "I gather she is slowly, gradually—and literally—tearing the bags apart."

"DAMN!" Whiskey exclaimed, shocked. "We might wanna run a quick check on HER, and make sure she isn't either injuring anything, or eating too little in the way of calories to heal properly after that kinda workout."

"It is a definite consideration," Dihl agreed. "Given she is my family now in every possible sense of the word, I would be appreciative if you would do that, actually."

"Consider it done, then," Whiskey said. "I can probably run a medscanner over her without her even knowing I've done it, if I need to an' I play my cards right. It got back to me that she didn't want to overload me by looking after Echo AND her. But that's my job, you know? And I care about you guys, too. I may not be part of that whole 'family' thing that you guys have put together, but for sure I'm a friend of that family! Which makes me think—how are YOU doing? You're part of our medical family, after all."

"I am doing reasonably well, except for the worry," Dihl

decided. "I know I need to sleep and eat on a regular schedule, and so I do...though the sleep is sometimes difficult, and my appetite is off because of that worry. For whatever it is worth, I am trying to keep Omega eating and sleeping as regularly as possible, too, so you have an ally on that. But yes, I understand her fretfulness over the lack of anything to do! I may not take down interstellar criminals as she does, but being a medtech is not exactly a sedentary job, either."

"Not at all," Whiskey agreed. "As for the worry, is it about more than Echo's sitch?"

"Yes and no. I worry about him, about Omega, about their relationship going forward..." Dihl sighed. "And about whether he will be able to do the job he loves so much, when all this is done."

"Unfortunately, I don't have answers for you on any of that," Whiskey said with a sigh of his own. "Not yet, anyhow. Do you have any specific questions?"

"Yes. Is his eye filling back out? The curvature of the lids... we have been unsure..."

Whiskey glanced at the door; seeing no one in it, he crouched next to Dihl and answered, keeping his voice low.

"Don't let on I said anything, okay?" he said. "Zar doesn't wanna worry you."

"No, of course not," Dihl declared. "I would not wish to put you in trouble."

"All right. To answer your question, it is, but slowly, and not nearly as much as we'd hoped it would be, by this stage of things," Whiskey admitted. "I know that Zarnix has consulted Doron a couple of times about it, but it seems that different patients can heal at different rates on things; sometimes even different parts of the same patient heal at different rates! So his hand and leg might be close to done by this point—and according to our instrumentation, they are, just about—but his eye, which is so complex and delicate an organ, might need a little more time. Or it might suddenly accelerate once it reaches a certain stage, and catch up to the arm and leg. Or..." Whiskey shrugged, giving her a regretful glance, "it might not."

"Mm," Dihl hummed, an unhappy expression on her face.

"I'm sorry not to have any better answer for you than that,"

Whiskey apologized. "Personally, I'm hoping that, as the forecast date for his decanting gets closer, his healing will accelerate, and everything'll go gangbusters. I DO think it's promising the way the area AROUND that eye is healing up right along."

"True," Dihl concluded. "I suppose we will just have to wait, and try to be patient."

"That's probably best, yes," Whiskey agreed. "Now, let me go make sure that your and Meg's dinners aren't forgotten again. They didn't remember to bring Meg's breakfast this morning, and bless her, she didn't complain or say a word. So nobody had a clue until, halfway through the morning, she became a little lightheaded and her poor stomach started rumbling so loud I heard it in the corridor outside. Granted, the door was propped open, but still."

"Oh gracious!" Dihl said in surprise and concern, putting a hand to her throat. "And with her 'enhanced' metabolism!"

"I know!" Whiskey said with a laugh. "Ain't it the truth!"

And he headed out to check on matters.

* * *

A little while later, Omega returned, seeming a little less restless for the workout and relaxing session in the hot tub. Dinner arrived, and she and Dihl shared the meal, chatting quietly as they ate.

Five minutes after the food services agent removed their trays, Whiskey came into the room.

"No, sit right there, Omega," he said as she made to rise, pulling out his medscanner and running it over her form, before adjusting the settings and doing so a second and third time. "I had some specific requests to check on you from your family members. I just wanna make sure you're taking good care of yourself, and not overdoing it on those venting sessions of yours. And if you're not taking proper care of yourself, then we need to do it for you."

"I'm fine," Omega protested.

"Actually, you're not, quite," Whiskey said, studying the readout on the device in his hand. "You have a couple of sprains and some pretty hefty bruising. And...shit! Girl, you have muscle strains all OVER your body! How is that not hurting?"

"I do?" Omega wondered, blank. "I guess I...do what?" She broke off and turned to the regen pod. "Hang on a sec."

Whiskey's eyebrow went up, and Dihl studied Omega, then noted the direction of her gaze, and behind her back, signaled Whiskey, then put her finger to her lips to signify he should remain quiet for a moment. His other eyebrow joined the first, then he nodded, and just waited. After a couple of minutes, Omega's gaze resumed a present light, and she turned her attention back to the physician.

"Sorry," she murmured. "Echo can sometimes communicate through the nd't'lq a little bit, even without really being fully conscious. And as he heals and the pain diminishes more and more, he can do more. It, um, it seems he's been aware for a few days of what you just discovered, Whiskey, and since we've been keeping him out of pain—since I've been one of the people keeping him out of pain, and he's connected to me via the nd't'lq bond—he's learned where that 'telepathic pain center' place is, and..."

"Ah," Dihl realized. "THAT is the reason you haven't hurt from your minor injuries; Echo has been returning the favor by keeping YOU out of pain."

"Something like, yeah," Omega confirmed. "Only he's been hoping one of y'all would recognize what I was doing to myself, and treat me for it."

"I can do that, so make sure he knows I'm on it," Whiskey agreed. "But what you need to do is to ease up on those workouts."

"If I do that, then you'll be treating me for something a whole lot more serious than a couple of strains and some sprains," Omega pointed out. "Like psychological issues and a completely busted hand, when I try to put it through a wall. I mean, I'm already doing some kinda-sorta remote counseling sessions with Zz'r'p, but..."

"Mm," Whiskey murmured. "Good point. Okay, let me go fetch some meds for you, for what you've already done to yourself, while I think on that some."

"All right. Echo says thanks, and so do I."

"Not a problem, either of ya."

Whiskey headed out.

* * *

He was back about fifteen minutes later with a vial of tablets. "Here," he said. "I ran into Zarnix and Zebra along the way to the pharmacy; Zee was giving Zar some sort of reaming-out, and threatening to call in Fox about some kinda thing, I dunno. Those two are like twins or something; either they get along fantastically, or they're arguing their heads off! Anyway, given Zee is your principal physician, Meg, I stopped 'em and told them about your special workouts, and how it was affecting you—in a positive fashion, mentally and emotionally; in a negative fashion, physically—and what we decided is this. We want you to continue doing what you need to do to vent and remain emotionally and mentally healthy—oh, and I'm supposed to ask if you've seen Ambassador Zz'r'p for a counseling session since you've come back?"

"If you mean have I been to his office for one, no, I've been here," Omega said, then held up a hand as Whiskey started to protest. "But that doesn't mean he and I haven't had a few sessions. That's the advantage of having a Deltiri for a counselor. I thought I mentioned that earlier." She grinned. "So yes, he and I have had a few sessions. Especially after he and the others took Echo's and my telepathic depositions for the trials. 'Cause he now knows exactly what happened, see, and being able to talk to him about it HAS helped. It's just that, until that lot gets what's coming to 'em..."

"Aha. I hear that," Whiskey said then. "Okay, that's good, that's real good. So keep doing those workouts, as hard as you need to, to ditch some of the anger and antsiness. BUT, we now want you to come by and see me or Zee and let us do a once-over on you after each workout. That way, we can determine if you've injured yourself again, and treat it right away. You have some damage in there that, according to my scanner, is nearly a week old, girl. A DIVISION week. And nobody treating it. You're gonna feel that, sooner or later, because you weren't giving it a chance to heal on its own before doing it all over again. And if you KEEP doing it, you're gonna wind up with some chronic injuries, maybe even torn tendons an' shit, and those are damn hard to heal properly, even with our techniques an' procedures."

"Oh," Omega murmured, considering the information he'd just presented to her. "Okay, yeah, I see what you mean. And sure, I can swing by and let one of y'all give me a scan. But how are you gonna treat it?"

"With this," he said, handing her the vial of tablets, each of which had a suspiciously familiar lavender hue. "It's a brand-new med. It took us a bit of work, and the project to make it has been going on for close to six months, but we managed it. This is an oral form of the IV we ginned out of the regen fluid stuff. I think they're calling it 'Regenic' or something like that, 'cause it's pretty similar to Rejuvic, which it turns out was ALSO based on the regen fluid, but Rejuvic is topical and more generic, an' really only for what you call 'boo-boos.' This is stronger, and oral, so it's systemic. We have to compound it for each patient individually, but it's a bit more convenient than coming down to the medlab and sitting around while we run a whole bag of the fluid into you."

"True," Omega agreed, accepting the pill bottle. "So... what? Do you want me to take one a day? One per meal?"

"No, no," Whiskey said. "Dihl said you were going to go sleep in a bit?"

"Yeah, once my dinner has digested a bit."

"Okay. Then take one now, since you just ate, and take one after breakfast in the morning, which I'll see to it you have, this time, if I have to fetch it myself," Whiskey said. "Then I'll come by before first lunch and give you a once-over, and if everything's healed up like I expect it will be, you're good until after your next workout. If you're not, then you'll take another after dinner tomorrow night, and I'll check you again. Breakfast and dinner, breakfast and dinner. Lather, rinse, repeat until the damage is healed."

"Oh, okay."

"BUT," Whiskey amended, "we do NOT want you doing another workout until AFTER you heal up all the damage from the previous one. Which should mean you can do them daily... ONCE we get you healed up from the cumulative damage, here."

"Which might mean you won't allow me to work out tomorrow, but I probably can the day after?" Omega verified.

"Exactly. But as between you, me, and Dihl? Zar, Zee and I told the pharmacy to prepare the strongest dosage for you for this particular situation," Whiskey told her. "So I fully expect that by tomorrow morning, you'll be back to normal. And I'll bet," he added, "that even with Echo having suppressed your pain, you'll feel better."

"Well, I won't complain about that, I suppose," Omega decided.

"GOOD," Dihl decreed. "Now, take your medication. We'll sit here and chat for perhaps forty-five minutes, and then it is off to bed with you."

"Okay, 'Mom,'" Omega said with a grin.

* * *

Several days later, the argument in Medical was still ongoing, as Zebra met with Zarnix in his office...again.

"...That doesn't give you the right not to TELL me anything!" Zebra told Zarnix in no uncertain terms. "India and I are the ones who worked on him within minutes of Omega rescuing him, after all."

"And you both came back traumatized by it," Zarnix protested. "India is still off medical duty because of it, mostly doing admin work in the Alpha Line Room for Romeo."

"I know, but that was my fault," Zebra noted, shamefaced. "I should have helped her clean the wounds, not left her to do it by herself while I treated the severed limbs. So I had the easier job, which means I'm good to go NOW."

"Zebra, I truly do not think it would be wise..."

"Zar, you're the nearest thing I have to a brother any more," Zebra said, earnest. "So you should know: Fox is now insisting on having an update. He's threatened to use Director authority, because you're not telling 'the rest of the family' ANYthing... which is not policy, and you and I both know it. But what you're forgetting is, YOU'RE part of that family now, too...and after sitting with the 'family' at the wedding, everybody knows it. Which means he can order you to remove yourself from the case, too, and leave it to Whiskey or Rglfrz."

"That is, I suppose, his prerogative as Director," an unhappy Zarnix admitted, shoulders slumping. "I think a more structured, broader base than that—as in, a team of physicians—is the better approach..."

"EXACTLY!" Zebra exclaimed. "And that means Echo's PERSONAL PHYSICIAN needs to be on the team! And that's ME!" She reached across the desk and took his hand in hers, patting it lightly. "Look, Zar. When Fox and I were first talking about it a few days ago, it was just, 'I'll come down and order him to tell you, bubeleh.' And it was 'half in jest,' as he puts it. But last night, it was, 'Enough is enough. I need to know what's going on with my top Agent, and if I'll still have him as top Agent after this, or not. I need to PLAN.' He was NOT happy, Zar. Remember, Echo isn't just his oldest friend, or his top field Agent; he's the head of Alpha Line, and he's the Assistant Director. So if I come home again and still don't know anything, he WILL meet with you directly, if he has to have Security fetch you and escort you to his office. If you put him off one more time..." She shook her head. "I can't promise he won't become seriously pissed. And then all bets are off. You're the best physician on staff. There's a REASON you're chief of staff! But there's a reason I'm the assistant chief of staff, too, remember. Let. Me. HELP. Brief me on how Echo is doing."

Zarnix sat back in his desk chair and sighed.

"All right, Zee," he said, defeated. "I have only been trying to protect you all, as befits a member of the family..."

"Oh no. That doesn't sound good," Zebra said, blanching a bit.

"It's been unaccountably slow, Zee," he admitted. "The trauma, both mental and physical...Doron says it has affected the healing rate. I think...I THINK...it might be accelerating a little, finally. Well, if you are going to rejoin the team, then I suppose you need to see the records and charts," he decided. "Hold on a few minutes while I fish everything out and pull it up."

* * *

Ten minutes later, Zebra had been read in on everything the Medical department had done to and for Echo since he arrived on Earth. She sat pondering what she had just reviewed for long moments.

"Well," she concluded after a minute or so, "there's good

news, and there's bad news."

"It appears that way, yes," Zarnix agreed. "Now perhaps you understand why I have not shared information."

"Yeah. It's almost, but not quite as bad as, 'There ain't no info to share,'" Zebra affirmed.

"Precisely," Zarnix confirmed. "I have been in daily contact with Doron, but he keeps telling me to be patient; Division One has never had these kinds of injuries to deal with in this procedure before, and he says it is naturally slow. I pointed out that I did not think Omega had what amounted to an exponential healing curve, but he responded that, given her personal history in light of what was done to her, she is not a good example to go by for non-augmented humans."

"Well, that's a good point, I guess."

"Yes, I had not thought about it quite like that until he said something, but we should not expect Echo to respond as Omega did."

"I just hope the end result is the same, or damn close to it," Zebra decided. "'Cause Meg came out of it pretty much physically back to normal. Oh, there's a couple small scar-type places on her lower back, where the skin color is a little bit different, but you have to really look close to tell; I'm hoping Echo turns out the same way. Let's go have a look-see at his current condition."

"All right."

* * *

Omega had just returned from her stress-relieving workout, and Whiskey was giving her a once-over with the medscanner, when Zarnix and Zebra came into Lab B to check on Echo. Dihl had gone back to her quarters to rest, and Omega jumped on the trio of physicians as they surveyed the pod's instrumentation and readouts.

"Zebra! Are you back on the team of doctors looking after Echo now?!" she asked.

"Sure am, honey," Zebra said with a smile. "I'm here so Zar can give me a bit of a look-see as to what's going on. I've already read over the charts and files. Zar needs a break anyhow; he's startin' to look a little ragged, himself."

"Great! So that means y'all can tell me how he's doing

now!" Omega exclaimed.

"I have been, Omega, I swear," Whiskey said, picking up the bottle of Regenic sitting on the end table and extracting one of the lavender tablets, handing it to her. "Here, take this, girl, and knock it back." Everyone paused while Omega accepted the pill, then washed it down with the glass of water sitting beside the pill bottle. "There. So, yeah, I've BEEN telling you. There's just nothing much to be TOLD."

"So far, that is largely true," Zarnix agreed.

"And I can confirm that," Zebra attested. "These are new types of injuries for us to deal with, Meg, at least with this technique. And one thing I can say for sure is that each type of injury or illness has its own timetable, and each patient responds with different degrees of rapidity to the treatment."

"But...how long are you gonna keep Echo in there?" Omega wondered, countenance falling.

"As long as it takes, honey," Zebra said, firm. "I'm already seeing a couple things I wanna discuss trying with Zar and the other docs, here."

"Oh, wonderful," Zarnix said, pleased. "I had not thought of that! Doron has always said you have excellent instincts for the regeneration process, Zee. If you have ideas we have not yet tried, this might actually be the start of the acceleration effect we have been wanting."

"Now THAT sounds good," Omega decided.

"Yeah, I'm betting I see some ways we can speed things along, and maybe even improve the outcome, honey," Zebra asserted. "Just hang in there, and try to be patient. I know it's hard."

"I'm tryin', here," Omega declared. "But yeah, I just wanna SEE him, you know?"

"He's right there," Whiskey said, pointing. "Just look in the window-thing. Whadda the techs call it? Oh—the viewing port."

"I HAVE been," Omega grumbled. "YOU look in there and tell me how much detail YOU can see. There's no lights, there's all that fluid between the window and him, and this particular fluid seems denser than usual..."

"It is," Zarnix said. "Given its composition to regrow the

missing parts, it has to be."

"But she has a point, Zar," Zebra observed. "You really can't see Echo too well down in there. I mean, you can see that there's a head with a face down there, but not much more than that."

"Well, we rather thought, given the eye..." Zarnix pointed out, tiptoeing gingerly around the damage to Echo's face. "But yes, now perhaps we can turn on the lights from time to time. It might even encourage him to respond, if he's as close to everything being closed and regrown as I hope."

"The thing has LIGHTS?!" Omega said in surprise. "Well hell, turn those suckers on and lemme see my guy!"

The doctors chuckled, and Zarnix flipped a switch. The interior of the regen pod lit with a soft blue-white light, and Omega bent over the viewing port.

"THERE you are," she murmured, expression softening. "Oh, Ace, I have really missed you, honey."

"Hold on a moment," Zarnix said, and he reached down and hit a small, almost-hidden switch on the side of the pod. A small padded platform extended from the side. "There you go, Omega. Have a seat, and talk to your husband for a while. We will slip out and leave the two of you alone...but let us know if he reacts to you. Turn the lights off before you go to bed, so it does not disturb him and he can sleep, too."

"I will," Omega said with a slightly watery smile, as she sat on the padded bench. "And thank you."

"Of course, honey," Zebra said, smiling back. "Your family has your backs."

"I know. But still."

"Shush. Talk to him."

"Okay. Hey, Ace. You awake in there, hon...?"

* * *

With Zebra on the team, and with her skills and experience in the procedure, as well as all the work she had done the previous summer on Echo's mother's cancer bolstering that experience, the team of four physicians began having brainstorming sessions on how to pick up the pace and intensity of Echo's healing. Soon the physicians began to smile when they read the pod's instrumentation.

318

"I still can't say how well it'll turn out," Zebra told Dihl and Omega only a few days later. "But it's progressing much better than it was, I gotta say. Faster, too."

"And that is a GOOD thing," Dihl declared.

"Amen," Omega averred.

* * *

A week later, Doron popped by for a brief check-in on Echo and the others.

"I cannot stay long, no more than two or three days at most," the little healer noted, "because I have a potentially bad situation developing in the Eriki system that needs my attention. But I was not so far away, and thought I would come by—how is it you say; ah! detour—and see how Echo is progressing."

"That's great," Zebra enthused. "Because Zar and I have been discussing the possibility of decanting him soon, but we're still trying to get a feel for whether or not he's READY to be decanted..."

"Ah. Well then, let me see," Doron said, sanguine.

"Right this way," Zarnix said, leading the Edeptan into Lab B.

* * *

No one was in the room at that precise moment; Omega had gone to bed. Dihl was late in arriving, but expected shortly; a minor household catastrophe had left her cleaning soggy coffee grounds from the counter and the floor of her kitchen, when the recalcitrant pod coffee brewer had unexpectedly popped open and flung the coffee pod and its contents across the room.

Doron headed straight for the instrumentation panel and surveyed the readouts. Then he turned on the interior regen pod light, extended the seat, and clambered up onto it, peering this way and that within the pod.

"Mm, yes, yes," he murmured to himself. "That will do, and that...yes, well, I understand your concern. But I think matters are proceeding as well as they can, under the circumstances. I think that, in about four or five more Earth days... uhm, perhaps two or three more Division days," he corrected himself, "Echo will be ready to remove from the bath. Give him plenty of time to reorient himself, however; with an injury of this type, there can sometimes be some visual and spatial disorientation. I hope he does not have such, for it has been my experience that the more disorientation, the...less well? the eye regeneration has gone."

"Do you expect it?" Whiskey wondered, having joined the party moments before, as it moved down the corridor toward the regeneration lab.

"Let me say it thus: I do not NOT expect it," Doron pointed out. "We cannot tell until he emerges. But I would say that there is little more that the regeneration can do for him. Let the healing finish its course, then decant him."

* * *

"It is done," Gwag Wuxullian told Omega as she sat in Fox's office the next day, looking at his face on one of the big wall screens. His call had come in only a few minutes earlier, and Fox had immediately summoned Omega at Wuxullian's formal request.

"Um...what's done?" Omega wondered, mildly confused; she had been napping in the recliner in Lab B when the summons came from Fox.

"She was asleep, Wux," Fox explained. "Not off-duty in bed asleep, but napping in her chair in the medlab with Echo."

"Ah. Forgive me for waking you, Omega," Wuxullian apologized. "I had no idea. Are you not sleeping well?"

"Not great," Omega admitted. "I do better when I'm more active, not sitting in a room in the medlab. But what's done?"

"Oh. The principals—both captains, the chief torturer, and the undercover kidnapping lead—have all been tried and convicted of war crimes—all charges," Wuxullian elaborated. "I feel rather sorry for the assigned defense attorneys; there is so much evidence against them that conviction is almost a foregone conclusion, but they try. The kidnapping team lead is undergoing extensive telepathic interrogation as we speak; three Deltiri and a Kartung are involved in that interrogation. We have hopes that all of the required information will be extracted from him by this time tomorrow, as they are not being quite as gentle with him as the interrogators were with you, though they are not cruel. 'Wringing him out' is probably a more appropriate term, however."

"Mmm," Omega all but growled the sound.

"The Cortians seemed surprised by the convictions," Wuxullian added. "They still do not seem able to see that what they did was wrong, on many levels. And they are inured in the idea that they, as slave holders and traders, are at the top of the food chain. I am still not certain they have grasped the fact that they are about to die for it."

Fox and Omega exchanged glances, then shook their heads in a tired fashion.

"Yes, I see and understand THOSE expressions, and feel the same," Wuxullian noted. "The execution squad is gathering right now. I anticipate notification that the chief torture expert and both captains have been executed within the hour. The rest of the tribunals will occur in order of shipboard rank, with charges and likely sentences commensurate with their degree of involvement. A shipboard janitor is not likely to know much about what business the ship conducts, after all...but the bridge crew would."

"Right," Omega said, nodding. "This all makes good sense to me."

"Good. Would you like for me to forward the notifications of execution to you, at least for those four?"

"I think...yes," Omega decided. "I...I think I just want to be able to tell Echo that it's done, they're gone, and they can never hurt him again. I'm sure that's what he wants right now."

"Mm," Fox hummed. "Very good, tekhter."

"Well, right now, Fox, that's all I really want, too," Omega admitted. "This might sound bad, given they're about to be executed, but I never want to have to see those sons of bitches, ever, ever again. I'm TIRED. I want it to be over."

"And it is perfectly understandable," Wuxullian averred. "Would you like the proofs of death sent to you?"

"No. No, I don't think so," Omega considered. "What I WOULD like is for YOU to verify the death, firsthand, please... if you don't mind. Or, or somebody you trust highly, at least. So that I can KNOW they're really dead. And then come back and let me know...or Fox, if it's more convenient. I know the chain of command means it should go from the Administration Chief to the Division Director, and then down to the Acting Department Chief."

"I don't have a problem, Omega, if he calls you, then you pass the message to me," Fox noted. "The personal need is more yours than mine. I may be one of Echo's oldest friends, a father figure, and his boss, but YOU are his wife. And I know you aren't trying to usurp the chain of command, nor would you."

"I think it would be good if I were present for the executions, yes..." Wuxullian decided.

"Yeah, 'cause somebody high up in PGLEIA needs to be able to say, for sure, those bastards are dead," Omega pointed out.

"Indeed. All right; I can do that. Do you need a formal face-to-face with me afterward?" Wuxullian asked.

"Not necessarily," Omega said. "I know you're awfully busy. If you've personally verified it, I'm good with a call to my cell phone, or even a text. Or a conference call with Fox, or just however works for you to do it."

"Very good, then," Wuxullian said, offering her a slightly wolfish smile. "Let me go take care of that. You should have a message from me on your cells in no more than an hour and a half."

"That works," Fox decided. "Fox out."

"Omega out," the Agent added.

"Wux out."

* * *

It only took forty-five minutes.

Omega was back in Lab B, dozing quietly in the recliner.

Dihl had been asleep in hers as well when Omega received the earlier summons from Fox, and the alert sound on Omega's phone had startled the older woman badly. Consequently Dihl had left a note that she had decided to go to her own, permanently-assigned down room and get horizontal for a couple of hours.

This left Omega alone in the lab with Echo's regen pod when her cell phone dinged with the *imperative incoming message* alert. Omega jerked awake, then fished out her cell phone, activated it, and pulled up the sophisticated galactic text messaging app.

Fox, Omega:
It is over. Both captains and the torture chamber manager have been executed. It was decided to do them together, rather than individually; the adjudicators and the firing squad commander concluded that their heinous crimes did not warrant individual attention.

I was part of the small team responsible for verifying death for each being. Therefore I can tell you conclusively that each one is dead—Captain Incke, Captain K'ti, and torture expert Acktrr. It has been decided that the bodies will be cremated and what ash remains disposed of in an undisclosed location on another celestial body, so that remaining Cortians cannot create some sort of martyrdom shrine.

Ttirrl, the kidnapper who was stationed on Tiniken, is nearly milked dry, and some half a dozen missing persons have been located already, as a result. I expect his execution sometime tomorrow morning.
~Wux

"Good enough!" Omega declared aloud, then looked over to the regeneration pod. "You hear that, Ace? They're gone. The bastards who hurt you are dead and gone, and they'll never hurt you, or me, or anybody else, ever again."

She sighed, finally beginning to relax, as the tension of waiting and the dread of future encounters ebbed from her body.

Then Omega replaced the phone in her pocket, grabbed the little pillow and the blanket off the bottom shelf of the end table, and curled up in the recliner to sleep in a way she had not since Echo had disappeared on Tiniken.

Chapter 12

As the time finally neared for Echo to be decanted from the regeneration pod, Zarnix and Zebra called a formal 'family meeting' to apprise the others of what to expect. This included Omega, Dihl, Fox, India, and Romeo; Zz'r'p was expecting an off-world vidcall of some importance from another system's embassy, and offered to 'sit in' using a remote telepathic link via Omega, though he noted that he was unlikely to comment—he simply wanted to know how his 'great-niece's spouse' was doing. The group gathered in the main medical conference room.

"Well, it's not looking like being perfect," Zebra said with a sigh. "I'm sorry, Meg, but even Doron's maxxed abilities can only do so much, and he's the expert—and he did pop back by a couple of days ago, on his way through to the next interstellar medical whatever, to check on things and verify our take. But yes...we did manage to put Humpty Dumpty back together again."

"How bad, bubeleh?" Fox wondered, seeing Omega's tight, pale face, and watching an equally-pale Dihl bite her lower lip.

"Not really that bad," Zebra decided. "We did pretty good, all in all. It was a bit different from Omega's situation, where, because she was burned by what was essentially ionizing radiation emanating from a specific locus, we were able to create a relatively smooth kind of contour—for certain definitions of smooth, at least—for everything to just grow back. Here, we had nonuniformities and abrupt truncations and things like that."

"Yes," Zarnix agreed. "It was a very different situation. Possibly we could have MADE a somewhat smoother contour, and we did discuss it, but that would have involved removal of viable tissue, not merely the removal of damaged or unviable tissue. And even then, it might not have...well, in the end, we came to a joint decision—unanimous across the entire staff of physicians, let me add—not to risk becoming 'too fancy,' as I think Whiskey put it one time, and leave the contours as they were. We did not want to risk making matters worse in our efforts to make them better."

"And of course, he doesn't have Meg's enhanced metabolism and healing abilities," Zebra added.

"How bad?" Fox repeated, a bit more forcefully this time. Zebra nodded and answered.

* * *

"His eye is back, with what seems to be full vision—"

"How do you know?" Omega wondered, insistent. "He's not awake..."

"When we built the new, specially-designed pods," Zarnix explained, "we made sure they were fully instrumented inside, from head to toe, for precisely this purpose—we want to KNOW how the healing is going on across the patient's full form. With these, we can see the entire body, in three dimensions, over multiple wavelengths of light, and also using technologies similar to x-rays and MRI."

"This thing is SO much better than that old hyperbaric chamber we cannibalized to put Meg in," Zebra interjected.

"...So in Echo's case, we have taken deep scans of the entire eye from multiple angles, including density readings," Zarnix continued his explanation. "Then we can measure the dimensions, plug them into a computer model, and ascertain the strength of the optic system. If we want, we can compare that to Echo's base medical records, and even to his other eye. And we have, and it all looks very good. Regarding the retinal function...have you ever used a circuit meter, Omega?"

"Once or twice," she said, letting the dry irony become apparent in her tone.

"And you know that the nervous system is basically electrical in nature, at least to a point," Zarnix reminded her. "You were not in the room when we placed him into the pod, but we outfitted him with numerous tiny sensors and probes, somewhat similar to acupuncture needles, so that we could determine the...mm, call it the circuit continuity, I suppose," he tried. "All of which tie into the instrumentation inside the pod. And we are able to tell that the nerves around the eye, including the optic nerve, are functioning well, and signals are getting through. He has actually opened his eyes once or twice, though there is no indication that he is awake, at least not fully, and in fact the Deltiri seeing to his pain levels at the time said he was of a certainty NOT awake. And it is our experience that that sort of behavior is not that unusual during the regeneration process, anyway. But it means that light did pass through the regenerated eye, fell on the retina, and created nerve reactions, for we did see nominal nerve response in and around the eye."

"This sounds...good," Dihl murmured.

"We think so," Zebra affirmed. "And his face is clear, with no scarring visible, though there might be a few places around that eye socket that could look a little odd in certain lighting, especially along the eyelids. His wrist and hand regenerated well, and judging by the scans and the nerve continuity, look to have pretty damn close to full mobility and dexterity by the time we're done with him—by which I mean, AFTER he finishes physical therapy, NOT immediately after he's decanted. Now, if it had been his RIGHT hand, I'd be a lot more worried, but for what he does with his left, and being a right-hander, I think we're gonna be good. There's a slight nonuniformity of the surface of the arm at the cleavage plane, but nobody except us docs, Meg, and him are apt to even see that, even if he wears short sleeves off-duty...it's just not gonna be THAT noticeable. It's the leg I'm most worried about."

"WE are most worried about," Zarnix reworded her statement.

"Why?" Omega managed to choke out. She had started to relax...until that point. Now she felt her gut tighten once more.

"That," Dihl agreed, her voice low and slightly tremulous.

Both members of Alpha Two simply nodded, faces tight, apparently uncertain what to say. Then they all—Omega, Dihl, Fox, India, and Romeo—leaned forward to listen.

"The tibia and the fibula were chopped off at different places, and at different angles, owing to the way they hacked on him," Zebra said, an angry light in her eyes. "It's our joint opinion, arrived at independently across the physician staff, that it took at least two blows with whatever blade they used to remove the leg, possibly more—Whiskey estimates more like four or five times. Which means the two main bones were like-ly NOT severed by the same blow, and in fact there was some shatter involved, as I think some of you have already heard. We figure, by that point, the blade may not have been as sharp as it needed to be for a clean sever...not that those bastards cared. And while we tried hard to recover all the chips, we probably missed some...which means the bone scaffolding wasn't quite complete despite our best efforts. So when the bones grew back in the regen pod, even with the fragments tacked onto the ends, the tibia and the fibula just...didn't grow back at the same rate, and we couldn't make 'em do so no matter how hard we tried; we're not quite sure why, but the human body is weird sometimes. Anyway, the tibia—that's the main shin bone—is a few millimeters shorter than it was originally. Not quite, but almost, a full centimeter...say, seven or eight millimeters. That works out to about a quarter to a third of an inch. Not much at all, really; it coulda been a lot worse."

"And likely would have been, had we not had the original bones to use as 'scaffolding,' if you will," Zarnix added.

"What he said," Zebra averred. "So your call to bring them back likely helped ensure the best possible outcome for him, Meg."

"Oh. Well...good. So his right leg is shorter than it used to be?" Omega wondered.

"No, just the tibia," Zarnix said. "Overall, laser scans of his body inside the pod indicate that that leg is essentially the same length it was before the trauma. Oh, it may be one or two millimeters out at most, but nothing significant in that respect; it is within the error bounds. But because the principal support bone of the shin is marginally shorter, the tendon attachments and the angles of effect are shifted. Not much, just a little. But in this instance, it does not take much to affect matters."

"Oh." Omega rubbed her forehead, considering the infor-mation just presented. "So the applied forces an' stuff have...a torque?...that's been added into the mix."

"Something like, yes," Zarnix confirmed. "And that will affect the function."

Zebra continued enumerating the condition of Echo's inju-ries, ticking off her fingers as she went.

"So. There's another nonuniformity in the surface of the leg in the region of the cleft, and because, like I said earlier, the Cortians took their damn blades to it at least twice that we could tell, it's a little more obvious than the one on his arm, 'cause it's not really linear like that one—it's more jagged. But the naturally different lengths between the right and left legs—which EVERYBODY has, to varying degrees; never mind the new one between the right tibia and fibula—which latter, by the way, we made sure wouldn't cause a problem down the road, by wearing at different rates or applying funky pressures or something, so we computer-modeled it in detail...well, by the time we were done? He's gonna have a limp, honey. It's all about the way the tendons attach through there, see, like you said. The good news is, neither Zar nor I think it's going to be such as would interfere with his full function as an Alpha Line Agent. By the time he's done with physical therapy, it might not even be noticeable to the average person...which, lemme note, none of you are. But it WILL be there, you guys are gonna see it and he'll see it, and it isn't gonna go away. Ever. Unless some serious miracle-working medical techniques crop up someplace in this big ol' spiral o' stars, in future."

"But with a little work—as Zebra said, we are talking lots of physical therapy, here—eventually he should still be able to run and maneuver essentially as well as ever," Zarnix noted. "He may notice the difference, but it should not slow him significantly. He will have to work VERY hard in the physical therapy, however, or that prognosis will change."

"Wait, now...but...it sounds like, once he's done with therapy, he can resume work at Omega's side?" Fox wondered, astounded. "In the field, even?"

Omega's jaw dropped; a lightly-trembling Dihl put her face in her hands. Romeo raked a hand over his face. India gripped her hands together tightly.

"That's the intent, yeah," Zebra pronounced the prognosis, smiling. "I can't say absolutely for certain that something won't crop up during P.T. to negate that, but right now, Zar and I aren't seeing signs of anything that would interfere with his duties, so you guys can all relax over THAT, at least. I'm just thinking that there's going to be more mental issues than that, over the whole pile o' shit."

"Zz'r'p has already offered to counsel Echo as well as me," Omega murmured. "I'mma do my damnedest to convince Echo to take him up on that, too. Somehow, I don't think it'll be that hard. The human counselor he had, after our first encounter with the Cortians, has transferred over to the London Office, and isn't available anyway."

"Good plan, tekhter," Fox agreed, and Dihl nodded; Alpha Two merely looked relieved. "I...have to say, Zebra bubeleh, I'm...surprised. Happy? Certainly! But very, very...surprised. Bluntly put, I expected to have to move him to an advisory role in Alpha Line, perhaps giving him a greater role as the Assistant Director, and move Omega into the department lead. I had already greased the skids to enable a smooth transition in that respect, if it came to it."

"Frankly, given what-all the damn Cortians did to him, I expected that, too," Zebra confessed. "But when Doron popped by—twice, no less—to help us work it all out, it helped a lot. It's always good when the procedure's developer and general expert comes by to help you set it up and work through it, when you have a bad sitch going."

"Is he still here?" Omega wondered. "Doron, I mean. I haven't seen him since sometime last night, and I need to thank him. And y'all."

"No, he hied him off to points unknown on another medical call, during your last sleep period," Zebra said. "I'd recommend dropping him a vidcall when you have a chance, if you want to. That little guy...I think he loves you and Echo to pieces, as you'd say, Meg."

"Yes," Zarnix agreed. "I cannot say for certain, but based on a couple of casual conversations I had with him, while he is revered as a healer on his homeworld, his diminutive stature... well. I fear that he may not have been treated well as a person, especially when he was a child and adolescent. And perhaps a little of that attitude toward his size has even held over into adulthood; certainly his sensitivity has, though he hides it well. But you and Echo accepted him, included him, appreciated him..."

"Aw," Omega murmured, touched. "Okay, I'll do that."

"As for thanking the rest of us," Zebra added with a smirk, "the team that worked on Echo voted, and decided if you'd fix us a big platter of your homemade shortbread at some point... when this is all over, maybe...they—WE—would be happy."

"Consider it done," Omega said, offering a slight—if wobbly—grin.

"That's better," Zebra, Fox, AND Zarnix said in unison, seeing the grin. "Now, have you gone home and rested lately?" Zebra appended. "I've seen Dihl coming and going, so I know she has, but it seems like I see you almost every time I'm in the medlab. How 'bout it?"

"No. I gather that our quarters have already been merged," Omega explained, "and I...oh, this may sound silly...I just didn't wanna take occupancy without Echo being with me."

"I hear that," India backed her friend. "I did something similar when Romeo and I merged our quarters...though for us, it was just for the duration of a shift, not days an' days. But I understand."

"...But after discussing it with him on, like, Echo's first day in the medlab," Omega continued, "Whiskey assigned me one of the cot-rooms that y'all medics use to crash in, and I've been napping in there...though I kinda prefer to stay in the room with Echo, at least until I get tired enough to fall over. But yeah, I've been resting. Sleeping, even. And I've been taking my meds," she added. "All of 'em. The xolafet for the anxiety, an' the Regenic for recovering from beatin' the shit outta fake Cortians in the gym."

"Oh, now I remember you mentioning something about the down room a while back. And the rest of that is good. Okay, I'm satisfied, then," Zebra decided. "And I understand, too. If you want to run over to our place to bake that shortbread, I don't have a problem with you using my kitchen, honey. Besides, it'll get you out of the medlab, doing something fun, for at least a little while."

"All right. I might just do that."

"Good." Zebra offered her a smile, and Omega returned it, though it was still a little wobbly.

"You are welcome to the use of my kitchen as well," Dihl offered.

"Make that three," India declared. "Hell, maybe we all oughta have a joint cooking party, and come up with a nice little spread to lay out in the break room for everyone."

"That ain't a half-bad idea at all," Zebra agreed, after a moment to consider. "Meg, what do you think?"

"Works for me," Omega said with a shrug. "I won't mind having company while I'm baking at all. Normally Echo and I cook together, so..."

"Ah," Dihl said with a smile. "Good point. That settles it, then."

"Now, as to the near future," Zarnix verbally nudged.

"Right. Fox, all things considered," Zebra pondered, "I don't think I want these two—meaning Alpha One, of course—on duty at all for at least a month. Given we're just about into the holidays, I'm thinking not until after the New Year, even."

"I would concur with that assessment," Zarnix agreed.

"Aw," Omega murmured again.

"Hush that," Fox ordered, but gently. "Echo is going to need that time to recuperate anyway, daughter. And you're going to be a big part of that recuperation, so you need to be with him."

"True..."

"And naturally, you've been wound tighter than piano wire from BEFORE the time the lot of us reached Eden after your distress call," Zebra pointed out, "so we want YOU to have some down time, too. You need to relax, and the two of you are gonna need some time to feel like nobody's breathing down your necks. Never mind time to put your heads on straight again. Hell, you didn't even get to finish your honeymoon! Look, Meg. We want YOU to relax for a change, sweetie. Yeah, you got a break for your honeymoon, but like I said, you didn't even have a chance to finish it before things went to hell in a handbasket...again! Kick back. Enjoy your new joint quarters, maybe go to the Ranch for Christmas with Dihl, go to Echo's beach house for some time off. Whatever you wanna do, go do it. Just no work."

"But..."

"No buts," Zebra ordered.

"Hey, now," Omega fussed. "I'M not gonna be in P.T., and

I need to at least check in with Alpha Line once in a damn while, just to see if Romeo and Golf need something! And Echo's gonna wanna do that some, too, once you let him outta the medlab. And if you tell him NOT to, he's not apt to take that very well, in a buncha different senses of the term."

"Mm," Dihl muttered, "she makes an excellent point, there."

"As his ex-partner, I gotta agree with that, too," Romeo added. "Underneath all that gruffness on th' surface, he's got a sensitive side. An' if you go tellin' him not to work, after all this shit done gone down, he's liable to assume it's 'cause he CAN'T work, no more. An' he ain't gonna be happy 'bout that, at all."

"Fair enough," Fox concluded. "They DO have a point, bubeleh. Why don't we try this: I'll sit down with Omega and the two of us will work up a VERY part-time schedule for her AND Echo, something that'll take them through until the New Year on an intermittent sort of basis, with plenty of time to get away from Headquarters for the assorted holidays and the like, then I'll run it by you for your approval, and to add in the various and sundry therapies he'll need to come back up to speed. Romeo's right, and so is Omega—and Dihl recognizes it, too. If we play this just so, it might provide some of the positive mental reinforcement Echo is going to need, as he pulls himself out of this entire mess."

"Yes, that makes sense," Zarnix agreed.

"Mmm...okay, fair enough, I think," Zebra decided. "I can definitely see it. Using work as mental therapy, huh?"

"Exactly," Omega confirmed.

"Okay, but run it by Zz'r'p, too," she agreed.

"Even as we speak," Omega said, with a hint of a smirk as she tapped her temple. "And he agrees. Telepathic counselors can be cool."

"I suppose so," Fox chuckled.

* * *

"Thanks for offering your place to gather and do this, Zee," India said, as she, Dihl, and Zebra prepared for a marathon cooking session in Zebra's big kitchen; Omega was expected momentarily. "Especially since you've been so busy taking

332

care of Echo, once you convinced Zar to let you back on the case."

"Well, Zar and I talked it over with Zz'r'p," Zebra noted, "and we all thought maybe it was time to take care of Echo's spouse an' partner for a little bit. You know, give her some focused family time, as it were. So we called in Whiskey and Rglfrz for a few extra hours, so I could come do this with all of you, and maybe take Meg's mind off things for a bit. Or at least, coax her to put Echo's condition into the background of her thoughts, instead of the forefront."

"Which I think is an excellent idea, and which does me good, as well," Dihl admitted, unpacking a small wicker basket of cooking supplies and putting the perishables into the refrigerator until they should be needed. The latter included sour cream, several varieties of cheeses, and a large stick of homemade chorizo; the former, a ripe avocado, a pack of tortillas, several varieties of peppers, tomatoes, an onion, a bunch of cilantro, and a jar of peach preserves.

"Make it three," India conceded. "I've really been shocked at how much working on Echo after his rescue did a number on me."

"Yeah, but I'm not—and we were hoping for that, too, for both of you," Zebra confessed. "Good for all of us, really. Lemme see, now...what-all did Meg say she needed...? Ah." She extracted several mixing bowls of various sizes from her cabinets, as well as a couple of measuring cups, a set of measuring spoons, one canister of flour and another of sugar, placing them along the rear countertop. Then she dragged an electric mixer out of the corner appliance garage. "There. And a big ol' container of butter is in the fridge. That ought to do for Meg's shortbread. Is it really an old family recipe?"

"She declares it is, yes," Dihl averred. "Possibly several hundred years old, no less. All the way back to Scotland."

"I've heard her say that, too. And I think getting her out of the medlab is nothing but a GREAT idea," India said. She was unloading a basket of her own, containing a jar of kimchi, wonton wrappers, a jar of minced pickled garlic, fresh bean sprouts, tofu, and a package of ground pork. She also extracted a package of raw, boneless chicken nuggets, and a little container holding several spice jars. Then she placed a pan on Zebra's stovetop and turned on the heat, preparing to begin cooking the meat. "And frankly, I think Romeo appreciated the opportunity to sit by himself with Echo in the regen pod. He cares an awful lot about Echo, but they're both, like, alpha male types, and he doesn't have much of a chance to EXPRESS that caring. It's not like he's gonna say so, even with Echo unconscious in there. But he'll probably talk to him like he was awake, and that'll give him a chance to...I dunno, express it the way guys like those two express it, I guess."

"Then this is good, all around," Zebra concluded. "How about you? Are you about ready to come back and do some doctoring with us again?"

"I...yeah, I think I am," India decided. "I just...I sat down with Zz'r'p for a couple counseling sessions, too, and he helped me see that I was projecting a little bit—Romeo, you know—and that made it hit so close to home for me that I couldn't maintain my objectivity. But he also pointed out that I didn't know that was gonna happen, and not to blame myself for what I didn't expect."

"An excellent piece of advice," Zebra noted, "especially when it was partly my fault for not helping you."

"No, you hush that," India demanded. "I had already determined I wasn't gonna let you, and that that distribution of duties was the proper and correct one for the jobs that needed doing."

"All right, if you say so."

"I say so." India pondered for a moment. "It woulda been good if we'd had at least one more physician on board, I guess... or known that Mm'l'n was a doctor, sooner, and had her AND another Deltiri in there, maybe."

"Good point," Zebra decided. "I think, when we debrief this, I'm gonna recommend—"

"New subject," Dihl decreed, deliberately interrupting. "Something NOT about medical work."

"Oh, okay," Zebra agreed. "What's everybody making?"

"Ah. I'm making kimchi dumplings and Korean popcorn chicken," India noted, gesturing at the items she was lining up on Zebra's island counter, as she added seasoned ground pork to the hot pan and began sautéing it. "I hope you have a buncha mixing bowls, 'cause I think we're gonna need 'em."

"I do," Zebra said with a grin. "No problem. Besides, I think Dihl brought over some extras."

"I did, just as you asked, to make sure, " Dihl said with a grin of her own, producing four more bowls, nested, in the bottom of the basket. "And I also have the makings of chorizo quesadillas, a big bowl of peach salsa, and a four-cheese queso fundido. I considered making a couple of Apache dishes, but could not find some of the items I wanted to make them truly authentic. And while frybread is quite tasty, it must be eaten hot and fresh; I have found that it does not take well to being placed on what amounts to a buffet, even with a stasis field around it."

"And Meg said she plans to make a huge batch of short-bread," Zebra observed. "We're talking monumental, here. A platter stacked several inches deep, she said."

"Ooo," Dihl hummed in appreciation.

"What about you, Zebra? Or are you just supervising and helping out?" India wondered.

"Oh no, I figured on making a couple of the dishes I've learned from Fox," Zebra said with a grin. "Jewish cuisine, especially the Ashkenazic variety, has a crap-TON of finger foods! But I'm gonna keep it relatively simple. I have all the stuff in the fridge to make potato knishes and some from-scratch hummus...which is WAY the hell better than store-bought. I figured I'd throw in a big bag of chips, or maybe a veggie tray, to dip in the hummus."

"Both," Dihl recommended. "I will have chips for the queso and salsa, in any event."

"Ah, right," Zebra decided. "I'll cut some veggies, then, while stuff cooks."

"That works," India averred. "This is gonna be one helluva buffet table. Lots of delicious flavors going here, but not too much of any one kind of flavor."

"Where is Omega?" Dihl asked, concerned. "I would like to wait until she is here before I begin..."

"She gave me a heads-up about fifteen minutes ago that she was 'handing over' to Romeo, and then she'd be up," Zebra said. "She oughta be here any—"

A distant knock sounded on the front door, and the household computer annunciated Omega's voice, *'It's me.'*

"Come on in," Zebra said into the air. A click sounded, and moments later Omega entered the kitchen.

"I made it, guys," she said with a smile. "Ooo, looks like y'all are all ready to go."

"Just about," Zebra said. "We were just waiting for you to arrive. I've still gotta get out the fixings for my stuff, but I have you set up over here on the counter, Meg, and the oven is preheating like you asked."

"Terrific," Omega said. "Do you have an extra apron? I usually manage to get flour everywhere..."

* * *

The cooking marathon ended up being fun for all four women, who chatted and laughed and stirred and tasted their way through an entire afternoon. By the end, even Omega was smiling again, at least for a while.

The delicious finger-food buffet that resulted, featuring Omega's homemade shortbread, was a huge hit with the entire medical staff, and since it was accompanied by a stasis-field table, stayed good for as long as the food lasted...which was not very long, all told.

* * *

A couple of days later, the medlab team decanted Echo. He was placed, naked, in a hospital bed until he woke; the physicians and medtechs had realized early on in the development of their regeneration-pod methodology that placing the patients in medical jumpsuits after decanting went better when they were awake to help, and not as limp as overcooked pasta, and still damp all over to boot. Omega sat patiently in a chair beside the bed, waiting for the sedation to wear off, and her husband/partner to awaken.

After some fifteen minutes, Echo began to stir. A few moments later, he blinked, then opened his eyes, staring at the ceiling tiles. He blinked several more times before he spoke.

"Well, that's working okay, at least..."

"Great," Omega said then, with a pleased smile. "That's AWFULLY good to know! It's a real good sign, according to

Doron. Zebra and the other doctors went to some effort to ensure it did. Doron even dropped by for several days, twice, to help out."

Echo flinched in surprise, having apparently just realized he was not alone and Omega was there. Then he turned his face away from her.

"All right, baby," he said, keeping his face averted. "Do me a favor, okay? Grab a hand mirror and give it to me, then go find Zebra. Or maybe Ma."

"Okeydoke," Omega said cheerfully, rising and fetching a hand-held mirror from the dressing counter of the hospital room. "I know how that feels. Here you go." She leaned over and kissed his near cheek as she deliberately placed the mirror...in his left hand.

The same left hand that already wore his wedding ring on the third finger.

He blinked again, and stared at his hand, then gripped the mirror's handle firmly.

"...But I'm not sure why you want me to go get somebody," she added. "I'll just hit the call button, and—"

"NO!" he cried, trying to turn away from her, but unable to quite manage rolling over in the bed, after so long in the neutral buoyancy of the regen pod. "Meg, honey, just...just go. I don't want you to, to see..."

"Oh. But it's okay if your mom sees?" she wondered, hurt.

"Not...not really, but..."

"Echo, answer me something."

"Um, okay, if I can."

"Do you remember me sneaking you out of the Cortians' ship?"

"I...no. You...you s-saw?"

"I saw." Omega was calm. "And yeah, you were probably in so much shock you don't remember much about that, even through the nd't'lq. I know the Deltiri who were helping said they were gonna keep you knocked out pretty good, to minimize the pain as I moved you. I just wasn't sure how deep under you were."

Echo seemed to slump in the bed.

"Damn," he breathed then. "So I got no chance of..."

"Just hold up the mirror and look, honey."

* * *

Echo did as she said, then did a double-take, running his free hand over the smooth skin of his face around the regrown eye. He winked that eye slowly, studying the eyelids, for several moments. Finally he spoke.

"That...that didn't..." he tried.

"No, it didn't," Omega soothed, leaning over to kiss his cheek again. "Oh, Zebra said there MIGHT be some odd skin colorations around the eyelids—you know, in the eye socket area—in certain lights. Emphasis on MIGHT. I haven't noticed anything yet, and I've been sitting here watching and waiting for you to wake up, never mind trying to study you through the viewing port of the regen pod for the last bazillion days—well, it wasn't, but it seemed that long, anyway. So...my handsome hubby is as handsome as ever. But you know something? I'd still love you, every bit as much, even if you HAD scarred. I'm just thankful you're here and alive, beside me, and okay. And you need to realize something."

"Realize what?" He looked at her askance, still not quite comfortable turning to look her full in the face, but wanting to watch her as she made what he sensed was an important statement.

"You need to understand that, if I had to, I'd walk into Hell itself to fetch you and bring you home. No matter what it took." She eyed him, her gaze steely, and he met those eyes as best he could, his face still slightly averted. "Got that?"

"Um, yeah, I guess so, baby." He gave her a sheepish half-smile. "I suppose you know, I'd do it for you, too."

"I thought you already sorta did," she noted.

"Huh?"

"Going to Edeptis the first time, to fetch Doron and bring him to Earth to keep me alive, last winter."

"Oh. Well, that was more like, I dunno, maybe an Iditarod run or something. You know, a breakneck race against time through unknown territory?" Echo shrugged. "On this one, you hadda literally have walked into an enemy spacecraft, right through their crew and the representative teams of...HOW many crime syndicates were represented?"

"I'm not sure," Omega admitted. "Around half a dozen, I guess, give or take. Mighta been more, but those were the main ones. 'Course, there were several factions of a couple of 'em, I'm pretty sure. There were some individual criminals there, too, I think. Not sure about that, though."

"Damn, baby! That's like running a gauntlet of demons through Hell on the way to find me!" Echo exclaimed, instinctively angling his face more toward her. "But...yeah, I appreciate it more than I got words to say. When...when that bastard... when he set to work on me? I thought I was done for. But you... baby, you hauled my ass out and took me to medical help. I dunno how the hell you did it, but I can't begin to express my thanks. An' absolutely I'd do the same for you, sweetheart. Whatever it took."

"Good. I still think we're already even, though." She cupped his left cheek in her hand and gently but determinedly turned his head to face her, gazing into the dark eyes, and this time, he permitted it. "Now that we have that settled, can I have a kiss? I've been waiting DAYS for one."

Echo studied her smiling face for long moments, seeing her unadulterated happiness at having him back, and the unconditional love in her eyes. Then and there, he decided to stop worrying so much about her reactions, and whether or not he would be acceptable to her as a spouse, going forward. Then he reached for her.

"C'mere, baby," he said then, easing his arms around her as she bent her head to his.

* * *

"Well, there's a little scarring, there," Echo decided a while later, as he fingered the slight depression along his left forearm that marked the cleavage line, after he and Omega had examined the hand and arm together. "But it's really not too noticeable. And," he added, flexing his fingers before drumming them on his thigh, "it feels normal. Oh, I might have a weak grip until I build the strength back in it, but that's to be expected. I'm not sure I'm even gonna need that much physical therapy to retrain the muscles an' such."

"Maybe not," Omega agreed, watching. "I hope not, for your sake. You might only have to just get past the trauma and regrowth stages. But I told you about the leg."

"Yeah, and that's a bit...troublesome," Echo decided, flipping back the covers to study his right leg, unconcerned about Omega seeing the rest of his nude body, given she'd had plenty of time to study it on their honeymoon...and had, by all appearances, enjoyed doing so. More, he had concluded—after rather intense but surreptitious scrutiny of her reactions to his face and arm—she wasn't bothered at all by what residual scarring was there. He pushed up to a seated position, drawing his right foot toward his crotch, so he could gingerly probe the scar below his knee with his fingers. "Hm. There's definitely a...kind of a, a dimply-thing there, but it's not THAT bad, I guess."

"I called Doron yesterday and talked to him," Omega told him, "'cause I wanted to thank him for all his help, and tell him how much I appreciated it, and we talked a little about some of this. He said that he fully expected that the scars will look their worst right now, but that as you go through P.T., and then start working out regularly again and build all the muscles back up, these depressions along the cut lines are gonna fill back out, at least a little."

"Really? That'd be nice." He flexed his foot. "An' it seems to work okay, too. Doesn't hurt, at least." He looked up at his partner and wife. "But you said that Zebra thought therapy would minimize the limp?"

"Yeah. The difference isn't THAT big, see—just a couple of millimeters, but the difference is right where it affects the tendon attachments an' shit; it's the physics of the applied forces and torques across the various joints—and I gathered it's more a matter of getting you used to it, I think." She shrugged. "I dunno; that little bit might make for some real soreness during therapy, at least while you get used to it, so don't be surprised on that account."

"Okay. Then I just gotta work hard. I've had to have work done on my legs before. Back years ago, when X-ray and I were a team, we took out a Froon, and it spit at me; I dodged, but the spit hit me across the shins and that acid saliva took off the meat, clear down to the bone in places. Never mind what it did to my Suit." He winced at the memory. "I kinda think that hurt almost as bad as the damn Cortian whackin' it off. Well, then again...maybe not."

"Mmm," Omega hummed, wincing with him. "But you never had any gait problems, the whole time I've known you..."

"No, that's right. 'Cause the medlab managed to grow it all back—way BEFORE we had the regen procedure," Echo explained. "O' course, back then it was a lot slower and more painful process to grow it back, but it was only a limited area, so that helped matters. An' the procedure seemed a lot more complicated, at least from my perspective. If he'd nailed me someplace else, it mighta been REALLY bad. But I hadda go through therapy after that, too. I just worked my ass off to make sure it all worked right after growing it back, so I did fine, and it didn't even scar other than a couple areas that tended not to tan quite as much as the rest of it. I'll do the same thing here, too. An' if it's sore after, it's sore. That just shows I worked it."

"Listen," Omega murmured, "I, um, I have a pretty good notion what you went through, honey—if anybody does, I do, you know? And...and Fox an' everybody knows it was, was bad. But, um, the counselor you used the first time, when I was the one that got hurt, has moved to the London Office, so Zz'r'p and I thought maybe...well, he'd like for you to come see him for a few counseling sessions...if you're okay with that..."

"I...think that's a damn good idea," Echo said in a very quiet voice. "Judging by how he's helped you, I think he's a helluva good counselor, anyway. Can I leave it to you to work out the scheduling for me?"

"Not a problem, sweetheart," Omega said, relieved at his immediate willingness and acceptance. "I'll get with him, and Zebra and Zarnix and Whiskey, and whoever is assigned to do your P.T., and work out the master schedule for everything you need to do. An' then I can keep up with it for you, if you want me to." He nodded affirmation, and she went on. "Okay, good. I been doing that on some stuff already, with a little as-sistance from Fox. You're on medical leave until further notice while we bring you back up to speed, and my main assignment for the duration is helping you, so that's no trouble. I'm also available for Romeo to consult in running Alpha Line, but he IS handling it, with help from India and Alpha Four, so we're good there, too. Once the medlab says it's okay, we can probably do some light duty stuff, you an' me, but they want us both on no MORE than that until after New Years."

"Oh," Echo said, nonplussed. "After New Years? What... this is stupid...what day is it?"

"It's not stupid; you were in the regen pod quite a while, honey. We're coming up on Thanksgiving in a couple days, I think." Omega shook her head. "I kinda lost track there, for a while, myself. I had to look at a calendar yesterday."

"So...what? We're on restricted duty for the next month, month an' a half?"

"Yeah. And Zebra wants us to clear outta Headquarters for at least some of that time," Omega noted. "Like, completely away from work, but someplace safe. And while we were discussing options on that, I think she had a bang-up idea about something."

"What?"

"How would you like to spend Christmas at the Ranch with your mom? Maybe kinda like it used to be when you were a boy, at least a little? Only with your wife along for the ride. I already discussed it with Dihl as a possibility, and she flatly loved and welcomed the idea..."

"I think that sounds great, baby!" Echo declared, eyes lighting up.

"Then that's what we're gonna do," Omega said with a brilliant smile.

* * *

"...No, I think it would be good for you both, all things considered," Zebra determined, and Zarnix nodded vehemently, as they sat with Alpha One in Echo's hospital room after his first—and very successful—session of physical therapy.

This first session was something of a test, with the medics setting up light work on Echo's hand and leg to determine capabilities, while also exercising the muscles of the eye and checking his vision. The left hand, in particular, was doing surprisingly well, though it lacked his usual grip strength, and the finer coordination movements were still awkward. The right leg was not in quite such good shape, but the walking coordination was still there; it was simply not yet strong enough to support Echo's full weight for more than a second or two. This, however, was still excellent, according to the team of physicians and therapists working with him, because it meant that, with the aid of a walker or crutches, he would not be bound to the bed for the immediate future. And the regrown eye was within a couple of percent of the original in terms of visual acuity; Echo had originally had 20/10 vision, and currently it was 20/12, with no noticeable limitation in terms of lighting, coloration, or the like. The muscles that moved the eye lagged just slightly, and had from the time he first opened his eyes after being decanted, but there was already evidence that the muscles that moved and flexed the eyeball were strengthening, and that this would be a temporary condition.

So Zebra and Zarnix had stuck around to discuss the schedule for releasing Echo into Omega's care, with the proviso that she bring him back to all of his therapy sessions in the medlab, as well as counseling in Zz'r'p's office.

"And I am in agreement," Zarnix averred. "After everything that has happened, I think you both need this. And sooner, rather than later."

"But...isn't it too soon?" Omega wondered. "We don't wanna mess up Echo's recovery, just to get us into our new joint quarters..."

"No, Zar and I have talked about this. I know it's really early, relative to when we usually release regen patients," Zebra continued, "but I still think that's good in this instance. You'll both be able to relax in your own home—"

"Which you both need," Zarnix interjected.

"—And neither of you has even seen your new merged quarters yet, 'cause Meg didn't wanna take possession without you being there, Echo," Zebra continued, as Omega flushed and Echo smiled. "Fox said to tell you both that he's sure a few things didn't go quite where you'll want 'em to end up, but he walked through personally after the merger, and not only did it go pretty damn good, it all ended up completely functional. And if you two want anything moved, he specifically said to tell you: one, it'll wait until Echo's stronger, and two, all you have to do is ask, and the whole damn family—well, except for the ones on Emdali and Aleancë, I guess—and most of Alpha Line will show up to move furniture for you two. And that includes Alpha Seven, who are back on active duty...and twelve kinds of happy to know you're BOTH okay."

"Indeed," Zarnix agreed. "Yankee has a completely different attitude toward Alpha One, from what I have seen—and India confirmed that for me. He has been by, with and without Tare, at least once a day, every day since you brought Echo home to Earth, Omega. He would not let us disturb you, nor do so himself, but he asked how you were BOTH doing, and if you specifically, Omega, were handling everything that had happened." He paused, then added, "We did not tell him about that one flashback dream; it was no one else's business, and we did not want it gossiped about. Someone should have thought about that possibility in any case, and Zz'r'p assured Zee and myself that the Deltiri embassy staff had added monitoring your sleep periods to their duties, until he could work with you in more depth to bring you past the nightmares. Which, he said, he wanted to start as soon as you could, after Echo was released from the medlab."

"Which means in the next couple days, dear," Zebra added.

"Um, okay," she murmured, shooting a surreptitious glance at Echo, who was watching her, but saying nothing. "So...what DID you tell Yankee?"

"We—well, it was Whiskey, 'cause he was the one looking after you, Meg—Whiskey told him you were doing amazingly well, considering, but that you have been getting counseling, and that was helping," Zebra added. "He was glad to hear it."

"Aw," Omega murmured, and Echo flushed slightly. "Thanks...to everybody."

"For all of it," Echo amended. "Flashback, huh? I vaguely remember something about you having a nightmare, while I was in the regen pod. Was that...?"

"Yeah," Omega confessed. "I had a screamin'-mimis fit, pretty much. Two parts Slug, two parts Cortian engines, one part Mark Wright, and three parts Echo-gets-tortured. Throw in blender and thoroughly combine."

"Damn, baby."

"Yeah. But I think half the medlab musta come running when I screamed, and they all stuck around until Zz'r'p an' your mom could settle me down again."

"All the more reason we need to thank everybody, then," Echo decided.

"Well," Zarnix said with a grin, "after that titanically-huge batch of shortbread Omega brought by a couple of days ago, one for the medlab AND one for Alpha Line, by way of saying thanks to both groups, I think the two of you are up to date on saying thank you. Never mind the nigh-banquet buffet that Omega, Dihl, India, and Zebra concocted together in Zebra's kitchen." He and Zebra laughed; Omega grinned, and Echo's eyebrows shot up.

"And you didn't save me any shortbread?" he demanded of his bride.

"No, because I figured I'd bake you some, fresh, once we got home," she pointed out. "Expect to be spoiled in that regard, for the next few weeks."

"Okay, then. That'll work," Echo decided. "No complaints outta me on that."

"Don't get used to it," Omega warned. "I said a 'few weeks,' not indefinitely."

"Right," Echo said, and chuckled. Omega's face lit up with a smile at his cheerful, affectionate response, and the two doctors watched, pleased, for several moments.

"So. What we are going to do," Zarnix finally tag-teamed Zebra, "is send Echo home in an antigrav wheelchair for his exclusive use for a week or so, along with a walker, crutches, and a cane—both of which latter should already be adjusted to his height, and awaiting you in the bedroom of your quarters. In fact, I think the cane is the same one you used last spring after the spacecraft crash, Echo. But we do not want you putting much weight on that leg and foot until the therapy ensures the strength is back in it, because you might fall. Which means try to do most of your perambulations in the chair, though the walker and crutches will be useful for bathroom visits and whatnot. The same restriction goes for the left hand, but you should be able to use it for light things. That said, do NOT bear down on the crutches OR the walker with that hand. Just use your left hand to steady things, and if you use the crutches, let your weight hang from your shoulders."

"Right," Echo said. "I understand what you're saying, and

I'll be careful."

"Later on, you can use the cane in your right hand," Zebra pointed out, "for short-distance stuff around your quarters, say from the bed to the bathroom, or getting from the couch to the bed, maybe. But it's going to take a good bit of physical therapy to reach that point, so DO NOT USE IT YET." She shrugged. "I dunno what they were thinking, and I don't really WANT to know, but the Cortians going after opposite hand and foot works out good for our purposes, now."

"I am merely thankful they did not try to, um, 'remove' anything else," Zarnix murmured. "Or rape you, or worse."

"Well, they were thinking about the rape part," Echo grumbled. "But they evidently no longer have the ability to, uh, 'salvage the genetics,' as they put it, in their former, technological fashion. And the genetics of the beings they had available as... we'll call 'em 'recipients'...weren't at all compatible to do it the, um, 'old-fashioned way,'" he added. "As for whacking off the family jewels or shit like that, they knew that was used for elimination too, never mind the potential for bleed-out, and I think they were afraid of outrightly killing me if they did too much. And since they wanted to make money by selling me to the highest bidder...to then turn around and kill...well, a dead slave is pretty worthless on the auction block." He shrugged, face tight. "They did actually give me enough medical care after...cutting things off...to ensure I didn't bleed out. Hurt like bloody damn hell, but it kept me alive, I guess."

"WHY did they do that?!" Omega demanded to know. "What in God's name were they trying to accomplish by torturing you? I was asleep when it all went down, and I dunno what led up to it..."

"Oh. They were trying to force me to give up some galactic classified info, including the sensor scrambler tech, before they sold me off," Echo explained. "They knew that the interested buyers were there for revenge, and that I likely wouldn't last long after being bought, so they wanted the tech to use for themselves. I wouldn't tell—actually, I couldn't even if I'd wanted to, 'cause I never bothered to find out how it works—so they tried to force me to tell. They figured chopping off body parts would break me."

"But it didn't," Omega said, a hint of pride in her voice.

"No. But you helped in that," Echo confessed. "If you hadn't helped me with your telepathic mental techniques, it might have. It was...bad." He bit his lip, then dropped his gaze.

Omega eased an arm around her mate.

"Ssh," she breathed. "It's over now."

"No, baby, it's not. Not yet. There's still the trials and shit. We'll have to appear as witnesses. Both of us."

"Nope. That's already been going on without us," Omega noted. "Zz'r'p and a couple of the other interrogators in the Deltiri embassy came to me and did what they called a 'sympathetic witness' interrogation...which meant they put me under and accessed all the memories, with my permission. They took my testimony, AND they took yours...through the nd't'lq... while you were in the regen pod—because, as your legal representative when you're incapacitated, I gave them proper permission. Then they wrote it all up as a formal report, and appended to it all their own reports of the incident, from across the embassy personnel. That package was then submitted to the tribunal in lieu of our direct testimony, in court, as a kind of formal deposition of the both of us, as well as the Deltiri reports providing corroboration. Given your condition, and the fact that I was on the team helping to suppress your pain through the nd't'lq, as well as helping to care for you as my spouse, the requirement for our in-person presence was waived." She paused, then added, "According to the info I've had from Fox, Chief Wux, and Uncle Pul, every Cortian brought to trial so far has been convicted, dead to rights, on the basis of our recorded testimony and that of several turncoats in the various crime syndicates. That includes the fake Ke!endarian on Tiniken, the ship captains, the slave handler who did this to you, the kidnapping team...the whole bunch. That lot were, in fact, the first to go to trial. The fake Ke!endarian is still alive ONLY because it turns out he was the focal point for a sentient-trafficking ring on Tiniken, and they're trying to find as many of his victims as they can, so the telepaths are milking him dry. But both of the ship captains, AND the one who personally tortured you, were all convicted and sentenced to be executed...and that joint execution has already occurred, days ago. He's GONE, honey.

Nothing more to worry about outta him. Ever. Again."

Echo seemed to relax a little bit at that information.

"So all the two of you need to do is to go home and relax, tonight," Zarnix confirmed. "Enjoy your new quarters, your new home together. There are even several ready-made meals in your refrigerator, provided by Dihl and India, never mind the frozen stuff the two of you have done, and which is still in the freezer—Zee says you have one of the big, oversized fridge/freezer combos now..."

"You do," Zebra confirmed. "It's practically walk-in, it's so big!"

"...So tonight, pick something, heat it up, and eat. Then do whatever you want to relax for the evening, THEN I want BOTH of you to go to bed early. Do not worry about ANY-THING else for the time being. We will start the various thera-pies tomorrow, first thing. Omega, you have and are maintain-ing the master schedule, correct?"

"Yup," Omega averred. "I sure do. Have it all worked out and in my outboard brain, with plenty of alerts and alarms to remind me of who goes where, when. So before you change the time on something, make sure you contact me and find out if the new time is actually available. Now, lessee..." She pulled out her cell phone, opened the scheduling app, and double-checked the next day's schedule. "Here we go. Tomorrow: we have hand therapy and more vision testing about mid-morning, so we can sleep in a bit; a joint session with Zz'r'p an' the nd't'lq expert guy is scheduled right after first lunch—Echo an' me both, together—then we're gonna go home and take a nice long nap. Leg and foot therapy is about an hour after second lunch, so we can actually slide second lunch a bit and sleep late for that nap, if we want to. THEN I'm gonna take Echo by the Alpha Line Room after the leg therapy, for a specially-sched-uled all-hands departmental meeting that Romeo asked for, to let everybody see Echo and say hi for juuust a few minutes before heading back home—fifteen or twenty minutes, max, so don't worry, y'all; I promise I'm not gonna let 'em wear him out. If he looks like bein' wiped after the therapy or something, I'll cut that in half. Then we go straight home, and the rest of the day is spent AT home, makin' like Brussels sprouts."

"Huh?" a puzzled Zebra wondered. "Brussels sprouts? What the hell does that mean?"

"Vegetating," Echo explained with a snort. Zebra's eyes widened as she grasped the pun, then she let out a bark of laughter, and clapped her hand over her mouth. Zarnix also laughed, allowing the laughter to taper into chuckles.

"Yes, to all that," Zarnix confirmed. "Very good. It is a busy schedule, but there are sufficient breaks in there that we should avoid overloading you, I think. If it proves too much for either of you, by all means, let us know, and we will adjust the scheduling going forward."

"Okay," Omega agreed, and Echo nodded.

"Zebra, what am I forgetting?" the Chesharilzi physician wondered. "There was something else..."

"Oh! Thanksgiving," Zebra said. "We haven't talked about the holidays yet. Meg, I know while Echo was in the regen pod an' you came over to my place for our big cooking session, you said something about having originally hoped to do a big 'family' dinner at your place, but you didn't expect Echo to be out of the medlab in time. Well, we're taking care of THAT; but with the schedule that you and Echo are going to have for counseling and therapy, plus your helping Echo deal with the things he's not strong enough to do yet, like bathing and dressing, you'll be pulling hair out by the handfuls if you try, and... well, I got together with Dihl and India to discuss it, and we had a proposal we wanted to put before you two."

Omega and Echo exchanged glances, then Echo said, "Shoot."

"We fully understand that you're wanting to be hostess in your new domicile, Meg. Your nice new joint quarters WILL be a good place for a big family-style meal, and Fox ensured that you had a big dining room like he and I, and Alpha Two, have...and a good-sized kitchen, too, with plenty of storage and workspace. But you won't have time or energy to cook, Meg, I swear you won't," Zebra pointed out. "So what we thought was this: Dihl can come over early in the day and help out with taking care of Echo and getting him cleaned up and dressed...and maybe a little core family thing, watching the parade on TV, if you want." The others watched, pleased, as Omega perked up at that, knowing that her own family had had special little holiday traditions. "After that, she can help you extend the table to the ten-seat length, then put out the place settings and such. But instead of you cooking your brains out in the kitchen to make a huge turkey dinner all by yourself, WE want to make it a big potluck meal, with Dihl and India and me doing the cooking—Fox, too, according to some things he's said—and bringing it over. It'll still be a full turkey dinner with all the trimmings, just divided between us three—uh, four—for the prep, so it won't be a big strain on ANYbody. Now, if you have something special you want to fix, or that Echo wants to fix—you know, like a 'family tradition' kinda dish or something—go for it, and if you need our help, we'll be glad to, but don't feel like you just HAVE to. And the Earth-based 'family' members will all be in attendance, including the 'new uncles,' Zar and Zz'r'p. That's nine—you two, me an' Fox, Romeo an' India, Dihl, Zz'r'p, and Zarnix. How does that sound?"

Echo and Omega looked at each other again, then grinned.

"It sounds great, Zebra!" Omega exclaimed. "Let's do it!"

"Alla that!" Echo agreed. "Damn straight!"

"Consider it done, then," Zebra said with a smile, and Zarnix sat back, pleased.

* * *

A couple of hours later, Echo was 'free of the medlab,' as he put it. Omega steered Echo's antigrav wheelchair through the back corridors into the housing section of Headquarters, aiming for their floor and corridor, and hoping to reach their quarters without being spotted and stopped. When they arrived, instead of two doors, side by side, there was only one, marked:

Alpha One:
Echo & Omega

"Don't take this the wrong way, baby," Echo observed, "but that looks...just really, really great, to me."

"Yeah, me too," Omega affirmed. "I remember when I first saw the door to my quarters, back when I joined the Agency, and it felt...weird. Like, 'Where did *I* go?' kinda weird. This? This just feels...right."

"Yeah. Yeah, it does."

Echo leaned forward in his antigrav wheelchair and grasped the doorknob in his right hand, opening the door as Omega eased his chair through it.

"Ohhh," Omega murmured, looking around as they went inside. "This looks lovely, honey."

"Yeah," Echo agreed. "It's even better than I imagined it when you and I worked it out. The color scheme turned out great. And I think maybe Fox put in a few ideas, too."

"Yeah. Kind of a homecoming gift, I guess."

"Yup."

They entered a central hallway, lined with tall oak bookcases full of the couple's myriad books. The entrance was parquet-floored in a golden oak that matched the bookcases, and which gave way to a medium blue carpet in the hall proper; the walls were painted a matching shade of lighter blue, with contrasting mushroom-tinted trim—not quite gray, and not quite cream. On their right, just inside the front door, was the coat alcove, with a cream-and-brass toned guest powder room opening off that.

Just down the hall and to the left was a comfortably-sized joint office in soft blue, with a simple, modernistic wrap-around-the-room oak desk/countertop, two workstations, two executive ergonomic desk chairs, multiple under-counter filing cabinets, and over-desktop bookshelves, the latter largely containing reference books for their work—everything from legal tomes and hardbound law codes, to star maps, maps of shipping lanes, various and sundry Division handbooks, and more.

The end of the hall was a square archway that opened onto the back of a great room on the left, with a huge sofa and two overstuffed recliners, complete with end tables and a big coffee table, and a kind of credenza backing onto the rear of the sofa; two reading nooks complete with chairs, side tables, and floor lamps; and a wide-screen flat television on the only black wall in the room, in front of the seating. A familiar sublimation-printed throw, depicting a certain nebula, was tossed casually across the back of the sofa.

Two huge, black-framed images of that same nebula, the Orion Nebula—one from Omega's Earth-based observatory the previous winter, the other taken by the pair from their spacecraft on the edge of the nebula the past spring—flanked the television...which was set in screensaver mode, with a selection of photographic images of numerous nebulae fading in and out on its screen. Overhead, the ceiling had been tinted in a kind of ombré pattern, extending from the black of the wall into progressively lighter shades of blue, and finally ending in a warm white at the back wall, which was a pale rose gold shade. Taken all together, the effect was that of looking into deep space as a sun rose to the rear.

A small planter of Echo's stargazer lilies occupied one corner, a little floating antigrav sunlamp hovering over it. The remaining two walls were lined with floor-to-ceiling bookcases that shifted hues much like the ceiling, from dark mahogany near the television, all the way to a pale golden oak near the back wall...which conveniently blended into the bookshelves in the hallway. The room was lit via overhead lighting recessed into the ceiling, as well as numerous smaller tabletop and floor lamps, which provided for softer, more individual lighting. The same plush blue carpeting from the hall covered the floor.

To the right, through a decorative sliding door, was a big, hardwood-floored dining room in soft neutral tones of tan, gray, and the same pale rose gold that tinted the great room's rear wall. Much of the framed artwork that had once adorned Omega's quarters' walls now hung here, mingling tastefully with several items Echo remembered from his youth on the ranch, including two woven Navajo rugs hung as tapestries, and which Dihl must have brought up and contributed to their furnishings. A big mesquite-wood, mission-style table for eight—expandable up to twelve—took center stage, with a small sideboard and china cabinet in the back corners; Omega's antique family china and crystal were already on display there. But in the near right corner was a cozy little breakfast nook for two in a matching style; next to this was an open archway into the kitchen.

Said kitchen was large and spacious, with professional-quality stainless-steel appliances, including a stove/oven combo with offworld settings as well as Earth-style. A central work island with overhead suspended cookpot rack allowed for plenty of brown-granite counter space, and there were under- and over-counter red cedar cabinets to store dishes and food-stuffs, the cedar blending nicely with the wrap-around terra-cotta brick backsplash, matching tile floor, and copper accents, the whole creating a lovely warm, homey, rustic look.

The pod brewer and a rack of coffee pods already took pride of place on the counter beneath the microwave. Two matching mugs sat beside it, ready for the newlywed couple to brew their first cups in their new domicile. An appliance garage, with the drip coffeemaker, food processor, mixer, and other odds and ends, occupied the nearby corner, ensuring efficient use of the volume while keeping the devices handy.

The master suite was at the back of the flat, and comprised a huge bedroom/bathroom combo with two closets. The bedroom contained a California king bed—to ensure Echo's tall and well-muscled frame fit in it, with comfortable room for Omega—two nightstands, a dresser with mirror, an armoire, a large overstuffed armchair, and a couple of short bookcases, as well as several images of the night sky, apparently selected by their 'family' for their enjoyment, for neither Echo nor Omega had had artwork on the walls of their bedrooms. The walls were tinted a soft medium-slate blue and the ceiling was indigo, soothing and relaxing. The right-hand wall contained two side-by-side, walk-in closets, both faced with mirrored sliding doors, enabling both Agents to get ready for work simultaneously and still check their appearances in the mirrors. The rear walls of both contained warp-tunnel access.

The left wall held the door into the master bath. This contained a tiny, walled-off water closet exclusively for the toilet and a little sink—rather like a powder room, for privacy—as well as a big, double-sink vanity in the main bathing area, along with a two-person shower with multiple-level spray heads, a large jacuzzi, and several storage cabinets for linens, medications and personal hygiene products, first aid kits, and other necessities. The bathroom was tiled throughout in cheery shades of aqua, gray, and white, with chrome fixtures and pearl-gray porcelain, and thick gray bath rugs on the tile floor to ensure wet feet did not slip. Décor included several large seashells, and a few small beach-themed, framed prints.

"Oh wow," Omega breathed. "This apartment is gigantic, Ace. When we were designing it, I didn't realize it was gonna be this big."

"Yeah, it's a sweet place. It's a good thing the building has that space warp; that's made it easy to do shit like this and not really have a payback, once the building was outfitted to handle it structurally."

"But..."

"Honey, remember: you and I rank. Division Assistant Director, here, never mind future Director. An' even if I don't come out of P.T. still able to run Alpha Line, YOU will. So... department chief into the bargain, one way or the other, never mind assistant department chief in you, if I CAN run it. All in one partnership. Plus, I think Fox fully expects the medlab to figure out your little genetic puzzle, an' enable us to have kids, eventually—he knows you love children, and I'm okay with the idea, too...as long as my kids' mom is you. An' I note that the place is set up so we can extend a corridor for additional bedrooms, if we rotate the master suite ninety degrees..." He pointed to several strategic spots, and her eyebrows shot up.

"Oh." Omega pursed her lips. "That'd be...good."

"Yeah."

"This is gorgeous, Echo."

"Yeah, baby," he agreed, as they peered into the bath from the bedroom door, "but I think I just spotted something. Turn off the overhead lights in the bedroom for a second."

Omega walked over to the wall switch in the bedroom, and flipped off the lights. The pre-installed little orange night-lights—there were two in the bedroom and one in the bathroom—came on automatically.

But a myriad of tiny spots on the ceiling illuminated, as well.

In the same pattern as stars of the night sky as viewed from North America in summertime.

"Oh!" Omega exclaimed, clapping her hands in delight. "THAT took some doing!"

"Not necessarily," Echo considered. "Knowing Facilities, it might have been as easy as 'printing' off a star map, or a photographic plate."

"Good point. Cool. But where on Earth did they get the idea?"

"Oh, that's easy. I think somebody took a look at your old bedroom on the Farm," Echo said with a grin, "and decided to give you the adult version. I expect Alpha Two showed Fox at some point, this past autumn."

"That makes a lotta sense," she agreed, matching his grin. "So. It looks like we're home, honey...together. Finally."

"I'd say so," Echo averred, then his face fell. "Sorry I couldn't carry you across the threshold."

"Oh, pissht. Hush that," she told him. "To be honest, I never once thought about it. I'm not gonna miss it, so don't worry about it."

"If you say so." His voice sounded resigned, and when she glanced at him, he appeared discouraged.

"I say so," Omega declared then.

"Listen, Meg..." Echo began, then averted his face.

"What?" Omega said, moving back to his side. "What's wrong, Ace?"

"I just," he began, then broke off. "Look. Y'all did a damn good job of puttin' me back together again, but I still got these scars, an' the limp..."

"So?"

"Huh?"

Omega crouched down beside the antigrav chair so she could look into his eyes easier.

"Look," she said. "You need to understand something, honey. You have a gorgeous body, and it really made me angry to see what the damn Cortians did to it—angrier than you know. Would I rather have had you whole, with no injuries and no scars? Of course. But given the choice of having you beside me with a few scars—"

"And a limp," Echo added.

"...And a limp," Omega amended, "versus not getting you back at all? Which one do YOU think I'd choose? Which one would you choose if the situation were reversed?"

"I already thought about that, when the Cortians torched you last winter," Echo admitted. "Granted, I hadn't told you I loved you yet, but I was gonna stick by you, baby, to my dying day, if the medics could only keep you alive."

"And so why would you think I'd feel any different?" she wondered.

"You sure?"

"I'm sure."

"Well, yeah, but..."

"No. Buts," Omega declared, determined to cheer him up. So she stood to enable the reach, then bent and caught his lips in a kiss, wanting to show him how much she meant it. It caught him off-guard, and he responded with intense fervor; she intensified it even further, deciding she was having some success in taking his mind off matters. Before too long, she decided to take her own mind off those matters and just enjoy having him there, kissing back. Eventually they broke off when her neck kinked and decided to protest.

"Mmph," she grumbled, rubbing at the twinge. "That wheelchair is NOT at the right height for this! So. Whatcha wanna do now?"

"Guess," he said with a smirk, commandeering the controls of the antigrav chair, and herding her toward the bed.

Author Notes

I want to thank the usual suspects, plus some, here. There's beta reader Evelyn Zinn, who also helped me brainstorm A LOT (including the whole business with the flerovium, noted below, because she loves chemistry and 'gets' it), and editor Courtney Galloway who also did a good deal of brainstorming with me, AND beta readers Randy Jones, Laura Peterson, and Alisa Russell. There's also my awesome graphics artist husband Darrell who does such dynamite covers, and my parents, Steve and Colene Gannaway, who brought me up to believe that I could do pretty much anything I set my mind to do. MANY additional thanks go to Shira Tomboulian, Paul Sparks and David DeLorme, who helped me figure out some of the medical matters, such as debriding the wounds prior to 'dunking' Echo, as well as David Hause, Perry Morrison Smith, James Coolman, Tatiana Murphy, Steve Poling, Jesse Walker, Bob Buelow, Sid Wing and Richard Evans, all of whom helped brainstorm some of that same info.

By the way, for what it's worth, flerovium is NOT a made-up metal. It happens to be the official, formal name for element 114 on the periodic table, a trans-actinide element. So far it's an 'artificial' element, only synthesized in particle accelerators, but there have been some atoms detected that have formed naturally from radioactive decay—which, in turn, means we may one day detect it in the detritus from a supernova explosion, though given the extremely short half-life, that's unlikely. Not impossible, though. It's a fascinating element; despite its large atomic weight (and likely very high density as a solid), it is apparently a gas at room temperature, making it similar to radon in terms of inhalation danger (which is why I had it collecting in microscopic pockets in the bulkheads, though it might not have been very healthy for the Cortians—we can hope), and while it's in the same periodic group as carbon, it has some properties of a metal in that group, but it also reacts as if it's a noble gas in many situations. The explanation for WHY it does that is a bit complicated, but half of the explanation is that the electrons in its outer orbital are experiencing relativistic-speed motion, and consequently act as effectively a full orbital. (Interestingly, the orbital BELOW that appears to be the one that may be capable of forming compounds.) There are a few chemical compounds it seems to form that are semi-sorta-stable, and those apparently include sulfates ($-SO_4$ radical) and sulfides (combines with pure sulfur), which is why I threw those in; those are not-uncommon combinations for many metal ores, anyway. Many crustal metal ores on Earth are formed in hydrothermal mineral deposits, meaning they are associated with magma someplace down there, and sulfurous gases are common volcanic gases, so would be dissolved in the same water that carried the metals—and so-called aqueous solutions of sulfides and sulfates tend to dissociate, forming ionized solutions, and often recombining with metallics in the solution, which then deposits on the surrounding rock. Voilà! A metal ore. That type of ore formation might or might not pertain to a metal asteroid, but sulfur isn't an uncommon element 'out there,' either; sulfur has a relatively high cosmic abundance.

Most of the isotopes for flerovium have half-lives of seconds or less (some as low as milliseconds), but one isotope, Fl-298, which has a 'double-magic' mass number—which tends to indicate higher stability—may have a considerably longer half-life (we don't know for sure, because it hasn't been detected yet). That said, based on what I already know, I figure that MIGHT be on the order of minutes, rather than seconds. What I decided to do was to throw it into an exotic alloy— a variation on a real family of alloys—and have it derived, and not-well-purified, from a cosmological source such as an asteroid. This means there could be some pretty wild isotopic abundances (ratios) in there, with some interactions of radioisotopes, daughter products, and more. So it turns out that 'real, live Fl-298' generates some interesting electronic fields in that particular alloy, and that, in turn, interferes with certain forms of telepathy...at least, in that universe, if not our own!

In addition, for those of you not into martial arts such as karate and whatnot, the term 'kipping' means using the body as a kind of spring to change positions, usually by arching hard, then powerfully reversing the direction of the arch. It's very popular right now as a means of doing things like pull-ups, but it originated (as far as I know) in martial arts as a way to swiftly change positions, often maintaining high momentum in the doing. I've usually seen it used as I used it, to move from a prone/vulnerable position into a standing/offensive one.

I have to confess something: This book was horribly rough to write. What with this being book 11, I'd had plenty of time to get to know and care about the characters—in ways that I hadn't, when writing in the first book of the series about what Slug did to Omega—so doing all that nastiness to Echo was HARD. I debated how much to show 'onscreen,' and in the end decided to have the worst of it occur 'offscreen,' because I'd like to keep this series YA-suitable. But when the whole plot came to me, I knew I couldn't pull too many punches on it, and just because I didn't put it 'onscreen' doesn't mean *I* don't know what happened, doesn't mean I didn't envision it to know where to go with what DID get depicted. As good an Agent as Echo is, he simply doesn't walk away from this one completely unscathed—and we'll get into the mental aspects, don't worry. But in the end, he'll be back to putting away bad guys alongside Omega very soon, so don't let it get you down, guys.

~Stephanie Osborn
March 2019
Huntsville, AL

About the Author

Stephanie Osborn is a former payload flight controller, a veteran of over twenty years of working in the civilian space program, as well as various military space defense programs. She has worked on numerous Space Shuttle flights and the International Space Station, and counts the training of astronauts on her resumé. Of those astronauts she trained, one was Kalpana Chawla, a member of the crew lost in the *Columbia* disaster.

She holds graduate and undergraduate degrees in four sciences: Astronomy, Physics, Chemistry, and Mathematics, and she is "fluent" in several more, including Geology and Anatomy. She obtained her various degrees from Austin Peay State University in Clarksville, TN and Vanderbilt University in Nashville, TN.

Stephanie is currently retired from space work. She now happily "passes it forward," teaching math and science via numerous media including radio, podcasting, and public speaking, as well as working with SIGMA, the science fiction think tank, while writing science fiction mysteries based on her knowledge, experience, and travels.

For more, or to subscribe to Stephanie's newsletter, go to http://www.stephanie-osborn.com/.

Other Books in the *Division One* Series:

1) *Alpha and Omega*
2) *A Small Medium At Large*
3) *A Very UnCONventional Christmas*
4) *Tour de Force*
5) *Trojan Horse*
6) *Texas Rangers*
7) *Definition and Alignment*
8) *Phantoms*
9) *Head Games*
10) *Break, Break Houston*
11) *Tourist Trap*

Planned for the series:
12) *Mega Moth*
13) *Everywhere Signs*
14) *Diplomatic Catfight*
15) *Shake, Rattle and Roll*
16) *Die Glocke*
17) *Forming Terra*

with more being brainstormed...

Don't miss any of these highly entertaining SF/F books by Stephanie Osborn!

The *Burnout* series by Stephanie Osborn:
The Fetish
Burnout: The mystery of Space Shuttle STS-281
Planned in the series:
Escape Velocity

* * *

Sherlock Holmes: Gentleman Aegis series by Stephanie Osborn:
Sherlock Holmes and the Mummy's Curse
Planned in the series:
Sherlock Holmes in the Wild Hunt
Sherlock Holmes and the Tournament of Shadows

* * *

The *Displaced Detective* series by Stephanie Osborn [being re-released by Enigma House Press, an imprint of Hydra Publications]:
The Case of the Displaced Detective: The Arrival
The Case of the Displaced Detective: At Speed
The Case of the Cosmological Killer: The Rendlesham Incident
The Case of the Cosmological Killer: Endings and Beginnings
A Case of Spontaneous Combustion
Fear in the French Quarter